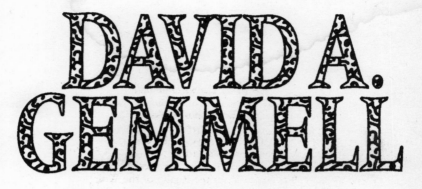

# DAVID A. GEMMELL

# STORMRIDER

BANTAM PRESS

LONDON · NEW YORK · TORONTO · SYDNEY · AUCKLAND

TRANSWORLD PUBLISHERS
61–63 Uxbridge Road, London W5 5SA
a division of The Random House Group Ltd

RANDOM HOUSE AUSTRALIA (PTY) LTD
20 Alfred Street, Milsons Point, Sydney,
New South Wales 2061, Australia

RANDOM HOUSE NEW ZEALAND LTD
18 Poland Road, Glenfield, Auckland 10, New Zealand

RANDOM HOUSE SOUTH AFRICA (PTY) LTD
Endulini, 5a Jubilee Road, Parktown 2193, South Africa

Published 2002 by Bantam Press
a division of Transworld Publishers

087578666

Typeset in 11/14pt Sabon by Falcon Oast Graphic Art Ltd.

Printed in Great Britain by
Clays Ltd, Bungay, Suffolk

3 5 7 9 10 8 6 4 2

*Stormrider* is dedicated with great affection to Big H – Harold Monger – and his wife Pat, with thanks for good memories and great stories

# ACKNOWLEDGEMENTS

My thanks to test readers Jan Dunlop, Tony Evans, Alan Fisher, Stella Graham and Steve Hutt, and to editors Steve Saffel of Del Rey and Selina Walker of Transworld.

# PROLOGUE

THE NIGHT SKY WAS LIT BY FLAMES, AND BLACK SMOKE SWIRLED across the valley as the town of Shelsans continued to burn. There were no screams now, no feeble cries, no begging for mercy. Two thousand heretics were dead, most slain by sword or mace, though many had been committed to the cleansing fires.

The young Knight of the Sacrifice stood high upon the hillside and stared down at the burning town. Reflections of the distant flames shone on his blood-spattered silver breastplate and glistening helm. The wind shifted and Winter Kay smelt the scent of roasting flesh. Far below the wind fanned the hunger of the flames. They blazed higher, devouring the ancient timber walls of the Old Museum, and the carved wooden gates of the Albitane Church.

Winter Kay removed his helm. His lean, angular features gleamed with sweat. Plucking a linen handkerchief from his belt he examined it for bloodstains. Finding none he wiped the cloth over his face and short-cropped dark hair. Putting on armour had been a waste of time today.

The townsfolk had offered no armed resistance as the thousand knights had ridden into the valley. Instead hundreds of them had walked from the town singing hymns, and crying out words of welcome and brotherhood. When they saw the Knights of the Sacrifice draw their longswords and heel their horses forward they had fallen to their knees and called upon the Source to protect them.

What idiots they were, thought Winter Kay. The Source blessed only those with the courage to fight, or the wit to run. He could not recall how many he had slain that day, only that his sword had been blunted by dusk, and that his holy white cloak had been drenched in the blood of the evil.

Some had tried to repent, begging for their lives as they were dragged to the pyres. One man – a stocky priest in a blue robe – had hurled himself to the ground before Winter Kay, promising him a great treasure if he was spared.

'What treasure do you possess, worm?' asked Winter Kay, pressing his sword point against the man's back.

'The Orb, sir. I can take you to the Orb of Kranos.'

'How quaint,' said Winter Kay. 'I expect it resides alongside the Sword of Connavar, and the Helm of Axias. Perhaps it is even wrapped in the Veiled Lady's robe?'

'I speak the truth, sir. The Orb is hidden in Shelsans. It has been kept there for centuries. I have seen it.'

Winter Kay hauled the man to his feet by his white hair. He was short and heavy, his face round, his eyes fearful. From all around them came the screams of the dying cultists. Winter Kay dragged the man towards the town. A woman ran past him, a sword jutting from her breast. She staggered several steps then fell to her knees. A knight followed her, wrenching the sword clear and decapitating her. Winter Kay walked on, holding his prisoner by the collar of his robe.

The man led him to a small church. In the doorway lay two dead priests. Beyond them were the bodies of a group of women and children.

The prisoner pointed to the altar. 'We need to move it, sir,' he said. 'The entrance to the vault is below it.' Sheathing his sword Winter Kay released the man. Together they lifted the altar table clear of the trapdoor beneath. The priest took hold of an iron ring and dragged the trapdoor open. Below it was a narrow set of steps. Winter Kay gestured the priest to climb down, and then followed him.

It was gloomy inside. The priest found a tinder box and struck a flame, lighting a torch that was set in a bracket on the grey wall. They moved on down a narrow corridor, which opened out into a circular room. There were already torches lit here, and an elderly man was sitting before an oval table. In his hands was a curiously carved black box, some eighteen inches high. Winter Kay thought it to be polished ebony. The old man saw the newcomers and gently laid the box upon the table.

'The Orb is within it,' said the captured priest.

'Oh, Pereus, how could you be so craven?' asked the elderly man.

'I don't want to die. Is that so terrible?' the prisoner replied.

'You will die anyway,' said the old priest, sadly. 'This knight has no intention of letting you live. There is not an ounce of mercy in him.'

'That is not true,' wailed the prisoner, swinging towards Winter Kay.

'Ah, but it is,' the knight told him, drawing his sword. The little priest tried to run, but Winter Kay sprang after him, delivering a ferocious blow to the back of the man's head. The skull cracked open. The priest crumpled to the stone floor. 'Is that truly the Orb of Kranos?' Winter Kay asked.

'Aye, it is. Do you have any inkling of what that means?'

'It is a relic of ancient times. A crystal ball, some say, through which we can see the future. Show it to me.'

'It is not crystal, Winter Kay. It is bone.'

'How is it you know my name?'

'I have the Gift, sir knight, though at this moment I wish I did not. So kill me and be done with it.'

'All in good time, priest. My arm is tired from constant work today. I'll let it rest awhile. Show me the Orb.'

The elderly priest stepped away from the table. 'I have no wish to see it. The box is not locked.'

Winter Kay strode forward. As he reached out for the lid he realized the box was not made of wood at all, but was cast from some dark metal. 'What are these symbols etched upon it?' he asked.

'Ward spells. The Orb radiates evil. The box contains it.'

'We shall see.' Winter Kay flipped open the lid. Within the box was an object wrapped in black velvet. Putting down his bloody sword Winter Kay reached in and lifted it out. Carefully he folded back the cloth. The priest was right. It was no crystal ball. It was a skull, an iron circlet upon its brow. 'What nonsense is this?' demanded Winter Kay. Reaching out he touched the yellowed brow. The skull began to glow, as if a bright candle had been lit within its hollow dome. Winter Kay felt a powerful surge of warmth flow along his fingers and up his arm. It was exquisite. It continued to flow through his body, up through his chest and neck and into his head. He cried out with the pleasure of it. All weariness from the day of slaughter fell away. He felt invigorated.

'This is a wondrous piece,' he said. 'I feel reborn.'

'Evil knows its own kind,' said the old man.

Winter Kay laughed aloud. 'I am not evil, fool. I am a Knight of the Sacrifice. I live to destroy evil wherever I find it. I do the work of the Source. I cleanse the land of the ungodly. Now tell me what magic has been placed in this skull.'

'Only what was always there. That . . . that creature was once a mighty king. A great hero destroyed him and freed the world of his evil. However, the darkness within him cannot die. It seeks to reach out and corrupt the souls of men. It will bring you nothing but sorrow and death.'

'Interesting,' said Winter Kay. 'There is an old adage: the enemy of my enemy must therefore be my friend. Since you are named by the church as the enemy, then this must be a vessel for good. I find no evil in it.'

'That is because its evil has already found you.'

'And now you begin to bore me, old man. I shall give you a few moments to make your peace with the blessed Source – and then I shall send you to Him.'

'I will go gladly, Winter Kay. Which is more than can be said for you, when the one with the golden eye comes for you.'

Winter Kay's sword swept up, then down in a murderous arc. Having been blunted by a day of murder the blade did not completely decapitate the old man. Blood sprayed across the room. Several drops splashed to the table, spattering the skull. Light blazed from the bone. As Winter Kay gazed upon it an ethereal face seemed to form for a brief moment. Then it faded.

Wrapping the skull in its hood of black velvet Winter Kay returned it to its box and carried it from the burning ruins of Shelsans.

# CHAPTER ONE

THE WINTER IN THE NORTHERN MOUNTAINS WAS THE MOST VICIOUS IN more than thirty years. Rivers and lakes lay under a foot of ice, and fierce blizzards raged across the land for days on end. Sheep trapped in snowdrifts died in their scores, and only the hardiest of the cattle would live to see the spring. Many roads were impassable and the townspeople struggled to survive. Highlanders of the Black Rigante came out of the mountains, bringing food and supplies, aiding farmers, seeking out those citizens trapped within lonely homes high in the hills. Even so, many died, frozen in their beds.

Few ventured out into the wilderness between Black Mountain and the craggy western peaks of the Rigante homeland.

Kaelin Ring was wishing he was not one of them as he struggled through the bitter cold towards the high cabin of Finbarr Ustal. Labouring under a heavy pack, to which was strapped a new long-barrelled musket, Kaelin pushed up the last steep hill. Ice shone brightly in his dark beard, and the long, white scar on his right cheek felt as if it was burning. His legs ached from the un-accustomed stride pattern necessitated by the wide snowshoes he wore. Kaelin climbed on, growing ever more weary. At twenty-three he was a powerful young man. In summer he would run, sometimes for ten miles over the hills, revelling in the strength and stamina of his youth, but at this moment he felt like an old man,

11

his muscles exhausted, his body crying out for rest. Anger flared. 'Rest here and you'll die,' he told himself.

His dark eyes scanned the hill ahead. The slope was steep and stretched on and up for another half-mile. He paused and clumsily readjusted the straps of his pack. Kaelin was wearing two pairs of gloves, one pair of lamb's wool, the second of rabbit fur, but his fingers still felt numb. A fierce wind blew down over the hills, lifting snow in flurries, stinging his face and eyes. The wind billowed his sheepskin hood, flicking it away from his face. With a curse Kaelin grabbed at it, hauling it back into place. The sky above was grey and heavy with snow clouds. Kaelin stared balefully at the slope ahead. He was coming to the end of his strength. To die here would be laughable, he told himself. Never to see Chara again, or his little son Jaim. 'It will not happen,' he said aloud. 'I'll not be beaten by a touch of snow.'

The wind picked up, roaring into his chest and almost throwing him from his feet. 'Is that the best you can do?' shouted Kaelin. Strengthened by his anger he ducked his head into the wind and began to climb again. The pain in his legs was growing now, his calves tight and cramping. As he struggled on he focused on Finbarr, and the welcome he would receive as he entered the warmth and security of the high cabin.

Finbarr had worked at Ironlatch Farm for several years, but last year had come to live in the north-west cabin with his wife and two surviving children. His oldest son had died two years ago. Employed by Maev Ring to watch over the stock in these mountain pastures Finbarr patrolled the high country, distributing bales of hay, and digging out sheep trapped in the snow. It was tough, demanding work. His wife, Ural, a strong woman, often worked alongside him, as did the two boys.

Kaelin had not seen the family for more than two months, and, caught within one of his wandering moods, had packed some supplies and set off for the cabin. In good weather it was a day's walk from Ironlatch, but in these conditions it had taken the powerful young highlander more than three times as long. He had been forced to spend one whole day in a cliff cave, sheltering from a fierce blizzard.

Exhausted now, Kaelin began to sweat from the effort of

climbing the hill. Fear touched him. In these conditions a man had to move slowly and carefully. At this temperature perspiration would freeze against the skin beneath a man's clothes, draining all warmth from his flesh.

'I am almost there,' he thought. 'The sweat does not matter.'

The sun was dropping low over the mountains as he approached the last quarter-mile, and he was now regretting that he had chosen to bring his new long-barrelled musket, and his two Emburley pistols. Kaelin had planned to do a little hunting with Finbarr and the boys, but now all he wanted was a chair by a warm hearth, and to be relieved of the weight of his guns and his pack. He shivered with pleasure at the thought of the heat from Finbarr's fire.

The boys, Feargol and Basson, would be delighted to see him. The youngsters loved his stories – stories he had first heard from the giant Jaim Grymauch when he was their age; tales of Connavar the King, and Bane, who had fought in the great arenas of Stone. Basson, the elder at ten, would sit at Kaelin's feet, his eyes wide, his attention rapt. Feargol, a six-year-old with an unruly mop of red hair, would interrupt the tales constantly, asking the oddest questions. 'Did Bane wear a hat?' he asked one day, just as Kaelin was telling the boys the story of a gladiatorial contest between Bane and a Stone warrior.

'Not while he was fighting before the crowd,' said Kaelin, patiently. 'So Bane drew his sword and stepped out before the emperor, a powerful man named—'

'What kind of a hat did he wear when he wasn't fighting?' asked Feargol.

'Will you be quiet?' snapped Basson, a slim young lad, who had inherited his mother's fair skin and blond hair. 'Who cares if he had a hat?'

'I like hats,' said Feargol.

'He had a woollen hat,' said Kaelin, 'just like yours, with ear protectors. When it was cold he would let them down and tie them below his chin. In the summer he would lift the ear flaps up and tie them at the top of the hat.'

'What colour was it?' asked Feargol. 'Was it white like mine?'

'Yes, it was white.'

Feargol was delighted. Scrambling up from the floor he ran back

13

into the bedroom and returned wearing his white hat. Then he sat quietly as Kaelin finished the story.

The memory lifted Kaelin's mood as he saw the cabin. He pictured the fire and the friendly reception, the boys running out to greet him. Kaelin paused in his climb. There was no smoke coming from the stone chimney. This was odd, for there was enough firewood to last the winter. He and Finbarr had spent weeks hauling and sawing logs, chopping rounds and stacking the fuel by the north wall.

As he came closer to the cabin he saw that the timbers of the west wall had caved in, and part of the roof had fallen. Then, out of the corner of his eye, he saw something red flicker in a nearby tree. Squinting against the fierce cold wind, and the flurrying snow, Kaelin focused on the tree. Finbarr's older son, Basson, dressed in a thin red nightshirt, was clinging to the upper branches. Kicking off his snowshoes Kaelin scrambled up the last part of the slope, his weariness forgotten. Even as he came to the tree he knew that the boy was dead.

The ten-year-old had frozen to death. There was ice in his blond hair, and his skin was blue. Great gouges had been torn from the trunk of the tree below him. Kaelin recognized the marks as the talons of a grizzly. They reached up almost nine feet.

Moving to the shattered wall of the cabin he saw the timbers had been smashed open. There were talon grooves in the shattered wood and blood upon the snow around the ruined door. Shrugging off his pack he pulled off his gloves. There would be no point trying to load the musket. The firing mechanism would be frozen solid. Opening his heavy sheepskin coat he pulled one of his long-barrelled Emburley pistols from its leather sheath and cocked it. He did not go into the cabin, but examined the bloodstained ground. There were bear tracks and a deep channel where something had been dragged towards the trees – something leaking gore.

With a sinking heart Kaelin Ring followed the channel. What he found, just inside the tree line, sickened him. The remains of the family were scattered here. Finbarr's head – half the face bitten away – was resting by a tree root. Of Ural there was part of a leg, and a ripped and bloody section of skirt. Kaelin had neither the heart nor the stomach to search for signs of the child, Feargol.

He returned to the cabin. There were deep claw marks on the outer, smashed walls. Inside, the table was broken in half, and two of the chairs were shattered. Several shelves had been torn from the walls, and the floor was littered with broken crockery. A discharged musket and a pistol lay close to the door of the back bedroom. A broken sabre was resting against the far wall, and a bloody kitchen knife had been hurled into the hearth. From what Kaelin could see – and the fact that Basson had scrambled up the tree in his nightshirt – the bear had come upon the cabin at night. It had smashed at the door and the frame, tearing out the timbers. This had not been done quickly. Finbarr and Ural had time to load and fire the musket and pistol. As the bear came through they had fought it with sword and knife. Spray patterns of blood upon the walls showed that they had died here. Basson must have ducked past the bear and run for the trees.

Kaelin moved to the hearth. Dropping to one knee he retrieved the bloodstained kitchen knife. Then he pressed his hand to the hearth stones. They were still slightly warm.

The attack had been last night.

Rising, Kaelin walked through to the small back bedroom. There was no sign here of disruption. The boys' bunk beds stood against the far wall, opposite the large double bed shared by Finbarr and Ural. Kaelin sat down upon the bed. This was a harsh land, and he had both killed men and seen others die upon the battlefield. Nothing like this, though.

It was unheard of for a bear – even a grizzly – to attack a cabin in this way. Often the beasts would scavenge around for scraps of food, but mostly they would keep away from people. Every highlander knew the two main rules when it came to dealing with such animals. Avoidance came first – especially if it was a mother with cubs, or it was feeding, or defending a kill. The second rule – if avoidance was not possible – was to remain calm and move slowly away from the beast. Given the choice bears tended to leave humans alone. Most attacks Kaelin had heard of had come when people had blundered upon a feeding bear and surprised it. The rips and tears in the timbers of the cabin showed that this grizzly had launched a frenzied assault in order to reach the people inside.

He glanced across at the bunk beds, and thought of little Feargol in his white cap. Finbarr had been over-protective of both his sons. He had already lost one child, his oldest boy, to a fever that was raging in Black Mountain. Finbarr had been determined to keep his other children safe. It was one of the reasons he had moved his family to this high cabin.

Kaelin shivered, his exhaustion returning. No time now to mourn the dead, he thought. The bear would be back to finish his feeding. Kaelin knew he should be long gone when that happened. Cold reality touched his mind. If he left now he would almost certainly die. He did not have the strength to make it back to the high cave. He cursed softly. In all likelihood the bear would not come to the cabin. It would eat its fill, and return to its lair. Kaelin fetched his pack and carried it back into the main room. Then he prepared a fire. Once the flames caught he removed his hooded cloak and sheepskin topcoat and squatted down before the blaze. The heat was welcome.

Outside the light was fading. If the bear *did* come now . . .

Fear touched the young Rigante, and he tried to quell it. 'If it comes I'll kill it,' he said aloud. The strength of the words calmed him, though only momentarily. Finbarr and Ural had discharged weapons at the beast. They had not stopped it.

Kaelin added more wood to the fire. His Emburley pistols were more powerful than Finbarr's weapons, and his musket was new. Picking up the weapon he rubbed at the mechanism with a fire-warmed cloth. Once it was working he loaded the musket and left it on the floor within easy reach. Warmer now, he began to relax a little as his strength returned. There was a bitter breeze blowing through the ruined wall. Kaelin found Finbarr's box of tools and began to make temporary repairs. The bear had torn out the timbers to the right of the door frame. The frame had buckled and snapped, tearing off the door and causing the roof to drop. Timbers had bent inwards, and the bear had struck them, snapping two completely as it entered the cabin. There was no way to repair the frame properly, but Kaelin managed to force some of the timbers back, and nail them, reinforcing the repair with sections of wood from the broken table. By the end of two hours he had created enough of a barrier to prevent the worst of the weather from freezing the cabin. Were the bear to return, however, it would be a matter of moments before it tore its way in.

Kaelin recovered Finbarr's musket and pistol, found the man's powder and shot and reloaded both weapons. Then he went to his pack, and removed some of the food he had brought to share with the family. There was a round of cheese, a section of honey-roasted ham, and two pottery containers of plum preserve, which the children loved. Sadness swept once more over Kaelin. They were good boys, and would have become fine men. Adding fuel to the fire he sat quietly, eating slices of ham.

Then he heard a noise. Rolling to his feet he snatched up his musket and cocked it. The sound had come from the bedroom. His heart began to beat more rapidly. Moving forward, he flicked the latch of the door and threw it open. There was no window here, and no way the bear could have gained entrance. Kaelin stepped inside. The room was empty. Dropping to one knee he bent and looked under the bed. A pile of folded clothing lay there. Kaelin rose, and scanned the small room. Apart from the beds there was a chest of drawers and, by the other wall, an ancient trunk, covered with carved symbols. 'Get a grip, Kaelin,' he told himself. 'Now you're hearing things.'

As he spoke he heard a soft sob coming from the trunk. Leaving the musket on the bed he knelt by the old chest and lifted the lid. Red-haired Feargol was curled up inside, still in his nightshirt. His face showed his terror. 'It's all right, boy,' said Kaelin, softly. 'It's Uncle Kaelin. You are safe now.' He reached into the trunk. Feargol squeezed shut his eyes and tried to burrow down through the clothes it contained. Kaelin paused. Instead of picking up the child he gently patted his thin shoulder. 'You've been very brave, Feargol. I am very proud of you,' he said, keeping his voice low and gentle. 'I think you should come out and have some food with me now.'

Leaving the boy he gathered up his musket and returned to the fire. He sat for some time, waiting, but Feargol did not come out. With a sigh Kaelin added more wood to the fire. The boy had moved beyond terror. He had listened to the roar of the bear and the screams of his parents. He had heard the snapping of bones and the rending of flesh. His world had been torn apart by the talons and teeth of a crazed beast. If necessary Kaelin would go and

17

lift him from the trunk, but he knew it would be better for the boy to make his own choice.

Years before, when Kaelin was just turned twelve, he and the giant Jaim Grymauch had taken part in a search for a lost Varlish boy. It was believed the child had wandered into the low woods, and search parties started out to find him. Jaim had doubted the prevailing wisdom, and, a long coil of rope on his shoulders, had set off into the hills.

'Why are we heading here?' Kaelin had asked him.

'It is said the boy was troubled, and fearful. Other boys had threatened him. In the woods you can hide – but you cannot see an enemy coming. Up in the hills you can also hide, but there are high vantage points. From them you can watch your pursuers.'

They had searched for most of the day. Often Jaim would stop and squat down, listening. Kaelin remembered it well. The big man would crouch, lift the band of black cloth around the socket of his ruined left eye, and scratch at the puckered, stitched skin of his eyelid. It was something he always did when he was worried. Towards dusk Kaelin heard a faint sound, and the two of them found a fissure, where the ground had given way. Moving to it Jaim called the boy's name. He was answered by a cry for help.

'Are you injured, lad?'

'No. Please get me out.'

'Can you stand? Are your arms still strong?'

'Yes. Please come and get me.'

'I'll lower a rope to you. You must tie it round your waist.'

'I can't,' wailed the child. 'Come and get me.'

'I can climb down there,' whispered Kaelin.

'I know,' said Jaim, softly. 'Maybe you will have to. Sit tight now, and be quiet while I talk to the boy.' Jaim transferred his attention to the fissure. 'I know you are a brave lad. So listen to me now. Up here the stars are about to shine, and the air is sweet. Have you ever heard of the magic eye?'

'No,' replied the boy.

And Jaim had told him a wondrous tall tale. 'Now my magic eye can always tell a hero,' he finished. 'And you, my lad, are a hero. A lesser boy would have died in this fall. I am going to lower the

18

rope now. Let me know when you can feel it.' Jaim uncoiled the rope and gently threaded it down the opening.

'I have it!'

'Put it round your waist. Nice and tight. Shout to me when you have done it.'

'Will you pull me up then?'

'I'm not a strong man, boy,' lied Jaim. 'You'll need to climb a little. I might be able to haul you to the first handhold.'

'I can't climb,' wailed the boy. 'It's dark and I'm not strong.'

'Well, we'll see,' said Jaim. 'Is the rope tight?'

'Yes, sir.'

'Then you start to climb and I'll take in the slack.'

It took about twenty minutes for the boy to make the climb. When he at last emerged Jaim clapped him on the back and told him how proud he was of him. 'You're a fine lad,' he said.

After they had returned the boy to his home, and were returning to their own, Kaelin asked: 'Why did you torture him so? I could have climbed down there in a minute. And you are not weak at all. You are the strongest man in the highlands.'

Jaim had paused in their walk. 'Ah, Kaelin, you have much to learn. There is no greater despair than to feel helpless. Had we merely pulled him out he would have carried that helplessness like a sack upon his shoulders. Any problem in his life would have seen him crying for help. We grow by *doing*, boy. We make ourselves men by our own actions. Yes, I helped him. But *he* climbed out. He took his own life in his own hands and he made a decision. It is a life lesson he learned today. He will be stronger for it.'

Sitting now by the fire in Finbarr's ravaged cabin Kaelin began to sing an old song that Jaim had taught him many years ago.

'*Lost by the roadside, happy in my hideaway,*
*Far from the troubles of when I was a runaway.*
*No-one can catch me, and not a man can match me.*
*I'm the cunning outlaw, all my troubles cast away.*'

He finished the song, and then called out. 'I have some plum preserve here for you, my little friend. And the fire is warm.' Then he began to sing again.

Just when he was starting to believe he would have to fetch the boy he saw the little six-year-old step into the doorway. His blue nightshirt was stained with urine, and he was wearing his white hat, with the ear flaps hanging down. Kaelin reached out and lifted a jar of preserve. 'I think we should eat a little something, my friend,' he said, his voice soft and soothing. Feargol turned towards the ruined wall, and stood staring at the broken timbers.

'The bear is going to come back,' he said.

'If it does I'll kill it,' said Kaelin. 'I'll let no bear come close to my friend Feargol.'

'Did the bear eat Basson?'

'No.'

'But it ate my daddy,' said the child, beginning to tremble. Tears spilled to his face.

'You and I are going to Ironlatch Farm tomorrow,' said Kaelin. 'It will be an adventure. You'll come and live with me and Chara and little Jaim. We'll be glad to have you. You know why? Look at me, Feargol. You know why?'

The little boy turned his gaze away from the torn wall. 'Why?'

'Because I like you. I think you are a fine boy. You are brave and you are bright. You are just like Bane. Come and sit by the fire. We'll eat, and we'll rest, and tomorrow we'll go home.'

Feargol walked across to where Kaelin waited. Then he sat on his lap. Kaelin put his arms round him and stroked his shoulder. 'Are you frightened of the bear?' the little boy asked.

'I was, Feargol. But not now. Trust me, boy. I'll not let it harm a hair of your head.'

'It has a horrible face, all scaly.'

After a while Feargol ate a little of the ham and cheese, following them with some sweet plum preserve. Then Kaelin took him back into the bedroom and found some clothes for him. The boy was very pale, his eyes wide and fearful. Kaelin dressed him in a warm shirt and leggings, chatting to him all the while. Then they returned to the main room, and Kaelin found a container of lantern oil. Filling an old jug with it, he placed it on the floor.

Feargol stayed close to him, watching him. Kaelin walked to the bedroom and cut a strip from a blanket. This he wrapped round a section of wood from a broken chair leg, and doused it with lantern oil. 'What are you doing?' asked Feargol.

'It's a surprise,' said Kaelin. 'Now I think you should rest. We have a long walk tomorrow, and you'll need to be strong.' Gathering blankets he laid them on the floor by the fire. 'You just lie down. I'll keep watch.'

Feargol did as he was told, but he didn't sleep. He lay very still, watching Kaelin.

'Am I really like Bane?' he asked.

'Yes. Very brave.'

'I don't feel brave. I feel very frightened.'

'Trust me, my friend. I know you are brave. I can tell. My uncle Jaim gave me a magic eye. I can always see the truth.'

'Where did he get it?'

Kaelin smiled, remembering the day Jaim told him the same story. 'He found it in a secret well, that could only be seen when the moon was new. It was left there by a mighty wizard.'

'Where do you keep it?' asked Feargol, suddenly yawning.

'Keep it?'

'The magic eye.'

'Ah! I keep it here,' said Kaelin, tapping the centre of his forehead.

'I can't see it.'

'That's because it's magical. You can only see it when the moon is new, and when a white owl flies overhead.'

Feargol yawned again. 'I have a magic eye,' he said. 'Daddy told me not to tell anyone.' The room was warm now, and dancing fire shadows flickered on the walls. Kaelin sat quietly as the boy fell asleep.

Kaelin Ring had no magical powers. He did not dream of future events, nor did he see ghosts. And yet he knew with grim certainty that the bear would return. It was not fear which filled him with this sense of foreboding. He knew that for sure. All his own fears had vanished the moment he had found little Feargol alive.

The bear would simply come back to feed. In doing so he would scent Kaelin and the boy. Like all the local highlanders Kaelin knew the bears which roamed his territory. In this area there was only

21

one huge grizzly. The locals called him Hang-lip. At some point in his young life he had been in a fight, and his lower lip had been half cut away. It hung now from his jaw, flapping as he walked. Kaelin had seen him often. He was big. On his hind legs he would reach almost eight feet – ten if he stretched his paws high. He lived alone. Finbarr had told Kaelin that Hang-lip had killed another bear in his territory – old Shabba. The news had saddened Kaelin, for Shabba had held a place in his heart. The old bear had once ransacked a camp of Kaelin's, and this had caused much merriment to Chara Jace, who, safe in a tree, had watched the whole scene. It was the first time Kaelin and Chara had been alone together. Old Shabba had ambled over to where Kaelin lay and sniffed his face before wandering off. And Hang-lip had killed him. 'I should have hunted him down then,' thought Kaelin. Bears would fight, but generally when one ran the other would let it go. Not Hang-lip. He was a killer. Now he had killed humans, and dined on their bodies. Jaim had once told Kaelin that in such circumstances bears developed a rare taste for human flesh, and would continue to hunt people. Kaelin had no idea if this were true. Jaim was a wonderful storyteller, and, like all storytellers, had a curious disregard for truth. What Kaelin did know, however, was that a musket ball was unlikely to kill such a beast instantly. The bear's ribs were immensely powerful, and any ball that struck one would bounce away. It would be a rare shot that found a way to a bear's heart.

The night wore on. Kaelin kept the fire blazing, and moved his position so that he was close to the entrance. From here he could see the edge of the trees, and listen for sounds of the bear's return. He was tired now, and longed for an hour's sleep. His mind wandered, and he thought of Jaim Grymauch, recalling the great fight he had had with the Varlish champion, Gorain. What a day that had been. The Bishop of Eldacre had invited Gorain and another champion, the legendary Chain Shada, to fight at the Highland Games. The bishop had wanted to see the clansmen humbled, and reinforce belief in Varlish superiority. It would have worked, too. But the one-eyed Jaim had fought Gorain to a standstill before knocking him out of the circle and into the crowd. It was a colossal moment, and Kaelin would treasure it all his life.

His own life had changed that night too. A girl who loved him had been murdered by a Varlish soldier and his nephew. They had raped her, then hanged her. Kaelin had found them both. In a night of bleak savagery he had killed them. Truth to tell he did not regret their deaths, nor his part in them. He did, however, feel shame at the way he had ripped at their bodies. Blind with rage he had cut off their heads and jammed them on the posts of a bridge.

Kaelin jerked to wakefulness. He had dozed, his head resting against the wall. He rubbed his eyes and stared out at the tree line. There was nothing there, and no sounds of crunching bone could be heard.

He pushed himself to his feet. Just as he did so a colossal black form reared into the opening, its huge head pushing over the newly repaired wall, its torn lip hanging. Kaelin hurled himself to the floor and rolled. Hang-lip let out a roar. Feargol awoke and screamed at the top of his voice. The bear lashed at a timber, which parted and flew across the room. Kaelin scrambled to the jug of lantern oil, grabbed the chair leg wrapped in cloth and held it in the fire. Flames leapt to the cloth. Carrying torch and jug he ran towards the bear, flinging the oil into its face. The beast lunged at him, but was hindered by a second timber, which groaned under its weight. Kaelin thrust the burning torch into the bear's mouth. The oil on its fur caught fire instantly, flaring up around its eyes. With a hideous roar it dropped to all fours and ran in flames towards the trees.

Feargol was sobbing by the fire. Kaelin moved to him. 'He's gone,' he said. The boy was trembling and Kaelin drew him into an embrace. 'I am very proud of you, Feargol,' he said, softly. 'I would never have been as brave as you when I was your age. I was frightened of mice, you know.'

'I *am* frightened of mice,' said Feargol, holding hard to Kaelin's shirt and pushing his head against the man's chest.

'Then we are alike,' Kaelin told him. 'Once I was frightened of mice – and now I fight bears.'

'He will come back. I know he will. '

Kaelin sat quietly for a moment. The boy was already terrified, and it was tempting to offer a small lie. It would relax him for a while. He dismissed the idea. 'Yes, Feargol, he will be coming back. He's not hungry any more. He just wants us dead. So I will have to kill him. But we will get to Ironlatch. I promise you.'

23

'Can you kill him?' asked the child. 'My daddy couldn't.'

'He took your daddy by surprise. Finbarr was a brave man, and your mother was a fine woman. But I will be ready for the beast, Feargol – and you will help me.'

'I can't fight bears, Kaelin. I can't!' Tears welled in the boy's eyes.

'You won't need to fight him, my friend. You will help me prepare. I want you to go to the kitchen and find any long knives. Then you can fetch your daddy's staff. We are going to make a spear. Off you go.' Kaelin gently eased the child from his embrace and stood. Feargol waited for a moment, then ran into the kitchen. Kaelin gathered up his musket and returned to the opening. A spear was unlikely to be more useful than his own weapons, but it would keep the child occupied.

The air was bitterly cold and it was snowing heavily. He knew the two of them would struggle to stay alive on the outside. If they set out soon after dawn they could reach the cliff cave by dusk. Kaelin had used it often, and had left a good supply of dry wood there. It would be a hard, strength-sapping walk. Yet what were the choices? When Hang-lip returned Kaelin would shoot him. Would the shots reach his heart? Perhaps. And *perhaps* was not good enough when he had a child to save. Picturing the long walk to the cliff cave he realized it was almost totally over open ground. If the bear came after them, as he feared it would, there would be nowhere to hide. The lack of options made him angry. To stay would be to invite disaster and death. To go would remove them from the only defensible position, and put them at risk from the awful cold.

Then there was the problem of clothing. Dressing to keep warm would involve many layers of wool, and this would restrict speed of movement. His snowshoes would help over steep drifts, but he would have to carry the boy as well as the pack and the musket, and – perhaps – the spear. Kaelin swore softly.

Looking out into the night he almost wished the bear would return now. Then he could take his shot, and see if he could bring it down.

Feargol came back into the main room, carrying three long knives. 'Will these do?' he asked.

One was too thin, but the other two were good, strong blades.

24

'Aye, one of these will be fine,' he told the boy, rubbing his hair. 'Now fetch the staff.' Finbarr's staff was just under six feet long, and fashioned from oak. Finding the dead man's tools Kaelin took a small hacksaw and cut a channel four inches deep in the staff's tip. Then, with a hammer, he smashed the horn handle of the knife, releasing the blade. This he inserted into the channel. Feargol watched him as he bound the new spear with twine. Once it was fully tied Kaelin tested the weapon. The blade was still a little loose. Cutting free the twine he retied it more tightly. Satisfied at last, he laid the spear on the floor.

The cold was becoming more intense and Kaelin told Feargol to add more fuel to the fire. The boy obeyed instantly. As soon as he had done it he ran back to sit close to Kaelin. 'It's cold over here,' said the man.

'I'm all right,' answered Feargol.

'What is your soul name?'

'Moon Lantern.'

'That's a good name. Mine is Ravenheart.'

'Why did your daddy call you that?'

'On the night I was born – so my uncle Jaim told me – there was a mighty stag at bay. Several wolves had cornered it. Just as they were attacking the stag my father's hound, Raven, came bursting out of the trees. He tore into the wolves and they ran away. He was a fine dog, Jaim said.'

'What happened to him?'

'He and my father died that night. Both had been shot in an ambush. Raven was dying even as he saved the stag.'

'I never knew Jaim. My daddy speaks of him. He says he was tall as a house, and the bravest Rigante ever.'

'He was tall, but only a few inches taller than me.' Kaelin chuckled. 'He did seem big, though. I miss him.'

'I miss my daddy,' said Feargol, blinking back tears. Kaelin put his arm round him.

'Aye, it is hard when those we love leave the world. No denying it.'

Outside the sky was lightening. Dawn was not far off. Kaelin took a deep breath. 'Go and find your warmest clothes, Feargol. We'll be leaving soon.'

'What about the bear?'

'We are in his territory. If we leave it maybe – just maybe – he will not follow.'

'I don't want to go.'

'Neither do I, my friend. But it will be safer.' All the while he was talking Kaelin kept watch on the tree line, his musket in his hand. There was no predicting the actions of this bear. Indeed, it was rare to see a grizzly out in such weather. In normal circumstances it should have been hibernating.

As the dawn approached Kaelin pulled on his heavy topcoat and climbed out of the shattered doorway. The world outside was white and alien, and unnaturally silent. Cocking the musket he moved out into the open and scanned the trees. The tracks of the bear headed off towards the north. Kaelin edged round the hut. By the wood store was a sled, about five feet long, neatly made with polished runners. He had seen Basson and Feargol playing on it last winter. Sadness touched him, and he glanced at the tree to which Basson's dead body still clung.

Returning to the cabin Kaelin helped Feargol to dress, placing a wool-lined, hooded coat over his clothes and finding him two sets of mittens. Outside once more he pulled the sled clear of the wood store, placing his pack inside it. The rope handles were frozen, but he brushed the ice clear and dragged the sled out onto open ground. It slid easily. Returning to the cabin he fetched out the spear and Finbarr's pistol and musket. These he also placed in the sled, the spear jutting out over the rear. Finding his snowshoes he strapped them on, and called Feargol. The little boy peeked out, then ran to stand alongside Kaelin.

'We are going to take the sled,' Kaelin told him. Feargol was not listening. He was staring horrified at his brother in the tree.

'Basson!' he called.

'Shhh!' said Kaelin, dropping down to kneel alongside the child. 'We must make no noise.'

'He won't come down!' wailed Feargol.

'Listen to me, little friend. Listen to me. Basson is dead. He can't be hurt any more. We must get you home. Then I'll come back and look after Basson.' Feargol began to cry. Kaelin drew him close and kissed his cheek. 'Be brave for a little while longer. Now climb in the sled.'

'Basson says he's frightened of the bear,' said Feargol. 'Tell him to come down.'

'He is safe where he is, Feargol. The bear cannot get him. I'll come back for him when I have you safe at Ironlatch. I promise. Now get into the sled.'

The boy slid in alongside his father's musket. 'Hold on to the spear,' said Kaelin. 'Don't let it fall out.' Carrying his own musket over his shoulder, Kaelin took hold of the rope with his left hand and began to drag the sled towards the long, downward slope, glancing back constantly to see if the beast had returned. After a quarter of an hour they reached the crest and Kaelin stopped. Ahead was a steep dip of around half a mile, ending in the frozen river. Removing his snowshoes Kaelin wedged them into the sled. He glanced back.

The bear was at the cabin. Around his head, and his sagging lip, the fur had burnt away, giving him a demonic look. He reared up on his hind legs, and saw the distant man and boy. With a savage roar he dropped to all fours and began to run at them.

Kaelin pushed the sled forward onto the slope. The snow was thick, and the sled did not begin to slide. Grunting with the effort he pushed harder. He did not dare look back. The sled began to move. Leaping onto it he grabbed for the ropes, losing hold of his musket, which fell to the snow. The sled slowed, then picked up speed.

Kaelin risked a glance back. The bear was closing fast, sending up great sprays of snow as it bounded towards them. The ground dipped more sharply and the sled gathered pace.

Then it was away, skidding and slithering towards the river below. Twice it hit hidden rocks and almost toppled. Kaelin wrestled with the rope guides, desperately trying to keep the sled upright. Halfway down there was a another dip, and a rise. The sled left the ground. The spear started to fall, but Feargol grabbed the haft, holding on tight. 'Good boy!' shouted Kaelin.

They closed on the river at terrific speed. Kaelin realized the sled would strike the ice with great force. If the surface gave way they would be plunged into the water, and swept below the ice. He tried to turn the sled and slow it, but to no avail. It hit the river bank, sending up a huge spray of snow. Finbarr's musket and pistol flew out. Feargol was hurled back into Kaelin, who grabbed him. This time the spear also fell clear. The sled rose into the air, landed on the ice and spun wildly. Kaelin and the boy were thrown out. Kaelin held tightly to Feargol, and managed to turn himself so that he struck the ice on his back, shielding the child from impact. They slid across the frozen river, slamming into the far bank. For a moment Kaelin lay still, his head spinning. Then he pushed Feargol to the bank and rolled to his knees. Far above on the slope he could see the bear. It was padding along the ridge, and making no attempt to follow them down.

Kaelin stood. His legs were trembling. 'Are you all right?' he asked Feargol.

'That was really fast,' said the boy.

'Yes, it was.'

Kaelin stumbled out onto the ice. The sled was lying on its side. He righted it, and saw that it was relatively undamaged. His pack was lying close by, as were the spear and Finbarr's musket. The pistol was nowhere in sight. Replacing pack, spear and musket he dragged the sled to the bank.

'The bear isn't following us,' said Feargol, happily.

'It looks that way,' agreed Kaelin.

It took some time to find a way out of the river bed, but eventually man and boy hauled the sled up onto more solid ground. It was here that Kaelin discovered his snowshoes had also been lost. His temper snapped and he swore loudly.

'Those were bad words,' said Feargol. Kaelin took a deep breath.

'Yes, they were.' He grinned at the child. 'Not a word to Chara about them.'

'She'll send you to bed without supper,' said Feargol.

'Aye – and more than that,' said Kaelin.

The journey to the cliff cave took more than six hours. Feargol was cold and trembling as they reached the cliff, and could not make the climb to the cave entrance. Kaelin swung the boy to his back. 'Hold on tight,' he said. Then, removing his gloves, he reached up for the first hold. The cliff face was ice-covered, but the holds were deep, the climb easy. The cave entrance was only some ten feet above the ground and Kaelin made it in moments, carrying the child inside and lowering him to the floor. There was wood stacked by the far wall. Kaelin prepared a fire, and, once it was started, sat Feargol beside it. Then he returned to the sled, removing the pack, musket and spear. The spear he threw haft first into the cave. The pack and musket he carried up. Feargol was lying beside the fire asleep. Kaelin shook him awake. 'Not yet, boy,' he said. 'First we must get you warm. Otherwise you'll die.' Removing the boy's topcoat and hat he rubbed at his arms and legs. The fire grew brighter and warmer. Feargol began to tremble and shiver. His lips were blue. His eyes closed. 'Stay awake!' roared Kaelin.

'S-s-sorry,' said the boy.

'I'm not angry,' Kaelin told him. 'You can sleep in a little while. First we let the fire warm our bodies. Then we eat a little. All right?'

'Yes, Uncle Kaelin.'

'You are a tough boy. You'll be fine.'

'Who left the wood here?'

'I did. A man should always be prepared. There are lots of places around these highlands where I have left fuel, or supplies. My uncle Jaim taught me that.'

Feargol's colour was better now, and Kaelin relaxed a little. Fetching his pack, he took out more of the dried meat and cheese and shared it with the child. The cave was warmer now. Some sixteen feet deep and fourteen feet wide, it had once been considerably larger, but, on the western side, a rock fall had collapsed part of the roof. One wall was now merely a wedged mass of broken stones, and several boulders had tumbled into the cave. Kaelin glanced at the wood store. He had spent the best part of a day last autumn bringing wood to the cave, and stacking it by the east wall. There was enough now to last through the night and tomorrow, if necessary.

It would still be a tough journey home, but if they travelled with care they would make it. Feargol lay down on the floor. Kaelin folded the now empty pack and made a pillow for the child. 'I've never been that fast in the sled,' said Feargol, sleepily. 'Daddy never let us go down the long slope.'

'A wise man, your daddy,' said Kaelin, ruffling the boy's red hair. 'Sleep now. It will be a tiring day tomorrow.'

Feargol closed his eyes. Kaelin covered him with his own topcoat

29

then sat by the fire. He dozed for a while, and dreamt of Finbarr Ustal. When first Kaelin had arrived at Ironlatch Farm Finbarr had been hostile. They had since become friends, and Kaelin had come to respect the highlander. To be honest he had never liked his wife. Strong though she was she had a harsh tongue, and was mean-spirited. Kaelin had never understood how Finbarr could have loved her. He noted that even the child had talked about Daddy, but not his mother. Still, mean-spirited or not, no-one deserved a death like that.

He woke several times during the night, and kept the fire going. It was good, dry wood, and there was little smoke. Even so his eyes felt gritty. In the firelight he gazed at the sleeping boy. He had his thumb in his mouth. Kaelin smiled. He would forever be Uncle Kaelin now. The thought was a sobering one. He wondered if this was how Jaim had felt about him, when he was the orphan child.

'Ah, Jaim, but I do miss you,' he said aloud.

Then came a crunching sound, followed by a roar. Kaelin rolled to his feet and ran to the cave entrance. Ten feet below the bear was tearing at the sled, his teeth crunching down on the wood. Rearing up, he flung the ruined pieces to the snow. Kaelin drew both pistols from his belt, cocked them, and called out: 'Eat this, you scum-sucking bastard!' He shot the right-hand pistol first, aiming at the bear's throat. The ball tore into the beast's shoulder. Hang-lip let out a fearsome roar, dropped to all fours and ran for the trees. Kaelin sent a second shot into him.

Little Feargol was sitting up, eyes wide and fearful. Kaelin moved back to the fire and sat down to clean his pistols before reloading them. Feargol was looking at him, but Kaelin could think of nothing to say.

'Did he break Basson's sled?' asked Feargol.

'Aye. With a vengeance. I put two shots into him though. Bet he's not happy now.'

'What are we going to do, Uncle Kaelin?'

'Tomorrow I'll sit in the cave mouth, lure him out, and keep shooting him until he is dead.'

'He wants to kill me,' said Feargol.

'Not just you, my friend. He just wants to feed.'

'No, he wants to kill me. He told me. I told Daddy. Daddy

didn't believe me either. Can you see his face, Uncle Kaelin?'

'Whose face?'

'The bear's.'

'Yes. His lip was torn in a fight when he was young.'

'No. His other face,' said the boy. 'The one with scales like a snake. The one with red eyes.'

'No,' said Kaelin, carefully. 'I can't see that face.'

'Not even with your magic eye?'

'I think you've had a bad dream, Feargol. Do you trust me?'

'Yes, Uncle Kaelin.'

'Then trust that I will kill the beast. If necessary I'll put shots into both its damned faces.'

The Wyrd of Wishing Tree woods watched as the three clansmen climbed the tree to retrieve the frozen body of Basson Ustal. She felt sick at heart. Of all the sad sights her eyes had witnessed during her long life she knew this one would stay with her to her dying day. A dead child in a thin nightshirt, clinging to a tree branch. Even in death his face was still contorted with terror. She glanced back at the cabin. The boy had seen the bodies of his parents dragged out, and then the bear had come for him, clawing furiously at the trunk of the tree.

The white-haired woman shivered, though not with the cold. The iron afterglow of evil hung in the air.

The figure of Rayster emerged from the tree line. Seeing the tall, fair-haired clansman lifted her heart momentarily. Moving past the Wyrd he walked to the tree and helped as Basson's body was lowered to the ground. Rayster's pale blue eyes met the Wyrd's green gaze. 'There's not much of them left to bury back there,' he said. 'I've gathered what I could upon a canvas sheet. We'll need to light fires to soften the earth before digging. You are sure the bear is gone?'

'Aye, clansman, the bear is gone. He hunts other prey now.'

'I cannot find trace of the youngest,' said Rayster.

'He is alive,' said the Wyrd. 'And with Kaelin Ring.'

'Ah, but that is good news,' said Rayster, with a broad smile.

'Aye. It was fortunate that Ravenheart chose this day to visit. Set the grave fires, Rayster, for the light is failing and I have much to do.'

31

She walked away from him then, and entered the ruined hut. The clansmen had relit the fire and, removing her wool-lined, hooded cloak, she sat before the flickering flames. Closing her eyes she thought of Kaelin Ring. 'Be true to your blood, Ravenheart,' she whispered. 'The bear is coming for you.'

She built up the fire and sat quietly. Hang-lip was always a cruel beast, and yet this action of his had baffled the clansmen. Not so the Wyrd. The beast was possessed. Somehow the enemy had managed to control him. Perhaps it was Hang-lip's twisted nature which allowed them access. Whatever the method their target was the child, Feargol. He had the Gift. The Wyrd had tried to explain this to Finbarr, but the clansman had angrily turned her away. 'You'll not fill my son's head with these ancient stupidities,' he had told her.

'Can you not see he is frightened, Finbarr? He is hearing voices. They are threatening him. I can help.'

'He is daydreaming. All children fear what they do not understand.'

'Not only children, Finbarr.'

'You stay away from my boy!'

She should have pushed him harder, she thought. Instead she had merely walked away from the cabin. The Wyrd sat now, feeling the ache in her bones. ' You are getting old and frail,' she said aloud.

'You'll never be old, Dweller,' said Rayster, using the name she had acquired here in the north. He moved alongside her and stretched out his hands to the fire. 'You look now just the same as when I first saw you. And I was a toddler then.'

'No, you weren't,' she told him. 'You were a babe, four days old. You were tiny, and yet braw. You should have been dead, but there was spirit in you. Mountain spirit. You gladdened my heart then, clansman. You do so now.' Rayster gave a crooked grin that was wondrously infectious. The Wyrd smiled back at him, and they sat in comfortable silence, listening to the crackling of the fire. The three other clansmen moved in, but they did not sit close to the woman they knew as the Dweller by the Lake. She was a witch, and she could – so they believed – read minds and hearts. They kept their distance. This amused the Wyrd, for she knew them all well, and there was little in their lives that could shame them. They

32

were brave, caring men, and good clansmen. Korrin Talis drank a little too much and became maudlin, and Potter Highstone crept away to an earth maiden once in a while, but they were small sins. She glanced at the youngest, Fada Talis. He was full of guilt, for his family were waiting for him to find a girl to marry, while in his heart he dreamt only of Rayster. Small sins – if sins at all. Yet sadly it was never the sin itself but only the weight men placed on it that counted.

'We've set the grave fires, Rayster,' said young Fada Talis. 'How long should we wait?'

'It'll be tough digging whenever,' said Rayster. 'But we'll wait an hour for the fires to soften the ground. Keep an eye on them, and keep them fed.'

'I will.'

'Did you see the deaths, Dweller?' asked Korrin Talis. In his mid-twenties he was losing his hair, which had receded at the temples giving him a sharp widow's peak above his brow.

'Aye,' she answered him. 'Finbarr and Ural put up a brave fight. They died swiftly.'

'Rayster tells us that Kaelin has the youngest,' he said.

'Yes, the boy is with Ravenheart. The bear is hunting them.'

'Why did you not say?' shouted Rayster, pushing himself to his feet. 'We must go and help him.'

'Sit down, man!' snapped the Wyrd. 'Do you think if that was a possibility I'd have dawdled here?'

'Will they escape it then?' he asked.

'No. It will come for them. Kaelin Ring will fight it. I cannot predict the outcome.'

'He's a bonny fighter,' said Potter Highstone. The oldest of the clansmen, Potter was powerfully built, and nicknamed Badger by his friends, after the heavy black and silver beard he sported. 'I'd wager my money on Ravenheart,' he said. 'Especially if he's carrying those Emburleys. Fine guns, by heaven.'

'I don't know,' muttered Korrin Talis. 'I've seen Hang-lip. Take a damned cannon to bring him down.'

'Where are they now?' Rayster asked the Wyrd. 'Can you see them?'

'No, I cannot *see* them, clansman. Yet I know where they are.

Kaelin has taken Feargol to the cliff cave. It is there the last fight will take place.'

'That's at least six hours from here,' said Fada Talis.

Rayster sat down again beside the Wyrd, who could feel the tension in him. He yearned to be able to aid his friend. He caught the Wyrd looking at him.

'I am sorry, Dweller. I did not mean to offend you.'

'Whisht, man. There is nothing you could ever do to offend me.'

The men chatted for some time, talking of the skills of Kaelin Ring and the stories of Hang-lip. The Wyrd stretched herself out on the rug before the fire. Closing her eyes, she carefully opened the eyes of her spirit.

Two demonic figures floated close by, their scaled faces but a few inches from her own, their blood red eyes watching her. Sitting up she reached into the pouch by her side, taking a pinch of the powder there and placing it under her tongue. Bright colours flared before her eyes and she felt fresh energy pulse through her veins. Beside her, Rayster got up and walked out of the cabin to help Fada with the grave fires. Even with the heat it would be hard work digging a grave in this winter soil, she knew.

'You look tired, Dweller,' said Potter. 'You should sleep for a while.'

Rising, she walked through to the small bedroom and sat on the broad bed. In here the residue was still strong, and she could feel the spirit echoes of Finbarr Ustal's fear. As the first crashes to the timbers awakened him he had rolled from his bed and gathered up his musket. Ural had stood with him. The Wyrd reached out and touched the carved wood of the trunk in which Feargol had hidden. It was old, but there was still power radiating from the symbols.

Something cold touched the Wyrd's heart and she shivered. In the old days there had been many of these spell chests, crafted and blessed to bring good luck to the owners. It had saved the boy. But not the parents.

Closing her mind to the awful images the Wyrd walked back to the main room. Rayster came in from the cold. 'Time to dig, lads,' he said. 'I've found a pickaxe and two shovels.'

Two hours later, the men exhausted, the grave dug, and filled

34

again, the Wyrd stood beside it. Holding out her arms she spoke in the ancient tongue.

> 'Seek the circle, find the light,
> Say farewell to flesh and bone.
> Walk the grey path,
> Watch the swan's flight,
> Let your heart light
> Bring you home.'

She stood silently for a moment, then shuddered. Her gaze flicked towards the tall, talon-gouged tree. 'They are not free yet,' she said. She swung towards the men. 'Go and rest now,' she said. 'I have work to do, and I need to be alone.'

She waited as they trooped back to the cabin, then walked to the tree and gathered her thoughts. Glancing up she looked at the bough to which the frightened boy had clung. Taking a deep breath she whispered a Word of Power. The air around her grew still. A shadowy figure began to form upon the bough. The Wyrd looked into the frightened eyes of the young boy sitting there. 'It is time to come down, Basson,' she told the child's spirit.

'The bear will get me!' he said.

'The bear is gone, boy. He cannot hurt you now.'

Basson shut his eyes tight and ignored her. Wearily the Wyrd walked away, entering the trees, and standing upon the blood-stained ground where the remains of Finbarr Ustal and his wife had been found. 'Finbarr!' she called. 'The Dweller needs you. Ural! Your son is frightened. Come to me now.' A mist seeped up from the snow, surrounding her. She felt a presence to her right, just out-side her line of sight. Then another. 'Follow me, Rigante,' she whispered, and walked back to the tree. The mist flowed with her.

At the tree she called out again. 'Look who I have with me, Basson,' she said. 'They have come to take you home.' The boy opened his eyes. All fear fled from him. 'I thought it had killed you,' he said. He began to climb down. As he did so his form grew paler, the lines increasingly indistinct. By the time he reached the ground he seemed little more than wood smoke. Ignoring the Wyrd the child's spirit flowed and merged with the mist, which then

35

rolled and moved back towards the trees. The Wyrd spoke the words again.

> 'Seek the circle, find the light,
> Say farewell to flesh and bone.
> Walk the grey path,
> Watch the swan's flight,
> Let your heart light
> Bring you home.'

Suddenly her legs buckled and she fell to the snow. Rayster, watching from the ruined doorway, ran to her, lifting her into his arms and carrying her back to the cabin.

'I will be all right,' she told him, as he laid her by the fire. 'I will be fine. As long as I do not sleep.'

# CHAPTER TWO

KAELIN RING SLEPT FITFULLY, WAKING OFTEN TO FEED THE FIRE. LITTLE Feargol, exhausted, lay in a deep and dreamless sleep. Smoke drifted lazily to the ceiling of the cave, then out into the night. Rising, Kaelin moved to the cave mouth. The night sky was clear of clouds, and he gazed at the bright stars. Moonlight gave the snow-covered landscape an ethereal quality, and he shivered, partly from the cold, but mostly from the awesome beauty of the land.

A bitter wind whispered across the cave mouth. Kaelin returned to the fire, and wrapped himself in his cloak. He had told the child he would lure out the bear and shoot it, but he doubted Hang-lip would be foolish enough to stand around and be repeatedly shot. At some point he would have to go out and meet the beast with musket and spear. The thought was not a pleasant one.

Chara had urged him not to travel to Finbarr's cabin. 'The weather is too fierce,' she said. 'It is foolishness.'

'Perhaps so,' he admitted. 'Yet I need the walk.'

'Then hold your son for a moment,' she said, her voice angry. 'And when you are lying in a snowdrift, and your life is slipping away, think of how you will never see him grow.' With that she had stalked from the room.

'Aye, you're a fool right enough, Kaelin Ring,' he told himself, as he added another chunk of wood to the flames. 'There's no denying it.'

Hunger gnawed at him. There was a little meat left, but no cheese and he had finished the last of his bread yesterday morning. The meat he decided to leave for Feargol. The child would need all his strength for the walk to Ironlatch. The fuel store was low now – enough perhaps for half a day. They could not wait out the bear.

Kaelin gazed around the cave, focusing on the jumbled stand of broken rocks that made up the western wall. Maybe men were sleeping here at the time of the roof fall, he thought. Perhaps their bodies are buried beneath those rocks. Cavemen dressed in furs, or ancient hunters sheltering from the snow.

'There are spirits of heroes wandering every forest and mountain,' Jaim had told him once. Kaelin wished it were true. Then perhaps he could talk to Jaim one more time, and say his farewells. Perhaps then he could put aside his grief.

'Is it morning yet?' asked Feargol, sitting up and rubbing his eyes.

'Almost. Did you dream?'

'No. I had a lovely sleep. Are you going to shoot the bear with your pistols?'

'No. I shall use your daddy's musket. It takes a bigger charge.'

Feargol stood up and looked around. 'I need to pee,' he said.

Kaelin smiled. 'Anywhere you please, my friend. There's no-one here to scold you for peeing inside.' The child walked to the cave mouth, then scampered back inside.

'It's too cold out there, Uncle Kaelin.' He ran to the rear wall and relieved himself. Then he returned to the fire. 'Will it take us long to reach Ironlatch?'

'It will. It will be very cold, and you'll need your hat.'

'I'll tie it down like Bane.' He looked across at Kaelin. 'Can I see one of your pistols?'

The boy had asked many times during Kaelin's visits to hold one of the Emburleys, but Finbarr had always told him no. Kaelin pulled one of the silver pistols from his belt. Reversing it he passed it to Feargol, who took it in both hands. 'It is very pretty,' said the boy, turning it over. 'What is that animal?' He pointed to the engraved pommel.

'Jaim said it was a lion – a ferocious beast who lives in the hot lands far to the south, across the seas.'

'Is it big then?'

'Jaim said they could be ten feet long, from the tips of their noses to the ends of their tails. And their teeth are as long as a man's fingers.'

'When I'm big I shall have pistols with lions on them. And I shall shoot all the bears.'

'That would not be good,' said Kaelin. 'The bears have a right to live their lives, to mate and rear young. They are not all as evil as Hang-lip. Don't hate the bears, Feargol. Hate is bad. Bane didn't hate bears.'

'Not even bears with bad faces?'

The question brought back the memory of last night's curious conversation. 'What did you mean when you said you told your daddy about the bear?' he asked.

'I told him it was coming. That I had seen its bad face.'

'What did you see?'

'I was playing with Basson and I saw this face. It was in the air. It had scales and red eyes. It spoke to me.'

'Did Basson see it?'

'No. He got angry and said I was making it up. The face frightened me and I told Daddy. He didn't believe me.'

'What did the face say to you?'

'He told me I was evil and I was going to die. He said a bear would eat me up.'

'And that is what you told your daddy?'

'Yes.'

'Have you seen the face again, Feargol?'

'No.'

'If you do then tell me.'

'Mm. Is there anything to eat?'

'You have a mind like a butterfly,' Kaelin told him, laughing. Just then there came a faint noise. Feargol was about to speak, but Kaelin hushed him. Then it came again – but not from outside the cave. Kaelin turned his gaze to the mass of broken rock. Suddenly the wall trembled, and a muffled roar sounded.

Hang-lip had found a way up into the cliff!

Kaelin scrambled up, gathering the musket. The wall trembled again, and several boulders tumbled into the cave. Dust filled the air. More rocks fell, and Kaelin saw Hang-lip's huge, scorched head. Raising the musket he fired. The shot hit the bear in the mouth, snapping one of its front teeth. Furiously the beast thrashed at the rocks. Kaelin dropped the musket and drew his second pistol, sending another shot into the bear's throat. A huge boulder gave way and Hang-lip surged up and into the cave. Kaelin let the pistol fall and swept up the spear. With a battle cry he leapt at the huge beast, plunging the spear deep into its chest, driving it on, seeking the heart. A taloned paw smashed into his shoulder. The spear snapped in two and Kaelin was hurled over the rocks. His left arm numbed by the blow, he rolled to his knees, drawing his hunting knife from its sheath. Without thinking he surged up and charged the bear. Blood was pouring from its throat, and the broken spear was wedged deep. Ducking under the beast's jaws Kaelin slammed his knife into its belly.

A shot thundered. The bear's head jerked up, and then its body sagged and fell across the young Rigante. Kaelin lay very still. The bear's head was on his chest, and he could hear its ragged breathing. Slowly the sound grew more rasping, until it was little more than a whisper. Then it ceased.

Kaelin eased himself from under the body. As he did so he saw that its right eye had been shot through. He turned. Little Feargol was sitting by the fire, Kaelin's pistol smoking in his hands.

'Did I kill it, Uncle Kaelin?'

'You did,' said the man. Feeling was coming back into his arm, and he flexed his fingers. He sank down next to Feargol, and retrieved his pistol. Then he put his hand on the child's shoulder. 'Did I not tell you I had a magic eye? You have killed Hang-lip and avenged your family. You are a hero, Feargol.'

'I don't want to be a hero any more, Uncle Kaelin,' said the child, tears in his eyes.

Kaelin drew the boy into a hug. 'I know. We shall go soon. I am very proud of you, little man. Your daddy would be too.'

Feargol began to cry. Kaelin patted the boy's back. 'All right, let us dress warm and take to the snow.'

*

A bitter wind blew across the waters of Sorrow Bird Lake, moon-light flickering on the crests of the tiny waves as they lapped against the ice forming around the shoreline. Snow lay thick on the branches of the pine trees bordering the shore, and a heavy silence hung over the winter land. The night sky was brilliantly lit by a full moon, around which stars glittered diamond bright against the impenetrable blackness of the heavens.

At the centre of the lake was a small, wooded island. Just within the tree line stood a roughly built, sod-roofed hut. Hazy smoke drifted from its cast iron chimney. In the open doorway stood a small, slender woman, a pale blue and green shawl wrapped tightly around her shoulders. Her white hair – normally tied in a single braid – hung loose, the cold breeze rippling through it.

The Wyrd's spirits were low, and she felt old and alone. The Redeemers had found the path to her spirit, and she was running out of tricks to thwart them. Spirit journeys now were fraught with peril. Despair touched her, and she fought it back.

Pulling shut the door she walked out to the frozen shore, the snow crunching beneath her booted feet. She shivered, though not with the winter cold. She could feel the dark spirits hovering around her, waiting. By now they would have sent killers to find her, cold-souled men who would ride north and seek to enter Rigante lands. They would not find it easy. Call Jace did not allow strangers to travel the inner passes. The Wyrd sighed. She did not doubt they would find a way. Circling the small island she returned to her hut. The fire was burning low, but she did not build it up. Too much heat and she would fall asleep. Then they would find her spirit as it wandered and, in her weary state, snuff out her life like an unwanted candle flame.

It was most galling. These Redeemers saw themselves as so deadly. They believed themselves all powerful. The truth was that the Wyrd could, if she chose, kill every one of them. Aye, that was tempting! She could become a creature of avenging fire, and burn their souls to damnation. Would it not advance the cause of good to destroy them, she wondered?

'Aye, and therein lies the path to your own destruction,' she said aloud.

The power granted to her by the spirit of Riamfada all those years ago had come at a price. 'It is born of love,' he had said, within the tranquil setting of the Wishing Tree woods. 'It is of harmony, and joy. You may use it to heal, to enhance, to bring together. Never to destroy.'

'I don't want to destroy anything,' she had told him.

'Let us hope that is always true.'

Oh, there had been times in the past when she had wished to cause harm. When the Moidart had betrayed Lanovar to his death. When the greedy Bishop of Eldacre had tried to have Maev Ring burned for witchcraft. Evil men who deserved death. Yet the temptation had never been as great as now. Is it just because my own life is threatened, she asked herself? Is my desire merely to save myself? The Wyrd hoped it was not.

She gazed around her small, single-roomed hut, her eyes lingering on the objects gathering dust on the shelves. There was an old green cap that had belonged to Ruathain, stepfather to Connavar the King, and a bronze cloak brooch Connavar's mother had given him when he was twelve. Alongside the brooch lay a bronze and silver wristband which had been worn by Vorna the Witch, long ago when the Rigante were kings of the highlands. There were other items: scarves, belts, jugs and cups. All had been owned by heroes of the clan. Nothing here was worth more than a single chailling in the markets, and yet they were beyond price. She had but to touch them, and her mind would fill with colour, and she would hear the voices of their owners drifting down through the centuries. Closing her eyes she would see fragments of their lives – Connavar fighting the bear to save his crippled friend, Ruathain holding his sons in his arms, Bane gathering the army to defend the homeland . . .

Moving to the nearest shelf the Wyrd reached out and picked up an old cloth, heavily stained with dried blood.

'Oh, Jaim,' she said, 'you were the best of them.'

The cloth had been used by Maev Ring to wipe the blood from Jaim's face after his epic fight with the Varlish fistfighting champion, Gorain. The one-eyed Jaim Grymauch had stood toe to toe with the champion, and – incredibly – had defeated him. 'You had a heart as big as the mountains,' said the Wyrd, a tear in her eye.

The greatest regret of her long life had come the day she had told Jaim Grymauch of the arrest of Maev Ring. Jaim had loved Maev, and had been determined to rescue her. The Wyrd had asked him to wait. He could have gone to the cathedral, where she was imprisoned for the trial, dealt with the guards and freed her. He would have lived then, and known happiness. But the Wyrd told him that the future well-being of the Rigante depended on his delaying the rescue.

So Jaim Grymauch had waited. They had brought Maev out to burn her at the stake, and Grymauch had marched through the crowds like a giant of old. He had scattered the guards, and killed three Knights of the Sacrifice. Then, having rescued Maev, and seen her free, he had been shot down by the muskets of the Moidart's soldiers.

Even now his death felt like an open wound to the Wyrd. Everything she had told him had come to pass. His heroism had forever altered the relationship between the northern Varlish and the Rigante. Before Jaim's death the highlanders were treated like an inferior race, and viewed with ill concealed contempt. A fog of hatred and fear blinded the Varlish. Jaim Grymauch had been the cleansing storm.

Now it seemed his death might be for nothing after all. War, destruction, plague and death were rampant in the southern lands. Malice hung in the air, touching all living things, disrupting the harmony of nature and poisoning the nature of all earth magic. It even affected the Wyrd. Normally tranquil of nature she found herself more swift to anger. Man had always feared spellcasters. Almost all societies had at one time or another burned witches. Yet, ironically, man himself could cast the most destructive spell of all. With his endless lust for war he could pollute the very magic that fed his world.

The Wyrd took a deep breath, then relaxed. She could feel the spirits of two Redeemers hovering near her. They hungered for her death, their minds overflowing with images of inflicted pain and suffering.

'You will not make me hate you,' she said aloud. However, even thinking of them brought anger to her heart. Best to think of nobler men, she told herself, turning her thoughts to Kaelin Ring.

The years since the death of Grymauch had been kind to him. Still in his early twenties he was admired by the Black Rigante, holding a position of honour in the council of their leader, Call Jace, and married to his daughter, Chara. Kaelin's first child had been born two years previously – a boy they had named Jaim. Life was good, and yet the black-haired young Rigante would often wander the lonely hills around Ironlatch Farm, camping out at nights in the woods, sometimes for days.

His need for solitude hurt his young wife, but she did not doubt his love for her. Had he not fought his way into the heart of an enemy castle to rescue her? Chara had spoken to the Wyrd about Kaelin's wanderings, on the day they had taken baby Jaim to Sorrow Bird Lake for the Blessing. While Kaelin sat holding the sleeping babe Chara and the Wyrd had strolled to Shrine Hollow and sat in the shafts of spring sunshine lancing through the trees.

'Sometimes he is so distant,' said Chara. 'His eyes get a faraway look, and then I know he will be gone. When he returns he is fine for a little while. I don't know what is wrong with him.'

The Wyrd had gazed affectionately at the slim, red-haired young woman. Even now she looked scarcely old enough to be a mother. Slight of build, and delicate of feature, she seemed almost childlike. 'His soul was pierced when Jaim died,' said the Wyrd. 'Grymauch was everything to him as a boy – a father, an older brother, a friend. He was the one constant in Kaelin's life. He was like a mountain. You could not imagine a day when he would not be there, filling the horizon.'

'Aye, I know he was a great man,' said Chara. The Wyrd laughed, the sound rich.

'Ah, Chara! He was a drunkard and he loved to go whoring. He was not stupid, but neither was he equipped for scholarship. Aye, he was a great man, but it was his humanity that made him great. Jaim was – believe it or not – ordinary. He was Rigante, and embodied the best and the worst of the clan. That is why he remains such an inspiration. Too many men are allowing his legend to grow out of proportion. He was not so much different from Rayster, Bael, or indeed Kaelin. Good men, strong men. Men to walk the mountains with.'

'I still do not see why Kaelin cannot let him go. He has his own family now.'

'Love carries burdens, Chara, my dear. And great love understands pain beyond bearing. As time passes Kaelin's grief will ease. It is not helped by the presence of Maev. She, I fear, will never recover from the loss.'

'Sometimes they sit in the evenings and talk about Grymauch,' said Chara. 'I can't contribute anything. I did not really know him. All I remember is that he was a big man who wore a strip of cloth over a blind eye. Why did Maev not wed him?'

'She *was* wedded to him,' said the Wyrd, 'only she did not know it. They shared everything except a bed. And, you know, that is not so important.'

As the two women talked the black-garbed Kaelin Ring came walking into the hollow, baby Jaim crying in his arms. 'If you two are finished gossiping,' he said, 'there's a little fellow here who needs his mother.' Chara took Jaim, opened her shirt and held him to her breast. The crying ceased immediately. Kaelin stood by, gazing fondly at his wife and son.

The Wyrd watched him, and felt pride swell in her. Kaelin Ring was all that a Rigante should be.

Taking his arm, the Wyrd led him back to the shores of Sorrow Bird Lake, and they stood together in the sunlight, gazing out over the mountains. 'You have done well, Ravenheart,' she told him. 'Jaim would be proud of you.'

'That is a good thought, Wyrd. Thank you for sharing it.'

'How is Maev?'

'Growing richer by the day. She deals now with the Moidart, sending cattle south to feed the Varlish armies.'

'I know she is rich, Kaelin, and you know that is not what I meant.'

Kaelin shrugged. 'What can I tell you, Wyrd? She talks of Grymauch endlessly.' He gave a wry smile. 'She seems to have forgotten all the times she lost her temper with him. He has become a golden man – almost a saint.'

'Understandable,' said the Wyrd. 'The man died for her.'

She saw a momentary spasm of pain cross his handsome features. 'Aye, he did that. Sometimes I dream of him, you know.

We'll be talking and laughing. Then I'll wake, and just for a heart-beat I think he's still here with us. It's like a wound that won't heal.'

'It will, Ravenheart. Trust me. Have you heard from Banny?'

Kaelin shook his head. 'There are few post riders now bringing mail from the south. I don't know what possessed him to join the army. He should have come here.'

'The war will come to the north, Ravenheart. When it does you must be ready for it.'

'We have had this conversation before, Wyrd. I listened then, and I am listening now. Call Jace has built new forges, making cannons, muskets and swords. We can do no more. If the Moidart comes north the Rigante will face him.'

A log in the fire cracked suddenly, jerking her mind back to the present. A burning cinder was smouldering upon the old rug. The Wyrd knelt down, pinched the cinder between her fingers and swiftly threw it back into the flames. Sitting upon the rug she stretched and yawned.

When would the Moidart and his army invade the highlands, she wondered? It had surprised her that the cruel and vengeful Lord of the North had not already joined the enemy. They were made for one another. They had approached him, she knew. The Moidart had requested time to consider their offer. The Wyrd shivered. He would be seeking a position of power among them. And he would get it.

Another face loomed in her mind – a handsome young man with golden hair and curious eyes, one gold, one green. The Moidart's son, Gaise Macon. The Stormrider. So much depended on him and his survival. She wished with all her heart that she could know just how much. It seemed sometimes that the Power had a mind of its own. On occasions – as with Jaim Grymauch – she had seen the future clear and bright. She had known what to do. The coming days of dread were like an awesome tapestry, ten thousand threads weaving in and out. Some she could see, some lines she could follow. But the whole was a mystery. In her spirit dreams she could see fragments. A hawk-faced Varlish lord – similar to the Moidart – and a skull within an ancient case, that burned with unholy light. Battles and deaths, some past and some still to come, raged in her visions.

All she knew, with grim certainty, was that the Stormrider was central to the survival of the Rigante, and that the Rigante were vital not only to the survival of the world she knew, but to the well-being of the world to come. Her eyes felt heavy with weariness and she pushed herself to her feet and once more ventured out into the night.

The Wyrd walked back through the trees to the remains of the old stone circle at the centre of the island. Only one golden column stood upright now, and this was cracked, the ancient runes worn away by wind and rain. The Wyrd shivered, and drew her shawl more tightly around her shoulders. The night wind whispered across the icy lake.

'*Soon, witch*,' came a voice in her mind. '*Soon your evil will be forever destroyed.*'

The Wyrd took a deep, calming breath and whispered the Words of Power. A bright light blazed and the world shifted beneath her feet. She stumbled – and fell to the earth of the Wishing Tree woods, hundreds of miles south of Sorrow Bird Lake. The Redeemers would find her soon. They knew almost all her tricks now.

Rising, she looked around her at the ancient trees. 'I need you, Riamfada,' she said aloud, her voice breaking. 'Help me!'

A glowing light formed, like a tiny candle flame flickering a few feet above the snow-covered earth. Slowly it swelled into a shimmering globe, like moonlit mist trapped in glass.

'What is troubling you, child?' asked the voice from the light.

'It is long since I was a child, Riamfada. Look at me. I am an old woman. My bones hurt and I can no longer – without a little magic – thread a needle.' The Wyrd sighed. 'It is forty years since first you took me into the Wishing Tree woods. Long years.'

'And *that* is what is troubling you?'

'No.' The Wyrd gazed at the globe of light floating some three feet away from her. For a moment her mind drifted away from her problems. 'Why do you not take human form these days?'

'This is what I am, child. I only take human form when I need to speak to humans who cannot understand my nature. It is tiring to do so, drawing particles from the air and shaping them like a sculptor. This is more comfortable for me. This is how

47

I am when I am with friends. What is it that you fear to say to me?'

'I am frightened, Riamfada.'

'Of the demons hunting you?'

'They are not demons – nor spirits like you,' she said. 'They are living men who have found a way to soar free from the flesh. They whisper to me of their hatred, and they seek to kill me when I am in spirit form. Thus far I have escaped them, but they are growing in strength . . .' Her words tailed away.

'You wish to fight them, Caretha? To kill them?'

'Would it be so wrong?'

'A simple question, but one of rare complexity. Your gift is to heal, Caretha, to enhance the fading magic of the world. When healers yearn to kill then hope begins to die.'

'Then I must let them kill me?'

'Better that than to become like them. *That* is the real danger, Caretha. Evil cannot be overcome by evil. The Seidh – at the last – understood that.'

'Why did they leave us?' said the Wyrd. 'They could have helped us, guided us. Then there would have been no wars, no plagues, no disease.'

'Once they too believed that,' said Riamfada. 'For thousands of years they tried. They saw man relentlessly devouring the magic, sowing the seeds that would inevitably lead to destruction and an end to all life. And slowly it dawned upon some of them that they too were parasites. The Seidh also fed on the magic, and were part of the cycle of destruction. Then the Seidh too went to war, Caretha. Among themselves and among humans. The most power-ful of them, a being known as Cernunnos, triumphed for a while. He took human form and became a king. He ruled for three hundred years, gathering massive human armies and waging wars across many lands. Then he was overthrown, his body destroyed. After that the Seidh slowly began to leave the world. The last to go was the Morrigu. I was with her when she passed – which pleased me greatly for she was the one who brought my spirit into the Seidh world, and I loved her.'

'Where did they go?'

'Far out among the stars. I do not know exactly what lies there.'

'Yet you remained.'

'I am an earthbound spirit, child. This is where I belong.'

Suddenly she sat upright, staring at the night sky above her. 'They are back,' she said.

'I see them. Stand between the stone pillars,' said the voice from the light.

The Wyrd pushed herself to her feet. Her shawl fell from her shoulders and she caught it and swung it back into place. Bright light blazed around her once more. For a time she floated weightless, spinning in the air. Then, with a lurch, she felt her body pressing down upon soft earth. The light did not diminish. Opening her eyes against the glare she saw that it was no longer night. The sun was low in a clear blue sky, and it shone down on a foreign landscape. All around her were trees of colossal size, their trunks red, their uppermost branches seeming to pierce the sky.

Beside her dust rose from the ground, swirling as if caught in a tiny whirlwind. Slowly it formed the shape of a man. Colours began to appear, blonding the hair, painting the eyes blue. A white-tipped eagle feather materialized on a shirt of painted buckskin. When the movement in the air had subsided Riamfada stood before her, dressed as she had never seen him. He wore a loincloth and soft moccasins, and there were painted symbols decorating his shirt – a handprint in red, and a series of circles in white, at the centre of which were depictions of birds and deer.

Before the Wyrd could speak she felt a ripple of earth magic flow across her, as if caught on a breeze. Dropping to her knees she stretched out her arms. The strength of the magic was awesome. It seemed to seep up from the ground, flowing out like mist.

'Is this paradise?' she whispered.

'It is at the moment,' he said. 'This is Uzamatte. You see that tree?' He pointed to her left. She looked round, and stared in disbelief at the redwood. It was ten times – perhaps twenty times – as thick as any tree she had ever seen. 'It is over two thousand years old,' Riamfada told her. 'This tree was ancient when Connavar fought the armies of Stone. The magic feeds it. There were trees like this in your world across the ocean, Caretha. No longer. Man has used up much of the magic there, burned it away in his wars, suffocated it with his greed. One day he will come here. He will look at these trees and will see no majesty. He will see timber. He will gaze upon the mountains and the waterfalls and he will see gold and silver. And far below the earth he will tunnel and burrow.' Riamfada sighed, and gave a small smile. 'But not yet.'

'There is still magic in my world,' said the Wyrd. 'Every day I try to summon more, to feed the land.'

'Yes, you do, child.'

'I know it is a losing battle,' she continued. 'In one day of war more harm is done than I can put right in ten lifetimes. It is said more than a hundred thousand have already died, and yet the war goes on. Gaise Macon is fighting in it now, and I fear for him. One day it will reach the north. I know this in my heart. It fills me with sorrow – and with terror.'

'You must rest now, Caretha. Absorb the magic. Strengthen your body and your spirit. You cannot stay here long. Sleep for a few hours, then I will return you to Sorrow Bird Lake. Once you are home you must find a way to reach the spirit of the white-haired swordsman. I do not have your gift for prophecy, but I sense he will be vital in the days ahead.'

'Could *you* not help us against this evil, Riamfada?'

'I *am* helping you, child. In the only way I can.'


Mulgrave the Swordsman trudged through the snow, a hood covering his prematurely white hair, a thick sheepskin jerkin and flowing cloak keeping the cold from his slender frame. He wandered through the market square. Most of the stalls were empty, but crowds were gathering around the few traders with food to sell. A brace of rabbits fetched a chailling – four times the usual price. The woman who bought them thrust them deep into a canvas sack and scurried away, her eyes fearful. Well she might be. Tempers were short now. Mulgrave wondered if all wars caused such a loss of simple humanity. Almost everyone seemed quicker to anger these days, and fights were commonplace among the citizens.

Armed guards were outside the bakery on the corner of Marrall Street, and a long queue of hungry people waited for the doors to open. There would not be enough loaves for all. It began to snow once more. The wind picked up, cold and searching. Mulgrave's grey cloak swirled up and he gathered it in, drawing it close around his chest. The raw chill caused his left shoulder to ache around the healing wound.

Despite the crowds in the square the small town was ominously quiet, footfalls dulled in the thick snow, whispered conversations swept away by the winds. Fear was everywhere. Not just from the threat of starvation, Mulgrave knew. The war was coming closer, and with it the terror. Only a few years ago the folk of Shelding would have argued in the taverns and meeting halls, debating the rights and wrongs of the Covenant. Some would have spoken up for the king's absolute right to rule. Others would have sided with the Covenanters, pointing out that every Varlish citizen should have equal rights under the law. Sometimes the debates would become heated, but mostly they were good-natured. At the close, the townsfolk would have gone back to their homes content.

After four years of war there were no more amiable debates.

Everyone knew of the fate of towns like Barstead, on the south coast. After one battle Covenant troops had entered the town, rooting out Royalist supporters. Sixty men were hanged. Three days later, the Covenant army in retreat, the Royalists had marched through Barstead. Three hundred and ten men with Covenant sympathies had been hanged. Then had come the Redeemers. Mulgrave shivered.

The town had been torched. No-one knew what had happened to all the women and children who had survived the murder of their men. But Mulgrave had heard from a scout who passed through the charred remains of Barstead. Blackened bodies were everywhere.

Pushing such thoughts from his mind Mulgrave continued on his way, cutting through alleyways and down narrow streets. A half-starved dog growled at him as he passed. Mulgrave ignored the beast, and the dog went back to chewing on the frozen carcass of a dead rat.

Crossing the curved bridge Mulgrave paused to stare down at the frozen stream. Some way along the bank, several men had cut holes in the ice, and were sitting, wrapped in blankets, their fishing lines bobbing.

Mulgrave walked on. The road was icy and treacherous, and he slithered as he reached the downward slope leading to the small church. It was an old building, with a crooked spire. For years there had been talk of repairing the spire, but Mulgrave liked it as it was. He paused in the cold to stare up at it. Some of the timbers had given way on the north side, causing it to lean precariously. It looked for all the world like a wizard's hat. Many of the towns-people predicted it would fall soon, but Mulgrave doubted it, though he did not know why. Gazing at the crooked spire lifted his spirits. It seemed to mock the straight, unbending Varlish values it had been built to commemorate.

A little way behind the church was Ermal Standfast's thatched cottage. Smoke was drifting up from the tall chimney. Mulgrave strolled to the front door and stepped inside, pushing the door shut against the swirling snow. The once portly priest was sitting by his fire, a black and white chequered blanket around his thin shoulders, a heavy red woollen cap upon his bald head. He glanced up and grinned as Mulgrave removed his cloak and stamped his booted feet upon the rush mat just inside the front door. 'It will get warmer soon,' said Ermal. 'Spring is coming.'

'It's taking its time,' replied Mulgrave, slipping out of his sheep-skin jerkin. The swordsman pulled up a chair and sat, extending his hands towards the fire.

'How is your shoulder?'

'Almost healed,' said Mulgrave. 'Though it aches in this weather.'

'It will. How old are you?' Ermal asked, suddenly.

Mulgrave had to think about the question. 'Thirty-four . . . almost thirty-five,' he said.

'When you are past forty it will ache all the time.'

'What an inspiring thought.'

Ermal Standfast chuckled. 'Two inches lower and that ball would have meant you never had to ache again. An inch to the left and you might have lost your arm. Give thanks for the ache, Mulgrave. Experiencing it means you are alive. Are you ready to rejoin your regiment?'

'No – though I will, for a while. I intend to ask Gaise for per-mission to quit the army.'

Ermal seemed surprised. 'My information is that you are a talented soldier. Why would a man turn his back on his talents?'

'My talents put men in the ground.'

'Ah, yes. There is that. The Grey Ghost will be sad to lose you. When he brought you to me he said you were his dearest friend. He sat by your bedside for fully two days.'

Mulgrave felt a stab of guilt. 'Gaise knows how I feel. I have seen too much death. Have you ever walked across a field in the aftermath of a battle?'

'Happily, no.'

'Luden Macks once said that the saddest sight in all the world is a battle lost. The second saddest sight is a battle won.'

'The man is your enemy, and yet you quote him.'

Mulgrave shook his head. 'I have no enemies. I just want to go . . .' He hesitated.

'Home?' prompted Ermal.

Mulgrave shook his head. 'I have no home. The place where I was born is deserted now.'

'What about your family?'

Mulgrave said nothing for a moment, but stared into the fire. 'I come from Shelsans,' he said. Ermal shuddered inwardly. He made the Sign of the Tree.

'How did you survive?' he asked. 'You can have been no more than nine . . . maybe ten.'

'I was in the hills when the knights came, visiting an old man who made honey mead wine. We saw the massacre. The old man took me to a cave high in the mountains.' Taking up a blackened poker Mulgrave absently stirred the coals of the fire. 'The closest I have to a thought of home lies far to the north. The Druagh mountains. It is good there. The air is clean. I like the people. There is something about the highlanders I warm to.'

Ermal rose. 'I have a little tisane left, and some honey. Warm yourself while I prepare it.'

Mulgrave leaned back in the chair and closed his eyes. His left shoulder was throbbing, and he could feel a prickling in the tips of his fingers. Luck had been with him on that dreadful day, as the grapeshot screamed through the air. A rider on his left – Toby Vainer – had been ripped apart, his face disappearing in a bloody spray. A second volley had torn through the men on his right. Yet only a single ball had punched into Mulgrave, and not one had

53

come close to Gaise Macon. The young general had ridden on, his grey horse leaping over the first cannon. The cannoneers had scattered and run as the cavalry broke through. Gaise and his riders had pursued them. Mulgrave had tried to follow. But his horse collapsed and died beneath him, hurling him from the saddle. Only then did Mulgrave see that the beast's body had shielded him from the worst of the grapeshot.

The wound in Mulgrave's shoulder – so small and seemingly insignificant – had festered badly. He had slipped into a semi-coma two days later.

He had returned to full consciousness in this cottage. According to Ermal Standfast Mulgrave had been taken to the field surgeon, and the man had shrugged and said: 'He will be dead within a week. The wound has gone bad.' Gaise Macon would have none of it. Having been told of a healer in Shelding, some thirty miles from the battlefield, he had commandeered a wagon.

Mulgrave had little recollection of the journey to Shelding. He remembered burning pain, and occasional glimpses of clouds scurrying across a blue sky. Odd snippets of conversation . . . 'I think he is dying, my lord.' And Gaise Macon saying: 'He will not die. I will not allow it.' He remembered the jolting of the wheels on the rutted road. But most of the journey was lost to him.

Ermal returned with two pottery jugs. Passing one to Mulgrave, he resumed his seat. 'So what will you do, my friend?'

'I don't know.'

'Have you lost faith in the cause?'

Mulgrave shrugged. 'What cause?' He rubbed at his eyes. He hadn't slept well for weeks. Nightmares haunted him, and he would awake several times a night, sometimes crying out in his anger and despair.

'Kings are chosen by the Source, so it is said,' Ermal went on. 'Therefore those who fight for the king could be considered godly. Is that not cause enough?'

'Anyone who believes that has not seen the work of the king's Redeemers.'

'There are always rumours of excesses in war,' said the priest. Mulgrave looked at him, seeing the fear in the man's eyes.

'Aye, you are right,' he said. 'Let us talk of other things.' He noted his friend's relief. Ermal relaxed back into his chair and sipped his tisane. A coal upon the fire split and crackled briefly. Several cinders dropped into the grate.

'Are you still dreaming of the white-haired woman?' asked Ermal.

'Yes.'

'Does she speak to you yet?'

'No. She tries, but I hear nothing. I think she is in danger.'

'What makes you think that?'

'In the last few dreams she has been on a mountainside, struggling to climb. She stops and looks back. There are . . . men . . . below her. Following, I think. Then she looks directly at me and speaks. But I hear nothing.'

Ermal added a thick log to the fire. 'Why did you hesitate?' he asked.

Mulgrave was nonplussed. 'I don't know what you mean.'

'Before you said *men*. Are they men?'

'What else could they be?' answered Mulgrave, suddenly uncomfortable.

Ermal opened his hands. 'It is a dream, Mulgrave. They could be anything. They could be fish on horseback.'

Mulgrave chuckled. 'I see. You think then that this is some trick of the mind? That she is not real?'

'I cannot say for certain. I once knew a man – Aran Powdermill. Strange little chap. Had two gold teeth in the front of his mouth. The man was crooked, a thief and a cheat who would do anything for money. Yet he could *see* events happening great distances away. He was also adept at finding lost items. He once located a child who had fallen down a forgotten well. He demanded two chaillings to find her. I also knew a woman who could commune with the dead. Truly remarkable talents they both possessed. Equally I once dreamed I was trapped inside a blackberry pie with a white bear. Absolutely nothing mystic there. I had eaten too much and fallen asleep on a bearskin rug. Some dreams are visions, some are merely the mind's fancies. You do not recall having met this woman?'

'No.'

'Do you recognize the mountains?'

'Aye, I do. The Druagh mountains in the north.'

'Perhaps you should travel there.'

'I have been thinking of it.'

'It might be best to wait until the spring. The war has displaced many citizens, and there are now said to be bands of thieves and cut-throats roaming the countryside.'

'It will be little better in the spring, my friend. This war is a long way from being won or lost.'

'I shall miss your company. So few of my parishioners play an adequate game of Shahmak.'

Mulgrave laughed. 'I have only beaten you once, Master Standfast.'

'Ah, but you have also drawn three games. It wounds my ego not to win.'

A comfortable silence grew, as Mulgrave watched the flames dance among the coals. Then he sighed and returned his gaze to the priest. 'They are not men,' he said. 'Their faces are grey and scaled, and their eyes are floating in blood.'

Ermal sat very quietly for a moment. 'Do they have circlets of iron upon their brows?'

'Aye, they do,' answered Mulgrave, surprised.

'Wait for a moment.' Ermal rose from his chair and walked through to his small study. He returned moments later with a slim silver chain. Hanging upon it was a small medallion, also silver, encased in a slender golden band. The medallion had been stamped on one side with the image of a tree. The reverse was embossed with a three-sided Keltoi rune. 'These were carried by the original Tree cultists back in the time of Stone. Each coin was blessed by the Veiled Lady, so it was said, and after her by Persis Albitane himself.' He placed the chain over Mulgrave's head, tucking the medallion inside his shirt. 'Wear it always, my boy.'

'Thank you. Do I take it you no longer believe that the dreams are a trick of the mind?'

Ermal spread his hands. 'I am not certain. The creatures you described are written of in the oldest scrolls. They were called the *Dezhem Bek*. Have you heard the name?'

'No.'

'It may be that you heard of them when you were a child in Shelsans, and the memory is what causes the dreams. I hope so.'

'What are they?' asked Mulgrave.

'I would imagine that depends on your perspective. To those who follow the Source of all Harmony the *Dezhem Bek* were men who had embraced the Shadow, given themselves over to evil in return for great powers. Some scrolls call them necromancers, others describe them as eaters of souls. In the old tongue *Dezhem Bek* means simply the Ravenous Ravens. Yet there are other books, written by those whose philosophies, shall we say, were at odds with the Source. In these the *Dezhem Bek* are described as achieving perfection of form, and strength beyond that of ordinary men. They were also said to be extremely long-lived.'

Mulgrave laughed. 'Perfection of form? I think not. Unless scaled flesh has become fashionable in the cities.'

'What you see in your dreams is their spirit form. You have heard of the Orb of Kranos?'

'Of course,' answered Mulgrave. 'A mythic vase or some such from ancient times.'

'No, not a vase,' said Ermal. 'Some say it was a globe of crystal through which men could see their futures. Others claim it was the magical pommel stone of a great sword. There is even a legend that it is the severed head of a necromancer. The *Dezhem Bek* were said to be guardians of the Orb. It made them near immortal.'

'I am not a great believer in magic,' said Mulgrave. 'I do not mock men who have faith. It gives them comfort, and oft times leads them to help others. Yet I have also seen great evils committed in the name of the Source. And never have I witnessed a miracle. Until I do I shall remain sceptical.'

'I cannot argue with that,' said Ermal Standfast. 'Nor will I try. What I will say is that I have heard rumours that the Orb was hidden in Shelsans. The Knights of the Sacrifice found it.'

Mulgrave sighed. 'My father used to talk of a great secret that was guarded in Shelsans. But then he used to tell many wonderful stories, fabulously embellished. He said that it was vital that we all learned to love. He said that love made friends of enemies and enriched the world. I wonder if he still believed that when the knights came and massacred those he loved.'

'Let us hope that he did,' said Ermal, softly.

*

Ermal Standfast had been a priest now for twenty-two years. He was loved within his community, for his sermons were gentle and often witty, and he was not judgemental with his flock. Also his fame as a healer was widespread, and many of his parishioners owed their life to what they perceived as his talent for herbal cures. It was this fame that had led Gaise Macon to bring the dying Mulgrave to him.

All in all the little priest should have been content – even proud of what he had achieved in Shelding during these last twenty-two years.

But even had Ermal been given to prideful thoughts, he would no longer be able to sustain them. He felt this strongly as he sat in his small living room, staring into the fading fire. Mulgrave was asleep upstairs, and the house – save for a few creaks from the ageing timbers – was silent.

'You are worse than a fraud,' Ermal told himself. 'You are a liar and a coward. You are a weak and loathsome man.' He felt close to tears as he sat in his deep armchair, a blanket around his thin shoulders.

Over the years he had gathered some knowledge of herbs, but all of his concoctions were actually based on camomile and cider vinegar, with just an occasional dash of mustard. There was no lasting medicinal benefit to be obtained from any of them. Ermal's talent came from within. When he laid hands upon the sick he could heal them. He would close his eyes and *know* what ailed them, and he could either draw it out or boost the patients' own defence mechanisms, causing them to heal themselves. At first he had kept this gift entirely secret. This was not originally out of fear, but more from a natural shyness and a desire to remain unnoticed. He did not want people to stare at him and consider him different. He did not wish to be unusual or special. As a youngster Ermal had desired comfortable anonymity. As he grew older – and more inclined towards the spiritual – he had felt that his gift should be put to use helping people. It took him a little time to come up with the idea of herbalism as a disguise for his talents. It seemed such a small lie, and one for which he believed the Source would forgive him. After all, was it not the Source who had made him shy and humble? On top of that there was the memory of his father –

an equally shy man. 'Do good in secret, Ermal,' he had said. His donations to charity were always made anonymously, or through a trusted intermediary who would not divulge the origin of the good fortune. 'All that we have comes from the Source,' Ermal's father claimed, 'and it is arrogance itself to claim credit for our ability to finance good deeds.'

For Ermal this became a life philosophy. And he was happy as a priest and a healer. He enjoyed the love of his parishioners, and the gratitude of those he healed.

All this had changed four years before, when the Redeemers had arrested old Tam Farley.

Guilt burned in Ermal's heart as he remembered the man. Tam had lived alone on a farm just outside Shelding. Ermal had visited him one morning, almost fifteen years ago. It was a bright, hot summer's day and Ermal had been walking his parish, knocking on doors and chatting to residents who did not – or could not through age or infirmity – attend services. Most of the people greeted him warmly enough. Occasionally he would be turned away by those who had no interest in matters spiritual.

At last he had come to Tam's cottage. The original farm building had caught fire some years previously, and was a burnt-out shell. The small farm had long since ceased to be a going concern, and Tam had sold his best fields to a neighbouring farmer. He lived alone in a cottage close to the derelict farmhouse, keeping only two dozen hens and an old rooster. The cottage was small, but tidily maintained and the front door, Ermal remembered, had a fresh coat of green paint upon it. He tapped at the frame.

Old Tam opened the door. He was a tall man, stooped by time, with an unruly mop of white hair, long and unkempt. Tam's face was heavily lined, but his eyes were a bright button blue, untouched by the years. They were the eyes of a young man, keen and still curious about life and all its hazards and wonders.

'I wondered when you would come, priest,' he said. 'Are you ready yet?'

'Ready for what?' Ermal had asked.

'Ready to let your talents grow. Ready to leave the prison of the flesh and soar through the sky. Ready to see the world with the eyes of spirit.'

'What on earth are you talking about, sir?'

Tam had peered at him, then grinned. 'I know what you are,' he said. 'I know what you do. When you use the magic I feel it. You healed Bab Fast. Took away his cancer. You carried the vileness home with you and had to find a way to dispose of it. That was tough, was it not? But the old hound was dying anyway.'

Ermal had been shocked. Bab Fast had been dying of a tumour in his belly. Ermal had never dealt with such a serious illness. Normally when he drew out an infection he would feel it in his own system for some days before it dissipated, but with Bab it had been different. Ermal had felt the tumour begin to grow within his own body. It had frightened him badly. He had known it would kill him and had – with less reluctance than he would have hoped – transferred the cancer to the body of an elderly hound who used to wander around the village, picking up scraps of food where it could. The hound had died the following day. How could Tam had known?

Ermal stood silently in the cottage doorway, unable to speak.

'Do not worry, man. I have told no-one. Come inside. We will talk awhile.'

Ermal sighed at the memory. He had sat with Tam for more than two hours. They had broken bread together, and Ermal learned that the old man was another who had been gifted by the Source. Tam's talent was of communication with the departed and – in a small way – prophecy. He also knew how to free himself from the confines of the flesh, allowing his spirit to soar free. In the months and years that followed Ermal too learned this skill. At first they would journey together, for, as Tam pointed out, it was easy for a soul to be lost in the vastness. But soon Ermal had soared alone, his spirit floating beneath the stars over foreign lands and strange cities, drifting above alien mountains and crossing vast oceans.

He and Tam had even witnessed the signing of the Covenant – the document that was supposed to end all fear of civil strife. The king had finally agreed to devolve some of his powers to a Great Council, the members of which would be elected from among the citizenry. It was a day of great jubilation across the realm. The king, dressed in a coat and leggings of magnificent blue satin, had entered the debating chamber, flanked by the Lords Buckman and

Winterbourne. The four hundred councillors present all rose from their seats and bowed deeply. The king moved to a heavily gilded chair and sat down. Luden Macks brought the document and laid it before him.

'This will end in blood,' said Tam.

Something cold touched Ermal's spirit, and he sensed a presence forming close by where they floated under the curved rafters of the chamber roof.

'Flee!' cried Tam.

Back in Tam's cottage Ermal had scrambled to his feet. 'What happened there?' he asked his friend.

'We are not the only ones with talent, Ermal. Best to avoid those we do not know.'

The days that followed proved golden and liberating for Ermal Standfast. He had found a friend with whom he could speak freely, and a mentor who could – and did – teach him to develop his talents.

The old man never came to church. He rarely left his cottage. But people would come to him there, requesting small prophecies, or wishing to communicate with the recent dead. It was this that led to Tam's death – and showed Ermal Standfast what a wretched creature he really was.

Four years ago, with the king revoking the terms of the Covenant and the civil war just beginning, a troop of Redeemers had ridden into Shelding. Within days they had arrested four people – one of them Tam Farley. He was accused of witchcraft. Fearing for his own life Ermal had fled the town, riding to the market town of Ridsdale and renting a room at a local tavern. From here he had used his talent to observe the fate of his friend. Tam was tortured for two days, but gave the Redeemers no names. They broke his fingers and put a fire beneath his feet. Still he would not speak – though he did scream. The other three prisoners were local farm workers who had come to Tam for prophecies. They too underwent torture. All four were sentenced to burn at the stake.

On the day of the execution a Redeemer stood in front of the crowd and asked if any would speak up for the accused, or offer reason why they should not die. No-one did. Ermal burned with shame and guilt.

For, as his spirit floated above the bound men at the stakes, Tam had looked up and seen him. The old man mouthed the words: 'I forgive you.' That forgiveness seared worse than any punishment Ermal could imagine.

Four years later the shame remained. 'I should have been there to speak for you, Tam,' he said.

And now it was strengthened by a new guilt. Today he had listened as Mulgrave spoke of spirits with scaled faces and Ermal had known what they were. Yet once more he had not spoken the full truth. The Redeemers were the new *Dezhem Bek*, and Ermal Standfast knew the extent of their powers.

Yes, he had given Mulgrave a charm that might keep him from spiritual harm, but he had not warned him of the true nature of the enemy.

Tears spilled to the priest's cheeks. 'You are a worthless craven,' he told himself.

# CHAPTER THREE

TAYBARD JAEKEL LAY FLAT ON HIS BELLY, HIS LONG RIFLE CRADLED across his arms. With great care he crawled through the undergrowth. He no longer cared about the mud smearing across his leaf green uniform jacket, or staining the silver embroidered Fawn in Brambles insignia. His jacket was now filthy, old tears clumsily stitched. Two years ago he had been so proud of this uniform, and eager to prove himself worthy of it. He had stood with Kammel Bard, Banny Achbain, and scores of other young men to take the oath of allegiance to the king, and had marched out of Eldacre to fight the evil Covenanters. There had been a band playing, and the sky had been blue and clear, the sun bright. Crowds had lined the roads, cheering the gallant young men.

Taybard pushed such thoughts from his mind as he reached the beginning of the downward slope into the valley. He crawled on, his rifle cradled across his forearms. A shot sounded. Taybard ducked instinctively, then swore as the hammer of his rifle dug into his left cheek, piercing the skin. Easing himself between two bushes he gazed out at the opposite slope. It was wooded, and several boulders jutted from the hillside. Taybard glanced down into the valley, where a squad of scouts from the King's Second Lancers were pinned down. Two men lay dead – evidence of the skill of the enemy musketeer – the other eight hunkering down behind what meagre shelter they could find. Another shot broke the silence. No-one was hit. The squad had no muskets, and could not return fire at this range with their pistols.

Taybard's blue eyes focused on the hillside opposite, locating the puff of smoke drifting from a large boulder just outside the tree line. Settling himself down he brought his own rifle to bear. It was a beautiful piece, the stock and butt of hand-polished walnut, delicately engraved and inlaid with silver. Gaise Macon had ordered twenty rifles from the legendary Emburley. Each one had cost more than a poor Varlish like Taybard Jaekel would earn in ten years. Taybard carried his rifle everywhere, and even slept with it alongside him. The guns were highly prized. One of Gaise's twenty riflemen had got drunk in Baracum, and had woken in the morning to find his rifle stolen. Gaise had hanged him.

Nestling the butt into his shoulder, Taybard waited. He gauged the distance between himself and the Covenanter musketeer at just over two hundred paces. An impossible shot for a regular musket, and a difficult one even for an Emburley with a rifled barrel.

The Covenanter sniper raised himself up, levelled his musket and fired at the soldiers below. Taybard did not shoot. He counted. The sniper had reared up swiftly, then taken three seconds to aim. Once he had fired he dropped back behind the boulder to reload.

Taybard eased back the engraved hammer and took aim.

On the opposite hillside the Covenanter came up into position. Taybard let out his breath, steadied his aim, and fired. The sniper jerked, dropped his weapon and fell against the boulder, sliding from sight. Taybard came to his feet, added a fresh charge of powder, ball and paper wadding to the barrel and rammed it home. Then he primed the flash pan, cocked the weapon and strode out from his hiding place. The soldiers below saw him and sent up a cheer.

Ignoring them, Taybard walked down the slope. As he went he caught a glimpse of a second Covenanter moving into sight. The man's musket came up. Taybard dropped to one knee. The musket ball screamed by him, and his own rifle boomed in response. The shot took the Covenanter through the bridge of the nose, snapping his head back. His legs gave way and he pitched to the earth. Once more Taybard calmly reloaded, then began to climb the slope. The first sniper lay dead, his throat torn away. Taybard sighed, and gestured to the soldiers. When they came up he ordered them to collect the two muskets and the powder and shot carried by the Covenanters.

The soldiers obeyed him gleefully, searching the bodies for any coin or valuables before pulling off their boots and belts. Taybard sat on a rock nearby. His hands were trembling now, and he rubbed the palms against his mud-streaked trews.

'You've got blood on your face,' said Jakon Gallowglass, moving to sit alongside him. Gallowglass was a lean five-year veteran from the south. No more than nineteen years of age, he had taken part in six major battles and a score of skirmishes. Taybard glanced at the man's pale features.

'Jabbed myself on my rifle as I got into position,' said Taybard.

'First shot was mighty fine. Took your time, though.'

'That's why it was fine.'

'Won't be no fresh fighting till the spring now,' said Gallowglass. 'With luck we'll be billeted in Baracum. Good whores in Baracum. You know where the Grey Ghost will be taking you?'

'Home would be good,' Taybard told him, laying his rifle against the rock. He rubbed his eyes. His hand smelt of black powder, acrid and unpleasant. Blood from his cheek was smeared on his palm.

'Aye, the war hasn't reached the north,' said Jakon. 'Must be good up there. Got a sweetheart back home?'

'No.'

'Just as well. After all the whores you've had you wouldn't want to be taking the pox home, eh?'

Taybard stared gloomily at the dead Covenanter. He was young, perhaps no more than eighteen. His face was boyish.

'Never seen no-one shoot as good as you,' said Gallowglass. 'Is it you or the Emburley?'

'A bit of both, I guess.'

'Ah, well. Time to finish the patrol. My thanks to you, Jaekel. That's the second time you've pulled my irons from the fire.'

'Your turn next time.'

Taybard watched as Gallowglass gathered the seven men. Within minutes they had entered the trees and were gone. Taybard sat for a while with the dead Covenanters, then rose and made his way back down the trail.

It began to rain. Pulling a leather cap from the pocket of his green jerkin Taybard held it over the hammer and flash pan of his rifle. Within minutes the rain had turned to sleet and then snow. Taybard trudged on, his feet cold.

The Covenanter sniper and his friend would not feel it.

Taybard covered the three miles to camp in just over an hour, reported his action to Duty Sergeant Lanfer Gosten, then made his way to the cluster of tents occupied by the Grey Ghost's company. Squatting down by a camp fire Taybard warmed his hands, then ducked into the tent he shared with Kammel Bard and Banny Achbain. The tent was empty. Taybard's clothes were soaked through. He removed his jerkin and shirt and rummaged in his pack for the spare woollen shirt he had purchased in Baracum the previous autumn. There were holes in it, but it was warm nevertheless. As he pulled it on the small pendant he wore caught in the cloth. Carefully he eased it clear, then gazed at it. Within a spherical cage of silver wire lay a perfect musket ball fashioned from gold. He had been so proud when he won it last year. The king himself had been present with his two sons, but the prize had been presented by his own general, Gaise Macon. Taybard had never expected to win. He was lying in seventh place after the standing targets.

A cold wind blew in from the tent entrance and Taybard tugged on his shirt, then donned the damp jerkin once more.

'*Won't be no fresh fighting till the spring now,*' Gallowglass had said.

Taybard hoped it was true.

Wrapping himself in his blankets he slept for a while, his rifle held close, like a sweetheart. He had hoped to dream of the mountains, and the cobbled roads of Old Hills. Instead he found himself once more running across the low ground after the Battle of Nollenby. Horsemen were chasing him, just as they had in reality, only this time Taybard was not fleet of foot. His legs felt heavy, his boots sinking into deep mud. He glanced back. Lancers were almost upon him, but they were not men. Their faces were skulls.

Then he realized they were no longer riding horses. The skulls were rammed upon target rails, just like those back in Baracum when he won the Golden Ball. The rails were greased, the targets pulled swiftly along the rails as the musketeers tried to hit them. Taybard had achieved a perfect score in the final, beating a rifleman from the Seventh Infantry. There were no other riflemen now. Taybard stood alone. The skulls on the target rails began to writhe, flesh forming over the bone. Taybard took aim at the first. It was the Covenant boy he had shot earlier. He was staring at Taybard. Then he began to weep and call out Taybard's name.

He awoke with a start, his face drenched in sweat.

'Taybard Jaekel!'

Taybard blinked. Someone was calling his name. Scrambling from his blankets he stumbled from the tent. The sun was going down, and cook fires had been lit. The burly duty sergeant, Lanfer Gosten, was standing alongside a young officer from the King's Second Lancers. Taybard saluted clumsily.

The officer chuckled. 'God's teeth, man, I must say that up close you don't look like a legend,' he said. He was tall and slim, his blue and gold uniform immaculately tailored and – more wondrous still – clean. Taybard glanced down. Even the man's boots were shining. The officer held out his hand. The gleam of gold caught Taybard's eye. 'Lord Ferson's compliments to you, musketeer,' said the officer, dropping the coin into Taybard's hand.

'What is this for, sir?' asked Taybard.

'For your rescue of the patrol. Lord Ferson was most impressed by your marksmanship. The second shot was a beauty.'

'You saw it, sir?'

'Yes. Lord Ferson had ridden out with a company of Lancers. We were on the far slope to you. So, well done.'

With that the officer strode away, picking his path carefully to avoid puddles.

'Did well for yourself there, Jaekel,' said Lanfer Gosten.

'Why in hell's name didn't the Lancers rescue their own men?' said Taybard, anger rising.

'Probably didn't want to get their uniforms dirty. Real question is, why did you?'

'I don't know what you mean, sergeant.'

'Oh yes you do, son,' said Lanfer, laying his hand on Taybard's shoulder. 'You were told to keep the patrol in sight and take out any snipers. You were also told to avoid risking yourself. From your own report the first Covenanter was shot from cover. All well and good. But then you walked out into the open. You know them bastards work in pairs. So what were you doing?'

Taybard shrugged. 'I wanted to draw him out. To finish it. That's all.'

Lanfer Gosten looked into Taybard's blue eyes. 'To finish it, eh? We're all tired of it, son. You're not alone in that.'

'What does that mean?'

'You know what it means. You've seen it before. That time when a soldier stops caring about living or dying. You can see it in the eyes. Then, in some battle or skirmish, they walk into the open – and they're gone.'

'I'm not like that,' said Taybard. 'I want to live. I want to go home to the mountains.'

'You hang on to that, Jaekel. I'm sick to death of burying Eldacre lads.'

The sergeant wandered away. Snow began swirling down from a brooding sky. Returning to his tent Taybard clipped a strap to his rifle and swung it over his shoulder. Then he walked out into the nearby trees to gather dry wood for the night fire. He could see other men engaged in the same enterprise. Some he knew, and these he nodded to, or exchanged greetings with. Others were strangers, newcomers from other companies. After several trips Taybard had gathered enough fuel to last the night. He piled it beside the tent, then relit the fire. Officers had iron braziers inside their double-leafed tents, and coal to keep their noble bones from freezing. Enlisted men like Taybard, Kammel and Banny had to make do with what they could find. Their tents were cheap canvas. Heavy rain would seep through them, dripping upon the sleeping men within.

Still, thought Taybard, as he sat beside his fire, with winter coming they would be billeted in some barracks somewhere, safe from shot and shell. It wouldn't be so bad.

And maybe – just maybe – the Grey Ghost would take them home.

The fire grew, licking at the dry wood. Taybard shivered as the heat flowed over him. The sky was dark now, with not a star shining. A powerful, round-shouldered figure loomed out of the shadows and slumped down by the fire. Taybard glanced up at the bearded face of Kammel Bard. 'Covenanters pulled back,' said Kammel. 'So I guess we won, after all. Any food?' he asked, leaning his rifle against a tent rope.

'Not yet. Where's Banny?'

'Lanfer sent him to guide the supply wagons in. Be more snow tonight, I reckon.'

'I don't think we won,' said Taybard. 'I don't think anyone won this time.'

Kammel pushed back the chunky woollen hood he wore and scratched at his thick, red hair. 'Well, we didn't pull back, did we?'

Taybard shrugged. 'How would I know? They say the battle stretched over nine miles. Some might have pulled back, I guess. Anyway, who decides?'

'What do you mean?'

'Well, who decides who has won or lost? It's not like Avondale any more. That was easy. We charged. They ran. We captured their cannon. Now *that* was a victory. Now we just charge each other, kill each other, and argue about who won.'

Other men began drifting into the camp, and from somewhere to the west came the smell of stew. The smell would be better than the taste, Taybard knew. Stale bread and a watery broth that would do little to dull the appetite. The fire began to hiss and splutter as sleet fell. Kammel pulled his hood back in place. Taybard stood and placed Kammel's rifle inside the tent. 'Did you get into the village?' he asked.

Kammel shook his head. 'Redeemers was there, questioning and such. No-one was allowed in. Doubt they had much food there, though. Covenanters would have taken most of it when they pulled out.'

The two men sat in silence for a while, ignoring the sleet, and enjoying what warmth they could absorb from the fire.

'You ever think back to old Jaim Grymauch?' asked Kammel, suddenly.

'Aye, often,' admitted Taybard. He glanced at his friend. 'You didn't like him.'

'I never said that.'

'He was a highlander. You always hated highlanders. Don't you remember? We once had a row because I said your grandmother was a clanswoman, and you called me a liar.'

'Well, I was younger then,' said Kammel defensively. 'But I always liked old Jaim. You remember that day, eh? Never seen the like. Knocked 'em all down, and cut Maev Ring from the fire.' Kammel swung round to stare across the camp. 'Damn, but I'm hungry,' he said.

'Won't be ready yet.'

'No, but they're already standing in line.'

'Let's wait for Banny. He shouldn't be long.'

Once more the silence descended. Taybard stared into the fire, thinking back to the day when Jaim Grymauch halted the execution of Maev Ring. It was something he would never forget. One lone highlander, surrendering his life to save the woman he loved. Jaim was a colossus that day, huge and seemingly invulnerable. He had scattered the guards, then drawn his massive sword and despatched three Knights of the Sacrifice. He had made it, with Maev, to the top of the cathedral steps. That was when the musketeers arrived. Taybard had run from the crowd, hurling himself at them, managing to ruin the aim of the nearest man. As the other musketeers fired Jaim had dragged Maev into a protective embrace. Lead shot ripped into him.

The death of a hero. Taybard would never forget it – even amid the sea of death that was this dreadful war.

'Here he comes,' said Kammel, pushing himself to his feet.

Taybard saw the slim figure of Banny Achbain striding through the camp. He approached the fire, crouched down and warmed his hands.

'You won't believe it,' he said.

'What?' asked Kammel.

'They say Lord Ferson has challenged the Grey Ghost to a duel. They're going to fight tomorrow.'

\*

As Mulgrave well knew, Gaise Macon was not a man given to out-bursts of temper. Though passionate by nature he rarely lost control. But he was coldly angry now as he paced the smoke-blackened ruin that had once been the country home of a rebel earl. The firelight glinted on his golden hair, and, for a moment, he looked again like the strikingly handsome youngster Mulgrave had trained on the Moidart's estates far to the north. He was still slim, though his shoulders had broadened in the last four years, and his face had lost that youthful glow. Still only in his early twenties Gaise Macon was a seasoned soldier, fighting a harsh and terrible war. His face was thinner, his curiously coloured eyes, one green and one gold, deeper set. The small, leaf-shaped burn scar on his right cheek shone white against his faded tan. Gaise removed his silver embroidered grey jacket and threw it across a broken couch. The white shirt he wore beneath it was stained by powder smoke at collar and cuff.

Mulgrave gazed around the ruined building. One wall had been blasted away by cannon shell, and fire had raged through the whole house. Here, in the rear hall, there was still part of a ceiling, which allowed some shelter from the swirling snowstorm outside. A fire was blazing in the undamaged hearth.

There were several chairs in the room. Mulgrave took one of these and reversed it, sitting down and resting his forearms on the high back. Gaise turned towards him. 'What kind of a fool would offer a duel at such a time?' he asked.

Mulgrave shrugged. 'It is surprising, right enough,' he said. '*Did* you call him a coward?'

'You know me well enough, my friend. Does it seem likely?'

Mulgrave shook his head. 'What *did* you say?'

'I asked why he had not led his heavy cavalry into the battle. The enemy were retreating in bad order. One major charge and they would have been routed. Yet he did not make it. And so another battle ended in a stalemate.'

'What did he reply?'

'He said he would not take criticism from a glory-seeking popin-jay,' answered Gaise. He smiled as he said it, his good humour flowing back. 'What on earth is a popinjay, Mulgrave?'

'A brightly coloured bird from the southern continents, sir. And how did you respond?'

71

'I pointed out that had my riders followed his example, and refrained from charging, the battle would have been lost.'

'Ah, then you did – in a manner of speaking – suggest he lacked nerve.'

'By heaven, Mulgrave, of course he lacks nerve. There's not an officer in the king's army who doesn't know that.'

'Yet he had the nerve to challenge you.'

'Aye, but not immediately. The challenge came the following day. We are due to meet on open ground at midday tomorrow. With pistols, if you please.'

'You have chosen pistols, sir?' asked Mulgrave, surprised. 'I would have thought swords more . . . suitable.'

'As would I. But his second informed me that Lord Ferson has an injured shoulder. He asked if I would object to pistols. It is all a nonsense,' said Gaise. 'Luden Macks will chuckle when he hears of it.' Gaise Macon drew up a chair, then dragged off his knee length riding boots. One of his socks boasted a huge hole, through which his toes could be seen. 'Popinjay, eh?' he said. 'By heaven, there are crofters back home with better clothes than mine.' He looked into Mulgrave's pale eyes. 'Will you be my second, my friend?'

'Of course, sir. I would urge you, however, to avoid any gallant gestures.'

'Such as what?'

'Do not try to wound him. Take him through the heart.'

Gaise sighed. 'I have no desire to kill him, Mulgrave.'

'It is not *your* desire that concerns me, sir. A wounded man is still dangerous, and I would far sooner see him below the earth than you.' Mulgrave fell silent. Gaise tugged on his boots and returned to the fire, adding fuel.

'Do you not find it puzzling, Mulgrave?' he asked.

'What, sir?'

'That a known coward should challenge me – and request pistols? Had it been swords I could have wounded him and honour might have been satisfied. Pistols are another matter entirely. As you can testify, my friend, even a shallow wound can corrupt and become mortal. Then there is the question of Winterbourne.'

'Winterbourne?'

'Aye, he is Ferson's second. Did I not mention that?'

'No, sir. I did not realize that Lord Ferson was so closely connected to the Redeemers.'

'Nor I – until now.'

Mulgrave rose from his chair and crossed the ruined room to the shattered north wall. Snow was falling outside, and the wind was chill. The open land beyond was lit by hundreds of camp fires. Mulgrave shivered. He had seen too many of these camps in the last four years. He scratched at his white hair and moved away from the wind. Kneeling by the fire he added a log. Gaise was right, the duel made no sense. And why would a cold-blooded killer like Winterbourne befriend a coward like Ferson? Mulgrave turned the events over and over in his mind. If Ferson was so aggrieved why had he not instantly issued a challenge? Why wait a day? His thoughts swung to the Earl of Winterbourne. Mulgrave detested the man, regarding him with a deep and perfect loathing. The acts of Winterbourne's Redeemers were unspeakable. Worse, by being unpunished and unchecked, they were condoned by the king. Mulgrave hated killing, but at least he had believed he was fighting on the side of right. Not so now. In this war there was no balance between right and wrong, good and evil. Both sides had committed atrocities.

'How is your shoulder now?' asked Gaise.

'Healed, sir.'

'That is good. I have missed you, Mulgrave. It is good to have you back.'

Mulgrave stayed silent. He wanted to tell his friend that he would be leaving soon for the north, but now that the moment was upon him he could not find the words.

An uneasy silence developed, and then Gaise spoke again. 'I think Winterbourne is behind the duel. I think he pressured Ferson into making the challenge.'

'For what purpose, sir?'

'I wish I knew. We do not see eye to eye on certain matters, but we both have the same objective, the defeat of Luden Macks and the Covenanters.'

'You stood against him after Ballest, sir. You refused to hand over those villagers.'

'Women and children, Mulgrave. They were not Covenanters. They were merely scavenging for food.'

'I agree with you, sir, and it does you credit that you fed them. Winterbourne would have killed them all. We both know that.'

'Aye, he is a hard, cruel man,' admitted Gaise. 'But that was a year ago and a small matter even then. He ought to have forgotten it by now.'

'Perhaps he has, sir. Might be safer, though, to assume that he has not.'

Gaise Macon chuckled. 'Were you always so suspicious of your fellow men, Mulgrave? Did you never learn the joys of forgiving and forgetting?'

'Indeed I have, sir,' answered Mulgrave, with a smile. 'I knew a man once – a gentle man. He took it upon himself to help a former convict rebuild his life. He took the man in, gave him the freedom of his home.'

'I can guess the end,' said Gaise. 'The convict killed him or robbed him.'

'No, sir. The convict became a carpenter, and worked very hard. He even repaired the good man's roof. He did this for no payment, in gratitude for all that the man had done for him.'

'Then what is the point of this story?' asked Gaise.

'He wasn't a very good carpenter. One day the roof caved in and killed the good man.'

Gaise Macon's laughter rang out. 'Now the moral of *that* story is worth debating. Another time, though. I must see if our supplies have arrived. Ride with me, Mulgrave.' Swinging his grey coat around his shoulders, he walked from the room.

With a sigh Mulgrave followed him.

Ice crunched under their horses' hooves as they negotiated the treacherous trail, their mounts slithering and sliding on the steep paths. Mulgrave's hands and feet were bitterly cold as he rode alongside the young general, and the winter wind stung like needles upon his face. It made him feel even colder to see that Gaise wore no gloves or hat, though his body was well protected by a long, sheepskin-lined cloak. Mulgrave glanced up at the sky. The snow clouds were clearing now, the stars shining brightly. It would grow colder yet before the dawn. His horse stumbled, then righted itself.

Ahead was a small slope, leading down to where the Eldacre Company had made camp. Gaise led the way, allowing his grey gelding to pick its own path through the mud and the ice.

A middle-aged soldier, wearing a hooded cloak, approached them and saluted. Gaise stepped down from the saddle and the soldier took hold of the grey's reins. 'Are the supplies in, Lanfer?' asked Gaise.

'Aye, my lord,' replied Lanfer Gosten. 'Less than half of what was promised. Even on short rations there's not enough to last a week. Four wagons was all we got.'

'Gather ten men and follow me to the quartermaster general,' ordered Gaise. Swinging into the saddle he touched heels to the grey and rode through the camp. Mulgrave followed, drawing alongside the angry young man.

'Are you planning something rash, sir?'

Gaise said nothing for a moment. 'Did Ermal like my gift?' he asked suddenly.

The question took Mulgrave by surprise. He recalled the little priest's delight at the bottle of apple brandy. They had sat on the last night staring at it, wondering how two whole apples could have been inserted through such a narrow neck. Then they had pulled the cork and filled their glasses. The liquor was sweet and warming.

'He was most grateful, sir,' said Mulgrave, 'though perplexed.'

Gaise grinned. 'As was I when first I saw them. Did he think magic was used?'

'At first he did. But by the time we had finished the bottle he had an answer.'

'What was it?'

'He thought the bottle must have been tied to the branches of an apple tree, with twig and blossom inserted into the neck. The apples would have grown within the glass. After they were ripe the twig was snipped and the brandy added.'

'The man is such a delight!' said Gaise happily. 'A fine mind.'

'What do you intend to do when we reach the quartermaster?'

'Find the wagons I paid for and see them delivered. I'll not have my men going hungry again. And not a word more about rashness,

75

my friend. There is nothing you can say that I do not already know.'

Mulgrave knew this was the truth. They had discussed the problem many times during the past year. The quartermaster general, a rich merchant named Cordley Lowen, had friends at court. Those friends were well paid by him from the huge profits he made from supplying food, gunpowder and weapons to the king's army. Not content with the fortune he was amassing from this – barely – legitimate enterprise Lowen was also engaged in reselling supplies to merchants from outlying towns: supplies already purchased by officers commanding private companies. The scandal was tolerated on two counts. First, Lowen shared his profits with the king's closest advisers. In addition, his list of contacts in the merchant community was second to none, which meant that Lowen could find supplies anywhere and at any time. A more honest quartermaster general would experience enormous difficulty supplying one tenth of the amount Lowen could provide. All of which made the man's position virtually unassailable.

Once before the Eldacre Company had received smaller shipments than had been paid for. Gaise had sent Lanfer Gosten to investigate. The sergeant had returned frustrated and angry. Order forms had been misplaced, ledgers had apparently been lost, and no-one could find details of the original supply orders. Gaise had written to Cordley Lowen, and received no reply.

Mulgrave rode on beside the silent Gaise Macon. It was after midnight now. The warehouses would probably be locked and guarded. There would be no stable hands or wagons ready.

The small town was full of soldiers, many of them drunk. Food might be scarce, but liquor was still plentiful. Gaise and Mulgrave rode slowly along the cobbled streets, cutting through the old market square, and on towards the merchant district. Three soldiers staggered across the street, singing a bawdy marching song. Two women approached the soldiers from the shadows, drawing them towards a darkened doorway.

The merchant district was quieter. Four musketeers stood guarding the warehouse gates. Gaise Macon rode past them, dismounting before a large terraced house, fronted with marble pillars. Trailing the grey's reins he called Mulgrave to him. 'High risk for high stakes, my friend,' he said. Taking a leather gauntlet from his saddle bag he tucked it into his belt.

'High risks indeed,' said Mulgrave.

Gaise smiled. 'Remain behind after I have seen Lowen. Speak to the man with comforting words. He will not want to die. He is a merchant, soft and spineless.'

Mulgrave sighed. 'A merchant with many friends in high places.'

Gaise Macon clapped him on the shoulder. 'It will all end well, Mulgrave,' he said. 'I will have my supplies.'

He walked to the front door and rapped at the bronze knocker. Moments passed, and finally the door swung open, to reveal an elderly servant in a nightrobe, a heavy cloak wrapped around his shoulders. He was carrying a lantern.

'What do you want?' he asked.

Gaise moved past him, gesturing Mulgrave to follow. Then he walked into the darkened, circular reception room, removing his cloak and draping it over a gilded chair.

'You can't come in here,' wailed the servant, holding aloft the lantern in a trembling hand. 'The general is asleep.'

'Best you wake him,' said Gaise, softly. 'Or I shall.'

'What is going on here?' came a woman's voice. Mulgrave swung round to see a dark-haired young woman coming down the curving staircase. She was wearing a robe of green velvet, but no shoes. She also carried a lit lantern, and even by its harsh and unflattering light Mulgrave could see that she was beautiful.

Gaise bowed deeply. 'My apologies for disturbing your rest, my lady. But I have urgent business with the general.'

'So urgent that it cannot wait for a civilized hour?' she responded, moving into the reception room and placing the lantern on a circular table.

'Indeed so, my lady, for I have hungry men to feed; men who risk their lives daily for the king; men forced to sleep in squalid tents on cold ground.'

'I think you should leave now and return in the morning,' she said, coldly.

Gaise turned to the servant. 'Wake your master, or I shall do it myself.'

'Did you not hear me?' demanded the woman. 'I asked you to leave.'

Gaise ignored her and swung towards Mulgrave. 'Go and wake the general,' he ordered. Mulgrave took a deep breath and moved towards the stairs.

'How dare you disobey me?' stormed the woman.

'How dare I?' replied Gaise, his voice angry. 'I dare because I have earned the right to dare. I fight for the king. I risk my life alongside my men. Aye, and I have to pay for that right with my own coin. I have to do that so that doxies like you can wear velvet robes and live in fine, stolen houses.'

Mulgrave winced as he heard the exchange, then started up the stairs.

'Stop!' ordered the woman. Her tone was commanding and Mulgrave paused and glanced back. She turned to the servant. 'Broadley, go and wake the general. Then get dressed and fetch the captain of the guard.'

'Yes, my lady,' said the old man. He scurried past Mulgrave without a glance.

'What is your name?' the woman asked Gaise.

'Gaise Macon, commander of the Eldacre Company.'

'Well, Gaise Macon, I shall see you humbled for your rudeness. The king shall hear of this unwarranted invasion.'

She moved away to the far wall, took a taper from a brass holder, lit it from her lantern, then walked to Mulgrave, who had descended the stairs. 'Be so good as to light more lanterns,' she told him. Mulgrave bowed, took the taper and obeyed her instructions, touching the flame to each of the five wall sconces. He glanced across at Gaise. The normally confident young general seemed ill at ease now, even nervous. Had the situation not been so fraught with future peril Mulgrave would have found it amusing. He had known Gaise Macon as both pupil and friend for almost six years. In that time he had been impressed by the young man's many skills; his confidence bordering on arrogance, and his endless good humour. But the one area in which the young general lacked all social skills came in the company of women. Mulgrave considered this to be a result of being raised by a widowed father. The boy had no sisters and no motherly influence. With women Gaise became

78

either self-conscious, or, as in this case, haughty. How could he have called her a doxy, wondered Mulgrave? Would a whore or a courtesan have issued such orders? Cordley Lowen's wife was living in a luxurious palace far south in Varingas. This girl was obviously his daughter.

With the lanterns lit Mulgrave stood silently by the far wall. Gaise Macon, studiously avoiding the beautiful girl in the green velvet robe, pretended to examine the many paintings on display. Ill at ease as he was he seemed much younger, his face boyish in the yellow light.

A tall man appeared at the top of the stairs, and began to descend. His hair was fashionably long, grey shot with streaks of black. His face was heavy set, the eyes deep beneath shaggy brows. He was fully dressed in black leggings and boots, and a braided red coat, with a general's yellow sash across it. As he reached the foot of the stairs he gestured to the woman. 'You may go to your room now, Cordelia,' he said. 'I shall deal with this.' His voice was firm, the tone cold, his anger barely suppressed.

'Yes, Father,' she said, offering him a curtsey.

Casting an angry glance at Gaise Macon she gathered the hem of her robe and climbed the stairs. Her departure brought a sense of relief to Mulgrave. It was also a tactical error from the quarter-master general. With the girl present Gaise would have remained uncertain, even defensive. Now Mulgrave could see the young man's confidence returning.

'Your explanation for this intrusion had better be good,' said Cordley Lowen.

'I am Gaise Macon, commander of the Eldacre Company.'

'I know who you are, young man,' snapped Lowen. 'I have heard the name – and the ridiculous nickname you have acquired. The Grey Ghost, is it not? What do you want?'

'I like a man who speaks his mind, general,' said Gaise smoothly. 'It makes matters so much more simple. I paid you for ten wagons of supplies. I received four. Last month I paid for twelve and received seven. At twelve pounds in gold coin per wagon that makes one hundred and thirty-two pounds you owe me. Or eleven wagons of supplies. I will take either. And I will take either *now*.'

Cordley Lowen's laughter barked out. 'How rare it is,' he said, 'to find such stupidity among the noble classes. Did you really think you could come here and cajole me into settling this . . . alleged debt?'

'No,' said Gaise Macon. 'I did not.' From his belt he pulled the leather riding gauntlet. Stepping forward he slashed it across Cordley Lowen's cheek. The sound was harsh, like a distant gunshot. Lowen staggered back. 'I knew you would not honour your debt,' said Gaise, 'but martial custom demanded that I offer you the chance. My man, Mulgrave, will discuss the details of the duel with you. The choice of weapons is yours.'

Cordley Lowen stood for a moment in astonished silence. Then he shook his head. 'I am not a nobleman. You cannot force me into a duel.'

'You are mistaken, sir,' Gaise told him. 'Perhaps you should have read the King's Manual before accepting the position of general. Noblemen *and officers* are covered by the conditions of the duel. We are both generals. I can challenge you. I *have* challenged you. Of course you can refuse the challenge. On page one hundred and four of the Manual you will find a section dealing with refusal. It states that the officer declining must resign his commission instantly. From that moment on he will be barred from all public office and lose the right to vote in any election, or to own lands above one acre. Harsh, is it not? But then we Varlish have no stomach for cowards.' Gaise stepped in close to the general, reaching out and tapping at his yellow sash. 'Swords or pistols, *General* Lowen. Your choice. I will leave you to discuss these matters with Captain Mulgrave.'

Gaise Macon stepped back, gave a short perfunctory bow, then gathered his cloak and left the house. Cordley Lowen swung towards Mulgrave. 'Is he mad?'

'A trifle hot-headed, sir. Will it be swords or pistols, and at what time and place tomorrow do you wish the duel to take place?'

'I am no swordsman.'

'Then it shall be pistols,' said Mulgrave. 'That is probably all to the good, sir. General Macon is an excellent swordsman. He is also a fine shot, of course, but there are many variables in pistol duels. A sudden gust of wind, heaviness or rain in the air. The ball might merely shatter a shoulder or break an arm.'

'I shall appeal to the king,' said Lowen, and Mulgrave could hear the fear in his voice.

'It will do no good, sir, I fear. In his twenty years of rule the king has only ever forbidden one duel, and that because of a technicality. As I recall, the challenger was a disgraced colonel who had been demoted to captain. He challenged his accuser, another colonel. It was decided that since the demotion made him the colonel's inferior the duel could not take place. It did, of course, for the colonel – that is the challenged colonel – arranged for himself to be demoted for a day. So they fought as captains. Shall we say an hour before noon, sir? General Macon has a second duel to fight tomorrow at noon.'

'A second duel?'

'Yes, sir. General Ferson has issued a challenge to him.'

'Ferson is one of the king's favourites,' observed Lowen.

'Indeed, sir. Is the time suitable?'

'Wait, wait, wait,' stammered the general, moving to a cabinet by the far wall and removing a crystal decanter. With trembling hand he filled a glass with brandy and half drained it. Turning towards Mulgrave he forced a smile. 'A drink, captain?'

'Thank you, sir. Most kind.'

Lowen filled a second glass, refilled his own, and moved back to stand before Mulgrave. The swordsman sipped his brandy. It was very fine. 'Surely you see, captain, how . . . disastrous such a duel would be? Who would supply the king's army were I to be killed? I am not afraid, you understand, but the king's needs must surely be considered paramount.'

'I agree with you, sir. Wholeheartedly. But the matter is set. You could, of course, arrange a time following General Macon's duel with Lord Ferson. It could be that Ferson will win. Unlikely, though.'

'Why?'

'When I said that General Macon was a *fine* shot I rather underplayed his talent. He is probably the finest pistol shot in the army.'

'Sweet heaven! This is a nightmare!'

'Once again I agree, sir. I do take your point about the king's needs. It is widely known that you have excelled in the role of quartermaster general.' Mulgrave paused. 'Perhaps I could prevail upon General Macon to reconsider.'

'Yes, that would be wise,' agreed Lowen.

Mulgrave sipped his brandy then sighed. 'I don't think I will be able to convince him.'

'But you will try?'

'I will, sir. Of course, had General Macon only waited until tomorrow we could have removed the cause of the problem.'

'In what way?'

'The warehouse would have been open and the mistake in supplies rectified. I'm sure that some ledger clerk merely made an error.'

'Of course,' said Lowen. 'You believe that he would withdraw his challenge if the supplies were available?'

'I'm sure I could convince him, sir. But it is after midnight, and the challenge is already made.'

'There are guards within the warehouses. And stable hands. I could write an order now, and the gates would be opened.'

'An admirable idea, sir,' said Mulgrave. 'It would have weighed heavily on me to have been party to the death of the king's quartermaster.'

An hour later Gaise Macon and Mulgrave led the convoy of eleven wagons down into the Eldacre Company camp. Gaise had said little during the ride, and once they were back in the ruined country house, the fire relit, he had sat staring sombrely into the flames.

'What is troubling you, my friend?' asked Mulgrave. 'You have your supplies.'

'The girl made me feel like a fool, Mulgrave. I did not like it.'

'All men are fools sometimes, sir.'

'Aye, I know.' The young man grinned. 'I am glad I didn't have to kill Lowen. Crooked as he is he is still the best quartermaster in the land. Without him the king's cause would be sorely damaged. I am grateful that he lacked the courage to fight.'

'Give yourself a little more credit, sir,' put in Mulgrave. 'You read him right. You knew he would crumble. Even so, it was . . . rash. You have also made another enemy.'

'A man is said to be judged by the enemies he makes,' replied Gaise.

'And by his friends,' observed Mulgrave.

Gaise placed a log on the fire. 'You are my only friend, Mulgrave. I do not know what I would do without you. These last six weeks have been ghastly. Now you are back I feel a burden lifted from me.'

Mulgrave's heart sank. 'Get some rest, sir,' he said. 'You'll need a clear head for the duel tomorrow.'

# CHAPTER FOUR

CHARA RING WATCHED HER HUSBAND AS HE WALKED TOWARDS THE milking sheds. Two-year-old Jaim was perched on his shoulder, while six-year-old Feargol walked alongside Kaelin holding tightly to his hand. Chara leaned against the door frame, a smile on her face. Behind her Maev Ring called out testily: 'The thaw may be coming, Chara, but it is still too cold to stand daydreaming in an open doorway.'

The younger woman stepped back inside and pushed shut the door, dropping the latch. Maev Ring was sitting at the pine table, carefully writing in a broad-leafed book. She was hunched over, peering closely at the page, a dark green shawl over her shoulders. Her red hair had more than a sprinkling of silver now, and there were harsh lines around her eyes. Yet still she was a strikingly attractive woman, thought Chara. If only she would smile more to soften her features.

'The boy adores Kaelin,' said Chara, moving past Maev into the long kitchen.

'He's a good lad, from good stock. I was always fond of Finbarr,' said Maev. Strange, how you talk only of the dead with fondness, thought Chara.

Taking a cloth, she wrapped it round the handle of the black iron kettle, lifting it from the stove and pouring boiling water into an iron pot. To this she added three teaspoonfuls of dried herbs gathered during the summer. The mixture was mainly camomile and mint, but there was also a sprinkling of dried stinging nettle, which Chara knew was good for the rheumatism that made Maev's fingers ache when she worked at her accounts. Allowing the tisane to brew she carried the pot into the main room and set it on a wooden mat. Then she fetched two cups, and a wax-sealed jar of honey. Maev liked to sweeten all tisanes.

The older woman leaned back from her account books and rubbed at her tired eyes. 'It seems that this winter has been hanging around for far too long,' she said. 'I think I shall go mad if I do not see blue skies and sunshine before long.'

Chara sat down and poured out the tisane. Maev sweetened hers, then sipped it appreciatively. 'It would also be good to get an uninterrupted night's sleep,' she said.

'Feargol's nightmares are still bad,' said Chara. 'It is not surprising. Heaven knows what the child went through on the night his parents were killed.'

'Yet he doesn't dream of the bear,' said Maev. 'He keeps talking about men with scaled faces and blood red eyes.' She shivered. 'Do you know he's even got me dreaming of them?'

Chara rose from her chair and moved to the fire, which was burning low. Adding three thick chunks of wood she glanced back at Maev. 'I have too,' she said. 'I wish the Dweller was closer. She would know what to do.'

'You've been listening to Senlic,' said Maev, with a mocking smile. 'That old man is as bad as the boy. Demons, he says. There are no demons, Chara. He just has bad dreams. They will pass.'

Chara said nothing. She had known Senlic Carpenter all her life. Everyone knew he was gifted with the Sight. Maev had spent too long in the Varlish town of Eldacre and had lost touch with the old magic. Senlic said the boy was visited by spirits who sought to do him harm. Chara believed it. She moved to the window and looked out at the melting snow. Soon the way through to the high passes of the Rigante would be clear. Then she would take Feargol to the Dweller – the woman Kaelin referred to as the Wyrd.

'Are you still planning to make the trip south?' she asked Maev.

'Yes. I still have business interests in Eldacre. And the Moidart wishes to see me.'

'The man is evil.'

'Aye, he is – and I do not need you to tell me.'

'Then why do you deal with him, Maev?'

Maev Ring sighed and finished her tisane. 'He is the Lord of the North. I can do no business without his goodwill. He is the power in the land, child. Since I cannot fight it and I cannot oppose it I have decided – for the moment – to flow around it.'

'And you intend to take Kaelin to see him?'

'Indeed I do. It is vital that he looks the man in the eye. Kaelin will one day rule the Rigante here. I know this. Your brother is a fine lad, but he is no leader. When Call Jace passes the Rigante will look for a strong man to take his place. That man will be Kaelin.'

'Or Rayster.'

Maev shook her head. 'Rayster is a fine Rigante. In some ways he reminds me of my Jaim. He is no leader, though – save by example. He is a fighter, brave and braw. He has a good heart. But most importantly he has no name. He was adopted into the clan. No-one knows who his parents were. Without a name he cannot rule.'

This was true, and a story Chara had known since she was a child in arms. A baby had been found by the Dweller on a mountainside just outside Rigante lands. The Dweller had carried him back to the clan, and there he was raised. The story had always confused Chara. The Dweller had mystical powers. Why then had she not used them to locate the child's parents? Chara had once asked Rayster about this. He had grinned and shrugged. 'I never asked,' he said.

'But do you not want to know your parents?'

'Why would I? They did not want to know me. I was tossed to a mountainside in a cold winter and left to die. I have no wish to look into the eyes of the woman who did that to me.'

It was the only moment she could recall that Rayster had ever spoken with bitterness in his voice. Back in those days, as a girl newly arrived at puberty, she had believed herself in love with the tall clansman. As the years passed, though, she realized he was like a brother to her, strong and loyal and loving. There was no passion to be kindled between them. Several of the clan girls had sought to entice Rayster to Walk the Tree, but he had gently declined them all, and from the age of sixteen had chosen to live alone in a cabin high above the clan valley. Now in his late twenties he was a confirmed bachelor. This saddened Chara, for Rayster was wonderful with children, and would, she was convinced, make a fine father. Little Jaim doted on him whenever he visited.

'You are miles away,' said Maev, pouring another cup of tisane.

'I was thinking about what you said about Rayster.'

'Don't misunderstand me. I was not speaking slightingly of the man. I admire and like him greatly.'

'I know that, Maev.'

'Kaelin needs to see the Moidart,' said Maev. 'He needs to know his enemy. One day – if the Source is willing – Kaelin will destroy the man and all he stands for. He will cut his vile head from his shoulders. Then Lanovar and my Jaim – and so many others – will be avenged.'

'The Moidart did not kill Jaim, Maev.'

'His men did. And the man murdered my brother, Lanovar. Shot him, having already given his oath on a truce. Hundreds more died later, hunted down and murdered on the Moidart's orders.'

The door opened and Kaelin entered. Lowering Jaim to the floor he strode to the fire. Feargol followed him, while two-year-old Jaim ran to his mother, arms outstretched. Chara hugged him, lifting him to her lap. His coat was wet through and she carried him upstairs to change his clothes.

'The Cochland brothers have been seen around Black Mountain again,' said Kaelin.

'Someone will be losing cattle,' said Maev.

'Not us.'

'No, they are not stupid men. Though I still think you should have hanged Draig. It would have been a harsher lesson.'

Kaelin drew up a chair. Feargol stayed alongside him. Kaelin absently put his arm around the boy's shoulder. 'Draig is a fighter, Maev, and I don't believe he is evil. Better to tackle him fist to fist.'

'Your face looked as if it had been kicked by a horse.'

'Was it kicked by a horse?' asked Feargol.

'No,' Kaelin told him. 'Draig is a big man and he punches hard.

However, my uncle Jaim taught me to fight with my fists, and, though Draig is strong and brave, he has little skill.'

'In short,' said Maev, 'Uncle Kaelin caught him with one of my bulls, beat him senseless and then let him go. The Cochlands do not raid here now.'

'Do they hate you, Uncle Kaelin?'

'I don't think so. One day maybe you can ask them. Now go off to your room and get out of those wet clothes.'

'Can't I stay a little while longer?'

'I need to talk to Maev. Go on with you. I'll still be here when you get back.' The boy hesitated, then ran up the stairs.

'He is like your shadow, Kaelin. You used to be like that with Jaim.'

'I remember. I've been thinking of this trip south. You don't need me, Maev. And I've no wish to see Eldacre again.'

'You think I have?' she snapped. 'You think I want to look down at that cursed cathedral? This is not a trip taken for pleasure, Kaelin. I need you. Trust me on that. I don't ask for much from you – or any man. Do this one thing for me.'

'What is so important?'

'I want you standing beside me when I visit Jaim's grave,' she said, her eyes suddenly glistening with tears.

Kaelin reached out and took her hand. 'I'll be there, Maev,' he said, with a sigh.

Chara was watching from the foot of the stairs. She felt a touch of anger at the older woman's manipulation. She didn't want Kaelin for a graveside visit. She wanted him to meet the Moidart.

Snow was swirling in through the shattered roof as Gaise Macon stretched out on the floor before the fire. He lay on his back, his head resting on a folded cloak. Despite his weariness he felt there was no chance of sleep. Seemingly random thoughts roiled in his mind. He found himself thinking of Eldacre Castle far to the north, and his father, the Moidart. There was no comfort in the memories. His childhood had been one of insistent sadness, struggling to find a way to make his father love him. He never had. Even now, as a fighting soldier in his twenties, Gaise Macon could find no reason for his father's lack of affection.

Lack of affection? It was more than that, thought Gaise. All his life his father had found ways to cause him pain. The young general wondered if his mother's death, so soon after giving birth to him, had caused the malice in the Moidart. But why should it? He was not responsible. His mother had been killed by assassins, who also stabbed the Moidart.

'It is a mystery you will never solve,' he told himself.

His mind drifted and he saw again the angry, flushed face of Lord Ferson, and the meeting of staff officers following the battle. The king had not been present. He generally avoided crowds, and the cramped conditions in the huge bell tent would have been abhorrent to him. Instead he had returned, with his family, to a nearby estate owned by Lord Winterbourne.

Four generals and eighteen senior officers had attended the meeting, and the first part had involved a discussion as to the battle's outcome. Many of the staff officers voiced the view that it was a great victory for the king's cause. Gaise had found this to be laughable. Luden Macks, outnumbered almost two to one, and expected to retreat, had attacked instead. Two divisions of the Royalist infantry had been swept aside. The advance had been halted by the steadfast courage of the elderly Lord Buckman, commander of the King's Guards. With troops streaming back through his lines Buckman had formed a fighting square, sending volley after volley into the charging Covenanters. It would not have been enough to stem the attack, but Gaise, from his position on the hills to the right, had led his four hundred cavalry in a furious charge. The Covenanters had broken. In pursuing them Gaise saw Lord Ferson and his two thousand Lancers on the opposite ridge. He sent a rider, requesting support. But the Lancers never moved.

In the bell tent Gaise had listened as a number of officers poured praise on their generals, obviously seeking to win favour. It was mildly stomach-churning. 'Surely, my lords,' he had said, 'the mere fact that we need to debate the issue at all shows that a full victory cannot be claimed? I would agree, however, that victory *should* have been ours. The enemy was retreating in disorder. One more charge would have routed them.'

'A matter of opinion,' snapped Lord Ferson, resplendent in a beautifully tailored battle coat of red wool, embroidered with gold thread. There was not a mark upon it, not a speck of dust, or a smear of mud. He was a small man, his reddish blond hair close curled and thinning at the crown. His thick moustache was waxed and raised into two points. It was said to be a new fashion in the capital, and Gaise thought it comical.

Gaise Macon had looked into the man's ruddy face, seeing the hostility in his small, closely set blue eyes. 'I disagree, my lord. I would be fascinated to know why the Lancers did not move. Did my request for assistance not reach you?'

Ferson's round face had flushed crimson. 'I'll not be criticized by a glory-seeking popinjay!' he thundered.

'Had that *popinjay* followed your example, general, we would not be discussing the merits of a dubious victory. The enemy would have overrun us.'

Before Ferson could respond General Buckman raised a hand. 'Gentlemen! Gentlemen! Let us not descend into rancour.' Past seventy, and a shrewd soldier, Owen Buckman was renowned for cool courage and total loyalty to the king. When he spoke his words were treated with respect. 'Our young friend is, in one particular, quite correct. It would be unwise to regard this battle as decisively in our favour. Luden's forces were intact at the close, and – eventually – withdrew in good order. By now he will have been reinforced by Dally's infantry. This was, it must be said, an opportunity missed.'

No-one spoke for a moment. Ferson sat staring malevolently at Gaise Macon. Then the cadaverous figure of Winter Kay, Lord Winterbourne, rose. In the lantern light his unusually pale skin seemed almost translucent, stretched tight across the bones of his face. His deep set, dark eyes were heavily shadowed, and showed no hint of emotion. He was wearing the heavy crimson cloak of the Redeemer Knights, and by his side hung a ceremonial short sword. The soldiers in the tent fell silent, waiting for Winterbourne to speak. Next to Buckman he was the most senior officer present. 'On current count the enemy lost more than a thousand men,' he said, his voice cold. 'He attacked, and was repulsed. In short he failed in his objective. My scouts report he has now pulled back into the hills. It is my belief there will be no major battles until the spring. We now have several months to gather reinforcements,' enlist fresh soldiers, and root out traitors from the surrounding towns.'

For the next hour the discussion focused on logistical issues: where the various units would spend winter, how they would be supplied, the gathering of fuel, and the sending out of recruiting teams.

As the meeting closed Lord Buckman drew Gaise aside. 'I thank you, young man, for your assistance in the field. That was a gallant charge, and a most welcome sight.'

'Thank you, sir.'

Taking Gaise by the arm Buckman led him further from the other officers. 'You are quite right about Ferson. His timidity was disgraceful. But be wary of drawing attention to it. The man – like all cowards – has a vengeful soul.'

'He should be dismissed, sir.'

'The king likes him, my boy, and we serve the king.'

Now, by the fire, Gaise was restless. His body was weary, but his mind would not relax. He sat up. The snow had stopped. Looking up through the shattered roof he saw that stars were once again bright in the night sky.

Suddenly a scent came to him. Summer pine. With it flowed a breath of warm breeze. Gaise turned towards the far side of the room. Gone were the smoke-blackened wall, the ruined paintings, the charred furniture. Instead tall pine trees were growing there, and beyond them Gaise could see sloping hills of verdant green. A small, white-haired figure moved into sight, sitting down upon a flat stone. Gaise smiled. He had not seen her in years – not since she had given him the Rigante soul-name of Stormrider.

Rising from the rug he walked across to the pine wood. 'It is good to see you, Wyrd,' he said.

The white-haired woman looked up at him and smiled. Her face was ageless, though she looked weary. 'I cannot stay long, Stormrider,' she said.

'How have you made this happen?' he asked, gesturing towards the trees. 'It is mighty magic.'

'No,' she said, 'not mighty at all. I have merely invaded your dreams. Look back. There you sleep by the fire.'

Gaise glanced round. His lean body was resting on its back, his

91

head on a folded cloak. He saw with surprise that the sleeping face was drawn and haggard, the eyes dark-rimmed. 'I look ghastly,' he said.

'Aye, you do. But you will wake refreshed. I'll see to that.'

Sunlight lanced through the trees. Gaise felt the warmth on his face. Sitting down opposite the Wyrd he watched as the ruined room shrank away, the threshold covered by a screen of bushes and trees. Birds were singing, and he heard the soft lapping of a stream running over rocks. It was as if a burden had lifted from his soul. 'Why have you come to me?' he asked the little woman. 'Is there something you need me to do?'

'I need you to stay alive, Gaise Macon.'

'I'll do my best,' he answered, with a smile.

'Have you found the answer yet?' she said.

'To which question?'

'Why would a coward challenge you?'

He shrugged. 'The nature of a coward is to avoid danger. If such a man courts peril there can be only two reasons. Either he is not a coward at all – or there is no danger.'

'Exactly. So, how could it be that a pistol duel would offer no danger?'

'The pistols would contain a charge and wadding, but no ball.'

'One of them would be loaded. Not yours, I fear.'

Gaise nodded. 'I know. Such treachery could not come from one coward. For such a foul enterprise to succeed there would need to be a conspiracy to murder me.'

'What do you intend to do?'

'I intend to win, Wyrd.'

'There is more to this than Ferson's conceit,' said the Wyrd. 'There is a source of evil, radiating its power. It is too strong for me to pierce. I have tried to find ways to read the future. All I see are fragmented images. I see you bearing a lost sword. I see a man with eyes of gold and green, yet he is not you. The more I search the less I find. I fear I am neither strong enough nor wise enough to find the way.'

Gaise heard the despair in her voice. Reaching out he took her hand. 'What can I do to help you?' he asked.

'I don't know. Enemies are seeking my death and I don't know why. The power of a great evil is at work and I don't know what it desires. Death is closing in on me, Stormrider. Day by day it gets closer. What I am sure of is that you must survive. It is vital.'

A cold breeze touched Gaise, and he saw a movement in the trees. The Wyrd sprang to her feet. 'They have found me,' she cried. Gaise rose alongside her. The sunshine disappeared. Two figures moved out of the gloom, dark swords in their hands. Their faces were grey and scaled. Iron circlets ringed their brows, and their eyes were swimming in blood. The Wyrd threw up her hands. Lightning flashed and a clap of thunder exploded. Gaise was hurled from his feet. He spun over and over, down through swirling blackness. He heard a shriek that chilled his blood.

He woke with a start, his heart pounding. Rolling to his feet he ran across the room to where his saddle was placed on a cracked bench. From the holsters stitched to the pommel mounting he drew two heavy pistols, and cocked them. Then he stood in the gloom and waited.

A lean figure moved through the doorway. Gaise swept up a pistol and pointed it.

'I'd be obliged if you would refrain from shooting me, sir,' said Mulgrave.

Gaise sagged back against the wall. 'What is wrong, sir?' asked Mulgrave, moving across to take the young noble's arm. He helped Gaise to the fire, and both men sat down upon the rug.

'I am all right now, my friend,' said Gaise, uncocking the pistols and laying them on the floor. 'I had a . . . nightmare.' He shivered and rubbed a hand across his face. It came away wet with sweat. 'What brings you here, Mulgrave? It is not dawn yet.'

'Sad news, sir. Word has just reached us that Lord Buckman has died in his sleep.'

Gaise sighed. He did not know the man well, but he felt a sense of deep loss. 'He was too old for campaigning,' he said. 'Yet without him we would have been ripped apart. Damn, but I liked the old man.'

'He was a fine gentleman, and a brave one. He'll be hard to replace.' Mulgrave reached out, placing his hand on Gaise's brow. 'You are very pale, sir, and you are still sweating. Perhaps I should fetch the surgeon.'

'It is not necessary. The dream was very real. I shall be fine now.'

'Would it help to talk of it, sir?'

Gaise shook his head. 'No.' Rising he pulled on his heavy grey topcoat. 'Let's see if we can find some breakfast.'

Winter Kay, Lord Winterbourne, was a warrior in the truest sense. The Lord of the Redeemers, and a Knight of the Sacrifice, he lived only for war. For such a man ultimate victory would be anathema. Victory would mean an end to war, a passing of glory and a life thereafter of tedious mediocrity. War was life lived to the fullest. It brought out the best in men.

As a younger man he had not fully understood this awesome fact. Deep down, however, he had sensed it. All his life he had lusted after combat. Before he was twenty he had fought three duels, two with sword, one with pistol. He had ridden with the Knights of the Sacrifice in the eastern wars, taking part in the sack of Alterin, and the Battle of Skeyne. He had been second in command at the massacre of Shelsans, when two thousand devotees of the New Tree cult had been put to the sword, or taken alive and burned.

It was here that the Source had blessed Winter Kay and delivered into his hands the Orb of Kranos.

In the years that followed he had taken the Orb on all his travels, gathering to him other knights pledged to fight for the honour of the Source. He had hoped his younger brother, Gayan, would have been among their number. But he had been slain by a Highlander at the cathedral city of Eldacre. It was a source of constant sorrow to Winter Kay.

In time he had formed the Redeemers; the finest of the knights. And he had learned how to feed the magic of the Orb, so that it in turn could empower his Redeemers. Mortal wounds healed overnight, strength and speed were enhanced. It was too early yet to tell, but Winter Kay also believed that even the ageing process was slowed. At forty-nine he could still ride, fight and react with the same speed and strength as when he was in his twenties. And, more than this, the power of the Orb allowed its followers to free themselves from the shackles of the flesh, their spirits soaring out into the skies, travelling wherever they wished. Winter Kay himself gained even more, for he was never far from the skull. At night visions came to him in his sleep, bright and vivid. He saw a great city, and palaces of marble. Then there were the blessed times that the ghost of Kranos himself would speak to him, filling his mind with promises of a golden tomorrow, a time of immortality and excess.

Only one small cloud marred Winter Kay's horizon.

Gaise Macon.

Was he the man with the golden eye the priest had prophesied? *'I will go gladly, Winter Kay. Which is more than can be said for you, when the one with the golden eye comes for you.'*

Winter Kay sat in his tent staring down at the walnut case, and the two silver-inlaid pistols nestling there. Gaise Macon would not be a danger after this afternoon. Jerad Ferson was a coward, but he was also a fair shot. At twenty paces he would put a ball into the young man's chest and that would be an end to it.

Two men, in red cloaks, approached the tent. Winter Kay bade them enter. Both were tall and lean. Removing their iron helms they bowed low.

'Did you kill the woman?' he asked them.

'No, lord. We failed.' Their faces were very pale and haggard, their eyes deep set. They looked exhausted. This was not uncommon following heavy use of the forbidden herb. He saw them looking longingly towards the metal box containing the Orb.

'Tell me what happened.'

The first man spoke: 'The trance was deep, lord, and, as you said, we could feel her energy. We entered her dream. She sensed us. Before we could strike she sent up a great and blinding light. Then she was gone. There was a spirit with her. A man.'

'What kind of man?'

The Redeemer glanced at his comrade. The second man spoke: 'I believe it was Macon, lord. I cannot be sure.'

Winter Kay rose from his seat and moved to the rear of the tent. Carefully he opened the lid of the metal box, drawing aside the black velvet. 'Come,' he said. The two Redeemers stumbled forward. 'Make obeisance,' he commanded them. Both men drew sharp daggers and cut the palms of their hands. Then they held them above the skull. Blood dripped to the bone. It began to glow.

95

The Redeemers waited for Winter Kay's order, then each lightly touched the skull. They stiffened. One of them gave a groan of pleasure.

'Enough!' said Winter Kay.

The Redeemers stepped back. No longer were their faces pale, and the cuts on their hands had sealed.

'In the name of the Source,' said Winter Kay, 'Gaise Macon must die. You will be the loaders at the duel. Whichever pistol he chooses must not be armed. You will appear to drop the ball into the muzzle, but keep it secreted in your hand.'

'Yes, lord. We understand.'

'The man is in communion with our enemy. He has sold his soul to evil.'

'Yes, lord.'

Winter Kay placed his hands on both men's shoulders, drawing them in close. 'If, by some freak of chance, Gaise Macon should survive this duel, you will make it your bounden duty to see him dead before the next full moon.'

'You wish us to challenge him, lord?' asked the first.

'No. Merely kill him. Do it quietly. Suffocate him in his bed, poison his food, stab him in a darkened alley. The method is immaterial. Just bring me, as a token, his golden eye.'

The snow clouds had cleared in the night, and the midday sky was now bright blue. The temperature had dropped to well below freezing, and ice had formed on the muddy path leading through to the area of the duel. Only a few months before this had been a secluded garden set within the grounds of one Lord Dunstan's private chapel. Dunstan would have walked here with his wife and his daughters after Holy Day services. They would, perhaps, have admired the roses that lined the paths asthey repaired to their mansion to enjoy a fine meal. Now Dunstan was dead, shot to pieces on Bladdley Moor, with most of his Covenant regiment. His fine house was a ruined shell, and the chapel – the last refuge of a group of diehard rebels – had been ripped apart by cannon shell, the spire lying in broken fragments across the northern tip of the garden.

Gaise Macon, dressed in a fur-lined charcoal grey jacket, grey breeches and knee-length riding boots, walked alongside the swordsman, Mulgrave, who had donned his high collared, leaf green uniform, and wore an officer's short cape. Both men could have been out for a pre-lunch stroll, and Gaise Macon was chatting amiably as they approached the area of the duel. A long trestle table had been set at the centre of the garden. Behind it stood two red-cloaked Redeemers. Lord Winterbourne was standing along-side the shorter Lord Ferson. Ferson's embroidered red topcoat was loosely draped across his shoulders. Beneath it he wore a beauti-fully crafted shirt of expensive white lace. Beyond the low wall round the garden stood hundreds of Ferson's men. Off to the right a number of Eldacre soldiers had also gathered.

'A fine day for such stupidity,' said Gaise Macon, approaching the two men.

Winter Kay gave a thin smile. 'Matters of honour are rarely stupid, young man. Perhaps an understanding of that from you would have spared us this duel.'

'I shall bear that in mind in future, my lord,' answered Gaise, with a bow.

A third man approached them. Wrapped in a heavy topcoat and scarf, the burly Lord Cumberlane bowed briefly to the two duel-lists. 'I am appointed by the king,' he said, 'as Master of the Duel. It is my duty to implore both of you to find an equitable solution to this matter.' There was ice forming upon his thick moustache, and his face was grey with cold. He swung towards Lord Ferson. 'Can you now, my lord, see your way clear to resolving this issue without recourse to bloodshed?'

'No,' replied Ferson, with a malevolent glance at Gaise Macon.

'Perhaps the offer of an apology?' insisted Lord Cumberlane.

'Honour demands satisfaction upon the field,' said Ferson. Mulgrave felt his anger rise. The man's confidence was such that the swordsman became ever more convinced that the duel was to be rigged. He glanced at Gaise Macon. The young man seemed per-fectly at ease, but Mulgrave knew him well, and could see that he was performing.

'Very well,' said Cumberlane, sadly. 'Let the matter commence. You will choose your weapons, and then stand back to back where I bid you. On my command you will advance ten paces and turn.

Once you have done so neither man will move. Not a step to the left or the right. I shall then give the instruction to fire. If either man shoots before I give the word he shall be deemed a craven, and shall face a charge of murder. Is my instruction clear?'

Both duellists nodded.

'Each man will fire a single shot. Should no-one be hit the duellists will remain in position while the pistols are reloaded.'

Ferson strolled to where two silver pistols had been laid upon the table. Gaise Macon followed him. Ferson waited while Gaise examined both pistols. They were Emburleys and handsomely crafted, the long barrels engraved with scenes of running deer, the butts boasting the Leopard Rampant crest of the Winterbourne family.

'Will they suffice?' asked Winter Kay.

'Admirable, sir. Admirable!' said Ferson jovially.

'Then choose, Master Macon,' said Winter Kay.

Gaise Macon made his choice. Ferson took up the second pistol. Both men then handed the pieces to the Redeemers behind the table. The Knights expertly primed the flash pans, snapping shut the covers, then tilted the weapons to add a charge of powder. The Redeemers then each took a round lead ball from a bowl set on the table.

'A moment, sir,' said Gaise Macon. 'I shall choose my own ball.'

'They are all identical,' said Winter Kay.

'Of course they all *appear* that way,' said Gaise Macon, smoothly, 'but I have learned to judge by feel.' Reaching into the bowl of shot he rolled several of them in his fingers. Then he produced one. 'This feels perfect,' he said. Reaching across the table he relieved his surprised loader of the silver pistol and dropped the shot into it. Lifting a small square of silk from alongside the bowl he pressed it into the barrel. Sliding the ramrod clear he tamped down the charge. 'I am ready,' he said, looking directly at Lord Ferson.

Mulgrave suppressed a smile. Ferson no longer looked confident. His face was ashen, and he was blinking rapidly. It seemed to Mulgrave that even the man's ludicrously waxed moustache points were about to sag. Ferson licked his lips and cast a glance at Winter Kay. 'Such behaviour is insufferable,' he said.

'In what way, sir?' asked Lord Cumberlane.

'He . . . he impugns the . . . the neutrality of . . . the competence of . . .' He stammered to silence. Sweat was showing on his brow.

'Ready yourselves, gentlemen,' said Lord Cumberlane. 'Back to back if you please.'

Gaise Macon removed his topcoat, handed it to Mulgrave, and walked out into the centre of the garden. Ferson lagged behind, staring at Winter Kay. Then he stumbled out to take his place. 'Be so good as to remove your uniform jacket,' Cumberlane told him. Winter Kay strode out and relieved him of the garment.

'Now, gentlemen, ten paces, if you please, and then await my instruction.'

Mulgrave moved back from the line of fire and watched as the two men slowly moved apart. His stomach was knotted now, and a great fear filled him. Both pistols were now primed, but, though a coward, Ferson could still win. One well placed shot and Gaise Macon could be lying dead upon the cold ground.

As the duellists reached the tenth pace Lord Cumberlane called out, 'Halt.'

Ferson spun and fired. Gaise Macon staggered to his left, then came upright. Blood was flowing from what appeared to Mulgrave to be the side of his head. A stunned silence followed. Lord Cumberlane stood staring at the wounded man. 'It was a hair trigger,' shouted Ferson. 'It went off early.'

'You were not told to turn,' said Cumberlane, icily. He began to walk towards the wounded Gaise Macon, but the young general waved him back.

'It is all right, my lord,' he said. 'The shot merely grazed my ear.'

'I am pleased to hear it,' said Cumberlane. 'Now you may take your own shot. If the knave still lives after you have fired I shall see him hanged.'

Gaise Macon readied himself. Ferson stood blinking in the sunlight, looking wretched. His pistol dropped from nerveless fingers. Mulgrave saw with deep embarrassment that the man was weeping. It was an appalling scene. In the background a large number of Ferson's soldiers had gathered to watch the duel. Some turned away in disgust. Others waited for the inevitable conclusion. Ferson fell to his knees, throwing his arms over his head.

Gaise Macon, the left side of his shirt drenched with blood, lowered his pistol and discharged his shot into the earth. As the sound thundered Lord Ferson screamed and threw himself to the ground.

Mulgrave ran to Gaise's side. Blood was streaming from the ruined earlobe. 'I am proud of you, sir,' he said. 'There would have been no satisfaction in killing such a cur.'

Gaise Macon sighed. 'We'll talk later.' Slowly he walked back to the trestle table, laying the pistol upon it. Then he approached Lord Cumberlane.

'I've never seen the like,' muttered Cumberlane. 'Damn, but it shames us all.'

'As the aggrieved party, sir, I wish for no action to be taken against Lord Ferson. It will satisfy me if he resigns his commission and returns to his home.'

'The knave ought to be hanged. By heaven, he's an affront to Varlish manhood. But I will do as you say.' Cumberlane held out his hand. 'I hope you don't live to regret your kindness, Gaise Macon.'

Gaise shook the general's hand. 'I hope I *never* live long enough to regret kindness, general. Though I am not sure it was kind. I think that for the coward every day carries a kind of death.' He swung away and found himself facing Winter Kay. 'I thank you for the use of your pistol, sir,' he said. Winter Kay said nothing, but he returned Gaise Macon's bow. With that the young general walked from the garden, Mulgrave beside him.

# CHAPTER FIVE

DRAIG COCHLAND WOULD DO MOST THINGS FOR MONEY. HE WOULD willingly steal and rob, and would think nothing of killing a man during the process of either activity. Draig was not a man to be fooled by those who established the rules. It seemed to him that the entire world was run by robbery of one kind or another. The whole structure of society depended on it. It always surprised Draig that other men couldn't see it. The poor hill farmer who struggled to survive through drought-plagued summers and harsh, bone-numbing winters still had to give one tenth of his crop to the Moidart's gatherers. What was that if not robbery? Give me one tenth of all you have or I will lock you away or hang you. Draig had voiced this many times in rowdy tavern arguments. It was always fun. People would get red in the face and argue about the need for taxes to build roads and maintain schools and such. Draig would laugh at them. 'Schools, eh? The Moidart wears silk shirts and you wear homespun cloth. *That's* where your money goes.'

It was as Old Gramps had always said: 'Steal a loaf of bread and they hang you, steal a land and they'll make you king.'

Draig's concept of good and evil was simple and easy to maintain. What was good for the small Cochland clan was good, and what was not was evil. Or so he had thought before the Varlish

101

rider had come into the high country settlement the Cochlands called home.

The man had ridden far, and he had come with promises of gold coin if the Cochlands would do a service for his lord. This *lord* remained unnamed, though Draig guessed it to be the Moidart, but as a gesture of good faith the rider had brought ten silver chaillings as a gift.

Draig did not like the man, but then that was not unusual. Draig didn't much like anybody. Except, perhaps, his brother Eain. Though truth to tell he wasn't *that* fond of him either. No, it was not the dislike that bothered Draig. It was something entirely different.

Even now, two hours after the rider had left, Draig could not quite put his finger on the cause of his disquiet. The man was Varlish and well spoken, which was enough to earn Draig's contempt. He was also cold, his eyes hard and flinty. But that wasn't it either.

Draig sat quietly by his fire, his heavy shoulders hunched over. After a while his brother came in and squatted down opposite him. Despite Eain's being a year younger they could almost have been twins, both green-eyed, large and hulking, their faces flat, their red beards matted and filthy.

'What did he want?' asked Eain.

'He wanted us to kill someone.'

'Good coin in it?'

'Aye, so he promised.'

'Excellent. Who are we to kill?'

'A child and a woman.'

Eain's eyes narrowed. 'Are you making a joke, brother?'

'No.'

'I'm not killing any child. Or any woman either,' he added, after a pause.

'No? Why?' asked Draig.

'What do you mean why? You just don't, is all.'

Draig sat quietly for a moment. Then he nodded. 'Aye, that's what I told him. He wasn't best pleased.'

'Who did he want killed?'

'The Dweller by the Lake, and the boy Kaelin Ring brought down from the hills.'

'The lad whose parents were killed by Hang-lip?'

'That's the one.'

'It makes no sense,' said Eain. 'Who'd profit by such a deed?'

'We would have,' observed Draig.

'You know what I mean.'

'Aye, I do, and I've no answer to give you.'

Eain took up a long stick and prodded the fire into life. 'I expect he'll go to Tostig and those Low Valley lads. They'll do it right enough.'

'I expect so. Ten pounds he was offering.'

Eain swore softly. 'I've never even seen ten pounds in one place.'

'You sorry I turned him down?'

Eain thought about it. 'Nah,' he said.

Draig rose from the fireside and walked to the doorway of the hut. Ducking his head he stepped beneath the sagging lintel and out into the clearing. Few of the Cochland clan were outside. Two scrawny children were throwing snowballs at each other, four others were hauling an ancient sled up the hillside. Only four of the men of the clan were in the settlement, the other twenty-three being off to the east, in two groups, seeking to steal cattle and head them south to Eldacre. Draig scratched at his beard. He wasn't sure exactly how old he was, but he felt too old to be chasing over the mountains after a few scrawny cows.

He felt strangely unsettled. Ten pounds was a fortune. A man could live well for two years on ten pounds. Yet he hadn't even come close to accepting the commission. The wind picked up and he shivered and returned to the fire.

Eain had set up the cook pot tripod and was mixing oats, salt and water into the old black pan, stirring it with a cracked and stained wooden spoon. 'I know what you're thinking,' he said.

Draig stared balefully at his brother. 'You don't even know what you're thinking half the time.'

'You're thinking of warning Kaelin Ring.'

'Why would I do something that stupid? The Varlish is a man of power. I don't need him as an enemy. And I wouldn't want Tostig and his crew creeping in here to cut my throat.'

'All right,' said Eain. 'Then what were you thinking of?'

103

Draig hawked and spat into the fire. 'I was thinking of warning Kaelin Ring,' he admitted.

'We don't even like him,' argued Eain.

'I don't like you either – but I'd tell you if there was a snake in your boot.'

'No you wouldn't. You'd just wait and laugh when it bit me. Like when that bloody tree branch fell on me. You could have shouted. Didn't though, did you?'

'Gods, man, that was fifteen years ago, and you're still on about it. I told you then it was funny.'

'Nothing funny about a broken shoulder.'

'No, you're wrong. That was even funnier.'

'Well, a pox on you and the horse you rode in on.'

'I don't know why you say that,' said Draig, settling down by the fire. 'You've never ridden a horse. Neither have I.'

'I like the sound of it. It's like poetry.'

'All the best poems have the word pox in them,' said Draig. 'Are you going to stir that porridge? I hate it when it's full of black bits.'

Eain grinned at him, showing stained and misshapen teeth. 'You really are in a strange mood, brother.'

'Yes,' agreed Draig. 'That's true, right enough. You remember when the Dweller came here and healed old Scats? We thought he'd lose that eye, but she put a poultice over it and all the pus just dried up.'

'I remember. You got angry because she wouldn't heal a boil you had.'

'It wasn't a boil, it was a cyst. Big as a damned goose egg.'

'Whatever. She said you were a man who deserved boils.' Eain laughed. 'Never thought to hear you let a woman talk to you that way.'

Draig shrugged. 'Didn't bother me,' he lied. 'She wouldn't take no payment from Scats. Made no sense. She'd walked twenty miles. Wouldn't even eat with us.'

'Probably didn't like black bits in her porridge,' observed Eain.

'Probably.' Draig suddenly swore. 'You know what's really liced my skin? That Varlish just assumed I was the kind of man who would kill a woman and a child. That's the reputation I have. No wonder the Dweller wouldn't heal my boil.'

'Cyst,' said Eain, gleefully.

'And the horse you rode in on,' said Draig.

Eain chuckled and stirred the porridge. 'You think Tostig will agree to kill them?'

'Of course he will. There's no Rigante in that man.'

'There's not more than a thimbleful in us,' Eain pointed out. 'And that was from Great-Gramps – which means it was three parts liquor anyway.'

Draig suddenly laughed. 'You are not wrong, brother. We're Cochlands now. And we look after our own. To hell with anyone else, eh?'

'Damn right.' Eain served up the porridge in two deep wooden bowls, and they ate in silence. Finally Draig put aside his empty plate and pushed himself to his feet.

He swore suddenly. 'Damn it, but I *do* like Kaelin Ring,' he said.

'You said you didn't like anybody.' Eain sounded aggrieved, and Draig laughed.

'The man's a fighter, and there's no give in him. When the Varlish took his woman and imprisoned her he walked into that fort and brought her out. Have to admire that.'

'He thrashed you and broke your nose,' argued Eain. 'We don't want to get involved in this, Draig. Tostig is an evil whoreson. Added to which he's good with sword and knife. Kaelin Ring can take care of himself.'

Draig shook his head. 'Not if he don't know what's coming. I think I'll walk to Ironlatch.'

'I'll not come with you on such foolishness.'

'Who asked you?'

'We're not full Rigante, brother. We don't owe anybody anything.'

'I never said we did.'

'Has it occurred to you that the Moidart is the one who wants them dead?'

'Yes,' said Draig, a sense of unease settling on him at the mention of the man's name.

'If he found out you'd gone against him, you know who he'd send.'

Draig shivered and did not answer. He knew all right.

Huntsekker would come, with that cursed scythe, and Draig's head would be in a bag.

'It'll be Huntsekker,' said Eain. 'He never fails.'

'Give it a rest, Eain! Anyway he did fail once. He didn't catch that fighter, Chain Shada. Word was that Grymauch took him out from under Huntsekker's nose. So he's human. He's not some demon of the dark to frighten me.'

'Well, the thought of him frightens me,' said Eain.

Draig moved across the hut, lifting an old bearskin coat from the floor. He shook it then swung it round his shoulders. 'We are not going to get involved in this,' he said. 'All I'm going to do is have a quiet word with Kaelin Ring. Then we're out of it.'

In the dark of the night Chara Ring stood at the upper bedroom window, staring out at the moonlit snow, and the sharp, jagged lines of the distant mountains. A blue and green Rigante shawl was wrapped round her slender shoulders, and her thoughts were deep and melancholy.

Five years ago she had been taken by Varlish soldiers and brought to the Black Mountain fort, and there had been brutally raped and abused. Often she would dream of being back in that bleak dungeon, listening to the laughter and grunts of the soldiers and the vicious words of the traitor Wullis Swainham. Many times since she had convinced herself she was over the worst, and that the vileness of that night had no power any more. Standing in the window she knew she was wrong. She knew that it would always be with her, like a wound upon the soul.

There was no doubting her love for Kaelin Ring, nor that she enjoyed the feeling of his arms around her. Mostly she could lose herself in the act of lovemaking, and occasionally it was even joyous. She had laughed with the Dweller about the importance to her of the physical closeness she had found with Kaelin. It was not strictly untrue. Chara needed to feel that Kaelin desired her. Often, however, as he held her, and entered her, she would see again the ugly, bestial faces of the men in the dungeon. The brutality of what she had endured would erupt from her subconscious, making her want to scream for Kaelin to get away from her. She would hold it back by picturing the moment that Kaelin came for her on that dreadful night.

In an act of breathtaking recklessness he and Rayster had entered the fort, killing the guards at the gatehouse and donning their uniforms. Then Kaelin had made his way to the dungeon and rescued her. She turned from the window and gazed at his sleeping form. He was lying on his back, one arm outstretched. In the moonlight the scar on his cheek shone bright. Chara remembered the sabre duel with her brother Bael that had caused it. It seemed a lifetime ago, as did so much of her life before the dungeon. It was as if she were two different people. Chara Then and Chara Now.

She no longer spoke to Kaelin about her memories. It was not that he did not care. It was that he cared too much. He wanted to find a 'cure' for her. In some ways it was touching, in others infuriating. On rare occasions she would open her heart to the Dweller. There was comfort there, for she would listen without seeking to offer remedies.

The worst moment had come just before this winter, when she and Kaelin had visited Black Mountain to bring in supplies. As the wagon was being loaded the two of them had walked through the town, and out onto the low meadow, by the stream. The day had been bright and clear, the sunshine warm. It was like a summer's day, and Chara had felt at peace. She was holding Kaelin's hand, and laughing at some little jest he made. Then she saw a man, also walking with his love. Three children were running alongside them, two tawny-haired boys and a girl with long auburn curls. Chara had stopped, her hand falling away from Kaelin's grip.

The man was one of the soldiers who had raped her.

She had thought them all killed in the battle at the Rigante Pass – a battle won by the brilliance of her husband, who led the Rigante in a night climb down a sheer rock face to emerge behind the besieging Varlish. She had *needed* to believe they were dead, punished for what they had done to her.

As Chara stood and watched the man and his family heading off towards the stream she saw him turn and look at her. He smiled and waved. Kaelin waved back. It seemed incomprehensible to Chara that the man did not recognize her, but she knew he did not.

She felt her heart would break. This man and others had all but ruined her life. Yet here he was, by a meadow spring on a sunny day, leading his own family out on a stroll.

A part of her longed to tell Kaelin of the man's deeds. A part of her wanted to see her husband march across the meadow and cut the man's heart out. Yet it was only a small part. The children with him were not guilty of any evil. Nor was the woman who walked by his side. Would it ease her own pain to see this woman widowed? She had turned away. 'What is wrong?' asked Kaelin.

'I have a headache,' said Chara, taking his hand once more. 'It is no matter. Why don't we go back into town and find a place to sit quietly and eat?'

In the faint light of pre-dawn Chara saw Senlic Carpenter move out to the far gate and lift the latch. His limp was more pronounced in the cold of the early mornings. He seemed to have aged badly since the stroke hit him in the autumn of last year. His hair was very white now, and he spoke with a slight slur. When he smiled, which was rare these days, the left side of his face did not move, and his left arm was near useless. She watched him clumsily open the gate. His dog, Patch, a black and white mongrel, ran out into the meadow.

'You are awake early,' said Kaelin, sitting up and yawning.

'Senlic shouldn't be working so hard,' she said. 'You should let him rest more.'

'I have tried,' he said. 'He needs to feel useful.'

Other men were moving into sight now, and she saw a team of horses being led off to the rear of the barn. 'I wish you weren't going with Maev,' she said.

He climbed out of the bed and moved to stand behind her. She felt his arms slide around her. 'Will you miss me?'

'That's a stupid question. Of course I'll miss you. As will Jaim and Feargol.'

'I'll be back within twenty days. Now why not come back to bed and give me something to remember you by?'

'You'll remember,' she said, spinning out of his grasp. 'And you have men standing out there in the cold waiting for you. So get yourself dressed. I'll go and prepare you some breakfast.' She left the room and walked downstairs. Maev was already there.

'Is there anything you want me to bring back from Eldacre?' asked the older woman.

'Just my husband,' answered Chara, coldly.

Senlic Carpenter was weary as he limped towards the main house, and his spirits were low. As a Rigante he had prided himself on his lack of fear, on his courage. But he was frightened now. Not of dying, for all men had, at some time, to pass from this life. No, Senlic's fear was of becoming sickly and a burden upon those he had served. He didn't want to end his life lying in a bed, incontinent and rambling. The stroke had almost killed him. On some mornings he wished that it had. He would at least have died as a man.

He paused at the gate. Patch sat down beside him. 'I wonder when I got old?' he said aloud, the words slurring. It seemed to have crept up on him almost unnoticed. Yes, his hair had greyed, and he found himself a little slower. He had noticed aches in his limbs during the coldest of the weather. Now, though, he felt so . . . so ancient.

He had bidden farewell to Kaelin and Maev, and most of the farm workers. Once he would have regretted not joining them on the journey to Eldacre. Senlic liked visiting cities occasionally, to marvel at the great buildings and to enjoy afternoons in taverns and evenings in whorehouses, where they played music. He didn't regret it now. A visit to a whorehouse would only fill him with shame. Patch caught sight of a rabbit out in the meadow and gave a low growl. 'You'll not catch him, boy,' said Senlic. Patch cocked his head and stared up at the man. 'You want to try though, eh? Go on then. Go get him!' Patch bounded off across the snow. The rabbit sat and watched him, then sprang away. Patch tried to turn and slithered on the snow. The sight lifted Senlic's mood. Yapping furiously Patch gave chase once more.

The sound of the dog barking brought little Feargol Ustal running from the main house. 'Will he catch the rabbit?' the six-year-old asked Senlic.

'No, son. Not a hope.'

'Has he ever caught a rabbit?'

'Not once in nine years of life. Doesn't stop him trying, though.'

Senlic thought about it for a moment. 'It's not strictly true, come to think on it. He did bring a rabbit back to me once. It had been struck by a hawk, but had managed to get away. It had a wound on one of its hind legs. Patch picked it up and brought it to me. Carried it like a little puppy – ever so careful – then laid it at my feet.'

'Did you eat it?'

'Funnily enough we didn't. I figured it had earned its life by escaping the hawk. So we kept it for a while, and fed it. The leg got better and I carried it back to the meadow and let it go.'

'Why didn't Patch kill it?' asked the red-headed child.

'Maybe he thought it deserved another chance at life. I don't know. Can't tell what a dog is thinking. You should have mittens on, boy. It's rare cold today.'

Feargol stared off to the south. 'I wish Uncle Kaelin had let me go to Eldacre,' he said.

'You still wearing that charm I gave you?'

'Yes,' said the boy happily, delving inside his coat and lifting out the small silver pendant.

'And all the dreams have gone, yes?'

'Yes, they have. It's wonderful. How did it make them go away?'

Senlic shrugged. 'It's magic, lad. Don't know how it works – only that it does. Do you still see pictures in your head?'

'Sometimes,' answered the boy, warily. 'Maev says they are day-dreams and of no . . .' he struggled for the word, 'condequinces,' he said, at last.

'Consequence,' corrected Senlic. 'It means importance. Maev is a person to listen to on most things. She's a clever woman, hard and bright. She's wrong on this, though, lad. I have the Sight too – or once I did. Tell me about the pictures.'

'Aunt Chara says you should come in and have a hot drink. She says it will do you good.'

'Aye, that's true. We'll go in together.'

Once inside Senlic struggled to remove his heavy topcoat. It wasn't easy with a left arm he couldn't lift. He saw Chara moving towards him and wanted to tell her to mind her business, but he was too tired, and her help was welcome. He sat at the breakfast table and sipped the hot, honeyed tisane she prepared for him. It had more than a dash of uisge in it, for which he was grateful. Feargol clambered on the seat beside him. 'Tell me about the pictures,' said Senlic.

'I saw a man with golden hair in a pistol fight. He had his ear shot off,' said Feargol.

'What else?'

'There's a place with trees, big huge trees, bigger than any trees in the mountains. They are red. One of them has a trunk almost as big as this house.'

'I think Maev is right about some of these visions,' said Chara, with a smile. 'Trees as big as houses. I have never heard the like.'

'Across the ocean,' said Senlic. 'I saw them once in a dream. There were people living there, and their skins were like the trees, reddish brown.'

'They have feathers in their hair and on their shirts,' said Feargol.

'That's right, lad. What was really strange was that none of them had beards.'

'You shouldn't encourage the boy,' said Chara. 'Big trees and men without beards.'

'It's true,' said Senlic. 'By the Source, it is. I always thought that one day I would cross the ocean and walk those mountains. What else have you seen, boy?'

'There's a sad man who paints pictures. He sits alone all the time. I watched him paint a picture. It was like magic. He dipped his brush in dark paint and smeared it on the . . . square. Then he dipped another brush in white paint, and mixed some blue in it. Then he dabbed at the picture, and all the dark smears suddenly became mountains with snow on them. He's very clever.'

'Why do you say he's a sad man?' asked Chara. 'If he can paint like that he should be happy.'

'He's not happy,' said Feargol. 'He hurts all the time. He has all these scars on his body, and they bleed and have pus in them. And he writes these long letters. Then he burns them.'

'Who does he write the letters to?' asked Senlic.

'I don't know. I can't read.'

'Does he have a wife?'

'No. He lives in a great big house. Much bigger than this one. And there are soldiers everywhere.'

'You should try to see happy things,' said Chara. 'Not sad men who paint pictures or people having their ears shot off.'

'I never know what I am going to see,' said Feargol. 'It's always a surprise. I would like to have one of the sad man's pictures. I would hang it in my room.'

Outside the house Patch began to bark again. This time it was not the excited yapping of the chase. Senlic pushed himself to his feet and walked to the window.

'What is it?' asked Chara.

'The Cochland brothers,' answered Senlic. 'Do you have a pistol?'

Eain Cochland was cursing himself for his decision to walk the eighteen miles to Ironlatch Farm with his brother Draig. He had been prompted to the action by simple boredom, and still had no real understanding of why Draig wanted to warn Kaelin Ring. Added to which he could still feel the stab of emotional pain he had suffered at hearing that his brother liked the man. In some ways it felt like a betrayal. He had long grown used to the fact that Draig didn't like him, but the hurt was lessened by the fact that he didn't like anybody.

Now, as well as his hurt feelings, his legs were aching, his feet and hands were cold, and he was hungry. It was vastly unlikely that they would be invited inside, and the whole enterprise was an enormous waste of time and effort. It was not that he wanted to see the little boy killed, nor that he didn't care. It was just that he didn't care *enough* to suffer cold hands and feet.

As they approached the gate a small black and white mongrel ran towards them, barking furiously. The dog ran towards Draig, who dropped to one knee on the snow and held out his hand. Eain stiffened. One of these days his idiot brother was going to have his fingers bitten off!

Not today, though. The dog did what all dogs did when Draig offered his hand. It stopped barking, stood looking suspiciously at the hand, then eased itself forward to sniff the fingers. 'Good lad,' said Draig softly, sliding his hand over the dog's head and ruffling its ears.

The farmhouse door opened and two people emerged. One was the old cattle handler Senlic Carpenter. Eain hadn't laid eyes on him for two years, and he was stunned at the change in the man's appearance. His hair, which had been dark grey, was now white and he looked about a hundred and ten years old. Beside him came Chara Ring. Eain felt suddenly uncomfortable. She was a mile beyond pretty! Her red hair was more closely cropped than was usually popular among highland women, but the style merely highlighted her beauty. Eain's thoughts plunged towards the carnal. Then he noticed the long pistol in her hand. He glanced back at Senlic and saw that he too was armed. His rising ardour vanished and he swung towards Draig. 'Looks like they won't be welcoming us with a pipe band,' he said. Draig rose to his feet and reached for the gate.

'No point opening that,' said Senlic Carpenter. 'You're not welcome here.'

'You look like you ought to be dead, old fool,' snarled Draig. 'Do not annoy me or I'll finish you where you stand.'

'Try it,' said Chara Ring, her voice cold. 'I'll put a ball through your skull before you've moved two paces.'

'That just about does it, Draig,' said Eain. 'Let's go home and leave these two to their day.'

'Aye, be off with you,' said Senlic.

Draig swallowed hard, and Eain could feel his brother's anger rising. 'I need to see Kaelin Ring,' said Draig.

'He's not here,' said Chara.

'Maev Ring then.'

'She's not here either.'

'Let's go home,' prompted Eain again. 'We're not welcome.'

'Aye, you're right,' muttered Draig.

A small red-headed boy appeared in the doorway. Eain glanced at him. He was pulling on a white cap, with ear protectors. Once it was in place he ran across the snow to stand between Chara and Senlic.

'You'd be Feargol, the boy who killed the bear,' said Draig.

'It killed my daddy,' said Feargol.

'Go inside now,' Chara told the child. 'This is no place for you at the moment. These two men are leaving.'

'They only just came,' said Feargol. Chara didn't answer, but she moved the pistol to her side.

Draig stared hard at Senlic Carpenter. 'It was once said you had the Sight, Carpenter. I see that's no longer true.' He glanced around at the farm buildings. 'Not many men here. I hope they're not gone long.'

Chara once more raised the pistol. Draig looked at her. Eain tugged at his brother's sleeve. There was no doubting her willingness to shoot. 'I also hope,' said Draig, 'that you are as good with that pistol as you claim. Chances are you'll need to be.'

'You should ask them if they want to rest,' said Feargol. 'You should give them something warm to drink.'

'Be quiet, boy!' snapped Senlic. 'Highland hospitality does not extend to rogues and thieves.'

'Would you like a biscuit?' asked Feargol, stepping forward, and pulling a crumbling oatcake from the pocket of his coat. He ran to the gate and pushed his hand through the gap in the slats. Draig dropped to one knee and took the offering. Then, with a sigh, he rose.

'Don't say anything!' urged Eain. 'We're not going to get involved!'

'The boy is in danger,' said Draig. 'That's why we came. That's why we walked twenty miles.'

'Eighteen miles,' said Eain.

'Whatever!' snapped Draig, casting a murderous glance at his brother. He looked back at Senlic. 'If you had the Sight you'd know I was telling you the truth.'

Senlic stepped forward and met Draig's gaze. 'I don't have it any more, Cochland. But the boy does.' He looked down at Feargol. 'You think these are bad men?' he asked.

'I think we should give them something hot to drink,' said Feargol. 'My daddy always did when people came to us from the cold.'

Chara Ring walked to the gate. 'Are you armed?' she asked.

'Aye,' said Draig, opening his long bearskin coat and showing her the butts of the two pistols in his belt. Eain saw the concern on her face.

'Walk ahead of me to the house,' she told Draig. 'I'll not have it

114

said I turned away any man in this weather – not even a Cochland.'

Eain wanted to tell her what to do with her damned hospitality, but the cold was really beginning to get to him now and he longed to sit down in the warmth. He followed Draig into the house, and shivered with pleasure as the heat from the fire touched his skin.

Draig sat down at the table and munched on the oatcake the boy had given him. Chara whispered something to Senlic, who went and stood by the far wall, his pistol now in his hand. Feargol clambered up on the bench seat alongside Draig and stared at him. 'Who is the man with the little beard, shaped like an arrow?' the boy asked.

'I see the boy does have the Sight,' Draig said to Senlic.

'He is coming here,' said Feargol.

'I know,' Draig told him. 'He's not close now, though, is he?' he added, suddenly nervous.

'I don't think so.'

Chara gave Draig a mug of warm tisane, then poured another for Eain. As Eain took it from her their hands touched. He felt himself blushing and looked away without thanking her.

'Now what is this danger you spoke of?' asked Chara.

'Maybe the boy should go upstairs,' said Draig.

'He is fine where he is.'

'I wouldn't want to frighten him.'

'Just say what you have to say,' Chara told him.

'Very well. A man – a Varlish man – came to me and asked me if I wanted to earn ten pounds. He said that his lord wanted two people dead.'

'I can see why he came to you,' said Senlic.

'Shut your trap!' hissed Eain.

'Leave it!' Draig ordered him. He sipped his tisane then turned to Chara. 'One he wanted dead was the Dweller, the other was this boy. I told him I wasn't interested. My guess – and the boy has just confirmed it – is that he then went to Tostig and the Low Valley scum he leads.'

'Tostig sports that beard style that was popular among the Varlish a few years back,' said Eain. All three adults swung to stare at him. 'You know the one, where the chin is shaved but you leave a small wedge of beard under the lower lip. Looks damn stupid, if

115

you ask me. Course you wouldn't say that to Tostig, him being a killer. Wouldn't catch me with a beard like that. Beards should be beards, I say. Proper beards.' Eain fell silent. They were still looking at him and no-one was speaking. Senlic was staring at him, bemused, and Draig had an expression of barely suppressed anger. Eain didn't want to look at Chara Ring. Even when she spoke.

'How did we get to talking about beards?' she asked.

'It's just that the boy mentioned an arrow-shaped beard,' said Eain, blundering on. 'It was a Varlish fashion, like I said, and—'

'Enough about damned beards!' thundered Draig. 'Gods, you're like a dog that won't let go of a bone.'

'Do you believe this story about hiring assassins?' Chara asked Senlic. 'Why would any Varlish want' – she glanced down at Feargol, who was listening intently – 'such a thing?' she concluded lamely. 'The Dweller has no links with the Varlish. And neither does Feargol.'

'The Cochlands steal cattle, Chara,' said Senlic. 'They are not subtle or clever men.'

'Thank you,' said Eain.

'That was actually an insult, brother,' said Draig, wearily. 'But let's move on.'

'Then you *do* believe them?' put in Chara.

'I do. It has the ring of truth,' replied the old man. 'And Feargol has *seen* that Tostig is coming here.'

'He is a bad man,' said Feargol.

'Yes, he is,' said Draig. 'As soon as Kaelin gets back I'd suggest you take the boy into the Rigante passes. Tostig won't be able to enter Call Jace's land. Now we'll be leaving you.' Draig rose. 'Thank you for the tisane.'

'Kaelin will be gone for three weeks,' said Senlic. 'He's taking a herd down to Eldacre. Most of the men are with him.'

'This is not our problem,' said Eain, sharply. 'We're not to get involved.'

'You don't need to be involved,' said Chara. 'I'll fetch you some food for your journey home.'

'Forget the food,' Eain told her. 'Come on, Draig. Our business here is done. Let's just go now. We'll get a bite in Black Mountain. At the Dog Tavern. Come on.'

'How many men are with Tostig?' Draig asked Feargol.

The boy closed his eyes, and Eain saw him counting his fingers. 'Seven,' he said. Eain swore.

'Can you see where they are?'

'Yes, but I don't know where it is.'

'What can you see, boy?' asked Senlic.

Feargol closed his eyes again. 'I can see a big building, all stone. And lots of houses. The man with the arrow beard is riding over a stone bridge. There are people fishing in the river.'

'Black Mountain,' said Senlic.

'That's no more than a two-hour ride in this weather,' added Chara.

Eain looked at his brother, and saw his features harden. 'Don't do this, Draig,' he pleaded. 'They don't want us. They hate us. It's got nothing to do with us now. You promised we wouldn't get involved.'

'The boy gave me a biscuit,' said Draig.

Eain's heart sank through his boots.

Chara Ring stood in the long kitchen, staring down at the pistol lying now beside the bread board. 'You can't stay, Chara,' said Senlic.

'I have weapons here, and I know how to use them,' she told him.

'There are eight of them, girl.'

Chara swung on him. 'Do not call me girl! I don't care how many there are. You think I'd be safer out in the wilderness with them?' she asked, keeping her voice low and pointing back towards the living room. 'I know men like them, Senlic. I spent a day and a night in a dungeon with men like them. Never again!' She leaned back against the work surface and began to tremble. Senlic reached towards her with his good hand. 'Do not touch me!' she told him sharply.

'I am sorry,' he said. 'I meant no offence. But Tostig will come here. There's nothing to stop him now. I expect he knows Kaelin and the men are gone. You'll not be safe, and neither will the boy.'

'I am staying in my home,' she told him.

Senlic sighed. 'Very well then. I'll load more weapons. I expect we'll hit a few of them. Then they'll stay back and pick us off as we leave the house over the next few days. Or they'll come at night. Then sooner or later, Chara, with me dead – and likely the Cochland boys too – you'll find yourself once more back in that dungeon.'

'I'll kill myself before I let that happen again.'

'Perhaps we could save the boy heartbreak and terror by killing him now,' said Senlic.

'Don't say such stupid things,' she told him.

'You need to be away from here,' he urged her.

'Then I'll go alone – just me, little Jaim and Feargol. I don't need the Cochlands.'

'Tostig and his men have horses. The snow is still deep and you'd have to carry Feargol and Jaim. You'll make no distance. You'll be exhausted within an hour and Tostig will catch you long before nightfall.'

'Has it occurred to you that all this is a trick? Ten pounds, Senlic. The Cochlands could be planning to murder me in the wilderness and collect the money themselves.'

'I don't believe that. Not once has Draig or Eain ever been accused of attacks upon women or children. They steal cattle, Chara. They are lazy men and thieves. You heard Eain. He wants no part in this. He is terrified of Tostig. They both are, though Draig would not admit it. With them you can get to the high country, where Tostig's horses will be useless. Without them we are all dead.'

'I can't do it, Senlic. I can't.'

'You can, Chara,' he said, softly. 'You are Rigante. We don't let fear rule us. Given a little time you would come to this realization yourself. But we don't have time. Every heartbeat of time we waste brings them closer.' He leaned in towards her, lowering his voice still further. 'The Cochlands are scum. I'll grant that. They may even desert you when trouble comes. They won't harm you, though. Or the boy. So use them like pack ponies until you are clear. Then send them on their way. And bear in mind that they too have Rigante blood.'

'So did Wullis Swainham,' she reminded him.

'Aye, he did,' admitted Senlic, 'and he shamed us all. The Cochlands aren't like him, though. I'd stake my life on that.'

118

'You are not staking *your* life,' she said, softly. 'You are staking mine and Jaim's and Feargol's.'

'I am aware of that, Chara.'

They stood in silence for several moments, and Senlic saw the trembling cease, and colour return to Chara's cheeks. She took a deep breath. 'Take the Cochlands to the supply store,' she said. 'Find them snowshoes and packs, and anything else you think they'll need.' She put her hand on the old man's shoulder, then leaned in and kissed his cheek. 'You are Rigante, my friend,' she said. 'I am sorry I spoke harshly.'

'Whisht, woman,' he said, then moved away.

Chara took Feargol upstairs to pack clothing, and Senlic led the Cochlands across to the supply hut. Eain was still complaining, urging Draig to reconsider. Draig told him he was free to return home alone. They continued to argue as they rummaged through the supplies, packing them untidily in canvas backpacks. Senlic left them to it and sat down upon a tack box.

'We'll need a musket each,' said Draig.

'Why do we need muskets?' asked Eain. 'I'm not fighting anybody.'

As they continued to argue Senlic leaned back against the wall of the hut. When the bright light obscured his vision he jerked. It had been years since the Sight had flared. He had thought it long gone now. In that moment he wished that it was. He suddenly groaned. Draig moved alongside him. 'Are you ill, old man?'

'I am all right,' said Senlic, struggling to his feet. 'You are right. You will need muskets, and a spare pistol each. We have some long hunting knives, bone-handled. Take two of those. You can keep them. You can keep it all once Chara and the children are safe. I don't doubt that Call Jace will also reward you for saving his daughter and grandson.'

'This isn't about rewards,' muttered Draig.

'I know, Cochland. I meant no offence. I am grateful you came, and I know Jace will be too. That is all I meant.'

When they had gathered all the supplies, and filled their packs Senlic picked out two muskets and a pair of pistols, plus powder and shot. Then he allowed both brothers to choose hunting knives. Once they had done so Draig hoisted his pack and moved towards the door.

'Wait,' said Senlic. 'There is something we must speak of.'

'You can trust us,' said Draig. 'Do not concern yourself.'

'It is not my trust that is lacking, Cochland. I *do* believe you.' He sighed. 'You know the history of Chara and Kaelin?'

'Aye, he rescued her from the Varlish. Walked into their castle and killed the guards.'

'Aye, he did. A grand deed it was. They had her though for some time before Kaelin got to her.'

'What is this about?' asked Eain.

'Quiet,' snapped Draig. 'You are saying they raped her?'

'More than that. They beat her, Cochland. They punched and thrashed her, kicked and bit her. It was torture. Their taunts and their vileness damned near broke her spirit. It haunts her still. Always will, I suspect. Now she has a fear of men. A great fear. You understand me? She is about to walk out into the wilderness with the Cochland brothers. By heaven, if I was a woman I wouldn't have that kind of courage.'

Draig stiffened. 'You think I would ever . . .'

'No, I don't,' said Senlic. 'What I am saying is be aware of her fears as you walk together. She is a strong woman. In this one area, though, she is as fragile as an ice crystal come the thaw.'

'I understand,' said Draig.

'I don't,' said Eain. 'And I'm getting damned cold standing here.'

Half an hour later Senlic stood at the farm gate, Patch beside him, and watched as the little group walked out across the snow. Draig was carrying Feargol on his hip, while Eain held two-year-old Jaim. Chara walked just behind them both, a musket cradled in her hands.

'You'll be all right, will you?' Chara had asked him.

'Aye, I will,' he had lied.

He waited until they had reached the first crest. His eyes were no longer good enough to see whether Chara or Feargol waved back at him, but he waved anyway. It was around three hours to dusk, and a sunset he knew he would not see.

Senlic Carpenter went back to the main house, and sat waiting, his pistol in his hand.

It had been a good life. He had not changed the world for the better, nor led a Rigante charge against the enemy. He had not sired a dozen tall sons. He would die now, as he had lived most of his life, alone. Yet he was content. Senlic had lived as a Rigante should, loving the land, and holding strong to the clan values of loyalty and courage. He would leave behind no ill will, no seeds of malice or hate to bedevil future generations.

He thought of loading a second pistol, but the vision had been clear. He would have time for one shot before they cut him down.

Actually this was not strictly true, he realized. In the vision he had seen two futures. In the first he had walked away from Ironlatch, and hidden until the riders moved on. He had then seen the eight men hunt down Chara and the others. In the second he did not hide. He saw himself murdered, and then watched as the scene shifted to the High Rigante. There he observed little Jaim clambering on to Call Jace's lap, Feargol standing close by, his white cap in his hands. Jace reached out to him too, and Feargol had smiled happily.

As he sat at the table, Patch beside him, he wondered why he had been offered such a ridiculous choice.

Was there a Rigante anywhere who would choose the first?

# CHAPTER SIX

CHARA RING STRUGGLED ON, HER LEGS WEARY. FOR THE LAST HOUR she had carried little Jaim. He was tearful now and cold and hungry. She also sensed his fear. He had never been carried out into such weather before and the biting wind and the wide, empty land frightened him. For the first two hours the hulking Eain had carried the child, but he was close to exhaustion now. Like most thieves Eain was a lazy man, and though he had enormous strength he was short on stamina. Draig too was suffering as they climbed yet another hill.

The snow here was thick and deep, and they had been forced to use snowshoes. Chara knew this area well, and, close to dusk, she headed them towards a cliff face where there were several shallow caves. At the first Draig began to remove his pack. 'Leave it,' said Chara. 'We will not be staying here.'

'Why?' asked Eain. 'It's shelter, isn't it?'

Chara was too tired to answer, and having checked the interior moved out once more into the wind and the snow. Draig followed her. Eain brought up the rear, too weary to complain. After a brief survey of the second cave she moved out again.

This time Draig asked her what she was looking for. Feargol, walking now beside the big highlander, looked up at him. 'She is seeking the cave where Uncle Kaelin left firewood,' he said.

A few minutes later Chara entered a third cave. Draig stepped in behind her, and saw a large stack of dry wood set against the far wall. 'Uncle Kaelin says a man should always be prepared,' said Feargol. 'He has hiding places like this everywhere.'

'A clever man, your uncle,' muttered Draig, slipping his pack from his shoulder. Pulling off his thick woollen gloves he rubbed at his fingers, trying to thaw them. Eain had slumped down by the wall, lacking even the energy to remove his pack. Chara glanced at Draig. Now they had stopped he saw the fear in her eyes. 'I wish it would snow,' he said.

'How can you want more snow?' muttered Eain. 'I've seen enough snow to last me a lifetime.'

'To cover our tracks,' Draig told him. 'A blind man could follow us.'

'There's a nice thought. Help me with the pack, will you?'

Draig stepped across to where his brother sat and eased the pack from his shoulders. Feargol had begun to build a fire. Draig moved alongside him, squatting down. 'No, lad, find the tiniest twigs first. You can't light a log with a spark. Logs come later.'

Within minutes a small fire was burning within a circle of stones. At first there was precious little warmth. Little Jaim came over and sat beside Draig, who ruffled the child's dark hair. 'Don't sit too close now,' he said. 'It might spit sparks.'

'My hands is cold,' said Jaim.

'They'll be warm soon.'

Draig added another chunk of wood to the blaze. Then he stood and wandered back to the cave mouth. It was already dark outside. He trudged through the snow for a short distance then turned to look back at the cave. Kaelin had chosen it well. It was deep and curved, the fire casting no flickering light against the wall close to the entrance. Not that it mattered, he realized, staring out at the tracks they had made coming here. The wind would eventually fill them in, but not before Tostig found their shelter, he knew. What then? Draig's mood was sombre as he made his way back to the cave.

'You see anything?' Chara asked him, as he slumped down by the fire.

'Only our tracks.'

Eain was at the fire now, preparing his cook pot. Feargol asked him if he needed more snow to melt. Eain nodded and the child took a wooden bowl and ran out past Draig, disappearing from sight. Jaim toddled after him, but Chara called him back. Draig removed his bearskin coat. Chara was still sitting by the far wall, her musket close by.

'Boy looks like his father,' he said, nodding towards Jaim. 'Though he has your eyes.'

Chara said nothing.

'I had a son,' he went on. 'A boy. Died when he was two.' He did not stare at her as he spoke, but out of the corner of his eye he saw her relax a little.

'I'm sorry.'

'Me too. Had a fever. Recovered. We were that happy, I can tell you. Then he just slipped away in his sleep. Fever took too much out of him, I guess.'

'I didn't know you were wed,' said Chara.

'Aye, I was. She left me . . . four years ago this coming spring. Don't blame her. Never was much of a husband.'

'Where did she go?'

'Lived with Eain for a while. Left him last year. Living with a crofter now, east of Black Mountain.'

'She was a sour woman,' said Eain. 'Not a good word to say about anyone or anything. Days were either too hot or too cold, too windy or too damp. I told her once she was the most complaining woman I'd ever met. Whacked a cook pot into my face, she did. Knocked out a tooth. Damn, but that hurt.'

'She must have loved you, Eain,' said Draig. 'Any other man had said that she'd have cut his throat in his sleep.'

'I do miss her,' admitted Eain.

Chara eased herself towards the fire, and Draig moved back to give her room, Feargol brought two more bowlfuls of snow before Eain told him it was enough. Jaim sat beside Draig, leaning in against him. 'You are good with children,' said Chara.

'Don't know why,' he said, with a grin. 'Can't stand 'em. All that noise and mayhem.'

'He's good with dogs too,' said Eain, stirring dried oats into the cook pot.

124

Draig called out to Feargol. 'Can you see the men chasing us now?' he asked. Feargol closed his eyes for a moment. Then his face crumpled and he sobbed. Chara scrambled across to him, taking him in her arms. Little Jaim began to cry too. Draig patted his shoulder. Eain sat nonplussed, idly stirring the porridge.

'What's wrong, Feargol?' asked Chara, stroking her fingers through the boy's red hair.

He looked up at her, tears falling from his eyes. 'They killed Senlic and Patch,' he said.

Draig felt a cold touch of dread and glanced at Eain. 'Shouldn't have got involved,' mouthed his brother, silently. 'Let's go home.'

Draig shook his head. 'Too late,' he mouthed back. Feargol was crying again. Chara kissed the top of his head and held him close. Jaim moved alongside her, his chubby arms reaching up. Chara drew him into the embrace and Draig sat silently watching them. It seemed to him that Kaelin Ring was a lucky man. This was a woman to walk the mountains with.

'Feargol,' he said softly. The boy looked up. 'We need to know where they are now.'

'They are coming,' said Feargol. 'Senlic shot one of the riders. He's hurt. They rode their horses after us, but then found the deep snow. The hurt man has taken the horses away, and the others are walking now. They are following our tracks.'

'Are you good with a musket?' Chara asked Draig.

'No. Neither is Eain, though he thinks he is.'

'What about pistols?'

'No. No good with them either.'

Chara sighed. 'This would be a good time to tell me something you *are* good at.'

'I don't quit,' he said. 'Tostig won't get you while I live. And I'm not the kind of man who dies easy.'

'Then let's you and I go out there and give them something to think about,' said Chara.

'What about me?' asked Eain.

Chara moved to the far wall and swung on her sheepskin-lined long coat. Then she took up her musket. 'You look after the children. Feed them and sit with them until we get back. And you should stir that porridge. It'll burn else.'

'Black bits in his porridge every time,' said Draig.

'And the horse you rode in on,' said Eain.

There were a number of surprises for Draig Cochland as he followed Chara Ring through the snow. The first was that despite his lack of rest he was no longer weary. The second was that the cold was not affecting him. The fur of his bearskin coat was bristling with ice. Crystals had also formed on his moustache and beard, where his hot breath had instantly frozen. Draig's heart was pounding wildly, and, at first, he could not identify what he was feeling. When he did it was the most surprising thing of all.

He was terrified.

Draig was not unused to fear. Any man who risked his life stealing other men's cattle or belongings understood what fear was. A chance shot could bring him down. Soldiers could surprise him. His life would likely be snuffed out on the end of a rope. These fears were common, and easily dealt with. Not so this unreasoning terror.

He stumbled on behind Chara Ring, following the line of tracks they had left earlier in the day, trying not to think about Tostig. But it was no use. The man's face was constantly in his mind, with its mocking half-grin. Draig had always been frightened of him. There was something unhinged about Tostig; something cold and empty.

He had come to the Low Valley around six years ago. At first he had been like every other outlaw; careful lest the Moidart's soldiers learned of him. However, since the war in the south had started there were few soldiers in the north, and Tostig had grown more reckless and more daring. Many of the vilest crimes of the last few years – rapes and murders – had gone unsolved. But Draig knew that Tostig and his men were behind them. One lowland farmer and his nine-year-old daughter had been killed in a raid two years ago. It had stunned the lowland community, for the child had been abused before being murdered. No-one had discovered the identity of the killers, though it was rumoured they were deserters from the army, passing through. Draig knew otherwise. One of Tostig's men had tried to sell him a silver engraved powder horn bearing the initials of the farmer.

Tostig was a man with no soul, and he had gathered to him like-minded men.

However, his evil deeds were not what bothered Draig Cochland. Draig was not responsible for the sins of others. What tormented Draig was that from the first moment he had met Tostig he had known fear. There was something in the way the man looked at him – the way in which a butcher might study a carcass, measuring the cuts and the joints with practised eye. For some time after that first meeting Draig had suffered nightmares. He had dreamt Tostig was coming to kill him.

They went away after a while, but returned after news came through of a traveller who had been robbed and killed. He had been tortured and partially skinned. Tostig carried a skinning knife, a small, crescent-shaped blade sheathed horizontally on his belt.

Ahead of him Chara ducked down behind a fallen log, and stared out over the snow. Draig moved alongside her. 'You see anything?' he whispered. Chara glanced at him. He looked away, knowing she had heard the terrible fear in his voice.

'I thought I saw movement,' she replied, pointing towards a stand of trees. The moon was bright, and high in the sky. Draig narrowed his eyes and peered at the trees. He could see nothing. 'Is your musket loaded?'

'Yes.'

'Make sure the action is not frozen.'

Draig tried to cock the weapon, but there was ice around the hammer. He rubbed at it to no avail. Lifting the weapon to his face he breathed against the action.

'I can't loosen it,' he said. Then he noticed that the action of Chara's musket was wrapped in a cloth. He felt foolish. 'I am sorry, Chara. I am unused to these weapons.'

'Keep working at the action,' she said.

Then he saw movement further down the slope. Three men emerged from the trees, following the tracks. Draig swore, and rubbed furiously at the cold iron. Eventually the hammer eased back.

'Check the flash pan,' ordered Chara. Draig flipped it open. There was ice on the powder within. Chara saw it. 'The weapon is useless.'

Four more men appeared, some twenty paces behind the first group. 'Which one is Tostig?' asked Chara.

Draig suddenly felt the cold wash over him. It was as if he had fallen into an icy river. His hands began to tremble. 'Which one?' said Chara again.

Draig sucked in a huge breath, letting it out slowly. 'At the centre of the second group. The one with the hood.'

Chara lifted her musket, removed the cloth then cocked the weapon. Resting the barrel on the log she brought it to bear. The shot boomed, and echoed across the empty land. Black smoke drifted around Draig, making his eyes sting. He rubbed at them, then scanned the slope. One man was down, but it was not Tostig. The figure tried to rise, then slumped back to the snow. The others were running, but not away from the gunfire. They were struggling through the deep snow towards the trees at the foot of the slope. Chara was calmly reloading her musket. A shot screamed by above them. Another thudded into the fallen log. Draig cast aside his musket and drew a pistol from his belt.

'Wait!' ordered Chara. 'You'll just waste the shot from here.' Drawing the ramrod from the barrel of her weapon she tamped down the ball and charge. Lastly she filled the flash pan, snapping the cover back into place.

By now the killers had reached the tree line below. Draig could no longer see them. Another shot boomed. This time Draig saw the smoke rise up. Yet still he could not see the shooter.

'We need to split up,' said Chara coolly. 'They'll be seeking to outflank us. You move right. Don't use that pistol until you are close.' As she spoke she rolled away from the log then ran into the trees to the left.

Draig lay where he was, panic sweeping over him. He struggled for control. 'You promised her!' he told himself. 'You said you'd die before you let them get her. Be a man!'

He swore, then rolled away to his right, coming to his knees and lurching upright. He almost slipped and fell, but made it into the trees. Keeping low he started down the slope, angling always to the right.

The moon vanished behind a cloud, and for a moment he was in near total darkness. A wave of panic rolled over him once more.

They could be anywhere. Within mere feet of him. Draig drew his second pistol and cocked it.

Another shot sounded from his left. A man's scream filled the air.

At that moment someone loomed alongside him. Draig raised his pistol and fired at point blank range, the barrel no more than a few inches from the bearded face. The man was hurled backwards. His body tumbled to the snow and rolled for several yards down the slope.

A second man appeared, a musket in his hands. Draig aimed his second pistol. It misfired. The musket thundered, the ball ricocheting from the tree by which Draig stood. Splinters stung his face. Dropping his pistols Draig charged at the man, slamming into him and knocking him from his feet. They went down together. Draig grabbed hold of the man's coat, and was vainly trying to punch him as they rolled down the slope. Both men slammed into a tree trunk. Draig gave a grunt of pain as the man head-butted him. Grabbing the assassin by the throat Draig reared up, then hammered a ferocious punch to the side of the man's head. Moonlight glinted on a knife blade. Draig grabbed the man's wrist. A wicked punch took Draig behind the right ear, but still he clung on to the knife arm. His own right hand scrabbled at his belt, pulling clear the long-bladed hunting knife Senlic had given him. The assassin tried to grab Draig's wrist. He was not quick enough. Draig's knife sliced into the assassin's neck. Blood sprayed out. Draig twisted the blade. The man's body spasmed, then went limp.

Dragging his knife clear, Draig rose unsteadily. Dazzling light blinded him and he felt a powerful blow to his head. He tried to turn, then realized he was lying on the snow, his leg twitching. With a great effort he rolled to his belly and tried to get his arms under him, struggling to rise. His head hurt; the pain worse than anything he had experienced before. He vomited to the snow, then tried to rise once more. His blurred vision began to clear. The dead man was to his right and he swung his head ponderously, wondering what had hit him.

There was a figure standing close by. Draig blinked, then squinted at the man. It was Tostig. 'I can't believe it's you, you oaf,' said Tostig. 'Did you think to rob me of my ten pounds?' He was holding a pistol. Smoke was still seeping from the barrel. He pushed it back into his belt and drew a second gun.

Draig peered around for his knife, but he could not see it. Tostig's left hand moved to his belt and Draig saw the crescent-shaped skinning knife slide from its sheath. 'I don't have time now to deal with you as you deserve, Cochland,' said Tostig. 'But I'll cut your eyes out and come back for you later.'

'Oh, I don't think so,' said a woman's voice. Draig looked up and saw Chara Ring standing in the moonlight, a pistol in her hand.

Tostig turned towards her. She was some twenty paces from him. Tostig began to move slowly to his right. 'Well, well,' he said, 'a girl with a gun. What is the world coming to?' He sheathed his knife. 'Why don't you run away, girl? This is a man's game. You know you are not going to try to shoot me. If you wanted that you would have fired when my back was turned. So just leave. See if you can escape me.'

Chara's pistol boomed, the shot ripping through Tostig's throat. He took two steps back, his pistol dropping from his fingers. Chara strode through the snow. 'I wanted you to see who killed you, dung breath,' she said coldly. Tostig fell to his knees, his life blood gushing from his ruptured jugular. Ignoring him, Chara moved to Draig. 'You've been shot in the head,' she said, probing the wound with her fingers. 'But it didn't crack the skull.' Draig swung away from her and vomited again.

'How many . . . did we get?' he asked.

'I got two plus that scum bucket. You?'

'Two. That makes . . . I don't know what that makes. Can't think.'

'It makes five,' said Chara. 'There are two more.'

'They must have got behind us.' Draig heaved himself upright, staggered, then righted himself. Chara was reloading her pistol.

From the distance came two shots.

'They are at the cave,' said Draig. More shots followed. Then there was silence.

Draig was in agony as he stumbled after Chara. His head contained a roiling sea of pain, and he stopped twice to vomit. By now there was almost nothing to bring up, but his belly continued to spasm. Blood was flowing down the left side of his face.

Chara was well ahead now, and Draig called out for her to wait for him. He stood and held on to an overhanging tree branch to help maintain balance. Chara did not pause, nor look back.

Got to help her, thought Draig, pushing on up the slope. It was then that he realized he had no weapons. His useless musket had been left behind at the fallen tree, his two pistols dropped when he fought the assassins, and his knife lost after Tostig had shot him. He was now as useless as the musket, and in no condition to help anyone.

Even so he fought his way up the slope and staggered, at last, into the cave. Eain was by the fire, adding fresh wood. Chara was sitting with Feargol and Jaim. Close by were two bodies. One had been shot through the head; the other appeared to have been hit from the side, a pistol ball having smashed through both cheeks of his face. Eain's knife was jutting from the man's chest.

As Draig turned the corner in the cave Eain looked up at him. 'Took your own sweet time,' he said. 'You want me to stitch that cut?'

'I'll do it,' said Chara.

'Can we go home then?' Eain asked Draig. 'I've had enough of this Rigante blood nonsense. I'm happy as a Cochland, you know that? I don't need any of this.'

Chara moved alongside Draig, and he felt her once more probing the wound in his skull. 'What happened here?' he asked her.

'Your brother killed the other two.' She said it so matter of factly that Draig found himself chuckling.

'Who would believe it?' he said.

'Sit still.'

He felt the prick of a needle in his skin. It was as nothing to the jagged pounding hammering in his skull. He closed his eyes, fighting to hold back another wave of nausea.

'The ball struck you at an angle,' he heard Chara say. 'You were lucky.'

'Oh, I feel lucky,' he muttered. He took a deep breath, which seemed to calm his stomach. 'We're an army, we Cochlands, you know. Unstoppable.'

Feargol came and sat beside him. 'There's lots of blood,' he said. 'Are you going to die?'

'I damned well hope not,' answered Draig.

'Are you going to stitch Eain's wounds?' the boy asked Chara. She paused, and stared down at the child.

'Eain's wounds?'

'The men who came in shot Eain as he was by the fire. He fell over. Then they came over to me and Jaim. One of them said: "Which is the one?" And the other one said: "Don't matter. Got to do them both anyway." Then Eain got up and shot one of them through the face. Then he shot the other one. The man with the bloody face ran at Eain and stabbed him. Then Eain took out his knife and stabbed him back. You ought to stitch up Eain's wounds.'

Chara swung round. Eain Cochland was sitting now by the far wall, his big overcoat drawn about his body.

Draig rolled to his knees then scrambled across to his brother. Chara was on the other side of him. Swiftly she opened his coat. Beneath it Eain's shirt was soaked in blood. Drawing her knife, Chara sliced away the cloth. Draig saw that Eain had been shot in the chest and belly. A bulging section of entrails was showing.

'Are we going home now?' Eain repeated.

Draig looked into his brother's face, and could think of nothing to say. Chara pulled the coat back into place, and sat quietly beside the brothers.

'Are you going to mend him?' asked Feargol.

'Shhh,' murmured Chara, rising and leading the boy away.

'Told you I could shoot,' said Eain.

'Yes, you did,' Chara whispered over her shoulder.

'Shouldn't have got involved, though. I'm going home.' Eain moved as if to rise, but Draig gently pushed him back.

'We'll just sit here for a while, eh? Gather our strength. Then we'll go,' he said.

'I'm starting to hurt, Draig. Did you kill Tostig?'

'No. Chara did that. Shot the bastard through the throat.'

'Like to have seen that,' said Eain.

'I'm sorry, Eain. I shouldn't have brought you with me. You were right. Not our concern.'

'You say that, but it won't make no difference. Next time you'll still go off pigheaded. You won't listen to me.'

'I will. Next time.'

'I'll hold you to that. Still, we won, eh? So no harm done then. Did you get any of them?'

'I got two.'

Eain smiled. 'Two each, eh? Your head looks bad.'

'Tostig shot me. Ball bounced off my skull. Feels like I've been butted by a bull.'

Eain groaned. 'I think they nicked me, you know. Bastards came running in as I was clearing away the pots. I fell over. Got 'em both, though. Think I'll sleep for a while. I'll feel better in the morning.'

'Yes, you sleep. You get some rest. You did well, Eain.'

After a while Chara came alongside Eain, and gently touched her fingers to his throat. 'He's gone,' she said. Draig reached out and stroked his brother's face.

'I know. Just leave me with him for a while. All right?'

'I am so sorry, Draig.'

'Don't matter,' he said, gruffly, his voice breaking. 'Didn't like him anyway.' His head dropped forward and Chara saw that he was weeping. She moved back quietly to where the children were waiting.

Jaim was trembling now from the shock of the attack. At two he had no sense of the reality of the danger he had faced. But he had seen men fall down and not get up. He hugged Chara tightly. 'Bad men, Mama,' he said.

'Yes, my sweet, they were bad men.'

Feargol sat very quietly. Chara settled herself down, Jaim on her lap, and reached out to the boy. He gave a sad little smile and leaned in to her. Chara closed her eyes, saddened that the vileness of the world should have scarred these two children. She could think of nothing to say to comfort them. In the background they could all hear the sound of Draig's weeping. Chara leaned back, resting her head on the cold wall of the cave.

'Someone is coming,' whispered Feargol.

Setting Jaim aside Chara eased her pistol from her belt, and cocked it.

A moon shadow fell across the cave entrance, and a small woman with white hair came into sight. 'Have you come to take Eain home?' asked Feargol.

'Yes, child,' said the Wyrd of the Wishing Tree woods. 'Now let us go back to the fire, where you can rest.'

'I'm not sleepy,' said Feargol.

'You will be,' she promised him. Chara lifted Jaim and they moved quietly back to the dying fire. Jaim stared at the bodies of the two assassins with wide, fear-filled eyes. The Wyrd spread out blankets for the two children. Jaim began to cry as Chara laid him down, but the Wyrd gently touched his brow and the child instantly fell asleep. She did the same for Feargol. Chara covered the boys with blankets, then added fuel to the fire. The Wyrd moved silently to where Draig sat, holding his brother's hand.

'Come to mock me?' he asked, his eyes red-rimmed from the tears he had shed.

'No, Draig. I have come to help Eain.'

'You're a bit too late.'

'He is still here, Draig. He is a little confused. He doesn't know why you are weeping, and he doesn't know why you can't hear him.'

'So you have come to mock me after all,' he said. 'Go away, woman. Leave us in peace.'

'Give me your hand, Draig Cochland,' she ordered. At first Chara thought he had ignored her, but then he looked into her eyes, and at her outstretched arm. Finally his own huge hand reached across and touched her fingers. 'Now look up.' Draig did so, and drew in a sharp breath. 'Aye,' said the Wyrd, softly. 'There he stands. Now, say these words after me. *Seek the circle, find the light, say farewell to flesh and bone.* Say them, Draig.'

The big highlander repeated them, softly, and the Wyrd spoke again.

> *'Walk the grey path,*
> *Watch the swan's flight,*
> *Let your heart light*
> *Bring you home.'*

134

Chara watched them both. She felt the hairs on the nape of her neck rise, and shivered. Both of them were staring at the far wall. There was nothing there that Chara could see.

'Where has he gone?' asked Draig.

'Wherever his heart light took him,' said the Wyrd. 'Now we have work to do, for when the children wake we do not want them frightened by the bodies. We must remove them from the cave.'

'I don't want Eain lying alongside them bastards,' said Draig, pushing himself wearily to his feet.

Together with Chara they dragged the bodies of the assassins out into the night. Draig loosely covered them with snow. Then he returned, and, with Chara's help, lifted Eain's body to his shoulders. With the Wyrd beside him he struggled further back along the cliff face to another cave, where he laid Eain down. Then he began to weep again.

'I can't just leave him here,' he said. 'He's my brother.'

'*He* is not here, Draig. In the spring we will return and carry his body back into Rigante lands. We will lay him alongside others of the clan.'

'He didn't want to come, Dweller. He didn't want to get involved. It should have been me who died.'

'Of course he wanted to come. Why else was he here? You didn't force him, Draig. He came because you were his brother and he loved you. He could have left at any time once the pursuit began. He made his own choices. Just as you did. Just as I knew you would.'

'Because I have Rigante blood?'

'In a way,' she answered. 'Now let us go back. You need to rest.'

Once by the fire again Draig lay down. The Wyrd touched his brow and he fell asleep. 'Would you like to sleep too, Chara?' she asked.

'Not yet, Dweller. There is so much here that I do not understand. Why would the Moidart want Feargol dead? Why would the Cochlands risk their lives for us? What is happening here, Dweller?'

'It is not the Moidart – though soon it could be. As to the Cochlands, well, they are highland men, Chara. Draig asked me if they had acted so because of their Rigante blood. The truth is they *wanted* to act so because of what the word Rigante had come to mean to them. Honour and courage, nobility of spirit. The Rigante are like a banner flying high above an army. Men look at that banner and feel inspired. What of you, though, Chara? How do *you* feel?'

'Confused,' she admitted. 'I did not want to walk out into the wilderness with these men. I was frightened by them. Now?' Chara sighed. 'Now I feel as if everything has changed. As if I have changed. I'll never forget that time in the dungeon. Never. Yet somehow its hold on me has gone. I know this. I feel . . . I feel like that time when the first sunshine of spring touches the face, and you know that winter has passed.'

'From now on you will be able to remember the dungeon without reliving it,' said the Wyrd. 'That is the gift the Cochlands gave you.'

'I am sorry that it took the death of a kind man to bring me that gift,' said Chara.

'Time for you to rest,' said the Wyrd. 'Tomorrow we will take Feargol to safety.'

# CHAPTER SEVEN

FOLLOWING THE DUEL GAISE MACON'S REPUTATION HAD GROWN among the soldiers of all units. Men talked of the Grey Ghost, and the soldiers of the Eldacre Company found themselves suddenly more popular. The name of the cowardly Lord Ferson was spoken with contempt. Ferson himself had left the camp the same day, and had not been seen since.

The body of the elderly Lord Buckman was taken to the Royalist city of Sandacum, for a state funeral, where the king spoke movingly of the general's courage and loyalty. Buckman's regiment was given over to Lord Cumberlane. Winter Kay became the Lord Marshal of all the king's armies.

A winter truce, negotiated between Lord Cumberlane and Luden Macks, was agreed and many of the twelve thousand militia serving the king were allowed to go home, with orders to re-assemble in the spring. The standing army of eight thousand men remained, some wintering in Sandacum, others in the regional capital of Baracum a hundred miles north.

Gaise Macon petitioned to be allowed to take his Eldacre Company home, with other militia regiments, but the request was denied. His cavalrymen and scouts were to patrol the truce lines west of Shelding, watching for incursions from Covenant skirmishers. A supply depot was also set up within the town, and in a time of famine and desperation this needed to be guarded. Billeting the men proved of little difficulty. As with most towns in the centre of Varlain there were many empty houses. Privation, sickness, starvation and the relentless drive for recruits from both factions had seen populations shrinking year by year. The arrival of six hundred soldiers for the winter was a boon for Shelding, though not necessarily a welcome one for all. New industries blossomed to service the troops. Plays were put on in the village hall, and older women took to sewing and mending for the soldiers. Younger women offered other services, and the men paid for their pleasures in food and clothing as well as coin.

Gaise Macon met with the town elders and churchmen to establish rules of behaviour for both townsfolk and soldiers during the winter, and to set down lines of communication between civil and military authorities. He also appointed Mulgrave as Watch Captain, with orders to select thirty men to act as a policing force to patrol the town and keep order. This was not an easy role. On the second night a group of rowdy young soldiers got into a fight with some of the townsfolk, following an assault on a young woman. Mulgrave and five of his men broke up the disturbance. A hasty hearing was called for the following morning. The woman gave evidence that two men had burst into her home and attempted to rape her. Her screams had been heard by neighbours who ran to her aid. A fight had taken place, and a townsman had been knifed in the leg.

Gaise Macon ordered the two men flogged, a punishment carried out in the market square, and administered by the veteran sergeant Lanfer Gosten. Each man suffered forty lashes. Both were unconscious by the conclusion, and needed to be carried from the square. One of them was Kammel Bard.

On the fourth day in Shelding a convoy of seventy wagons arrived from Sandacum, bringing supplies for the new depot. With them came Quartermaster General Cordley Lowen, a company of dragoons, and two Redeemer Knights. Mulgrave was there to greet the new arrivals. Cordley Lowen, his daughter and three servants were assigned a pleasant house overlooking a mill stream. The dragoons rode back to Sandacum. The two Redeemer Knights approached Mulgrave. He recognized them as the loaders from

Gaise Macon's duel with Ferson. Neither man wore battle armour, and both were dressed instead in dark tunics and leggings, and long, black coats bearing the White Tree of the priesthood upon collar and cuff. Many of the Redeemer Knights, Mulgrave knew, took holy orders in the first three years of their service.

'Good morning to you, gentlemen,' said Mulgrave, coolly.

'And to you,' replied the first, a tall, broad-shouldered young man, with black hair and deep set eyes. 'I am Petar Olomayne, and this is my cousin, Sholar Astin.'

'Welcome to Shelding,' said Mulgrave.

'We are on our way south, to the shrine at Meadowlight,' said Petar Olomayne.

'A long journey. Will you be staying overnight in Shelding?'

'Possibly, captain.' The two knights offered a bow, then led their horses away towards the village square. Mulgrave watched them go. He had heard of Petar Olomayne. The man was a noted swordsman, having fought five duels. He had also been decorated for courage following the Battle of Nollenby. The other one – Sholar Astin – he did not know, though he knew his type. Cold-eyed and heartless.

Mulgrave thought of Ermal Standfast, the little priest who had saved his life. The two Redeemers wore the same priestly garb as Ermal, and had studied the same texts, passing the same examinations. Yet where one lived to love, the others loved to kill. It was baffling to Mulgrave.

Later that day, in the rectory behind the crooked church, he spoke to Ermal regarding his confusion. The priest sipped his sweet tisane. 'No need for confusion, my dear Mulgrave,' he said. 'Beautiful wine and sour vinegar come from exactly the same source. Curiously if one leaves a bottle of wine open for long enough it will become vinegar. Happily in this house wine never survives long enough to go bad.'

'I was raised in Shelsans,' said Mulgrave. 'The priests there used to preach the words of the Veiled Lady. They talked of human life being sacred, and told of how the early cultists refused to fight. They believed in love and forgiveness.'

'As do I,' said Ermal.

'Does it not strike you as strange that the people of Shelsans were massacred not by pagans who believed in gods of death and violence, but by people who professed to follow the same religion?'

'Not strange, Mulgrave. Infinitely sad. Are you still having the nightmares?'

'No. She does not appear to me any more.'

'Is this why you are still a soldier?'

Mulgrave shook his head. 'Gaise Macon is my friend. I cannot desert him now.'

'Friendship does carry responsibility,' agreed Ermal.

'I sense a *but* in that comment,' said Mulgrave.

'But a man needs to look after his own soul, Mulgrave. Your upbringing in Shelsans taught you that killing is to be abhorred. And something is calling to you.'

'Aye, I know.' Mulgrave finished his tisane and rose to leave. 'Is there anything you need?' he asked.

'I am content, my friend,' answered Ermal. Then he grinned. 'Though if another bottle of apple brandy should find its way into your possession I would be delighted to share it with you.'

In all his twenty-two years of life Gaise Macon had known few moments of true happiness. His childhood had been spent in the gloomy environs of Eldacre Castle, under the baleful eye of the Moidart. No playmates to run with, no toys to brighten his days. His youth had been no less strained. He had known one day of enormous pleasure when he had joined the local Varlish school, but then, seeing the boy's pleasure, the Moidart had taken him from it, hiring a series of tutors to teach the boy.

Reading proved his salvation. In books Gaise could travel far from the cold misery of Eldacre. He could journey back in time, to the great days of Stone, and read the campaigns of the legendary Jasaray. He could ride with the Iron Wolves of Connavar, and fight again the wars of the Battle King Bane. He did not outwardly glory in these pursuits, for had he done so the Moidart would certainly have removed these pleasures also.

His greatest happiness had been supplied by two very different men, one a soldier, the other a teacher. Mulgrave had been the first shining light to enter the boy's life, brought to Eldacre to teach him the arts of personal warfare: to ride a war horse, and to use the

140

sword, the pistol, and even the bow. Mulgrave had soon learned of the Moidart's cruelty towards Gaise, and the teacher and his student had entered into a secret friendship. They did not laugh together in public, nor were they seen to be outwardly affectionate. But on long rides together Gaise would open his heart to his friend. The second man to impact on the life of Gaise Macon was a skinny schoolteacher named Alterith Shaddler. He taught Gaise history and arithmetic – but also smuggled into Eldacre books of verse, and works of imaginative history, in which the characters spoke, one to another, leaving the reader convinced he was in the same room with them. These *fictions*, as Alterith called them, were the water of life to a parched soul. Gaise devoured them. Here he found what was lacking in his own life: stories of honour and chivalry, friendship and love. Gaise dreaded to think what kind of man he would have become without these yardsticks to measure himself against. Even now he found himself having to rein in the more ruthless side of his nature. One of his deepest regrets was hanging the soldier who lost the Emburley rifle. One moment of anger. One careless command and a man's life had been snuffed out. Such was the legacy carried by the Moidart's son.

No-one would ever know just how much he had longed to put a ball through Ferson's face, to smash his skull to shards, to watch his body crumple to the ground. Gaise sighed and felt shame even now at the crude pleasure the thought gave him.

'I am not so different from you, Father,' he whispered.

He had longed for the day when, reaching Varlish majority at twenty-one, he would be free of the Moidart's malign influence. Free to know happiness. Free to live his life as he chose. Yet here he was, a year later, in a rented house, heavy of heart and filled with an indescribable loneliness.

Gaise knew that Mulgrave longed to be free of this war. He knew also that only the man's love for him held him here. If I were truly his friend, Gaise thought, I would let him go. I would wish him well, and be happy that he was free of this madness.

For madness it was. Gaise knew that now. Scores of thousands had died, their blood soaking into the earth, their cries unheard or unheeded. And for what? The vanity of a king, and the ambitions of a few nobles. Gaise tried to shake himself clear of such treasonous thoughts. Rising from his desk he walked to the leaded window, pushing it open to allow the cold night air to seep into the firelit room. From here he could see the silhouetted line of the western hills. Beyond them was the army of Luden Macks. There, as here, the soldiers would be sheltering against the winter night, keeping their weapons clean, giving prayers of thanks for the truce that would see them alive for a few more weeks. They would be drinking and whoring. Living for the day.

Some distance away Gaise could see two men talking. They were dressed in dark clothes. They glanced up, saw him, and moved away into the shadows. Three soldiers of the Watch came into view. Gaise recognized Taybard Jaekel. His mood lifted. He had been tempted to reject Jaekel when first he had tried to enlist. Gaise remembered him as one of three young men who attacked a highland lad back in Old Hills. It was a cowardly assault, and only the arrival of Gaise and Mulgrave had prevented the highlander being knifed while held.

Gaise had been sitting at the recruitment desk when Jaekel stepped forward. 'I know you,' he said, coldly.

'Yes, sir,' said Jaekel. 'I am in your debt.'

'How so?'

'You prevented me from committing an act I would have regretted all my life.'

'What happened to that highland lad? Ring, wasn't it?'

'Kaelin Ring, sir. He went north.'

'Is he still your enemy?'

'No, sir. He is my friend.'

'Good enough. Make your mark.'

Gaise smiled at the memory. Taybard Jaekel had proved an exemplary soldier, cool under fire, and utterly reliable. He was also the finest shot with a musket Gaise had ever seen. In standing competition he was merely excellent, but in the field his talents were beyond extraordinary. Mulgrave – who was himself a marksman of quality – called it *deflection targeting*. This involved shooting at a point ahead of a moving target so that ball and victim arrived at the same place at the same time. The judgement involved had to be instant and instinctive.

Gaise wondered if Jaekel still had the golden musket ball he had won. Probably not, he thought. Soldiers tended to spend what they had as soon as they received their pay. A golden musket ball, in a sphere of silver wire, would be worth more than two months' wages.

The three soldiers moved out of sight. Once more Gaise Macon felt alone. Mulgrave was probably with Ermal Standfast, enjoying a pleasant tisane by a roaring fire. Alterith Shaddler would be asleep in his bed, at the school house in Old Hills. And the Moidart? The man's hawklike features flashed into Gaise's mind. Probably torturing some poor soul deep in the dungeons of Eldacre.

Gaise chided himself for an unworthy thought. The Moidart was probably also asleep. To Gaise's recollection the Moidart had only personally tortured one man to death, many years ago after a failed assassination attempt. Gaise could still remember the man's screams.

Thoughts of assassination made him think of Ferson and the duel. Mulgrave had been right to think that Winter Kay hated him. There was no doubt in Gaise's mind that the loaders had been ordered to misload the pistol. Gaise had known it from the moment he had taken the gun from the loader's hand and inserted the ball himself. Ferson's face had betrayed the plan. From cocky confidence to abject terror in the space of a heartbeat. The loaders were Redeemers. They would not have taken it upon themselves to sentence Gaise to death. No, Winterbourne was behind it.

No matter how hard he tried Gaise could not come up with a reason for the man's hatred. Yes, he had prevented Winter Kay killing a few villagers, but the truth was that from the first moment the two had met face to face, after the Battle of Nollenby four months ago, Gaise had sensed the man's dislike. Most odd, he thought. He had received a written invitation to dine with the earl and his friends – an invitation graciously constructed, congratulating Gaise on the courage of the Eldacre Company. Gaise had ridden with Mulgrave to Winterbourne's castle outside Baracum, and had entered the dining hall. Winterbourne had been talking with some other guests, but, on seeing Gaise, had walked towards him, smiling, his hand extended. Yet, at the point of the meeting, something changed. Winterbourne's smile had faded. The conversation was stilted and abrupt. For the rest of the evening they exchanged barely a word. Even the normally astute Mulgrave had been unable to come up with a reason.

Now it was no longer a small matter of one man's dislike for another. Winterbourne had connived in a plot to murder him. Would there be another? Mulgrave thought it likely, and Gaise trusted his instincts. One thing was sure – should there be another challenge Gaise would insist on swords.

The room was growing cold now, and Gaise pushed shut the window, dropping the latch. It was late, and he thought of taking to his bed. Dismissing the idea – his mind was too full – he gathered his heavy, fur-lined topcoat and swung it round his shoulders. A walk in the crisp night air would relax him. There were many wild dogs roaming the town now, and Gaise took up the silver-topped cane Mulgrave had given him on his birthday. With this in hand he walked downstairs and out through the front door. The night was bitter cold, though the wind had dropped. Gaise took a deep breath and strolled through the garden to the small, cast iron gate. Stepping out into the street he walked towards the old bridge, snow crunching beneath his boot heels.

Up ahead there were lights in the tavern. Gaise had released four barrels of brandy from the supply depot, and many townsfolk had gathered for an evening of merriment, a temporary release from the fear of war. They were all living on the edge of the abyss now. Next year's seed corn was being eaten, most of the cattle had been slaughtered to feed either the townsfolk or the army. It would not be long before the wild dogs were also hunted for meat.

Four years ago it had seemed to Gaise to be an almost holy war. The king's authority had been challenged, and the army mustered to defeat the traitors. Along the way the objectives had subtly shifted. Both sides claimed to have the king's best interests at heart. Both claimed the moral high ground. The Covenanters maintained that the king had granted them certain rights of self rule, which he had. Then, on bad advice, he revoked those rights. The Royalists claimed the Covenanters sought the abolition of the monarchy, and the destruction of the noble classes. They cited the growing influence of Luden Macks, a farmer from the south, with barely a trace of noble blood in his veins. Macks now largely controlled the

Covenant cause. Yet Macks had begged the king to restore the Covenant, and had pledged allegiance to his cause should he do so.

Gaise paused on the old bridge, staring out over the frozen water. The armies were tearing the land apart, with no side close to victory. Meanwhile the citizens faced starvation, disease, and terror.

Movement to his right caught his eye. A large black dog had padded out onto the bridge. It was gaunt, its ribs clearly showing in the moonlight. Gaise gripped his cane, ready to strike the beast if it approached. The hound bared its fangs. Gaise suddenly smiled, and dropped to one knee, holding out his hand. The black dog backed away at first, then stood its ground. 'Come on, boy,' whispered Gaise. 'Let us be friends.' The dog stood for a moment, then ambled forward a few steps, sniffing at the outstretched hand. 'Life is tough for you too, eh?' said Gaise, stroking its long nose, then patting its emaciated flank. 'I'll tell you what. You can come home with me and I'll find you a few morsels. You can sleep before my fire. How does that sound?' The dog moved in closer, arching its neck and licking at Gaise's face. Gaise grinned. Mulgrave would have been furious to have witnessed the scene.

'Must you always take risks, sir?' he would say. 'The dog could have ripped out your throat.'

Moving slowly, Gaise came to his feet and turned. Two priests were walking towards him. He was about to offer a greeting, but something stopped him – something about the way they were moving. Their hands were thrust deep into the pockets of their long black overcoats, and their eyes were fixed upon him. Suddenly one of them threw open his coat, drawing a sabre. The other pulled a long knife from his pocket. Gaise twisted the silver handle of his cane, pulling clear the narrow sword blade it contained. The knife-man leapt forward. In that instant Gaise recognized him as one of the loaders from the duel with Ferson. Beside him the hound gave a deep growl and leapt at the knifeman, huge jaws clamping down on the man's arm. The second man's sabre slashed through the air. Gaise swayed back, parrying the blow with his sword stick. The knifeman had fallen to his knees and was hammering his fist into the dog's head, trying to dislodge the beast's grip. The Redeemer with the sabre moved round his fallen comrade and advanced on Gaise.

'You have given yourself over to evil, Gaise Macon,' he said. 'The reward for such sin is always death.'

He attacked with great speed. Gaise parried and moved. The sword stick was shorter than the sabre, and half as thick. A solid blow from the Redeemer would shatter it.

Disadvantaged in this way most swordsmen would have faced defeat and death. Gaise Macon, however, was not *most* swordsmen. Blessed with great balance and speed, he had also been trained by one of the finest blade masters in the realm. Even so the fight was one-sided, all the advantages lying with the Redeemer. He attacked again, always perfectly in balance. Gaise blocked and slid away to his left.

'You move well, Macon,' said the Redeemer. Beyond the two swordsmen the second Redeemer had battered the hound senseless and was now standing by the bridge wall, holding his shattered arm.

'Kill him, Petar,' he called. 'I am bleeding to death.'

'Would you be Petar Olomayne?' asked Gaise.

'I would. It is gratifying that you have heard of me.'

'I had heard you were a man of some skill with a blade,' said Gaise. 'Now I see you are naught but a clumsy bludgeoner.'

Petar Olomayne's mouth tightened. 'For that I'll carve my initials in your heart,' he said.

Launching an attack with blistering speed he forced Gaise back along the bridge. Both men needed to move with care here, for there was a gradient, and ice underfoot. Olomayne slipped. Gaise lunged. Olomayne parried and sent a slashing riposte that cut through Gaise's coat.

Now the pace quickened, the blades clashing together in a whirl of flashing steel. One tiny misjudgement from either man would see sharp metal piercing soft flesh. Back and forth they fought on the treacherous footing, neither man giving ground. Now it was a true duel, as they probed for weaknesses, reading each other's moves. Gaise fought coolly and with patience. As Mulgrave had taught him, all duels followed a pattern. They began with heat and fury, then settled into a contest of wills. With two equally matched opponents there would come a time when the worm of doubt entered the equation. The truly skilled recognized such moments, and fed them. It was at this time that the endgame would begin.

Petar Olomayne had the advantage of a superior weapon, giving him added reach. Yet he had not been able to breach his opponent's defences. Gaise fought on, watching his opponent's eyes, waiting for the moment.

Olomayne launched a frenzied attack. Gaise ducked beneath a murderous cut, his own blade flickering out and cutting Olomayne's cheek. The Redeemer swore and the two men moved apart for a moment.

'Damn, but you are an oaf,' said Gaise, his voice full of contempt. 'Am I too heavily armed for you?' Olomayne's eyes widened, and his lips drew back in a primal snarl. The insult cut through his reason and he leapt forward, the sabre lancing for Gaise's heart. Gaise sidestepped, plunging his sword deep into Olomayne's chest. The point slid between the Redeemer's ribs, skewering both lungs and exiting beneath his left armpit. Olomayne gave a strangled cry and fell against the bridge wall. Gaise tried to drag the blade clear, but it was wedged tight. Olomayne's breath was coming in bubbling gasps, blood spraying from his lips. Gaise reached down and gathered up the Redeemer's sabre. Then he walked back to where the second Redeemer waited, still holding his shattered arm.

'We were ordered to this deed,' said the Redeemer, backing away. 'I demand to be treated as a knight, and ransomed to my lord.'

'You will take this message to Lord Winterbourne,' said Gaise. Then he paused and gazed down at the still form of the black hound. Anger surged through him, and his control over his inner demons melted away. He looked the man in the eye. 'Never mind, I expect he'll get the message.' The sabre swept up and lanced through the Redeemer's throat. Gaise watched as the dying man sank to his knees, then pitched sideways to the cold stone of the bridge.

Kneeling by the hound, Gaise placed his hand on the dog's chest. The heart was still beating. Heaving the unconscious dog into his arms he staggered back to the house. Behind him other starving dogs were gathering, drawn by the smell of blood.

Inside the main room Gaise gently laid the hound on the rug by the hearth. Then he lit the fire, and in its light examined the beast for wounds. The dog had fastened its fangs to Astin's knife arm, and the Redeemer had beaten it with his fist. There were no knife cuts. With luck it was merely stunned. Gaise walked to the kitchen. There was a little broth left in the pan and he heated it until it was lukewarm, when he poured it into a shallow bowl. Carrying it back into the living room he saw the hound was stirring. Gaise stroked it, speaking soothingly. It gave a low growl and tried to lift its head. Gaise moved the bowl closer. The hound's nostrils twitched. It tried to rise, but fell back. Gaise straddled the beast. 'Come on now,' he said, leaning down and lifting it to its feet. Its legs were unsteady, but Gaise supported it. The hound's huge head dipped towards the bowl. Its tongue lapped at the juices. Then it began to eat more hungrily. With the broth finished the dog sank back to its haunches. Gaise sat beside it. 'That will do for now, eh?' he said, patting the great head.

The dog licked at his hand, then stretched out on the rug and fell asleep.

Within the hour Mulgrave was sitting in the living room. Two soldiers of the Watch had disturbed a pack of wild dogs feeding on the corpses. Mulgrave had been summoned, and had recognized the sword stick he had given Gaise Macon. Ordering the torn bodies to be carried away he hurried to the general's house. There he found Gaise sitting by the fire, alongside a sleeping black hound.

'I shall call him Soldier,' said Gaise, absently. 'You recall me telling you about my first dog?'

'I do, sir. The Moidart shot it. What happened out there?'

Gaise sighed. 'I fear there is more of the Moidart in me than I realized.' He shook his head. 'Odd, don't you think, that one can despise a man for his cruelties and then commit just such an act oneself?'

'I cannot judge, sir,' said Mulgrave, quietly. 'I don't yet know what you did.'

'Did the dogs dine on them?'

'Partially.'

Gaise rolled to his feet. The hound stirred. Gaise patted its head.

'You rest, Soldier. I'll see you get more food in the morning.' He strolled to the window and drew back the curtain. There were still dogs upon the bridge, squabbling over the patches of blood on the stone. 'The Redeemers attacked me, Mulgrave, one with a sabre, one with a knife. Soldier grabbed the knifeman. The other one was Olomayne the duellist.'

'I know, sir. I saw them when they arrived yesterday. They claimed to be on their way to the Meadowlight shrine. Olomayne was said to be a fine swordsman.'

Gaise shook his head. 'He was adequate. Ah, Mulgrave, I am sick at heart.'

'You did what you had to do, sir,' said Mulgrave.

Gaise shook his head. 'No, I did not. I killed Astin unnecessarily. He was unarmed and demanded to be ransomed. Damn it, Mulgrave. I expect the Moidart would be truly proud of me.'

'You are not like the Moidart,' said Mulgrave. 'Believe me, sir.'

'I wish I could. I have been sitting here, replaying the events in my mind. I cannot forget how I felt when I slid that sabre through the man's throat.' He looked at Mulgrave, and the swordsman saw the anguish in his eyes. 'I enjoyed it,' he confessed. 'There, it is said. I killed an unarmed man, and I took pleasure in it.'

Mulgrave said nothing for a moment, then he rose and placed his hand on the young noble's shoulder. 'I know you, Gaise,' he said, gently. 'I have known you since you were a boy. You are not the Moidart. And, no, you are not perfect either. You are a man. As men we are all cursed by the violence in our natures. Men like the Moidart – aye, and Winterbourne – revel in that nature. We do not. We struggle to overcome it. Sometimes we fail.' Stepping away from his friend he moved to the fire, adding fuel. The dog stirred and growled at him. 'My, that is an ugly beast,' he said. 'Why did it come to your aid?'

Gaise smiled, and shrugged. 'I petted him. Long time since anyone has, I suppose.'

'You petted a wild dog?'

Gaise laughed. 'Just as well I did.'

Mulgrave shook his head. 'You will never lose your love of risk, I think.'

'I hope not, Mulgrave.' The nobleman's smile faded. 'What now, do you think?'

The white-haired swordsman walked back across the room. 'Winterbourne wants you dead. It will not end here.'

'I do not understand it,' said Gaise. 'How could denying him the deaths of a few villagers result in such hatred?'

'The cause of his bile does not matter now, sir. The question is: how do we respond?'

Gaise thought about it. 'The options are severely limited. I cannot challenge him. I am a junior general, in charge of a small company. He is a field Marshal. I cannot fight him. Equally I cannot run. That would make me a deserter. I would be hunted down and hanged.'

The two men talked on for some time and Mulgrave was heavy of heart when he finally left the young general. Winterbourne controlled not only the five hundred warrior priests of the Redeemers, but also the ten thousand heavy cavalry of the Knights of the Sacrifice, and three regiments of infantry. Alongside Cumberlane he was one of the most powerful men in the realm. Securing the death of a minor noble like Gaise Macon would not be difficult. He could be poisoned, shot from ambush, knifed in the street, or – more likely – once the truce was over ordered to attack an impossible position, charging his men against a line of cannon.

Mulgrave walked down the cobbled main street to the undertaker's yard. Three soldiers were waiting outside, huddled in their cloaks. He recognized the first as Taybard Jaekel. The sandy-haired young soldier saluted.

'We've got the bodies wrapped in canvas, sir,' he said.

'Good. At first light see them buried.'

'Yes, sir. Who were they?'

Mulgrave gestured for Jaekel to follow him, then walked away a few paces. 'What I am about to tell you is for you alone. This information is not to be shared. I have watched you, Jaekel. You are a good soldier. More than that I sense you are loyal to Gaise Macon.'

'I am that, sir.'

'So I am going to trust you. The dead men were Redeemers. They tried to assassinate Lord Gaise.'

'Why?' asked the astonished Jaekel. 'They are on our side.'

'That in itself is a stain on us all. However, it doesn't matter why. What does matter is that there are likely to be other attempts. From tomorrow you and your squad will guard Lord Gaise. You will accompany him wherever he goes. You will watch out for strangers, and you will allow no-one to get close enough to strike a blow. You understand? The official story will be they were Covenant spies. You understand?'

'Yes, sir.'

'You will pick a second squad to guard the general's house during the night. You will tell them of assassins seeking to harm Lord Gaise.'

'Aye, sir, I can do all that,' said Jaekel. 'Won't make no difference, though, if they send a marksman. We need to get away from here. Back home to our own country.'

'You'll get no argument from me on that,' said Mulgrave wearily. He glanced back at the other two men. 'They are friends of yours?'

'Yes, sir. Banny and Kammel. We're all from Old Hills.'

'The big one was flogged recently.'

'Yes, sir. He got drunk and . . .' Jaekel shrugged.

'I remember. He made unwelcome advances to a woman. Does he bear the Lord Gaise any grudge for his punishment?'

Jaekel chuckled. 'Even if he did he wouldn't let any harm come to him. Trust me on that, sir. Kammel's not the brightest of men, but he's highland.'

There were two great halls in Castle Winterbourne. The first was where Winter Kay entertained his secular guests, a massive room on the ground floor, boasting two huge fireplaces, and decorated with fine paintings and splendid statues. It had an oak gallery on three sides, and a fourth for use by musicians or, at times of religious festivals, a choir.

The second hall was below ground, and this was not open to casual guests. The entrance was hidden by a cunningly crafted panel, and led to a secret stairwell. The hall itself was hung with trappings of red velvet, the room lit by curious brass lanterns boasting crimson glass. At the centre of the huge room stood a beautifully wrought table of dark oak, which could seat more than a hundred men. No paintings adorned the walls here, and no servants carried food, or refilled goblets. The hooded men who came here did not eat or drink. They came to pay homage to the Orb of Kranos, and to listen to the words of their lord, Winter Kay.

Tonight there were one hundred and forty Redeemers. The veterans took the one hundred seats, the other, newer recruits standing silently by the walls.

At the north end of the hall, some ten feet to the rear of where Winter Kay sat, stood a wooden cross. Hanging from it was the pitiful, naked, gagged figure of Lord Ferson, blood oozing from around the long iron spikes impaling his wrists and feet.

Winter Kay pushed back his crimson hood and turned towards the dying man. 'This was a fascinating method of execution,' he told the silent Redeemers. 'You will note that the victim continually seeks to draw himself up, then sags back. This is because death comes from suffocation. As the body hangs upon the arms air is denied to the lungs. Therefore, to breathe, the victim must push himself up with his legs. This, of course, causes extreme pain where the nails pierce the feet. Such pain cannot long be endured. So the victim – to alleviate the agony in his lower limbs – hangs once more on his arms. Unable to breathe he forces himself up again. A continual circle of agony until exhaustion overcomes his will to live. Quite exquisite.'

He swung back towards the Redeemers. 'All actions have consequences,' he said, his voice calm. 'Ferson suffers for his cowardice. As a result of that cowardice two of our number have also passed to the other side. Petar Olomayne and Sholar Astin failed in their assigned task. Against the great strides we have made in the last two years these are tiny reverses. Yet we must not be complacent. Our mission is a great one, far beyond the petty desires of earthly kings and princes. We are the Chosen, the Elite. Failure of any kind is abhorrent to us.'

A low, strangled moan came from the body on the cross. Winter Kay ignored the sound.

'We stand on the verge of immortality. To achieve our goal we must be steadfast, our hearts filled with courage. Do not be dismayed by delays. All great causes suffer some reverses. It is how we overcome them that dictates our greatness.' He stared out over the red-robed warriors, then took a deep breath. 'Return to the dining hall and eat, my friends. Enjoy the evening. There is much work to be done during these remaining winter months, and much hardship to be endured. Go now. Relax and enjoy yourselves.' He turned towards the two men closest to him and signalled them to remain. The other Redeemers filed slowly from the hall.

Winter Kay twisted his chair and sat down facing the dying man. Ferson had bitten through his lip and blood now flowed through the gag and down over his beard. 'You really are a disgraceful spectacle,' said Winter Kay. 'There is nothing about you that is remotely admirable.'

'A shame about Petar,' said Marl Coper. Winter Kay transferred his gaze to his aide, and stared hard at the thin-faced young man.

'I thought you did not like him, Marl.'

'I didn't, lord. He was, however, a fine duellist and had performed adequately in the past. He was also appallingly bad at cards, and I shall miss the vast amounts I won from him.'

'What do you wish us to do about Macon now, lord?' asked the second man, a sandy-haired, middle-aged nobleman named Eris Velroy. He seemed ill at ease, and his eyes kept darting towards the dying man on the cross. Winter Kay held his gaze, noting the sheen of sweat on the man's brow.

'Is something troubling you, Velroy?'

'Not at all, my lord.'

'Ferson was your friend, was he not?'

'Not exactly friends, my lord. More . . . acquaintances I would say.'

Winter Kay gave a cold smile. 'It never ceases to surprise me how few friends the doomed have. One moment they are surrounded by smiling faces, the next they are utterly friendless.' The man on the cross suddenly cried out. His scream, though muffled by the cloth, was shrill. 'Oh, he is really beginning to bore me now,' said Winter Kay, rising from his chair. Leaning against the cross was an iron club. Hefting it Winter Kay smashed two blows to the dying man's legs, snapping the bones. Ferson screamed again. He tried to draw himself up on his arms, but his strength gave out and he sagged down. Within moments his breathing had ceased. 'Now, as to

153

Macon,' said Winter Kay, laying down the club. 'He has proved more resilient than one would have hoped. Had he died during the duel with Ferson we could have closed the matter quietly. Indeed, had Petar and Sholar succeeded the issue would have been over. However, we cannot continue to send individual assassins. Macon will be wary now.' Winter Kay sighed. 'Unfortunately we must take decisive action of a larger nature. This will necessitate some planning, for it will first involve the elimination of a secondary threat.'

'From what quarter, lord?' asked Marl Coper.

'Gaise Macon is the son of the Moidart. It was my hope to enlist him to our order. He has all the qualities we seek: courage, single-mindedness, and an abhorrence for weakness and the endless stupidity of compassion. Those same qualities, however, would ensure his enmity once his son was killed. It is essential, therefore, that the Moidart is dealt with before we sentence Macon. Choose two men, Marl. Go north with letters from me to the Moidart. He will welcome you. While at his castle kill him, and make it appear the work of assassins. The Moidart is no stranger to assassination attempts. Once he is dead we will deal with his son.'

Marl Coper remained silent for a moment. Winter Kay knew what he was thinking. The Moidart's reputation was unparalleled. Harsh and deadly were the two words most often used, but even these did not come close to doing him justice.

'He is older now,' said Winter Kay, softly. 'His body is a mass of burn scars that plague him constantly, and he has a festering wound in his groin, that will never quite heal. He is merely a man, Marl.'

'Aye, my lord,' said Marl, doubt still in his voice. 'However, you yourself have just spoken of his qualities. There have been many assassination attempts. None of them have succeeded. He is sharp and canny, and he has the Harvester.'

'The Harvester is a middle-aged farmer, Marl, with an eye for the dramatic. I met him once. He is a large man, and a tough one. But were it not for the fact that he beheads his victims with a shortened hand scythe he would be no more than another hired assassin. That is one of the Moidart's skills. He makes people *believe* that he – and to a lesser extent the Harvester – has almost mystic qualities.

154

They do not. The Moidart understands that fear is essential to control the masses. Therefore he finds devious ways to feed that fear. I do not suggest that you underestimate either man. However, they are but men. Kill the Moidart – and the Harvester if he interferes. Then we can wipe out the son with impunity.'

'The will of the Orb be done,' whispered Marl.

'Even so,' agreed Winter Kay. 'Now, once the Moidart is dead, you will go to the Pinance and instruct him to lead his army into the north. Stay with him, Marl. See that Eldacre is held for the cause.'

'You may rely on me, my lord.'

'I do, Marl. Though I am displeased with your failure to kill the demonic child. Did I not instruct you to find suitable assassins?'

'You did, my lord. My researches showed that the Cochlands were such men. I apologize for my failure in this matter.'

'Your methods were flawed. Tostig should have been the first choice. You chose Draig Cochland because he had been thrashed by Kaelin Ring. You believed this would make him an enemy of Ring and his family.'

'Yes, lord. It was an error.'

'One such error can be forgiven, Marl. We often learn by making mistakes. This is why I have given you this new task. Do it well, and you will be restored into my good graces.'

After the two men had gone Winter Kay sat quietly in the meeting hall, staring up at the corpse of Lord Ferson. He had always known the man was weak and cowardly, which is why he had never allowed him to join the Redeemers. An order destined to change the world needed to be strong. Yet Ferson had proved useful. He had been rich, influential, and a close friend of the king and his family. Winter Kay had never enjoyed the king's friendship and had needed Ferson to draw him into the inner circle. Now he virtually commanded the king's armies, and his power was close to total.

*'The will of the Orb be done.'*

The words of Marl Coper echoed in Winter Kay's mind. Even now, after all these years, he found them disturbing. He had coined the phrase in this very room just over six years previously, to focus the minds of his Redeemers on the source of their power. He had not thought of it as a literal truth, merely as a device. As the years passed he had begun to wonder, and to worry over it.

The skull possessed great power, but – he had tried to convince himself – it was not sentient. Yet when he held it in his hands, and the dreams began, he found his mind focusing as never before. As if, without the Orb, his normal understanding of the world was that of a bird in a cage in a single room of a small house. With the skull in his hands he became an eagle, soaring high above the earth, seeing all. It was then that his plans were formed. It was then that he understood.

The skull did not *speak* to him. Rather he would see shapes and colours, outlines and structures, each pointing out areas of danger or success. In some ways it felt like the child's game his father used to set for him and his brother, Gayan, on feast days. Father would hide objects and clues around the huge gardens, and the boys would hunt them down, finally arriving at their reward. The method was the same now. While holding the skull Winter Kay could see some problems almost before they arose.

Like the recent battle. The plan was for Luden Macks to inflict some damage on the Royalist army, to come close to victory, by overpowering and killing the elderly Lord Buckman and his Guards. As Macks and his forces cut through towards the enemy centre they would be attacked by the Knights of the Sacrifice, hidden in woods close to the king's headquarters. Luden Macks's army would be repulsed – though not destroyed – and Winter Kay's standing with the king, following the death of Buckman, would be enhanced. It was, in essence, a simple plan. He had come upon it while holding the skull in his hands. The images formed in his mind like shining steel. Potential problem areas were seen as a corrosive red, like rust forming on the beauty of the steel. In this second phase of his vision he had seen the one flaw in the plan. Buckman was a fighter and a charismatic leader. His line would hold long enough for reinforcements to be brought up.

Winter Kay had then prepared his strategy. Lord Ferson was sent to the right flank, with strict orders to avoid action unless directly attacked. All other regular units were positioned in such a way as to be useless to Buckman once Luden Macks broke through.

It would have worked, but for one small rogue element.

Gaise Macon.

Because of him Buckman scored a partial victory, and Winter Kay had been forced to have the man poisoned – a deed which did not sit well. The old warrior deserved to die on the battlefield.

Now, as he sat beneath Ferson's contorted body, Winter Kay found his anger rising. When first he had seen Gaise Macon at close quarters, and looked into those odd eyes, he had remembered the curse of the old priest back in Shelsans. '*I will go gladly, Winter Kay. Which is more than can be said for you, when the one with the golden eye comes for you.*'

I should have had him killed then, thought Winter Kay. And he would have – but for the Moidart.

The source of unlimited power lay in the north. Winter Kay understood this, though he did not know *why* he understood it. It was like an aftertaste from holding the skull. Once his plans were formed he would drift into strange dreams, that always melted away upon awakening, leaving him drained. For days afterwards he would find himself thinking about the high north lands, and picturing mountains he had never actually seen. At such times he would be filled with an indescribable longing.

He had, during the last year, tried to court the Moidart, inviting him south. Always the man refused. The refusals were courteous. Winter Kay had planned to visit him next spring, to take the skull and heal the man's scars, drawing him into the Brotherhood. The Moidart would have proved an invaluable ally.

Such a pity that a fine man should have been cursed with a son like Gaise Macon.

# CHAPTER EIGHT

APOTHECARY RAMUS PONDERED ON THE NATURE OF IRONY. A SMALL man, near sighted and balding, he had never wished harm on any living soul. His life had been one of service, the gathering of herbs and medicines for the relief of pain and the curing of disease. He was also – though he had been surprised to discover it – well loved in the town of Old Hills.

In short, were anyone who knew him to be asked, they would say: 'Ramus is a good man, a kind man.' Those with a keener eye – like Alterith Shaddler, the spindly schoolteacher – would add: 'He is a shy man, with no understanding of malice or evil.' They would be able to say little more than this, for no-one knew him well. In his fifty plus years Ramus had, until recently, made no friends. He encouraged no visitors to his tiny cottage home, and engaged in no small talk or gossip. Ramus was invariably polite to all he met, doffing his grey woollen cap to the women, nodding or bowing briefly to the men. His shyness gave him a neutrality which allowed his patients to discuss intimate details of their conditions without embarrassment. Ramus would sit quietly, listen intently, and then prescribe adequate medication or herbal remedies.

Had anyone been asked to nominate a friend for such a man they would probably have opted for Alterith Shaddler, the teacher of highland children. He was also shy, and, though taller than Ramus and round-shouldered, another man of gentle disposition. In fact the two men rarely spoke.

No, the friendship Ramus finally formed in the middle years of his life, was not with Alterith Shaddler. For some time the little apothecary had been meeting a man known for his ruthlessness, his disregard for human life, and his merciless treatment of those he considered enemies.

Sometimes Ramus lay awake at night wondering just how such a ridiculous situation should have come to pass. He wondered still, as he sat beneath the paintings in the gallery of the Moidart's winter residence, waiting for his audience with the ruler.

It had all begun in a bizarre way four years ago. The Moidart had summoned him to the manor, ordering him to bring fresh ointments and salves for the unhealed burn scars that festered on his back and arms. In the Moidart's private rooms the earl had shown Ramus a painting – a magnificent landscape of mountains, woods and a lake. It was like nothing Ramus had ever seen. All works of painted art, however skilfully they represented the images the artist desired, were mannered and two-dimensional. The medium, Ramus considered, was calm and detached. This painting, however, was vivid and raw. The snow on the mountains had been applied with a knife, the paint unthinned. The trees were vibrant with cold winter colour, and, staring at it, Ramus could almost hear birdsong. He had looked into the Moidart's dark, emotionless eyes, at the harsh lines of the man's hawklike face, then back at the awesome beauty of the landscape. How could a man of such evil have created a work of such beauty?

Even now the conversation that had followed was burned into Ramus's memory.

'The hardest part was the water upon the lake,' said the Moidart, 'and obtaining the reflection of the mountains and trees. I discovered it by error. One merely pulls the bristles of a dry brush down in sharp motions. Would you like this painting?'

'I could not afford such a . . . a masterpiece, lord,' said Ramus, astonished.

'I am not some peasant who needs to sell his wares. It is finished. I have no more use for it.'

159

'Thank you, lord. I don't know what to say.' He paused. 'Are there others? I would love to see them.'

'No.'

'But what of the paintings you have completed over the years?'

'Time for you to go, master apothecary. I have much to do. I will send the painting to you.'

The work now hung in the small living room of Ramus's cottage, and it was this extraordinary painting which had set in motion the curious chain of events that now had Ramus sitting outside the Moidart's rooms.

A nobleman known as the Pinance – a rival earl to the Moidart, from the lands immediately southwest – had visited Ramus the following year, suffering from what was delicately known as 'a social complaint'. The visit had been in secret. The Pinance had arrived late one evening, accompanied only by two armed retainers. Ramus had greeted the earl courteously, and examined him while his men waited outside. The Pinance was well known for his voracious sexual appetite, and it was his love of the company of whores that had led to the painful – and to Ramus mildly disgusting – condition. Ramus applied a poultice to the area, then prescribed a treatment he had perfected some years before. As Ramus was preparing the herbs, and writing out his instructions, the Pinance glanced up at the painting. 'I like this greatly, apothecary,' he said. 'Would you sell it to me?'

'I cannot, lord. It was a gift.'

'I will give you fifty pounds for it.'

Ramus had been astonished. It would take him years to earn fifty pounds. It was a colossal sum.

'I . . . I am sorry, lord. The price is not the issue.'

The Pinance, a heavy set man with dyed black hair, smiled. 'Then direct me to the artist. I desire his work at my castle.'

'He is a very private man, lord, but I shall contact him on your behalf,' said Ramus.

The Pinance stood for a moment. 'If he paints me a scene such as this the fifty pounds stands. I never met a rich artist, so tell him I require the painting before the autumn. Lots of mountains, mind. I like to look at mountains.'

'I will, lord,' said Ramus miserably.

After the Pinance had gone Ramus sat quietly by the fire, wondering how to extricate himself from such an invidious position. The Pinance was near as ruthless as the Moidart himself, and not a man to defy. Yet the Moidart loathed him. There was no way he would paint a picture for him.

Even so Ramus had gone to Eldacre Castle and requested a meeting. He had arrived in the Moidart's private quarters on the topmost floor, and had stood nervously before the earl's desk. Always before it had been the Moidart who had summoned the apothecary, and Ramus felt ill at ease having initiated the meeting. The Moidart sat back in his chair, his dark eyes watching the little man.

'Make this brief, apothecary, for I have much to do today.'

'Yes, lord. I . . . I have a problem that I am unable to resolve . . .'

'Your problems do not interest me.'

'Indeed no, lord. A patient visited me two nights ago . . .'

'His name?'

Ramus had dreaded this moment. He took a deep breath. 'It was the Pinance.'

'I know. He arrived with two retainers. What is the problem?'

'He wanted to buy the painting you gave me. He offered me fifty pounds for it. I told him no.'

'That was stupid.'

'Perhaps so, lord, but I would not part with it for any amount of money,' said Ramus. It was no lie, and Ramus was no flatterer. The transparent honesty of the statement took the Moidart by surprise. For a moment only the shock registered on his gaunt face, then he rose from his chair.

'It seems the problem is therefore resolved,' he said.

'No, lord. The Pinance has instructed me to contact the artist and commission a painting for him. He wishes to hang it in his castle.'

Ramus had never heard the Moidart laugh, nor even seen the man smile. But he laughed now. 'The Pinance wants to hang one of *my* paintings in *his* castle?' His laughter boomed out. 'Ah, Ramus, what a fine treat.' He walked to a tall window and stood staring out over the northern hills. Then he swung back. 'Write to him. Tell him the artist is working on a larger painting and requires seventy-five pounds for it.'

161

'Seventy-five, lord?'

'Tell him you will have it delivered in two months.'

'You . . . you will paint a picture for the Pinance?' asked Ramus, aghast. 'It is said you . . . dislike him.'

'Dislike does not begin to describe it. It will please me greatly, however, that he will unknowingly hang *my* painting on *his* wall. One day – when the time is right – I will let him know the name of the artist.' The Moidart laughed again. 'And now you must go.'

Two months later Ramus stood again before the Moidart, handing him a bulging money pouch containing seventy-five gold coins. This time there was no laughter. The Moidart spread the money out on his desk and stared at it, his face pensive.

'Is there a problem, lord?' asked Ramus.

'Did he like the painting?'

'He was awed by it, sir, as was I. It was majestic.' It was another mountain scene, only this time it was of a storm in a bay, waves crashing upon black rocks, gulls wheeling in the sky. 'The Pinance stood and stared at it for the longest time. His relatives were there also, and many retainers. They were all stunned by it.'

The Moidart sighed. 'In all my life this is the first money I have ever earned with the skill of my hands. A most peculiar feeling. That will be all, Ramus.'

And yet it had not been. Other nobles had visited the Pinance, and, similarly awestruck, had contacted Ramus. The word spread south about the mysterious artist and his magnificent work. The apothecary was inundated with requests. Not wishing to annoy the Moidart with another meeting Ramus sent the letters on to him.

He had been summoned to the Moidart's summer residence in Eldacre Castle, and this time led through to the earl's private living quarters. They were surprisingly spartan, lacking adornment of any kind. The furniture was comfortable, but far from new, the rugs threadbare. There were no curtains at the double aspect windows, and the frame of one window was split, water dripping through from the heavy rain outside. Despite the fire the room was draughty and cold. It seemed strange to Ramus that a man as rich as the Moidart should live in conditions akin to poverty. But then the man was cloaked in contradiction. A cold-hearted killer and an

162

artist who produced works of dazzling beauty. Why should there not be other contradictory indications, he wondered?

The Moidart bade him sit – which was also surprising since he had never before offered Ramus a seat. It was with some trepidation that the apothecary sat in the earl's presence.

'I have decided to accept another commission,' said the Moidart, lifting one of the letters Ramus had sent him. 'You will arrange it.'

'Of course, lord.'

'You may keep two per cent of the commission.'

'Thank you, but that is not necessary.'

'I will decide what is necessary, apothecary.'

'Yes, lord.'

The Moidart reached across to a small table, upon which stood a flagon of water and a single goblet. He poured himself a drink, and sat quietly for a while. Ramus did not know what he was supposed to do. He had not been dismissed. So he sat awkwardly, waiting for the Moidart to speak. When at last he did, he did not look at Ramus. 'I was taught that to earn money with one's hands was below the dignity of a nobleman. Yet I took great pleasure in the Pinance's commission. I thought perhaps it was because he was my enemy and that I had fooled him in some way. This was not so. Now I shall paint again. I do not however desire anyone to know that the work is mine.' His cold eyes held to Ramus's gaze. 'It is against my instincts to trust anyone, apothecary, and yet it seems I must trust you.'

'And you can, my lord.'

During the next few years the Moidart earned more than two and a half thousand pounds through his paintings. They were hung in great houses all across the Varlish realm.

Now the two men met once a month. There was little in the way of easy conversation, and yet Ramus had come to look forward to the encounters. Indeed he had come to *like* the Moidart. It remained a puzzle to the little apothecary.

As he sat in the gallery he found himself admiring the portrait of the Moidart's grandmother. He had last seen her just before her death fourteen years before, a bent and heavily wrinkled woman nearing ninety. In this portrait she was young, and incredibly beautiful. What captivated Ramus was her eyes, one green one gold, just like her great-grandson's. Ramus had always liked Gaise Macon, and had often wondered how such a charming young man could have been sired by a monster like the Moidart. Now he felt he knew, for when they discussed painting the Moidart seemed human – almost affable at times. The coldness left his voice, and he spoke with passion and feeling about light, shade and colour; about shadow and perspective, composition and texture. In the beginning Ramus would say little. The Moidart was a touchy host at best. One did not initiate conversation. One merely responded. On one particular afternoon, however, Ramus – enduring a pounding headache which cut through his usual caution – had ventured a criticism of a particular work. 'It seems crowded,' he said. Almost as soon as the words were uttered he felt a chill go through him.

'You are right, apothecary,' said the Moidart, peering at the landscape. 'Too much is happening there. Excellent. I shall repaint it.'

Now Ramus felt at ease speaking frankly about the paintings, though he never made the mistake of speaking frankly about anything else.

The captain of the castle, Galliott the Borderer, came out of the Moidart's office and greeted Ramus. Galliott was a handsome middle-aged man, broad-shouldered and every inch the soldier. 'Good day to you, apothecary. I trust you are in good health.'

'I am, sir, and it is kind of you to ask.'

'The lord will see you now.'

Ramus offered a short bow and entered the office.

The Moidart was standing by the window, dressed in his habitual black riding shirt and breeches, his long black and silver hair tied in a pony tail. He swung towards Ramus and nodded a greeting. As usual he did not begin with any pleasantries.

'Do you hear news from the war, apothecary?'

'Sometimes, lord.'

'Does it ever concern my son?'

'Indeed so. He is much lauded for his daring cavalry tactics.'

'Has anyone spoken to you of his having enemies?'

'No, lord.'

'Ah well, it matters not. Come and see the new work. I have to admit I am pleased with it.'

It was a winter scene, cold and brilliant, snow clouds deep and threatening, crowning the majestic peak of Caer Druagh. A tiny figure could be seen, toiling through a blizzard, head bent against a fierce wind. Small though it was against the majesty of nature the figure radiated an intensity of purpose, a determination to survive and prevail. For a time the two men spoke of the use of colour, the addition of a dash of midnight blue giving life to the arctic white of the snow. Ramus was more interested in the forlorn figure. Every line and curve of the work seemed to draw the eye towards him. Never before had the Moidart introduced a human form into his work.

Ramus peered more closely at the painting. There was something about the figure that was vaguely familiar, but he could not quite place it. He stepped back and looked again. There was just the suggestion – the merest speck of grey – to suggest a beard. Then he had it.

'That is Huntsekker,' he said. The Moidart seemed surprised. He too re-examined his own work.

'I suppose it could be,' he admitted, 'though it was not a conscious plan. The figure was an afterthought. The piece seemed to lack focus without it.'

Ramus was less comfortable now. Huntsekker was a reminder of the Moidart's darker side. The man was a killer, known throughout the north as the Harvester. He hunted down the Moidart's enemies, removing their heads with a wickedly sharp sickle blade. The little apothecary shivered.

The Moidart noted his distaste and said nothing. Ramus was that rarest of men, gentle and absurdly honest. There was no malice in him, and – more astonishingly – no understanding of malice. But then he did not exist in a world of danger and treachery. He did not have enemies at every turn, subtle and vicious, waiting for their moment to strike.

The Moidart glanced back at the painting. Yes, the man facing the deadly blizzard *was* Huntsekker. It seemed so obvious now. Who else could survive such a storm?

Huntsekker paused at the crest of the hill and gazed down at the small row of shanty houses at the edge of the river. There were boats moored just beyond them, long flat-bottomed craft, garishly painted. Huntsekker had never understood the appeal of living on water. He liked his feet to be on solid ground, his home to be fashioned from wood and stone.

The moon was high and bright, its light gleaming on the silver spikes of his forked beard, the night wind ruffling the ankle length coat of shaggy bearskin he wore. Huntsekker leaned on his staff and ran his gaze along the river front. Several open fires had been set on the shore, and a crowd of river men and women sat around them. They were drinking cheap spirits, and Huntsekker could hear laughter. Several children were playing at the water's edge, skimming stones out over the icy water.

The big man hoped there were no trouble-making strangers among them. Though he would never admit it he was tired, and the cold wind had brought on a headache that was drumming at his temples.

Slowly and carefully he made his way down the hill, heading for the house of Aran Powdermill. It stood a little beyond the other homes, and Huntsekker could see the glare of golden light coming from the lower window.

Reaching level ground he tried to skirt the revellers. There were maybe thirty people in the group, roughly dressed, many of them with bright scarves around their heads. Two of the men saw him and called out. Huntsekker ignored them and plodded on. But he heard them run after him and turned to face them.

'It is customary for strangers to visit our fire,' said the first man, with a wide, challenging grin. He was powerfully built and tall, maybe twenty years younger than Huntsekker. A red scarf was tied around his head, and he wore a heavy topcoat of faded crimson. The second man was leaner. He too wore a red scarf, and sported a thick, shaggy black beard. He had moved a little to Huntsekker's left, and his hand was resting on the hilt of a knife at his belt. Some things never change, thought Huntsekker wearily. He would be invited to join them. They would ply him with drink. At some point he would be asked to pay for his enjoyment. The amount – curiously – would be exactly the number of coins in his money pouch.

'I am not the stranger here,' he said coldly. 'You are. Now go back to your fire and your women and leave me in peace.'

'We don't like your tone,' snapped the second man.

'Do I look like I care, rat breath?' said Huntsekker.

'Well now,' said the first man, his smile fading. 'It looks like we have someone here who thinks he's tough. Is that what you think, fat man?' he asked, stepping in close.

Huntsekker smiled. Reaching up he idly tugged the spikes of his beard. Then his left fist snapped forward, slamming into the big man's face. Dropping his staff Huntsekker followed this with a right cross that spun the river man from his feet. He lay there unmoving. Lazily Huntsekker turned towards the second man who was staring in stunned amazement at his fallen comrade. The man swallowed hard, glanced back at the watching people by the fire, then reached for his knife.

'Do not be foolish,' said Huntsekker, so softly that the crowd could not hear. 'You are gutless and frightened. You know that if you draw that blade I will kill you. So pick up your friend and take him back to the fire. Then ask some of the others who did this to him. When you hear my name try not to piss in your breeches.'

The man swallowed hard. His hand came away from the knife. Huntsekker gathered up his staff and walked on to Powdermill's house. He was angry now, and his neck felt stiff and sore. In the old days throwing a punch would have loosened him up. Now he had pulled a muscle. Still, the headache had gone.

Coming to the front door he rapped on it with his knuckles. 'Who is it?' called a thin, reedy voice.

'A real wizard would know already,' replied Huntsekker. 'But then you're just a miserable fake.'

The door swung open and a small man peered out. He had long white hair, thinning at the crown, and small, button blue eyes. He gave a wide grin, displaying two golden teeth. 'I don't use my powers lightly, Huntsekker,' he said.

'Or cheaply. Invite me in. It's damned cold out here.'

Aran Powdermill stepped aside. Huntsekker eased past him, removed his bearskin coat, and strode across to a deep chair by the fire.

'Make yourself at home, why don't you?' said the little man. Huntsekker gazed around the room. Books and manuscripts filled the shelves, and littered the long table by the only window. Powdermill dragged a second chair to the fire and sat down.

'You are looking old and tired,' he said.

'I am both,' agreed Huntsekker. 'So let us cut to the chase.'

'The Moidart is troubled,' said Powdermill, before Huntsekker could continue. 'His son is threatened, and he wants to know the nature of the enemy.'

'Makes no sense to me,' said Huntsekker. 'You don't know who is at your door, but you know the thoughts of a man twenty miles away.'

'Life is a mystery,' said Powdermill, with a gold-toothed grin.

'It is that, right enough,' agreed Huntsekker.

'Your farm is prospering, I hear. Cattle to feed the armies of the south. You must be almost wealthy by now, Huntsekker.'

'The Moidart wants—'

'—me to travel with you to Eldacre. I won't do it.'

'That is not wise, Powdermill. The Moidart is not a man to disappoint.'

'You misunderstand me, big man. I will come – but not with you. The Moidart is watched. Not all the time. They missed his meeting with you. Which is just as well, for if they had not I would have turned you down flat, threat or no threat.'

'No-one watches the Moidart. I would have seen them.'

Powdermill shook his head. 'Not these you wouldn't, big man. They float in the air, unseen by normal eyes. They have great powers.'

Huntsekker smiled. 'I am not one of your marks. Spare me the nonsense.'

The little man shrugged. 'The Moidart spoke to you in the uppermost room of the Winter House. He was standing by the window, facing south-east. He asked if you knew anyone with *power*. A seer or a mystic. You hesitated. Then you spoke my name.'

Huntsekker shifted uncomfortably in his chair. 'All right, tell me the trick. How do you know this?'

'Not through trickery, Huntsekker. The simplest way to explain is to say that a seer always *hears* when his name is mentioned. Now, as far as I have seen, the Moidart is watched at times during the day. But never after he has taken to his bed. When you return to Eldacre go to him after midnight. Tell him I will come to him, but that I will require ten pounds.'

'Are you mad, Aran? This house isn't worth ten pounds. By heaven, he'll pluck your eyes out for your impudence.'

'Without my skill he will not survive the winter. Neither will you, big man. You are occasionally watched too. You will be on their death list. That is why I will not travel with you. As to the ten pounds – that is the value I put on my life.'

'Who are *they*?'

Aran shook his head. 'Do you not listen? I will not speak their name. Nor should you. Nor should the Moidart. Merely say *the enemy*. Tell him my price. I will come to him tomorrow. After midnight.'

'And that is all you can tell me?'

Aran Powdermill grinned. 'I can tell you that the man you hit is now waiting in the shadows outside, seeking revenge.'

'At last! A useful piece of mystical information.'

'Not really. I saw him duck under my window.'

Huntsekker laughed aloud. 'Well, it will be amusing to see you barter with the Moidart. I will see you tomorrow.'

'If the Source is willing,' said Aran, with no trace of a smile. Huntsekker rose and pulled on his coat. 'You are welcome to stay the night.'

'I have matters to attend to.' Taking up his staff Huntsekker strode to the door. Opening it he stepped outside. Someone rushed from the shadows. Huntsekker's staff whirled and cracked against the man's skull. He slumped to the snow. 'River men used to be tougher than this in my day,' Huntsekker told the little mystic.

'Things were *always* better in the old days,' answered Aran, with a smile.

As befitted a dutiful son Gaise Macon sent a letter home once a month, informing his father of his movements, and aspects of the campaign he felt might interest him. Truth to tell Gaise had little idea of what might or might not interest the Moidart. His father had never replied – until now. Gaise sat in the main room of his house, Soldier asleep at his feet, and read the letter again.

*Word has reached me of the duel with Ferson. The information is sketchy. Write now and inform me of all the events that led up to it – and any that have followed it. Leave nothing out. Keep Mulgrave close and avoid strict routine in your movements. When possible resign your commission and travel north.*

It was signed *M.*

Gaise shook his head and gave a wry smile. Not a word of affectionate greeting. Not a mention of life back in Eldacre.

Tucking the letter into the pocket of his blue silk jacket Gaise moved to the small mirror on the wall, and carefully tied his white cravat. This too was silk – bought in the capital four years ago, when life was simpler. He looked at his reflection. The clothes were bright and stylish – superbly cut jacket, edged with silver embroidery, over a white shirt, with lace collar and extravagant cuffs, grey leggings merging with highly polished black riding boots. The clothes spoke of calmer days – times of nonsense and trivia, balls and parties, visits to the theatre or fine dining establishments. The face, however, was a stark contrast. The eyes were tired and had seen too much. The features were drawn and tense.

*When possible resign your commission and travel north.*

How good that sounded. Gaise made a final adjustment to his cravat and turned away from the mirror. Soldier lifted his great black head and watched the man. His tail wagged.

'You have to remain here, my friend,' said Gaise, crouching down and stroking the hound's head.

But Soldier followed him to the front door, and Gaise had to push him back as he eased himself out. The hound barked furiously as Gaise walked away. Taybard Jaekel and his friend, the powerfully built Kammel Bard, were waiting outside. Both men saluted.

'Have you heard from home?' asked Gaise, as he walked out onto the main street.

Jaekel fell in alongside him, his rifle cradled across his chest. 'Not in a month, sir. They said the winter is harsh.'

'I'd still sooner suffer our winters than spend any more time here,' said Gaise.

'Amen to that, sir.'

'You still have that golden musket ball?' asked Gaise.

'Yes, sir,' answered Taybard, tapping at his chest. 'Seems a long time ago now.'

'It was a good day, Jaekel.'

They strolled through the town. Gaise did not even glance at the bridge.

Guests had already begun arriving at the mayor's large house. Gaise was welcomed by the man's wife, a small and once pretty woman with rapidly blinking eyes, and a sad expression. Gaise bowed to her, and kissed her hand. She led him through to the main reception room, where some twenty people had already gathered. The mayor moved away from a small group of residents and bowed deeply. He was red-faced and – amazingly, considering the food shortages – overweight. 'Welcome, general,' he said, affecting a broad smile that did not reach his eyes. 'You are *most* welcome. Allow me to introduce you to my friends. Some of whom I believe you have met.' Gaise followed the man round the room, shaking hands, making agreeable comments. He was ill at ease, but masked it well. It was not his intention to stay long. This party had been arranged in haste to honour Quartermaster General Cordley Lowen. There was no way Gaise could refuse to attend without causing further offence.

Lowen, dressed in full military uniform of braided crimson, was standing by the fire, chatting to several of the town's leading citizens. They were hanging on his every word, nodding and smiling. His dark-haired daughter was standing close by, in a figure-hugging gown of green satin. It seemed to shimmer in the lantern light.

The mayor led Gaise to the group. Lowen saw them, and his eyes narrowed. His smile, however, remained fixed.

'Good evening, General Macon,' he said.

'And to you, sir. I trust you are well.'

'As well as one can be in these dreadful times.' He stepped aside. 'You remember my daughter, Cordelia.'

'I do, sir.' Gaise felt his stomach tighten as he met her eyes. He bowed deeply. She made no attempt to disguise her contempt for him, her face remaining set, her dark eyes angry. An uncomfortable silence grew. Gaise could think of nothing to say. The fat mayor blurted out something meaningless, and one of the other guests mentioned the weather, and the moment passed.

171

As soon as he could Gaise moved away from the group towards the long table on which a punch bowl had been set. He felt foolish, and a little angry. Filling a glass with cider punch he sipped it.

'So, who are we challenging tonight, general?' asked Cordelia Lowen, appearing alongside him. 'The mayor perhaps?'

Gaise reddened, but this time kept a firm hold on his temper. 'I was rather hoping for an uneventful evening, lady,' he said. 'Though I am glad of this opportunity to apologize for my boorish behaviour.'

Her expression softened, but only marginally. 'I heard of your duel with Lord Ferson.'

'Despite appearances I am not a duellist,' he said. 'Lord Ferson challenged me. I did not desire it.'

'People say otherwise,' she observed, reaching out and filling a crystal cup with punch.

'Really? What do they say?' he asked.

She sipped her drink. Gaise took a deep breath, determined to maintain composure. It was difficult, though, in her company. He found himself staring at her lips, the tiny movement in her throat as she swallowed, the creamy beauty of her skin. 'Is it customary to stare at a woman's breasts where you come from?' she asked. Gaise's head jerked up. He reddened, which made the small, white burn scar on his right cheek stand out.

'I . . . am sorry, lady. Truth to tell I am not comfortable in the presence of women. I seem to develop two left legs and the manners of a village idiot.'

'Your mother must have been a ferocious woman to leave you so daunted by female company.'

'She was murdered when I was a babe. My father never remarried.'

'Then how do you overcome this affliction, General Macon? You are a mildly presentable young man, and I would imagine have enjoyed the company of at least a certain kind of woman.'

Gaise was shocked. He looked into her green eyes, and saw that she was mocking him. Yet it seemed to him that her manner was more gentle, and there was no malice in it. 'I have never sought the company of such women,' he said.

Her surprise was genuine. 'Let me understand this, sir. You are unused to the company of polite women, and you do not frequent the company of the other kind. Does this mean, sir, that the legendary Grey Ghost, the dashing cavalry general, is in fact a virgin?'

'I am, lady,' he told her, blushing furiously.

'Do you not know how to lie?' she enquired. 'All men do it.'

'Of course. But why would you wish me to lie to you?'

'It is not about lying to me, sir. In my experience men are boastful and full of vain pride. I can think of no man who would so easily admit to his inexperience.'

'It was not *easy*, lady.'

She looked into his eyes, then glanced away. 'Perhaps you are one of those who prefer the company of men . . . in all things. It would not be surprising.'

Gaise laughed. 'It would surprise *me*. If I was so inclined, lady, I doubt you would be having the extraordinary effect on me that you are.'

Now it was Cordelia who blushed. She recovered her composure swiftly. 'That was very smoothly said, general. Especially for a man who professes to be uncomfortable with women.'

'I know. I cannot explain it.'

'I understand you come from the north. They say it is pretty there.'

'Aye, it is a beautiful land. Majestic mountains, and lakes of exquisite beauty. Will you be staying long in Shelding?'

'We had expected to stay longer, but my father has received new orders. We leave in four days.'

'I am sorry to hear that.'

'I am not,' she told him. 'I long to return home.'

'Yes, of course.'

'Enjoy your evening, general,' she said, and, with a delicate bow of her head, moved away from him.

Gaise finished his punch – which was over-sweet – and located the mayor. Thanking him for his hospitality he explained that there were military matters to attend to and left the gathering. Jaekel and Bard joined him outside.

Mulgrave was waiting back at the house. 'How did it go, sir?' he asked.

At that moment Soldier bounded from the rear rooms, his tail wagging. Gaise knelt down and patted the over-excited animal. 'Be calm now,' he said. 'Settle down.' Eventually the hound quietened. Gaise sat by the fire, the dog at his feet.

'It was interesting,' said Gaise.

'Was she there?'

'Aye, she was. She is enchanting, Mulgrave. And I barely stumbled in my speech.'

'Will you be seeing her again?' The question was asked too innocently. Gaise looked up at his friend.

'What is bothering you, Mulgrave?'

The swordsman shrugged and forced a smile. 'This is not a good time to fall in love, sir. We are surrounded by enemies.'

'Fear not, my friend. She and the general are leaving in four days. He has fresh orders.'

'I thought he was to stay for a month to establish the depot.'

'So did I. But that's the army for you, Mulgrave.'

'The army,' muttered Mulgrave, with a shake of his head. 'What we are facing here, sir, is not about armies at war. By heaven, you'd be safer if you led the men to join Luden Macks. At least then you'd know the enemy would be in front of you.'

Cordelia Lowen stood patiently as the elderly maid struggled to unfasten the twenty small mother of pearl buttons at the back of her gown. Cordelia loved the gown, but it was definitely impractical. Without a servant to hand she would have been forced to cut the garment clear. She had made this point to her father, when he bought it for her. He had laughed.

'That is entirely the point, my dear. Peasants wear dresses that are easily removed. Only the rich can wear this gown.'

It still seemed stupid to Cordelia. The buttons were beautiful, but they could just as easily have been placed at the front.

'Can't seem to get this one, my dear,' said Mrs Broadley. 'Sorry to keep you waiting so.'

'That's all right, Mara. It is loose enough now.' Stepping away from the woman Cordelia undid the buttons of the sleeves then began to tug the waist upwards. The old woman tried to help.

174

After a few moments of useless struggle Cordelia suddenly burst into laughter. 'This is not a gown,' she said. 'It is an instrument of torture. Cut the damned button off.'

'Oh no, my lady,' wailed Mrs Broadley. 'It will ruin it. Let me try one more time.'

Cordelia's good humour faded as she heard the terror in the old woman's voice. If the dress was ruined she would be blamed, for being too arthritic to unbutton it. That then might be the end of her employment. She, and old Broadley her husband, had been with Cordley Lowen for almost twenty years, having served his father before that. Cordelia wondered what they would do when their time of service was at an end. Did they have money saved? If they did it wouldn't be much.

'I've got it,' said Mrs Broadley, happily. 'Stand up, my dear.' Within moments the garment was laid upon the bed and Cordelia breathed a sigh of deep relief.

'I could scarcely breathe in that thing,' she said. 'I felt faint the whole evening.'

'I expect you were the centre of attention. All the men there were dumbstruck by your beauty.'

Cordelia moved to the chair by the mirror. Mrs Broadley removed the pins from the young woman's hair, allowing it to tumble to her shoulders. Then the servant took up a silver-backed brush. 'Have you seen General Macon?' asked Cordelia, as her hair was being brushed.

'Unpleasant young man,' said Mrs Broadley. 'I remember Mr Broadley telling me of his rudeness back at the old house.'

'Yes, yes, but have you *seen* him?'

'Yes, my lady.'

'What do you think?'

'Of what, my lady?'

'Do you find him presentable?'

'It has never crossed my mind. He is handsome, I would say. He carries himself well. Though I don't know why he should march everywhere with an honour guard.'

'There was an attempt on his life. Luden Macks sent two assassins to kill him. He fought them and killed them.'

'That is what soldiers do, I suppose. Kill people,' said Mrs

175

Broadley, primly. 'He is a noted duellist as well. He shot that Lord Ferson.'

'No, he didn't. Lord Ferson was not shot. Gaise did not kill him.'

'Oh, Gaise is it? Best not to let the general hear you use his given name, my lady. Mr Broadley says the general does not hold this soldier in high regard. He was very rude, you know.'

'I do know, Mara. I was there.'

'Of course, my lady.'

'Would you fetch me my robe? I think I shall join the general in the study.'

Moments later, in a white evening robe, Cordelia Lowen descended the stairs. Her father, having shed his uniform coat, was sitting at his desk, reading. Cordelia entered the room and poured herself a goblet of mulled wine. It was too heavily spiced, but still good upon the tongue. 'What are you reading?' she asked.

Cordley Lowen glanced up. 'Letters outlining the finances of the Southlands Company. Molion sent them by rider this morning.'

'I expect they say you are richer than ever, Father.'

'Indeed they do. It makes happy reading,' he said, though she noted his voice sounded far from happy. 'Did you enjoy the party?'

She shrugged. 'It was better than I expected.'

'I saw you talking to young Macon.'

'He apologized for his boorish behaviour.'

'He is young and impetuous. He did what he believed was right.' Cordley Lowen shook his head and gave a wry smile. 'Indeed, he *was* right.'

Cordelia was shocked. How could such behaviour be considered right? She sipped her wine, and settled down into a padded leather chair by the fire. Cordley Lowen glanced at her and sighed.

'I don't want to lose your love, my child.'

'You never will, Father.'

'*Never* is a long time. I have done well for the king's forces, finding food and supplies, ensuring that shipments arrive and that the army is never short of powder and shot.'

'Of course you have. The king could not have found a better man.'

'To do this I have needed to bribe officials, and perform many unsavoury deeds.'

'Such is the nature of the army, Father. Why are you talking like this?'

'To finance those bribes – and to line my own pockets – I have double sold some supplies. Meats and produce paid for by independent officers were – diverted.'

'You did what you had to do, I am sure. Let us not talk about this, Father. Please!'

'I have become a thief, Cordelia. On a grand scale. Macon paid for supplies he did not receive. That is why he came to the house. That was the reason for his anger.'

'Why are you telling me this? I did not need to know.'

'I need you to know, and I cannot really explain why. Not even to myself. I think, perhaps, it is because you are the one true person in my life. You are, indeed, the only object of true worth I will leave behind me.'

'Stop it!' she cried, running to him and throwing her arms around him. 'You are frightening me with this talk.' She kissed his cheek. 'You are just tired, Father. You need rest.'

Taking her hands in his own he kissed them. 'You are right, of course. I am tired, and I am becoming maudlin. But I have been foolish these last few years. My eyes are open now, though. By heaven they are. I don't know how I could have been so blind.' He turned away from her and stared out of the window at the moon-lit snow covering the small garden at the rear of the house. Cordelia stood quietly, watching his face, reading the pain she saw there. It was an unsettling sight. The one great constant in Cordelia's life was the power that emanated from her father. He was always sure, always confident. He radiated purpose.

Cordley Lowen sighed and ran a hand through his leonine hair. 'Gaise Macon could have killed me. I would have thought that the child of such a father would have done so without hesitation.'

Glad of the opportunity to change the subject Cordelia asked: 'His father is an earl somewhere in the north, is he not?'

'His father is the Moidart, Cordelia. Tales of his savagery abound – though I would hope that the worst of them have never been repeated to you.'

'I have heard of the Moidart,' said Cordelia, 'and some of the legends surrounding him. I do not believe them to be true. No

177

Varlish lord would behave in so despicable a manner. The king would not allow it.'

'There you are wrong,' said Cordley Lowen. 'The area under the Moidart's rule has a history of rebellion, which is why his disgusting methods *were* allowed by the king, and his father before him. His treatment of the clans, the tortures, the dismemberments and the hangings, are, sadly, a matter of public record. Though they pale into insignificance compared to some of the atrocities being perpetrated now in this war.'

'Luden Macks has much to answer for,' said Cordelia. 'He will be brought to account for them.'

Cordley Lowen said nothing for a moment. He leaned back in his chair and pinched the bridge of his nose. 'Do not make judgements about matters which are beyond your knowledge, Cordelia. Not all the atrocities . . .' he faltered, then swore softly. This surprised Cordelia, for she had never heard her father use such language. 'Damn it, girl, not a tenth of the atrocities can be laid at Macks's door. Men, women and children have been ruthlessly and horribly butchered by soldiers riding under the king's banner.' He fell silent for a few moments, and she saw that he was struggling for control. He closed his eyes and took several deep, slow breaths. 'Come the spring I shall resign my commission and we will go back to Varingas. Possibly even cross the water and head east to the Middle Sea. You always liked the estates there, I recall.'

'I thought you were happy in the army, Father. Only recently you said you had been invited to join a select order of knights. It was a great honour, you said.'

'We will talk no more of it. Do you like Macon?'

'Yes, I do,' she admitted.

'He is doomed, Cordelia. He has enemies in very high places. His death is assured.'

She stared at him. 'There must be something we can do.'

'Aye, there is,' he said, sadly. 'We can leave. And that is what we will do in four days.'

'No, that is not what I meant. We must warn him.'

'These are forces far beyond our ability to tackle. We cannot save him, Cordelia. I will be hard pressed to save myself.'

'How can you talk this way?' she cried, stepping back from him. 'It is contemptible.'

'As I said but a moment ago, *never* is a long time,' he told her, sadly.

Huntsekker had never been what he would describe as a deep thinking man. His needs were simple, and he rarely bothered with concepts or philosophies that required dedicated thought. Conversations revolving around politics bored him. Talk of religion mystified him. Love? Well, that was totally baffling. He had seen grown men, tough men, reduced to whimpering dolts because some doxy refused their attentions.

For Huntsekker the world was essentially a remarkably simple place. A man should earn enough to fill his belly, build a home to keep out the cold, and survive for as long as he could before death took him. Then he was worm food. These were the basics. If a man was lucky he would also find a little happiness. Even that, however, was not guaranteed.

But as he trudged on through the melting snow he found himself thinking about life. This was no longer unusual and all the more disquieting for it. It had tended to happen more frequently in the last four years. Huntsekker even knew the exact moment it began.

When Jaim Grymauch died saving Maev Ring. Huntsekker had been there, and had watched as the huge highlander stalked across the cathedral square, scattering the guards with his quarterstaff. Then the four Knights of the Sacrifice, in full silver armour, had run at him. Grymauch had dropped his staff and drawn a huge, old-fashioned broadsword from a scabbard between his shoulders. He killed two in swift fashion, threw the third into the execution fire, and left the fourth unconscious. In the crowd Huntsekker had felt a soaring of the heart as the one-eyed clansman had cut his lady free.

It was a moment of joy unmatched in Huntsekker's long life. It was pure and unselfish. It spoke of something beyond the Harvester's narrow vision of existence. It shone like sunlight after the storm.

Then the musketeers had pushed through the crowd and shot Grymauch. Huntsekker had run to him, gently lowering him to the

179

ground. There was nothing to be done. The big man was dying. Huntsekker had pulled Maev Ring clear, taken her through the cathedral and out across the back fields. He had done this in a moment of reckless passion. Not for her. But for the memory of the hero who gave his life to save her.

His actions had surprised him. Not since the long ago days of his youth had such absurdly romantic notions touched him.

Now, as he walked through the winter night, he could no longer summon the precious feeling he had experienced.

One fact was sure, though. Huntsekker's world had been subtly changed by Jaim's death.

Not just because life was more interesting while Jaim prowled the highlands, stealing cattle. The man had style, and more than that. He had heart. Huntsekker had not even realized that he himself lacked that quality. Not until he met Jaim.

In all the years Huntsekker had lived in the north he only had two dealings with Jaim Grymauch. On the first occasion Jaim stole his prize bull. Huntsekker knew he would try, and had set traps around the paddock. Then he had sat for night after night, his blunderbuss loaded, waiting for the raid. One night he dozed. When he awoke the bull had gone. Huntsekker and his men scoured the highlands all night and found nothing. When they returned to the farm at dawn they found the bull back in the paddock, a sprig of heather tied to its horn. That memory still made Huntsekker smile.

The second occasion had been more deadly. The Moidart had demanded the death of the fistfighter Chain Shada. Grymauch had spirited him away. Huntsekker guessed their destination and set a trap.

It had not worked. Jaim took to the river and swam behind the ambushers. The first moment Huntsekker realized he had been tricked was when a knife blade pricked at his throat. He was holding his blunderbuss, but there was no way he could turn it.

'Best be putting that dreadful thing down, Harvester,' came the voice of Jaim Grymauch. 'I'd hate to be cutting your throat on such a fine night as this.'

Huntsekker smiled at the memory. He had carefully laid the gun down then looked at Grymauch. The man's clothes were drenched.

'You'll catch a chill, Grymauch,' he said. 'You're not as young as once you were.'

'Maybe I'll take that bearskin coat,' replied Jaim. 'That'll keep me warm.'

'It's too big for you, son. Takes a man to wear a coat like this.'

Huntsekker had thought his life would be over that night. As well as the massive Chain Shada there was a youth with Grymauch, dark-eyed and carrying two Emburley pistols. Huntsekker looked into his eyes and saw the ferocity there. Kaelin Ring was a killer. Huntsekker knew the type. Hell, Huntsekker *was* the type. There was no doubt about it. Death waited for Huntsekker, and the only one of his men still conscious, the sharp-featured Boillard Seeton.

But instead Jaim had asked them their intentions. Huntsekker had offered to say nothing about the encounter. Seeton was quick to agree. Huntsekker did not expect Jaim to believe the promises. Boillard Seeton was a man without honour, and Grymauch had no reason to believe in Huntsekker's word.

'Well, that's it, then,' said Grymauch.

'The hell it is!' stormed Kaelin Ring, his voice shaking with anger. 'I say we kill them.' Huntsekker saw the pistol come up. It was pointed at his face. He stood very still.

'We'll kill no-one!' said Jaim.

'We can't trust them. They'll betray us as soon as they get to Eldacre.'

'Aye, maybe they will. That's for them to decide,' said Jaim softly, moving to stand between Huntsekker and the youth. 'Killing shouldn't be easy, boy. Life should be precious.'

Kaelin Ring hadn't been convinced, but he had acceded to Grymauch's wishes. Chain Shada crossed the bridge, and Grymauch and Kaelin Ring moved off into the woods.

Huntsekker had watched them go. The boy had been right. The most sensible course of action would have been to kill them both. Still, Huntsekker had thought, maybe Boillard Seeton would for once justify the faith reposed in him. That hope was short-lived.

'By the Sacrifice I'll see him swing and I'll piss on his grave,' Seeton had said, once Grymauch and the others had left.

'No, you won't, Boillard. You gave your word.'

181

'Under duress,' argued Boillard. 'Don't count.'

'Mine does.'

'Well, I'm not you, Harvester. You do as you wish. Nobody shoots Boillard Seeton and gets away with it. Damn, but I'll enjoy seeing them hang.'

'I don't think so.'

Huntsekker had drawn his scythe and sliced it through Seeton's heart. The man was dead before he knew it.

Just the three occasions. A stolen bull, an ambush by a stream, and a death near the cathedral. A few sentences had passed between them. No more than that. Yet Huntsekker constantly caught himself thinking of the highlander, the memories tinged with a massive regret that he had not known him well.

He walked on, cutting down through a gully and clambering up the other side. He was breathing heavily as he reached the top, and the old familiar ache in the lower back had begun.

He stretched, then looked for a place to sit. He was still some five miles from Eldacre, and was beginning to regret turning down Powdermill's offer of a night's lodging. Leaving the trail he found a small hollow and sat with his back to a tree. His thoughts drifted to the Moidart. Huntsekker had never liked him. He was not a man who would ever inspire devotion. Too cold, too self-contained. Too deadly.

Just like you, Huntsekker, he thought. Ah well, we are what we are.

The Moidart was troubled. Huntsekker had known the man angry, and filled with a cold, murderous rage. Never troubled, though. Always confident in his talent. What had changed? After the meeting with Powdermill Huntsekker thought he knew.

'They float in the air.'

Huntsekker shivered and glanced around the hollow. As always when troubled he tugged at the twin silver spikes of his beard. Thoughts of magic left him uneasy. Twenty years ago the church authorities had set out to destroy magickers and witches. There were burnings across the land. Huntsekker was one of those who had kicked down doors, dragging out suspects for questioning. Dark and bloody times, with many an innocent flayed or put to the fire.

Now there were few who admitted to the dark arts. Huntsekker had come across Powdermill eight years ago. The man was known as a *finder*. Huntsekker had been tracking a rapist and a killer, but the man had gone to ground somewhere. In desperation Huntsekker had listened to the advice of one of his men, Dal Naydham, and sought out Powdermill. He had no great expectation of success, but anything was better than returning to the Moidart with news that the killer had escaped him.

Powdermill went into a trance while holding a glove owned by the killer. When he opened his eyes he told Huntsekker about a cabin in a valley in the shadows of Caer Druagh, some sixty miles south. He described it, and the route to it.

Huntsekker found the man, removed his head and carried it back to Eldacre. He had earned nothing for the trip. Powdermill's price had been exactly the bounty. Two pounds, eight chaillings. He was a canny little bastard.

His back eased, Huntsekker rose and returned to the road. Something was still troubling him, but he couldn't put his finger on the problem.

The answer came to him just a fraction too late: why had Powdermill refused to travel with him?

The first shot struck him between the shoulder blades, slamming him forwards. The second shot hit him in the lower chest. Instinctively Huntsekker threw himself to the right, and over the edge of a steep drop. He fell heavily, then pitched head over heels, gathering speed until his body splashed into an icy stream.

The moon disappeared behind thick clouds. Huntsekker, semiconscious, dragged himself clear of the water and crawled into thick undergrowth. There he passed out.

When he awoke it was dawn. His head pounded, and there was dried blood on his scalp. With a groan he sat up, struggling to remember how he came to be there. Had he fallen? Then he remembered the shots from the darkness. With an effort he opened his bearskin coat. There was blood on his shirt, which was ripped, and the wooden hilt of his double shot pistol was dented and split. Huntsekker pulled it clear. The second shot had struck the weapon, then cannoned off across the flesh of his left side, tearing the skin.

The big man scanned the upper tree line, seeking out the

183

assassins. There was no-one in sight. Rising, he grunted with pain as he took off the heavy bearskin coat. As he did so a flattened ball dropped away from the narrow, double mesh chain mail that was expertly fitted to the lining of the shoulders, extending down to his hips. Two of the outer mesh rings had snapped, but the second layer had saved his life.

Bruised, bleeding and angry Huntsekker donned the coat. He would not go straight to Eldacre. Instead he would go home first.

And fetch his scythe.

# CHAPTER NINE

JAKON GALLOWGLASS HAD FEW FRIENDS. A NATURALLY TACITURN MAN, he had little time for socializing, and no inclination at all to sit gossiping around camp fires. Only two activities interested the young southerner, fighting and whoring. At nineteen he had been in the army for five years, at war now for four. In that time he had developed a taste for battle. Where most soldiers spent their lives caught between boredom and terror Jakon Gallowglass enjoyed his to the full. He was neither introspective nor imaginative. He listened as his comrades spoke of their fears of death or mutilation, but let the words wash over him. Jakon would wrap himself in his cloak and think of better things. There was a new whore at Mellin's tavern, a buxom youngster from the eastern shires. Three daens for a swift ride, and half a chailling for an entire night. Jakon could not imagine why a man would want a whore for an entire night. He'd spent an evening with one once. The ride had been most enjoyable, but afterwards all she'd wanted to do was talk. Endlessly. There had been a buzzing in his ears for days afterwards. It was amazing how many words had flowed out of her. She told him her life story, and by the end of the evening Jakon felt he had lived it several times over.

No, give him the swift ride every time.

He had enjoyed just such a ride this very evening, and was on his way back to camp. Snow had been falling hard, and Jakon trudged slowly through it, climbing a steep bank to cut across the fields. As he approached a small wood he saw a horseman enter the trees. It was his commanding officer, Barin Macy, in his uniform of scarlet and gold, partially obscured by his fur-lined cloak. Jakon paused in the moonlight, idly wondering what the general would be doing at this time of night in such a desolate place. In normal circumstances Jakon would not have gone a single step out of his way to find out. Curiosity was not one of his vices. On this occasion, however, the general was riding across the path Jakon was to take. This posed a problem, in that he had slipped out of camp without a pass, and, were he to be seen, he'd have to endure a flogging. So he hunkered down beside a bush and waited for the rider to exit the trees.

Only he didn't.

Jakon was growing cold, and decided to see if he could creep past the small wood without being noticed. Keeping low he angled his way down the slope to the edge of the trees. He could hear voices now, and paused again.

'They're northerners. There'll be few tears shed,' he heard someone say.

'Even so, they are good fighting men. It'll not be easy,' came the reply.

'I think you are wrong, Macy. They'll be expecting nothing. Your men will get in close, and at the first volley the Eldacre men will panic and run. Keep your cavalry in reserve to mop up stragglers. And bring back the head of the traitor Macon.'

'Damn it, Velroy, this is hard to believe. The Grey Ghost has been our finest cavalry leader. He's turned several battles. Why would he defect to Luden Macks? It makes no sense.'

'It is not for us to question orders. Pick your men carefully and ride out late the day after tomorrow. Attack the town the following morning. Come in on all four sides. No-one must escape.'

'What of the townsfolk?'

'The Redeemers will take over after the battle. They will question the citizens and deal with any deemed to have Covenant sympathies.'

'By heaven, Velroy, this feels like a dirty business.'

'Do it well and you will be given command of Ferson's Lancers.

Lord Winterbourne also offers a thousand pounds as a gesture of his continuing goodwill towards you and your family.'

'That is most generous.'

'Lord Winterbourne makes a very good friend, Macy. It is worth remembering.'

'A man can never have enough friends,' answered Macy. 'Convey my thanks to the earl, and tell him he can rely upon me and my men. And now I must go. This cold is eating into my bones.'

Jakon ducked down. He heard the creak of leather as the general mounted. Then he saw the rider swing his horse back towards the camp. Jakon waited until the other officer also departed, then he rose from his hiding place.

Jakon Gallowglass did not have many friends. But two years ago, a ball lodged in his thigh, he had waited to be killed by Covenant scouts. He had been hunkered down on a stretch of open ground, two dead comrades alongside him. Dragging himself behind one of the bodies he had lain there quietly as shots rained in on him. He could hear some of them thunking into the corpse, and others kicking up dirt close by. Then he'd heard a shot from behind him. With a curse he rolled to his back, scrabbling for his pistol. There were no Covenanters there. It was a young, sandy-haired musketeer wearing the leaf green tunic of the Eldacre regiment. He was kneeling on the ground some fifty paces behind Jakon's position. Shots peppered the ground around him, but he coolly loaded and fired. Then a horseman on a huge grey gelding came thundering across the open ground. A young rider, wearing a wide-brimmed grey hat and a long grey greatcoat, leapt to the ground alongside Jakon, hauling him upright and lifting him into the saddle. Vaulting up behind him the rider had kicked the gelding into a run. A shot screamed by them, ripping the hat from the rider's head. The gelding took off and was soon out of range of the muskets. The rider drew up and helped Jakon to the ground. Other cavalrymen moved past them, galloping out towards the high ground and the Covenant snipers. The officer knelt beside Jakon, examining the wound to his thigh. 'Broke no bones, and missed the major artery. You're a lucky young fellow. I'll put a tourniquet on it until we can get you to a surgeon.'

'Thank you, sir.'

The man laughed. 'Don't thank me. Thank that idiot rifleman of mine. He's too good a man to lose. If I hadn't pulled you out he'd still be there in the line of fire. As it is I've lost a damn good hat,' he said, pushing his hand through his long, golden hair.

'You're the Grey Ghost.'

'One of these days I must find out where that name originated,' said Gaise Macon. 'Now what can we use as a tourniquet?' The Grey Ghost had untied a white silk scarf from his neck, and, using Jakon's pistol as a lever, had tightened it around the wounded thigh. 'That should hold you, lad. I'll leave you in the capable hands of young Jaekel here.' Patting Jakon on the shoulder he had returned to his mount and ridden away towards the hills.

Jakon eased himself up into a sitting position. The rifleman sat beside him. 'Thanks,' said Jakon.

'Don't mention it,' said Taybard Jaekel, and they sat in silence for a while. Jaekel had pulled a plug of smoked meat from his hip pouch. With a small knife he cut it in half and handed a section to Jakon. 'Need to loosen that tourniquet,' he said. 'Leg'll rot if you don't.'

'Did you hit any of them Covenanters?' asked Jakon.

'Two.'

'You only fired twice.'

'That's why I only hit two.'

The leg was beginning to pain him, but Jakon still managed a smile. 'I'm Jakon Gallowglass. I owe you one.'

'If I see you near a tavern I'll let you buy me a tankard of ale,' said Jaekel.

It was a good memory.

Now Jakon Gallowglass, cold and angry, stood at the edge of the woods, staring at the twinkling fires of the camp not two hundred paces distant. Given the choice he would have preferred to arrive five minutes after the officers had gone, to have heard nothing of their plans. That way when he had heard of the death of the Grey Ghost and Taybard Jaekel he could simply have experienced a little grief, before resuming his life of fighting and whoring.

Gallowglass swore, long and loudly, his anger rising. He had spent many evenings in the company of Taybard Jaekel. He liked

188

the man. He didn't fill your head with questions. Added to which he had saved Jakon's life twice. 'Damn and perdition,' he said.

If he headed off towards Shelding he could be there by late morning. At which point he would have moved beyond desertion and become a traitor.

Jakon Gallowglass was not a fool. Even if he warned the Grey Ghost it was unlikely the man or his company would survive. If they did they would become hunted men, hundreds of miles from their homeland.

'Best you look after yourself, Gallowglass,' he whispered.

Then he turned his back on the Shelding road and returned to his barracks.

Marl Coper had always been ambitious. As a child living on the south coast with his widowed father he had dreamed of a life of power and riches. In that order. His family had been poor, though not poverty-stricken. His father was an army surgeon, and had received a tract of land and a good house upon his retirement. After that he tended to the citizens of Lord Winterbourne's southern estates. He would not have seen himself as poor. There was always food on the table, but clothes had to be mended, shoes repaired. They owned only two horses, both old and swaybacked. Marl needed more than this.

He was a good student at the local school, reading endlessly, studying Varlish history. It seemed to Marl that the greatest attribute of history's giants was ruthlessness, combined with a single-minded goal. Closer examination, however, showed that all the great men had also learned the craft of politics. They had acquired mentors, patrons who could lift them, supply them with contacts, and ease their way through the treacherous alleyways of power.

Marl's first mentor had been a canny old man who ran Lord Winterbourne's southern manor. The thirteen-year-old Marl had run errands for him, seeking to please him at every turn. The old man took a shine to him, and began inviting him to his home. Here Marl performed services of a more disquieting nature.

By the time Marl was nineteen he had learned all that he could from the old man. It had not occurred to him at that time to engineer his death, and thus take over his role. Marl was still young and unsure of his skills. One day, however, fate intervened. They were crossing the ice-covered River Tael, when suddenly the surface cracked. The old man was spun from his feet, landing heavily, his legs slipping under water. He scrabbled to hold on to the tilting ice. Marl threw himself flat and instinctively reached out for his mentor. In that moment he realized they were totally alone. Unseen. Slithering forward he reached the old man. His lips were already blue with cold. 'Pull me out, boy. Be careful, though. If we both go under we're doomed.'

Marl reached out, pushed aside the old man's questing hand and thrust his head down under the ice. The old man fought hard, but the current dragged him down to his death.

Marl Coper made a fine steward. He reorganized the running of the manor, and introduced a new breed of cattle, purchased from the north, which were more hardy and supplied more beef. He improved the horse herds, acquiring three fine stallions from across the sea. The manor house itself had fallen into disrepair, as Lord Winterbourne spent little time there, but Marl brought in carpenters and stonemasons to renovate the building. Despite the expenditure the profits from the estate doubled in three years.

He worked tirelessly, with one aim in mind. To impress the Winterbourne family. Initially this meant catching the eye of Sir Gayan Kay, Lord Winterbourne's younger brother. Impressing him was not easy. The man was a Knight of the Sacrifice, boorish and arrogant. He had a habit of speaking his mind, no matter the hurt or the offence caused. He maintained that this was the duty of a knight, to speak the truth. As always with such people, were any to speak *their* minds to *him* he would fly into uncontrollable rages. Marl observed him quietly for more than a year. He noted that Gayan Kay professed a hatred of sycophants, and yet surrounded himself with the most appalling toadies.

Marl organized hunts for Gayan Kay and his friends, arranged the balls and gatherings he was so fond of, paid his overdue bills, and kept largely in the background until he had studied the man fully. He learned to read Gayan Kay. The man had an ego the size of a mountain, but he was no fool.

Except for his belief that he was a poet of distinction.

Often he would invite his friends to listen to his latest compositions. They were mostly maudlin and trite, but his hangers-on would applaud wildly. Marl joined in, and waited his moment. One evening he listened as Gayan droned on, and noticed that the knight was not offering the piece with his usual verve. Marl sensed that he was unsure of the poem – as well he might be. It was singularly awful. At the close all his companions told him how wonderful it was. Marl took a deep breath. 'I do not think, sir,' he said, 'that it is worthy of you.' A stunned silence followed. Gayan Kay's face went pale. Marl pressed on smoothly. 'Had any other poet offered such a piece I would have praised them to the skies. It is wonderful and vibrant. But your work, sir, is normally touched with greatness.'

Gayan Kay stood silently for a moment. 'Damn,' he said, 'but I do love an honest man. He's right. The piece is not worthy of me.'

Within a remarkably short space of time Marl became Gayan Kay's best friend.

As a result he was drawn into the close circle of men who gathered around the powerful Winter Kay. Their first meeting had been inauspicious. Winter Kay had nodded in his direction then moved away. He was not like his brother. Marl watched him closely. He did not suffer fools, and he was immune to flattery.

It was another year before he saw him again. Winter Kay arrived in the south, took a tour of the manor house, then summoned Marl to the newly refurbished rooms in the southern wing.

'You have done well, young Coper,' said Winter Kay. 'It seems to have been fortunate for my family that old Welham vanished beneath the ice when he did.'

'I am happy to serve, my lord.'

'Tell me how he died.'

Marl looked into the man's cold eyes. 'The ice cracked as we crossed the river. He was swept away.'

'Could you have reached him.'

'I did reach him, my lord. He died though.'

'My brother is impressed with you, sir. He is easily impressed. I am not.'

Marl said nothing as Winter Kay observed him. 'From all I have heard you are a thinking man. From what I have seen you are an ambitious one. Ambition is a fine thing. How far, however, will you go to achieve your ends?'

'As far as is necessary, my lord.'

'Would you kill?'

'I would obey the orders of my lord, whatever they were,' he answered smoothly.

'I think you would. Find a replacement for yourself here. Train him for a month, then join me at Baracum.'

Marl had expected his first mission for Lord Winterbourne to be tough, but the nature of it caused him his first serious doubts. Winter Kay had a mistress, who had given birth to a son. She wanted him to marry her, and threatened to take the matter of her son's birthright to the royal court. Marl's orders were simple. Kill the woman and the brat and dispose of the bodies. Marl had stood outside the woman's home in the midnight darkness, thinking back to his youth and his father's teachings. Killing old Welham had been a spontaneous act. This was calculated murder. In the end Marl reasoned that if he did not do it, someone else would. And that someone else would reap the rewards. Therefore, if the woman was effectively dead anyway, why shouldn't he be the one to benefit from it? He had strangled her and the child, and dragged the bodies down into front room, which he doused in lantern oil.

He could still see the flames as he topped the furthest rise.

Now, as he rode with his two retainers into the grounds of the Moidart's Winter House, he was what he had always desired to be – a man of power and influence. Winter Kay ruled the Redeemers, and virtually the land. The king was a straw in the wind, nothing more than a human banner to be waved when necessary.

One day, perhaps soon, Marl would find a way to supplant even the dread Lord Winterbourne. But first there was the problem of the Moidart.

Few among the ruling classes had not heard of the Lord of the North. He had survived numerous assassination attempts during his thirty-year reign. He had been shot, stabbed, and almost burned to death when the old manor had been set ablaze. Marl drew rein and looked beyond the present house to the blackened timbers and collapsed stones of the old building some distance away within the trees. No attempt seemed to have been made to remove the ruins.

A middle-aged officer with a heavy jaw and tired eyes stepped from the manor house and strode down to meet the riders. He exchanged a few words with the two sentries who had accompanied the Redeemers from the gates, then turned towards Marl.

'Good afternoon, gentlemen. I am Captain Galliott and I welcome you to the Winter House. I shall show you to your rooms, but first, as is the custom in the north, would you please hand over your weapons to the guards. No knives, swords or pistols are allowed in the earl's presence.'

'By heaven, sir,' said Marl, who had been forewarned of this rule, 'we are Redeemers and Knights of the Sacrifice. It would be unseemly to surrender our weapons.'

'Indeed it would, sir,' said Galliott smoothly, 'but do not consider it a surrender. You are merely offering a mark of respect to the Moidart. The weapons will be well looked after, and offered to you upon your departure.'

'Very well,' said Marl, with a sidelong glance at the slender figure of Kurol Ryder. He carried two knives within his riding boots, long, sharp disembowelling blades. These would suffice.

The three Redeemers dismounted, removed their sword and knife belts and left their pistols in the scabbards upon the pommels of their saddles.

Galliott led them up the steps to the main doors, and then onto the first floor gallery. Here each of the men was assigned a room. Marl's was the largest. It was comfortably furnished, with a fine bed, fashioned from pine, boasting an ornate headboard. There was a writing desk set by the window, and in the hearth a fire was glowing. 'I shall have a servant bring you some refreshment, Sir Marl,' said Galliott.

'Just a little water, captain. I need to pray and continue my fast until this evening.'

'Of course, sir. The Moidart is busy at present, but I will send a servant when he is free.'

'Most kind, captain.'

As Galliott withdrew Marl removed his black riding cloak and draped it over a chair. Then he lay down on the bed and closed his eyes. Despite the training Winter Kay had offered him, and the added energy supplied by the Orb, Marl had never found it easy to break free of the confines of his body. It was always an effort involving intense concentration, and not a little discomfort. Searing head pain always followed. However, he managed it and his spirit floated above the bed. For a moment he gazed down on his form, then slowly drifted through the door and out onto the gallery. Galliott was standing at the bottom of the stairs talking to a soldier. Marl floated closer.

'They gives me the creeps, captain, and I don't mind admitting it,' said the man. 'All dressed in black and pretending to be holy. I've heard stories about them bastards. Freeze your blood it would.'

'You shouldn't listen to stories, Packard. They are Knights of the Sacrifice and they are fighting a war on behalf of the king. More than that, though, they are guests of the Moidart, and will be treated with the utmost respect.'

'I'll do that right enough, captain. But the sooner they're gone the better.'

Marl floated on, down the long corridor and through the empty dining hall. He heard voices and entered a room containing two men. One was sitting at a desk, the other standing before him. The conversation was of little note – something to do with tax revenues and the shortfalls caused by the severity of the winter and the death of more livestock than expected. Marl took the opportunity to study the Moidart. The man was slim, the skin of his face drawn tight over high cheekbones. He had long hair, drawn tight over his skull and tied in a pony tail. His clothes were well cut, a jacket of black satin over a white shirt with lace cuffs. He wore no jewellery. Marl moved closer, staring at the man's face. It was cruel and haughty. Here was a man very much like Winter Kay, a natural ruler who expected instant obedience. Marl could see arrogance in him, and a steely determination. Not a man to flatter unnecessarily. He would read it instantly and feel contempt for the flatterer.

Marl moved on, finally reaching the Moidart's private chamber. It was less well furnished than the guest room he himself occupied. As he floated there he felt another presence. His spirit spun.

The spirit of Kurol Ryder hung suspended in the air, scanning the room. In the flesh Kurol Ryder was a good looking man, but Marl had never quite adjusted to the spirit features; the pale, sickly scaled faces and the blood eyes. Happily, spirits generated no re-flection in mirrors and Marl had never had to see himself in such a light.

'No problem here,' said Kurol Ryder. 'The lock is old and will be easily picked. If I suffocate him it might look as if he died in his sleep.'

'No,' said Marl. 'Cut his throat as he sleeps. Less possibility of anything going wrong.'

'As you wish, sir.'

Marl could feel the pull of his body. Unlike the other Redeemers he could not hold this ethereal form for long. Dizziness touched him, and he returned to his body with a start. His head was pound-ing painfully and he took a pinch of willow powder from his pouch, placing it on his tongue. He felt a little sick and rose from the bed. From the window he could look out over the mountains to the north, towering peaks, crowned with snow. Marl closed his eyes and breathed deeply, waiting for the nausea to pass.

He heard a light knock at his door. After a moment it opened and the powerfully built Kannit Persan stepped inside. For a big man he moved gracefully, always in balance. Kannit spent an in-ordinate amount of time on honing his body. Whenever time allowed he would be found running through the hills, or heaving weights. He maintained that had he not been from a noble family he would have become a circle fighter, like the great Chain Shada. Marl was not so sure. Kannit Persan – a handsome man with fine aquiline features – had a habit of pausing by mirrors and enjoying his reflection. The thought of a broken and twisted nose, or scarred brows, would be anathema to him.

'It is a fine house,' said Kannit. 'A shame we will not be staying long. The grounds are extensive and there is a track leading up into the hills. One of the servants told me it extends over four miles through some beautiful country. I'd like the opportunity to run it.'

'Another time,' promised Marl. 'Kurol is prepared. Are you?'

'Of course. It will be simpler without the Harvester.'

'I would be happier had we seen his body,' said Marl.

'One shot in the centre of his back, one in his chest. Even if he survived he's not going to be in any condition to save his master,' pointed out Kannit.

'What do you make of Galliott?'

Kannit shrugged his massive shoulders. 'An ordinary soldier, no more no less. I could take him in a heartbeat. There's an interesting painting on the gallery,' he said. 'A beautiful woman – with one green eye and one gold. Just like Macon. Must be something that runs in the family.'

'The Moidart's grandmother, I understand,' said Marl. 'She was a real beauty in her day.'

A servant arrived, bowed, and requested them to join the Moidart in the dining hall.

Marl and Kannit strolled down the stairs. Kurol Ryder was waiting for them, and the three Redeemers followed Galliott to the doorway of a long room, where a fire was blazing in a deep hearth. Here the officer left them, drawing shut the door behind him.

'Welcome, my friends,' said the Moidart. 'Please be seated.' He glanced at Marl. 'You, I think, are Marl Coper. Be so kind as to introduce your friends.'

Marl did so. Both the Redeemers rose and bowed as he named them. 'Kurol Ryder,' said the Moidart. 'Are your family from the Deppersom manor?'

'Yes, lord.'

'I knew your father many years ago. He served at Eldacre back during the first clan rising. A fine soldier. Utterly ruthless and totally dedicated. Such men are rare. Is he well?'

'He died, lord, five years ago.'

'But you follow the family tradition of service to your lord. Commendable. It is what raises the Varlish above lesser races.' He swung to Kannit. 'You, sir, I do not know, but you have the look of the Varlish about you. Cold eyes. Most becoming.'

The Moidart seated himself opposite the three Redeemers, who were sitting side by side and facing the window. Servants brought food. A pie of good steak and braised kidney, some fresh baked bread, and three flagons of strong ale. Marl noted that the Moidart did not partake of the ale, and so he too refused, requesting water. The meal was finished in near silence. Once the servants had cleared away the dishes the Moidart leaned back.

'I do miss the life at court,' he said, 'the intrigues and the politicking. It makes one feel alive. Enemies who become friends,

friends who become enemies; each person desperately trying to read the runes and see where the ebb and flow of power will take them. I understand you are particularly adept at such games, Master Coper. I congratulate you. Not an easy life.'

'I am just a simple man, my lord,' said Marl, 'serving my lord as best I can.'

'And how is Lord Winterbourne?' asked the Moidart. 'I hear he has been having problems of late.'

'Problems, my lord?' queried Marl.

'A troublesome general who just does not seem to want to die. Is that not so?' The smallest of smiles touched the Moidart's lips, but his eyes remained emotionless. The room suddenly seemed very still.

'You have the advantage of me, sir. Of whom are you speaking?'

'Why, my son, sir. Gaise Macon. Is that not why you are here?' The question was asked innocently and Marl thought fast.

'I think someone must have overstated the situation to you, sir. The quarrel was never between Lord Winterbourne and your son. Lord Ferson issued the challenge. Lord Winterbourne was merely acting as his second. The matter is now resolved. There is certainly no ill feeling between the two men. Lord Winterbourne speaks highly of General Macon, who is a masterful fighter and a fine cavalry commander. He is a credit to you, sir.'

'We come from a family of fighters, Master Coper,' said the Moidart smoothly. 'More than that we are intriguers. I have forgotten more about treachery and malice than you have ever learned. So let me tell you how I see the situation. Were I Lord Winterbourne, and I desired the death of Gaise Macon, I would – as he did – try to arrange it in a way that could not be laid at my door. I would do this because I would be concerned about the Moidart. I would think, what do I know about this man? The answer is simple. The Moidart is a killer. He has no sense of remorse, is not held back by principles of honour or chivalry. If I kill his son he will find a way to kill me. Are you following me so far?'

'I hear your words, my lord, but they have no meaning for me.'

The Moidart gave a small smile. It did not reach his eyes. 'Bear with me then, young Coper. Think of it as a political lesson. A duel

197

is arranged. This is an excellent plan. If Macon dies all is well. If he lives? Well, other plans can be hatched. The idea of pistols is a pleasing one. So much can go wrong – and pass undetected. A misfire, perhaps. Or . . . who knows? A badly loaded weapon? Yes, I think that is the route I would have followed.' The Moidart filled a goblet with water and sipped it, his pale eyes watching the three men intently. 'Yet it failed. Plans do, you know. The best of them. Rogue elements appear. They cannot be planned for. Are you a student of history, young Coper?'

'I am, sir.'

'Then you will recall the legendary Battle of Vorin Field. The Keltoi battle king, Bane, had been betrayed and his forces led into a trap. Yet he won. History tells us it was because of his bravery and his heroic leadership. This is only partly true. He won because an officer leading a cavalry troop got lost. The man had been sent, with six hundred riders, to intercept a supply caravan. In the maze of canyons and valleys he took a wrong turn. This brought him and his troops out behind the Stone army. Bane was hard pressed, but when the officer led his men to attack the enemy rear the battle was turned. Rogue elements, you see? Now, where was I? Ah yes, the killing of the troublesome Gaise. The duel failed to achieve its purpose. Now comes the first error. Killers are sent. One of them is a noted swordsman, the other a backstabber. Surely no rogue elements can spoil this plan?' The Moidart shook his head and laughed. 'Who could have foreseen the arrival of an ugly dog? Hmmm? Most amusing. Added to this Gaise Macon is also a fine swordsman. I take the credit here, for long ago I hired Mulgrave to teach him. However that is by the by. For now the snake is out of the basket. The killers were Redeemers. Only one man could send Redeemers. Now his problem has truly doubled. Once the Moidart discovers the plan he will become an enemy far more deadly than the naive young general. Therefore – speaking still as Winter Kay – before I can take my vengeance on the son, I must see the father slain. How does that sound to you, Marl Coper?'

Marl sat very still. He could feel the tension in the two men on either side of him. Here they were, three Redeemers in a room, alone with the man they had come to kill. And he was taunting them.

'An interesting story, my lord,' said Marl. 'Respectfully, however, there are flaws in it.'

'Pray, enlighten me.'

'First, the duel with Lord Ferson followed Gaise Macon's accusation of cowardice. Lord Ferson had no alternative but to issue a challenge. Second – though I know of no attack upon the Lord Gaise – if two Redeemers did seek to kill him they could have done so for their own reasons. It does not follow that they were instructed to harm him. The Lord Gaise has a habit of speaking his mind. Perhaps he insulted them. All I know is that I have been instructed to come to you, offering the friendship of my lord.'

'Splendid,' said the Moidart. 'I congratulate you. Had you come alone I might even have been tempted to allow myself to be convinced. Unfortunately you brought these two fools with you,' he said, waving a hand towards Kurol Ryder and Kannit Persan. 'Their eyes betray them. Young Ryder is like his father. When threatened his face adopts the look of a frightened rabbit.'

'Hell! Let's do it now!' snarled Kurol Ryder, pushing himself to his feet and drawing a knife from his boot.

Something bright and shining slashed through the air. Blood splashed from Kurol's open throat. His head lolled absurdly, and his body crumpled. A huge hand grabbed Kurol's hair. The scythe slashed down again, and the head came clear.

Marl's heart was hammering, and he felt dizzy. Glancing to his right he saw the huge figure of Huntsekker, a bloody scythe in his hand. Beyond him a hidden panelled doorway lay open. Another man was standing there, small and white-haired. He smiled at Marl, who saw a flash of gold teeth. Huntsekker tossed Kurol's head to the table top. It rolled to the left and lay there, the sightless eyes staring at Marl.

'Ah, I see the rogue element has arrived,' said the Moidart. Kurol Ryder's headless body toppled to the floor.

Kannit Persan, his face drenched in sweat, was staring at the Moidart, and the long pistol he had produced from beneath the table. 'So now,' said the Moidart, with a cold smile, 'we find ourselves in a pretty fix. Three assassins come to my home, sent by the king's foremost general. What am I to do with them?'

The small white-haired man moved out from behind the

panel, and approached the Moidart, leaning in to whisper in his ear.

'Ah,' said the Moidart, glancing up towards the ceiling. 'Apparently we are joined by Winterbourne himself.' Transferring his gaze to Marl he asked: 'Do you wish to commune with your lord? Perhaps he can offer some way out of this predicament.'

'I feel certain, sir,' said Marl, 'that there has been a great misunderstanding. I am sure we can resolve this matter without further bloodshed.'

'I don't think so,' said the Moidart, lifting the pistol. The shot sounded like a thunderclap in the enclosed room. Kannit Persan, his throat torn out, surged to his feet, staggered several paces then pitched to the floor, where he lay for several moments noisily drowning in his own blood. The Moidart laid down the pistol and poured himself a goblet of water. He spoke to Marl, but his words were drowned by the gurgling gasps of Kannit Persan.

'I did not hear you, sir,' said Marl.

'I asked if you would like a little water, sir. You seem pale.'

A growing sense of unreality gripped Marl Coper. He shook his head. 'No, thank you.'

At last Kannit was silent. The Moidart sipped his water, his gaze never leaving Marl's chalk white face. 'I have always been a vastly unforgiving man,' said the Moidart. 'I have no ill feeling concerning the attempt to kill me. As I have already said, I would probably do the same if the circumstances were reversed. What does irritate me, however, is the fact that it was organized with such a blatant lack of subtlety. It insults my intelligence.' The white-headed man spoke quietly to the Moidart once more. 'Ah, you are alone now, Master Coper. Apparently we have bored Lord Winterbourne.'

Marl took a deep breath, and summoned the last of his courage. 'As you are aware, sir, your son is in the south. His life hangs by a thread. Release me and I shall see that no harm comes to him.'

'No, no, no,' said the Moidart, shaking his head. 'You cannot guarantee that, Marl Coper. My son will live or die depending on his skill and his luck. I cannot shape those events. Neither can you. If I could I wouldn't have killed your comrades. I would have found some other way to deal with Winterbourne. As it is I am extremely displeased. I am a king's man, and have no sympathy for the Covenant rabble. They were always going to lose. Now I am forced to their side. My own lands – mercifully free of the in-efficiency of war – will now see battles and disruption to trade. My wealth – gathered by my family for generations – will be squandered on armies and guns and swords. It is most vexing.'

'Please don't kill me, lord,' said Marl, tears dropping to his cheeks.

'I won't be killing you yet, Master Coper. Oh no. First there is much you can tell me. I need to know all there is to know about Winter Kay and his plans. My man Huntsekker will show you to your new quarters. I will join you there presently. Then we can talk.'

'I'll tell you anything you need to know, lord. I swear it.'

'I know. People in my dungeons always do.'

# CHAPTER TEN

TWO HUNDRED AND TWENTY-THREE CATTLE HAD SURVIVED THE LONG drive to Eldacre. Fourteen had been slaughtered en route to feed the nine herders, and sundry other folk who had begged food along the way. Five had been stolen, and Maev had forbidden Kaelin to lead his men after them. This had galled the young Rigante.

'They are *my* cattle, Kaelin,' she said, quietly. 'If anyone is entitled to be outraged it is me.'

'Maybe so,' Kaelin told her. 'But what would you have said had I been leading this trip and had come home to tell *you* that I had decided to allow a few cattle to be stolen?'

Maev Ring suddenly smiled. Her hard face softened, and she seemed years younger. 'I would have berated you, nephew. Long and hard.'

The answer eased Kaelin's anger. 'So why this unaccustomed softness?'

Maev climbed down from the long supply wagon and strode out to the edge of the trail. Far below they could see the towering grey castle, standing proud above the town. Maev gazed down onto Eldacre, seeking out the Five Fields, where every year the Games were held. She felt her throat tighten as she remembered Jaim Grymauch giving the fight of his life against the Varlish champion, Gorain. Maev sighed. 'A long time since I've been home,' she said.

'Didn't think I could face it before this. Not sure I can even now.'

Kaelin moved alongside his aunt, placing his arm round her shoulder. 'I can still remember the pride I felt when Grymauch knocked the man out of the circle. I can hear the roar of the clansmen, and see the stunned astonishment on the faces of the Varlish crowd.'

'Aye,' said Maev. 'The man could punch.' She shrugged off his protective hug. 'I need no mollycoddling,' she said. Kaelin grinned and shook his head.

'You're the least huggable woman I ever met.'

'Aye, that's true enough,' she agreed. The last of the sunlight fell upon her red and grey hair. Maev Ring at forty was still a handsome woman, straight-backed and tall. She had put on a little weight in the last four years, but still walked with the easy grace of the highlander. Hitching up her heavy green skirt she climbed back to the wagon. 'Join me,' she said, sliding across the seat. 'We need to talk.'

Kaelin stepped up alongside her and took the reins. The four horses leaned into the traces and the wagon trundled towards the sloping road. Behind them the herders prodded the cattle forward.

'Two weeks we've been on the road and *now* you need to talk?' said Kaelin.

'I'll be seeing the Moidart tomorrow. I thought you might like to come with me.'

Kaelin Ring said nothing. Carefully he guided the wagon forward, keeping his foot poised above the brake. Maev watched him closely. 'Has the Morrigu stolen your tongue?' she asked at last.

The wagon slipped towards the edge of the trail. Kaelin steered it on. There was ice here and the road was steep, the horses tired. He coaxed the team, calling out to them as he flicked on the reins. Slowly the wagon rumbled over the worst of the slope, coming out onto steadier ground.

'Why would I want to meet him?' he asked.

'Because he is the ruler of this land, Kaelin. And one day you will be a man of power. It is wise that you should meet. A man should know his friends, but it is vital that he knows his enemies.'

'What do I need to know? He betrayed my father and murdered him. His men then slaughtered the Rigante. My mother was among them. Were it not for you those same men would have lifted the babe I was and smashed my head against a wall.'

'It is all true,' said Maev. 'Yet when that same man was pressed to have me executed he declared me innocent.'

'Pah! Your skills were creating riches, and he took his share in taxes. Are you trying to convince me there is good in the man? He is a creature of hatred and bile.'

'Aye, he is. You know why he hated your father?'

'Of course. He was the leader of the Rigante and the Moidart could not defeat him.'

'That is not the whole story, Kaelin. The Moidart had a wife. It was said he adored her. She was a fickle woman, however. She met with your father in secret.'

'That is a lie!'

'Jaim saw them one day. He kept it secret for many years, but one night, when drunk, he told me of it. Lanovar was a great man in many ways. He was bonny and brave, and bright and witty. He could not resist a pretty face though.' Maev laughed. 'Truth to tell he could not resist them whether they were pretty or not.'

'Are you saying the Moidart killed him for sleeping with his wife?'

'Oh, how proper! Sleeping, indeed! I doubt they slept much. But, yes, that's why the Moidart hated him. Have you ever seen Gaise Macon?'

'I met him once,' said Kaelin.

'Did you see his eyes?'

'Of course I saw his eyes . . .' Kaelin faltered, remembering their curious colour, one green one gold.

'Lanovar's eyes,' said Maev.

The words hung in the air. Kaelin said nothing, his mind reeling. Out of nowhere he remembered the Wyrd talking to him years ago, in what seemed a different age. Jaim was alive, the future seemed bright, and he had just had a scrap with some local youths. Gaise Macon had come to his rescue. The Wyrd seemed fascinated by this. She had pressed him for his views on the young nobleman. 'Did you like him?' she asked.

'He is Varlish,' he had answered, as if that were the end of the matter. The Wyrd had then spoken of Maev, but her words burned in him now.

'She is Rigante, Ravenheart, and in her flows the blood of Ruathain and Meria, two of the great heroes of our past. Aye, and Lanach and Bedril, who held the pass. Maev is old blood. As are you. As is Gaise Macon.'

As is Gaise Macon!

Kaelin's stomach tightened. Lifting the reins he tossed them into Maev's lap, then leapt from the wagon. He wanted to hear no more.

'Wait, Kaelin!' called Maev.

He swung round. 'Wait? What for? More lies?'

'I am telling you the truth.'

'Maybe!' he raged. 'But what of all the lies until now? Jaim knew. You knew. The Wyrd knew. Only Kaelin had to be kept in the dark. Damn you, Maev, you had no right to keep it from me. And worse, you had no right to tell me now.'

Maev jumped from the wagon and ran to him. 'I am sorry. Truly, Kaelin. I would do nothing to cause you pain. Yes, I kept it from you. Not for as long as you think, though. Only two years. I saw Gaise Macon when he visited the barracks at Black Mountain. He rode by me. I looked into his face – and I saw Lanovar's eyes. I wanted to tell you then, but little Jaim had just been born, and I couldn't find a way to broach it with you.'

'Now you have,' he said. 'So leave me be.'

With that he strode off into the gathering darkness.

Kaelin Ring was still angry as he entered the outskirts of Eldacre, but it was tinged with a deep sorrow. He had never known his father, and all the stories of him had come from Jaim, or Maev, or the Wyrd. He had heard of Lanovar's courage, and his compassion, of his love for practical jokes. He had been told how handsome he was, and how admired. In Kaelin's mind Lanovar had become a kind of god – or at least a man of infinite nobility and honour. That image was now tarnished. What man of honour would steal another man's wife?

He wondered if Lanovar himself had known the reason for his murder. As he lay dying on that mountainside, Jaim beside him, did he consider that his own treacherous behaviour had brought him to this?

Kaelin paused at the edge of the Five Fields, and leaned against the old separation fence. Here highlanders had to queue and show their passes. No Rigante or Pannone was allowed to enter the Varlish areas. No-one had bothered with that rule for the last two years, so he had been told. Other rules, though, remained in force here in the south. No highlander could own a horse over fourteen hands, nor carry a sword, nor own a pistol.

Even as he thought it he realized he still had his Emburley pistols, hidden in concealed pockets within his ankle length leather coat. 'You idiot,' he chided himself. He had intended to hide them in the wagon before they entered the town. Four years away, and now a husband and father, and he had committed a hanging offence in his first moments in Eldacre.

Kaelin walked on. The town had grown in the last four years, spreading out over the hillsides. New homes had been constructed on the ridge meadow, and the avenue leading to the town centre and the cathedral had been widened. Tall, cast iron lamp pillars had been set in the road, and Kaelin saw a lamp lighter moving along the avenue carrying a set of steps. There were many people in the town centre, heading off towards taverns or dining establishments. Only a few of the older people still wore the white wigs that once typified a Varlish gentleman.

Kaelin came to the towering cathedral, and paused to watch people crossing the square. Here, four years ago, Jaim Grymauch had fought his way to Maev Ring's side and cut her free from the execution pyre.

The tall young highlander closed his eyes, and pictured the face of his friend and mentor. All anger left him then. It was no surprise that Jaim had never told him about Lanovar's weaknesses. Jaim rarely spoke ill of anyone, and Lanovar had been his greatest friend.

Leaving the cathedral grounds Kaelin spent an hour wandering the streets, revisiting places he remembered from childhood. Grimm's Bakery was no longer at the corner of Weaver's Street. It had been replaced by a clothing store. That was a shame. On feast days Maev would often take Kaelin to Grimm's, and buy a slab of raisin bread, topped with spiced icing. He paused at the shop front, remembering the joys of those bygone days.

'That is a fine coat, sir,' said a young man standing in the doorway. 'I'll warrant the leather was not crafted on these shores. The stitching is exceptional.'

'It was made by my wife,' said Kaelin, coolly.

'She has great talent, sir. We have many new items on display inside. Some splendid gloves have just arrived from Varingas.'

'Thank you, no,' said Kaelin. 'Tell me, what happened to Grimm's?'

'The old man died, sir. Two years ago. His widow sold the business.'

Kaelin strolled away, back through the town centre, making his way to the Black Boar Inn, where Maev had reserved rooms. The inn was one of the oldest buildings in Eldacre, and, though it had been renovated and expanded over the centuries, still retained some of its original features. Part of the stables at the rear – so the owner maintained – had once been the meeting hall of the Long Laird, a contemporary of the great king, Connavar. Kaelin had never stayed at the Black Boar, but he and Jaim had once dined there. Jaim had got into a fight with two timber men, had downed them both, and he and Kaelin had been forced to sprint away into the night to avoid the Watch soldiers.

The inn was crowded, and Kaelin eased his way to the bar. Here he gave his name to a round-shouldered man with a short-cropped grey beard. The man led him through to the rear of the building and up a short flight of stairs.

'You want me to tell the lady you've arrived?' asked the man.

'No. I'll see her later.'

The room was small, but a fire had been laid in the hearth, and the innkeeper lit a lantern, which he placed on a table by the bedside. Once alone Kaelin walked to the window and stared out into the street below.

Maev wanted him to meet the Moidart, to stand face to face with the man who had murdered his father. The thought was abhorrent to him. And yet Maev was right. It was vital to know one's enemies. The Moidart was an evil man, cold and deadly. He hated the Rigante, and, had it not been for this awesomely stupid

207

war, would have led his forces against Call Jace and the clans. One day we'll have to fight him, thought Kaelin.

On that day I will avenge Lanovar.

*What of Gaise Macon? What of your brother?* The thought leapt unbidden to his mind. Kaelin sighed. 'He is not my brother,' he said aloud. 'And if he comes against me I'll kill him.'

Aran Powdermill once had a cat. It was an exceptional rat killer. Grey and sleek it would sit quietly as the rat showed itself, its golden eyes watching unblinking. There seemed to be no tension in it, no desire or bloodlust. It would watch and wait. When it pounced Aran would always jump. The movement was so swift, sudden and deadly. The cat never played with its prey. It moved in and killed. Then it would pad away to its resting place beneath the window, and wait for another victim.

Aran could not help thinking about the cat as he stood in the company of the Moidart. The earl had spent most of the day with the unfortunate Marl Coper. The screams had been quite chilling. When the Moidart finally emerged he went to his rooms and bathed and changed. He was now wearing a grey silk jacket, embroidered with silver, over a white lace shirt, trousers of charcoal grey and knee length boots. His black and silver hair was neatly combed, though Aran struggled to avoid looking at the small splash of blood on the hair at the Moidart's right temple.

'What do you know of the Orb of Kranos?' asked the Moidart.

'Might I sit, lord? I have a near permanent ache in my right leg. It is hard to concentrate while in pain.'

The Moidart gestured to a chair. Aran sat and massaged his calf. The pain had been growing worse of late, especially if he had to walk any distance, or stand for more than a few minutes. 'The Orb is said to be a vessel of some kind, perhaps a—'

'It is a skull,' said the Moidart. 'What does it do?'

'A skull! Yes, that was the description given by Prassimus in one of the oldest texts. He maintained it was the skull of a great king – a man who believed he was immortal. According to Prassimus he was a vampire of great power. He was destroyed in a war thousands of years before the dawn of our history.'

'Where did he come from?'

'Prassimus?'

'Kranos.'

'No-one really knows, lord. There have been some archaeological finds across the narrow sea. One hundred years ago a burial mound near Goriasa was found to contain three gold tablets, upon which was a script no-one could translate. There were also items that pre-dated our own civilization. A vase I recall that was crafted from volcanic rock. To this day no-one has been able to ascertain how it was created.'

'Vases do not interest me. Could this Kranos have been from my lands?'

'Why would you think so, lord?'

'Coper tells me that Winter Kay has spent years acquiring maps of the highlands north of Eldacre. He has also studied Rigante history and is fascinated by their myths.'

'I suppose Kranos *could* have come from the north,' said Aran. 'There are certainly the remains of ancient structures in various sites.'

'We'll think of that later,' said the Moidart. 'What powers does the Orb possess according to your study?'

'Regeneration and renewal are most mentioned. The healing of wounds, the increase of physical strength. Delay of the signs of ageing. These virtues were said to be enjoyed by the *Dezhem Bek* – the servants of the Orb.'

'The Ravenous Ravens,' said the Moidart.

'You are well read, my lord.'

'Not at all. Young Master Coper explained it to me.'

'Ah yes.'

'Why were they called ravenous?'

'I had always thought it was alliteration, lord. Poetry,' he added.

'I know what alliteration means. The word ravenous, however, is interesting. Eternally hungry. For what? Power? Bloodshed? The Redeemers have built a reputation for excess. Is it because they desire it – or they need it? Coper talks of touching the skull and feeling a thrill of power – a satisfaction unlike anything he has experienced before. He says the feeling is most exquisite after violent activity. By which he meant torture and murder. I fancy he did not find it quite so exquisite today – as the victim.'

I expect that you did, thought Aran, miserably.

'Give the matter some thought, Master Powdermill. I need to know the limits of their power, and the drawbacks to it. Do you know the Wyrd of Wishing Tree woods?'

Aran jerked. The change of tack was sudden. He struggled to gather his thoughts. 'I have met her, lord. She is of the Old Way. There are not many left now.'

'Fewer since Winter Kay began seeking them out and killing them. She is one of the last. Why would he want her dead?'

'I have no idea, lord.'

'Then use your brain,' snapped the Moidart. 'I do not expect you to be able to answer these questions instantly. I pose them so you can consider the answers. These *Dezhem Bek* must desire something. In order to achieve it they need to kill a mad woman of the forest. Looked at another way, they fear her. As matters stand, Master Powdermill, we cannot win against these Redeemers. They not only have the power of the Orb, but are masters of the army. Therefore we need to know what knowledge this woman possesses. Not so?'

'I see your point, lord,' said Aran. 'According to the legends Kranos was slain by a great hero. Some even say it was his son. He cannot again return to the world of blood and flesh. Yet his body was invested with enormous powers, and so his Orb – his skull – carries great magic. It seems inconceivable that such magic could be threatened by a Rigante Wicca woman.'

'I do not believe it is necessarily the magic which is threatened,' said the Moidart. 'The magic is merely the power which drives them towards whatever they desire. It is that *goal* which the Wyrd threatens. If a man has a race horse and someone seeks to cripple it he does not do so because he does not like the horse. He does it so that it will not win a race. It is the race we must identify. In legend what do these *Dezhem Bek* desire?'

Aran considered the question. He had not studied the texts for many years. 'I do not think I can help you with this problem, my lord,' he said, at last. 'You need a scholar of greater wit than I.' He took a deep breath. 'I was rather hoping to return to my home, having fulfilled the service I promised.'

'Your hopes are immaterial to me. And you are not thinking

clearly. Do you believe you can appear at my side, engineer the deaths of three Redeemers, be seen by Lord Winterbourne himself, and then depart to your home with no fear of reprisal? God's teeth, man, they will be hunting you till the day you die. Believe me, you will be safer in my service.'

'As you wish, lord,' said Aran, determined to be gone from Eldacre as soon as the household was sleeping.

'I will also supply you with an extra ten pounds for every month you serve me up to a full year. If we are both alive at year's end I will double the entire amount and give you lands and a fine house. It is up to you, Master Powdermill. Serve me and become rich, or run off into the night and answer to the Redeemers or the Harvester – whichever finds you first.'

'A difficult choice, lord. I'll need time to think on it.' Aran looked into the Moidart's eyes, and felt a shiver go through him. 'I have thought on it and will accept your kind offer,' he said.

'Wise,' said the Moidart. 'Now, these ward spells you have placed around the manor. How far can we rely on them?'

'They will need to be recharged daily, lord. I cannot guarantee they will keep out all the spirits. It would be advisable not to discuss plans of action unless I am present to *see* whether any Redeemers have breached my defences. What we need are holy relics. True relics, not the dross held in the cathedral. Charms blessed by the Veiled Lady or Persis Albitane are the strongest. There are not many in the north.'

'Can you find them?'

'Given time, lord. Time, however, is not with us, I fear.'

'That is true. I expect another attempt on my life any day now. The Redeemers can communicate with each other over vast distances. They have people in the north. They will have been primed to come after me. The Pinance is also allied with Winterbourne. I expect he will be raising an army even as we speak.'

'You seem to be taking this matter very calmly, my lord,' said Aran.

'Go and rest, Master Powdermill. Then set to work finding out what Winterbourne really wants. Find out why he fears the Wyrd. This, I believe, is the key.'

'I will, lord,' said Aran, rising. 'Did you want me to spirit-travel south and find out what is happening with your son?'

'Can you communicate with him?'

'No, lord.'

'Then he is on his own. Concentrate instead on what will keep *us* alive.'

Back in his own room Aran Powdermill pondered the questions set by the Moidart. Could the Wyrd truly be so powerful that she could prevent the Redeemers achieving their goal? Aran doubted it. Why then did they hunt her? The reason men have hunted our kind since the dawn of time, he thought. Fear. We have a natural power they neither possess nor understand. The Wyrd knew the old magic, Powdermill believed. It could both heal and kill. The fact that she hesitated to use the darker spells would not placate the Redeemers. Merely knowing she possessed greater power than they would be enough to make them want her dead.

And me, thought Powdermill, miserably.


Kaelin Ring had never been close to the Moidart's Winter House. Few highlanders ever had – unless to be taken to the lower dungeons, never more to see the light of day. The building was impressive, without a trace of gaudiness, and crafted in the style of the country manors found in the south. Three storeys tall and built of stone, faced beneath the eaves with white-stained timbers, it was an elegant structure of some forty rooms. The grounds were extensive and bordered by a high wall. Entry to the manor was through a huge set of wrought iron gates, guarded by four sentries in bright yellow uniforms.

Both Maev and Kaelin were searched for weapons, and then escorted through to the inner buildings.

As Kaelin walked alongside Maev he glanced at the many soldiers patrolling the grounds. The precautions seemed excessive. The Moidart was not a popular man, but he was not as hated as he had been back in the days of the clan uprisings.

Galliott the Borderer came out to meet them at the main doors. He offered a bow to Maev. It seemed to Kaelin that the soldier was uneasy in the presence of his aunt. As well he might be, since he had commanded the soldiers at her abortive execution and it had been his musketeers who had shot down Grymauch.

'Welcome to the Winter House, Maev Ring,' he said.

'Thank you, captain,' she replied coolly. 'You remember my nephew, Kaelin.'

'I do. You have grown, young man. Life in the north obviously agrees with you.'

'Aye,' said Kaelin.

A huge figure emerged from the doors above them. Huntsekker, in his old bearskin coat, came walking down the steps. He bowed as he saw Maev. 'You are looking well, lady,' he said. 'It is good to see you again.' Maev nodded in his direction, but did not speak. Huntsekker glanced at Kaelin, and he smiled broadly. 'Well,' he said. 'Another familiar face. Last time I saw you it was with that old rascal Grymauch. Damn, but I miss him.'

Kaelin was surprised by the sincerity in the man's voice. 'We all miss him, Harvester,' he said.

Galliott led them inside. A small, white-haired man came out of a side room and walked up the stairs. He glanced back at Kaelin and gave an awkward smile, showing gold teeth. Galliott showed them to a waiting room and summoned a servant, ordering the man to fetch refreshments for the Moidart's guests. Maev sat in a deep armchair, but Kaelin remained standing and strolled to a window. Through it he could see a stretch of lawn leading to a meadow. Beyond that he watched a squad of soldiers patrolling the perimeter wall. Galliott left them and Maev let out a sigh. 'Relax, Kaelin,' she said. 'You are making me nervous.'

He turned from the window and smiled. 'It is hard to feel comfortable when one is this close to evil,' he said. 'The last time I saw Huntsekker I held a pistol to his face. Had Jaim not stopped me I would have sent him to hell.'

'I know. And yet it was Huntsekker who escorted me from the execution square. Had he not done so I would now be dead.'

'I never understood that,' admitted Kaelin. 'The man is a cold killer.'

'He liked Jaim. He did it for him.'

'How could he like him? Jaim stole his bull and made a fool of him, and he stopped him catching Chain Shada. It makes no sense to me.'

'You of all men should know that Jaim touched hearts. No-one hated him. Not even Galliott. When those musketeers came Galliott tried to stop them shooting. Even he didn't want to see Jaim dead. Beware the Harvester, Kaelin. But don't hate him.'

'Have you noticed how many guards there are?' said Kaelin, transferring his gaze back to the window. 'It is as if they are expecting a siege.'

At that moment the door opened and a servant told them the Moidart would see them. Maev pushed herself to her feet and Kaelin followed her and the servant along a panelled corridor, up a flight of stairs, and into a long study. A fire was burning in the hearth. Kaelin found his heart beating faster as he gazed upon the Moidart. The man was sitting at a desk by the window, his black and silver hair drawn back tightly from his lean face. His eyes were hooded and pale, his lips thin. He did not rise from his chair as Maev approached, but gestured for her to take a seat. Kaelin he ignored.

'Welcome back to Eldacre, madam,' he said. The voice was deep and cold. There was a controlled tension in the man that put Kaelin on edge.

'I trust you are well, my lord,' said Maev. 'This is my nephew, Kaelin.'

The Moidart's eyes flickered towards the young highlander. 'The son of Lanovar,' he said. 'I have heard of you.'

At the mention of his father's name Kaelin felt a rise of anger. All colour fled from his face. He stood staring at the seated man, and, in that moment, wanted nothing more than to leap across the room and tear out his throat. He looked into the Moidart's eyes, and knew that the older man understood his feelings. He could read him as easily as a child's book. Kaelin also saw that the Moidart's right hand was hidden below the desk top. He took a deep breath. 'Aye,' he said, 'the son of Lanovar. Though, sadly, I never knew him.'

The malevolent gleam left the Moidart's eyes, and he transferred his attention back to Maev Ring. For a little while they spoke about the business of cattle, the improvement of stock and the shipping of herds. In that time Kaelin regained his composure. Maev had been right. It was wise to have taken this opportunity to

214

meet the Moidart. He was not like any man Kaelin had ever met. It was not just that he was chilling; there was about him a fierce intelligence that should never be underestimated.

The meeting ended and Maev rose and curtseyed. The Moidart thanked her for taking the time to visit. As Kaelin turned away towards the door the Moidart spoke. 'Give me a few moments of your time, Master Ring.' He walked to the door, opening it for Maev, who glanced back anxiously at her nephew. The Moidart gave a thin smile. 'No harm will befall him, madam, I can assure you.' He pushed shut the door and returned to his seat.

'You are an able and astute young man,' he said. 'Some years ago you entered the barracks building at Black Mountain and freed a prisoner. A brilliant and well thought out action, requiring initiative and nerve.' Kaelin stood very still. 'I mention this to show a little goodwill,' continued the Moidart. 'On another day I would have had you arrested and hanged, but – happily for you – this is not another day.' The Moidart looked away from Kaelin and called out, 'Come in and join us, Master Powdermill!'

A panel behind Kaelin slid open, and the little man with the gold teeth entered the room. 'Are we alone?' asked the Moidart.

'We are, my lord.'

The Moidart swung back to Kaelin. 'My understanding is that you are acquainted with a woman known as the Wyrd of the Wishing Tree woods.'

'She is a friend of mine,' said Kaelin.

'Good. There are those who want her dead.'

'Are you one of them?'

'Not today. My enemies want her dead. Therefore I want her alive. These enemies have great powers, Master Ring. They can attack her through magic, and through might. You cannot protect her from magic. You can, however, use your strengths and your skill to ensure no assassin reaches her. You can also tell her that she has an ally in the Moidart.'

'An alliance she would not welcome,' Kaelin pointed out.

'I dare say you are correct. Have you heard recently from Call Jace?'

'No, but he was well when last I saw him. I shall tell him you asked about his health.'

215

'He is not well now, Master Ring. Two days ago he had a stroke, and is paralysed down his left side.' The Moidart gestured towards the little man with the gold teeth. 'This is Master Powdermill. Like the Wyrd he has an ability to see events over great distances. The Black Rigante are, at this moment, leaderless. The timing is unfortunate. By the spring an army will be marching on us. I can raise perhaps three thousand good fighting men, two thousand more in chaff and cannon fodder. Ten times that number will oppose me. A force of Rigante would be most welcome.'

Kaelin suddenly laughed. 'I find this hard to believe,' he said. 'The man who murdered my mother and father, and hundreds of other Rigante men, women and children, believes the clan would fight for him. I admire your gall. If an army is coming against you I hope they take you, and rip your heart out.'

'Yes, yes,' said the Moidart. 'I am sure you feel better for that. Now that it is out of the way let us look coolly at the facts. The army that will come will devastate the land, butchering the people of the north in their thousands. *All* the people, not just Varlish. Destruction, terror and chaos will sweep the land. For some reason – though I have yet to ascertain why – the enemy is fascinated by Rigante history and myth. Their leader has been gathering maps of Black Rigante lands for some years. It is he who seeks to kill the Wyrd. Why her death is important to him I have – as yet – no idea. It is my hope that she will. All I require from you is to protect her as best you can. Powdermill will contact you, and perhaps, together, we can find a way to thwart the enemy.'

'Who is this enemy?' asked Kaelin. 'Luden Macks?'

'No, the threat will not come from the Covenanters, but from Lord Winterbourne, the marshal of the king's armies, and his Redeemers.'

'You are standing against the king?' said Kaelin, amazed. 'But your own son is a part of that army.'

'Indeed he is – if he still lives. Fate, Master Ring, often displays a grim sense of humour – as evidenced by this conversation. You are my natural enemy. I do not deny it. Both blood and history make us what we are. Should we both survive the coming blood-shed – which, sadly, is highly unlikely – we will become enemies again. I would certainly enjoy watching you hang. At this moment, however, you are important to me. Will you protect the Wyrd?'

'I shall. She is my friend. I do not desert my friends in their need.'

'Most touching. Think also on what I said about the Rigante, Master Ring. If Eldacre falls you cannot stand alone. I will also supply one thousand pounds in gold to distribute among the Rigante warriors and their families should you decide to fight alongside me.'

Kaelin Ring felt tension easing from his frame. 'You need to be a little more persuasive,' he said. 'All I have is your word that these things are happening. You say an army is coming against you. This I believe. Perhaps the king has finally decided to rid himself of your evil. Or perhaps it is exactly as you say. The problem is that your word is worthless. A long time ago you promised my father safe conduct at a meeting to make peace. You murdered him there.'

'He actually died a little later,' said the Moidart, 'but that is by the by. Interestingly enough that is the only time I have ever broken my word. I won't say that I have been haunted by it ever since, or any other such nonsense, but it was regrettable. I will say that because of this – small – regret I did not later seek out and kill the big fool who tried to rescue him on that day. Grymauch was his name. He charged in, wearing a scarf wrapped round his face. It was a ludicrous disguise. He was the biggest clansman in the area, and everyone knew he was Lanovar's right hand man. However, this is also irrelevant. I do not dispute, Master Ring, that in the eyes of the Rigante I am evil. It is a matter of perspective. History is largely concerned with achievers, men who change the course of their nation. To the people of Stone the Emperor Jasaray was a great man and a hero, and Connavar was a vicious and evil savage. To the Rigante Jasaray was a vile conqueror and Connavar a hero. Heroes and villains, Master Ring, are largely interchangeable depending on historical circumstance. It is almost amusing. I loathe the clans. Always have. Their independence of thought prevents any cohesion of purpose. They were conquered because of this. And conquered peoples are weak. I abhor weakness. Yet – and here is the sweet irony, Master Ring – if we succeed in this venture we will protect the Rigante, and future generations will talk about the blessed, heroic Moidart who stood tall against the forces of evil. The Varlish in the south will view me – a man who admires them above all races – as a grotesque traitor. Perspective, Master Ring. I cannot convince you of the truth at this time, but I expect the Wyrd – if she still lives – will do so.'

'Then you had better pray she does live,' said Kaelin.

'I don't pray, Master Ring. I act. Given the choice I would now be allied to the enemy and on the verge of becoming richer and more powerful. Unfortunately that enemy chose to threaten my son. They sent men to kill me. So here I am getting ready to battle in a cause I do not believe in, against an enemy with superior forces, and superior powers. The one advantage I have is that the enemy has displayed stupidity. My hope is they will do so again.'

'That stupidity would be . . . ?' enquired Kaelin.

'Coming against *me*, Master Ring. Oh, and the small matter of trying to kill the child . . . Feargol. They failed not once but twice.'

'Twice?'

The Moidart swung to Aran Powdermill. 'Tell him.'

'They sent killers out to murder your wife and son and Feargol Ustal. They did not succeed,' he added swiftly. 'Draig Cochland and his brother got to them first and helped them escape into Call Jace's territory.'

'They are safe?'

'Aye, they are,' said Aran Powdermill. 'Though your man Senlic is dead, as is Eain Cochland.'

'I shall return north,' said Kaelin. 'If the Wyrd tells me your words are true I will do all I can to raise a Rigante force and march them to Eldacre.'

'Very good, Master Ring,' said the Moidart, extending his hand. Kaelin Ring stared at it, then looked into the man's pale eyes. The Moidart gave a wry smile. 'Yes, I suppose that the sweetness of irony can only be pushed so far.'

Mulgrave was tired as he strolled across the bridge towards the little church. He had slept poorly these last few nights, his mind roiling with unresolved questions. Outlying scouts had been reporting troop movements, which made little sense during a cease-fire, and yesterday sixty wagons had arrived, removing all powder and supplies from the new depot constructed on the orders of Cordley Lowen. It seemed to Mulgrave a waste of time, money and

218

effort to construct a depot and then almost immediately abandon it. Added to which it meant that the soldiers of the Eldacre Company now had only the ammunition and powder they were carrying. Should Luden Macks break the ceasefire the Eldacre men would be unable to fight for more than a day. Mulgrave had put these worries to Gaise Macon. 'We will probably be ordered else-where within the next few days,' the young general had said. 'Obviously the high command have decided to move the lines.'

'The high command, sir, is Lord Winterbourne. Do you feel comfortable knowing that our men now have no source of ammunition? Tomorrow they are removing the food supplies.'

'No, I don't feel comfortable, my friend. It is most galling to be left in a reactive situation. We can do nothing. We must await orders. However, we can ensure the scouts move further afield. I want to know of any further troop movements in the area.'

'Why so, sir?'

'The line is being drawn back. Save for us. We are now sitting out in the open, with no reinforcements to call upon. The nearest Royalist forces are now six miles east of us. I can make no sense of it. If Macks was to attack we could be surrounded and wiped out before any help arrived.'

'*If* any help was ordered to arrive,' said Mulgrave.

'Tell the scouts they are to avoid being seen.'

Mulgrave had smiled. 'That is the point of being a scout, sir, surely?'

'I mean by our own allies as well as the troops of Luden Macks.'

The words had chilled Mulgrave.

Now, as he made his way to Ermal Standfast's cottage, he found himself relaxing. The little priest's company was always a joy. Yet when he arrived he saw a small wagon outside the door. As he approached it he found it was packed with items of Ermal's furniture, and a great many boxes. There were bundles of books tied with string. Two men emerged from the house carrying an old leather chair. They nodded to Mulgrave as they passed.

The swordsman entered the cottage. The main room was almost empty now, and Ermal came into sight from the lower bedroom, carrying yet another bundle of books. He saw Mulgrave and gave a nervous smile. The two men returned. Ermal handed them the books, asking them to place them in the wagon. After they had done so he gave them each a silver chailling. The men touched their caps and walked out.

'What is happening here?' asked Mulgrave.

'I am . . . er . . . leaving for the south, Mulgrave.'

'This is a swift decision. Only yesterday you said you were looking forward to the spring.'

'Yes, it is a little swift. But the decision is made.'

'What is wrong, Ermal?'

'Nothing. Nothing at all. I have a sister in Varingas. I . . . feel the need to put the fears of war far behind me.'

'It seems to me that you are frightened, Ermal.'

The little man's shoulders sagged. Mulgrave saw him glance nervously towards the ceiling. 'Yes, I am frightened. Wars do that to me. I would like to live quietly in the capital. You remember telling me of your dreams of the white-haired old woman . . . who lived in the south by the sea? Yes, of course you do,' he added swiftly. 'She felt that death was hunting her. I have been having those same dreams, Mulgrave. The very same ones that you told me about. I am not a young man any more. I just want to live out my life, and study my books, and help people where I can with a few medicines and powders. I am not a warrior. I want no part in the violence that is all around me. I don't want hungry carrion birds pecking at my eyes. You understand? They are here. You only have to look in the trees around us to see them waiting to feed. I wish you well, Mulgrave. Now I must go.'

He moved towards Mulgrave and shook his hand. The swordsman saw the sheen of sweat upon the old priest's features.

'May the Source be with you always,' said Mulgrave.

Ermal Standfast's eyes shone with repressed tears. 'I do not think He cares overmuch about weak men like me,' he said.

Then he took his old coat from its hook and struggled into it. Mulgrave walked with him to the wagon. They spoke no more and Mulgrave stood silently as the vehicle trundled over the snow. Ermal did not call out a farewell. Nor did he wave.

Mulgrave returned to the silent house. The fire was still burning, though there were no chairs to sit upon. Even the old hearth rug was gone. The swordsman sat down upon the floor. Ermal's words

220

had been strange. Mulgrave knew he was trying to tell him something, but had spoken as if they were being overheard. The white-haired woman was in the north, not the south. She had not been hunted by death, but by the *Dezhem Bek*.

'*I have been having those same dreams, Mulgrave. The very same ones that you told me about.*'

Ermal had also dreamt of them.

'*I don't want hungry carrion birds pecking at my eyes. You understand? They are here. You only have to look in the trees around us to see them waiting to feed.*'

Hungry carrion birds. The Ravenous Ravens. The *Dezhem Bek*. *They are here.*


Winter Kay had long believed himself to be above rage. He saw the outpourings of violent anger as indications of a lesser intellect. Which was why he was struggling to control the volcanic state of his own temper. How could Marl Coper have been so stupid? Could he not detect the simple ward spells around the manor? And to shoot the Harvester without bothering to find the body? Such complacency deserved torture and death. Winter Kay poured himself a cup of cold water and sipped it. Calm yourself, he thought. Think!

All of his plans over the years had been meticulously orchestrated, with almost complete success in every quarter. Orders had been given and carried out. Good men had been recruited, while the weak and the difficult had been brushed aside or killed. The king was now an irrelevance, the Covenanters about to be destroyed, and the wonderful wholeness of the strategy on the verge of a triumphant completion.

He wandered to the window and stared down at the castle grounds. Some of his guests were wandering the gardens. Several riders were cantering across the open land beyond the western wall on a hawking venture. The lead rider, wearing a purple sash, was the king. The sun was shining now with the promise of spring. Winter Kay took a deep breath.

Let us seek a little perspective here, he told himself. I was complacent in the question of Gaise Macon. Ferson was a cowardly fool, Macon brighter than I had anticipated. It will not save him

221

now. Thoughts of Macon's impending demise helped relax him. Yet what of the Moidart? This was a real source of regret. The man would have been a great help in the cause. I should have gone to him sooner, thought Winter Kay. I should have healed his burns and made him one of us.

Too late now.

A light tapping sounded at the door. 'Come in, Velroy,' he called.

Eris Velroy entered and bowed. The man looked tired, his face ashen. His eyes darted to the box on the table, containing the Orb of Kranos.

'Sit down, man,' said Winter Kay. Velroy pushed a hand through his thick, sandy hair, then rubbed at his dark-ringed eyes. He slumped to a seat. 'You managed to break through the ward spell?'

'It was not necessary, my lord. The Moidart had no spell placed over the dungeon. I think he wanted us to see the torture of Marl. It was ghastly.'

'No doubt. The Moidart is highly skilled in such practices. He frightens you, doesn't he?'

'He does, my lord,' admitted Velroy.

'Where is the Pinance now?'

'He is gathering his forces. They will march on Eldacre at week's end. Twelve thousand men, boosted by a division of five hundred knights. They have few cannon, though, as yet. The Pinance believes that the Moidart will move his men into Eldacre Castle and seek to hold out there.'

'As soon as Macks is destroyed we will deploy three more regiments in the north. What of Macy and his men?'

'They will attack Shelding tomorrow morning at dawn.'

'Always dawn,' said Winter Kay. 'I have often wondered why it is never midnight or dusk.'

'Yes, my lord,' said Eris Velroy, wearily.

'Macy has two thousand men. How are they allocated?'

'Three hundred musketeers, fifteen hundred cavalry and two hundred heavy infantry with pike and sword.'

'And Macon?'

'Just under six hundred, my lord. One hundred musketeers, four hundred and fifty cavalry and forty riflemen.'

'Most of whom will be asleep when the attack begins. Very well. You made it clear that I want Macon's head delivered to me?'

'I did, my lord.'

'Excellent. Tonight the world order changes, Velroy. Tomorrow a new age begins. It will be the Age of the Redeemers. I shall be riding with Kalmer and his knights – after saying my sweet farewells to the king and his family.'

'Will you take the crown yourself, my lord?'

Winter Kay looked into Velroy's tired eyes. 'You know, young Marl was always asking me such questions. He wondered why I never answered them. I suspect, having watched him die, you now know why.'

Velroy swallowed hard. 'Yes, my lord.'

'Come, make obeisance to the Orb. Restore your strength. The night to come will be long and bloody.'


Gaise Macon scanned the reports from his scouts. Columns of mounted soldiers had been seen heading west, some three miles north of Shelding. This was most odd. Luden Macks – who was camped some twenty miles west – had agreed a truce and a four-mile-wide neutral area between the armies. Shelding was at the western edge of this area, and if cavalry units were heading west they would be in danger of breaking the ceasefire.

And it was not only cavalry that had been identified. Taybard Jaekel had seen units of artillery on the southern road the previous night. Major movements of this kind would usually have followed meetings of the General Staff, and yet Gaise had not been summoned to any such gatherings.

Not only was the Eldacre Company now apparently excluded from such meetings, but with the withdrawal of supplies they had been left with food that would not last more than another two days.

Had it not been for a moment of luck they would also have lost their horses. This last incident had angered Gaise and he had written a letter to Lord Winterbourne. Earlier in the afternoon he and Mulgrave had decided to ride out and scout the countryside. They had walked to the long meadow where the four hundred and fifty cavalry mounts were picketed – and arrived to find the grey-haired sergeant, Lanfer Gosten, involved in a furious argument with an officer of the Second Lancers. A troop of twenty riders were sitting their mounts close by.

'What is going on, Lanfer?' asked Gaise, as he approached the group.

'This gentleman says he has orders to remove our horses to new locations, sir,' said Gosten. 'It's not right. You can't leave cavalrymen without mounts.'

'Indeed you cannot,' agreed Gaise. He walked to where the officer sat a handsome grey gelding.

'I am Gaise Macon.'

'I have orders, general, to remove—'

'Get off your horse.'

'Sir?'

'You are in the presence of a general. Now get off your horse and salute.'

The man stepped down from the saddle and offered a swift salute. He was tall and slender, and wearing the red tunic, emblazoned with gold epaulettes, of a captain in the King's Second Lancers. 'Your name?'

'Konran Macy, general.'

'You are related to General Barin Macy?'

'I am his brother, sir.'

'Very well. Now what is this about the mounts?'

Macy handed Gaise his orders. They were explicit. All mounts in Shelding were to be taken to Lincster, four miles east. The order was signed by Macy's brother.

'There seems to be an error here,' said Gaise Macon. 'First, the Eldacre Company does not come under the control of the Second Lancers.'

'Lord Winterbourne has put General Macy in command of this section of the front, sir,' said the officer, smugly.

'And second, the Eldacre mounts are private property, owned by myself, and not the property of the army. Should General Macy wish to commandeer my mounts he can seek a written order from Lord Winterbourne. Such an order would be challenged by me, and subject then to a decision from a military court of inquiry.'

'My orders are to take the horses, sir. I intend—'

'Be silent! Your intentions interest me not at all.' Gaise swung to Lanfer Gosten. There were some fifteen musketeers close by. 'Sergeant, gather your men.' Lanfer Gosten barked out an order and the musketeers ran forward. 'Are those weapons primed?'

'Yes sir,' answered Gosten.

'Very well.' Gaise returned his attention to Konran Macy. 'Remount your gelding, captain. Return to General Macy and tell him I do not appreciate discourteous behaviour. Now get thee gone.'

Konran Macy stood for a moment without moving. His face had lost all colour and Gaise could see he was struggling to control himself. His blue eyes shone with anger. 'Are you deaf, or just stupid?' asked Gaise, stepping in close.

At that moment a rider behind Macy edged his horse forward. 'Konran!' he called out sharply. 'Let's go.'

Macy blinked and relaxed. Turning on his heel he walked to his horse and stepped into the saddle. With one backward glance, burning with hatred, he rode away, his men following.

Mulgrave approached Gaise. 'I think that man does not like you, sir,' he said.

'And I shall never sleep again for worry,' muttered Gaise.

'I think we should put off our ride, sir,' said Mulgrave. Gaise nodded agreement.

'Move the horses into town, Lanfer. Picket them on the common land beyond the market square.'

'Yes, my lord.'

Now, as he sat in his small study, Gaise was growing more concerned. What if Lord Winterbourne was intending a surprise attack on Luden Macks in violation of the truce? What if Macks were to break out? He would head due east – directly towards Shelding. Without mounts, with little ammunition and only one hundred and forty musketeers and riflemen, the Eldacre Company would be overrun.

As evening approached Gaise pulled on a fur-lined topcoat and, with the black hound Soldier padding at his side, left the house. Taybard Jaekel and another rifleman – a big fellow with a bushy red beard – both saluted as he came into sight.

'Warmer tonight,' said Gaise.

'Aye, sir,' answered Taybard Jaekel. 'Spring's coming.'

'Taking its bloody time,' muttered the bearded soldier. Gaise struggled to remember the man's name, which he acknowledged was a symptom of his weariness.

'Bard, isn't it?' he said at last.

'That's right, sir. Kammel Bard. You had me flogged.'

'You seem to have recovered well,' said Gaise, with wry amusement. He wished Mulgrave could have been here to witness the moment. What on earth was the proper response to a man you've ordered lashed?

'Breed 'em tough in the highlands,' said Bard. 'Rigante blood, you know.'

Gaise laughed. 'Only a few years ago it would have been an offence to say that. Now I can tell you that my own family is equally blessed. My great-grandmother was half Rigante. Fine woman, so the legends have it. Even the king now talks of his grandfather and his Rigante heritage.'

'That's why we're unbeatable, sir,' said Kammel Bard. 'We're a Rigante army.'

Gaise smiled and strolled past the soldiers, who fell in step behind him. As they reached the gate Gaise saw Cordelia Lowen walking towards him. She was dressed as if for riding, with a heavy split skirt and boots, and a tunic coat with a fur collar. Her dark hair was hanging free. Gaise felt his breath quicken and his heart begin to pound.

'Good evening to you, general,' she said.

'And to you, lady. May I introduce my guards, Taybard Jaekel and Kammel Bard – two fine lads from my homeland.' Both men bowed clumsily. Soldier padded to her. Cordelia dropped to one knee. 'Best be careful,' said Gaise. 'He's nervous around strangers.'

Cordelia tilted her head to one side and flicked her fingers. The hound instantly settled down on his haunches at her feet. Cordelia patted his head. 'He seems perfectly sweet to me.'

'Indeed so, lady.'

'Are you going to invite me inside for a hot tisane, or do I stand in the cold?' she asked.

'Inside? I . . . er . . . have no servants.'

'Is it beyond the skills of a general to fill a kettle with water and hang it over a fire?'

'I did not mean that. I meant we would be . . . alone.'

'Oh, I see. Well, do not worry, general. I am sure if I attack you your guards would swiftly come to your aid.'

Gaise sighed. He noticed both soldiers struggling not to smile. 'Very well, lady.' Turning to Taybard he said: 'If I call for help come running.'

'We'll be there in a heartbeat, sir.'

Despite her apparent confidence Cordelia Lowen felt confused and uncertain. Her normally rational mind had been in turmoil since the meeting with Gaise Macon at the mayor's gathering. It was most unsettling. She could not seem to push him from her thoughts. She kept picturing those strange eyes, of gold and green, and his quick nervous smile.

For most of the day she had found herself thinking of him, and had managed to convince herself that it was concern for his safety that was unsettling her. After all, he was a servant of the king, and if danger loomed it was her bounden duty to assist.

Now, as he led her into the little house, she knew this was only partly true. At nineteen Cordelia Lowen was no stranger to the exquisite joys of physical attraction. There had been young officers whose presence quickened her blood, and handsome men who caused thoughts which were quite wicked. No-one, however, had come close to affecting her in the same manner as this young noble-man. The thought that she would leave tomorrow and perhaps never see him again was truly ghastly.

'There is a kettle somewhere,' she heard him say.

'Pray do not concern yourself with tisane, general. I was only teasing. Might I sit by your fire?'

'Of course. May I take your coat?'

'It is a little unconventional for a single woman to enter the home of a bachelor,' she said. 'It would be considered even more unseemly were she to undress there.'

'Yes, indeed. Would you object if I removed mine? It seems uncommonly hot.'

She laughed then at his discomfort. 'Ah, to the Void with

convention,' she said, unbuttoning her jacket and removing it. Beneath it she wore a shirt of heavy silk, and a brocaded riding waistcoat of shimmering green. Gaise took the jacket from her, and hung it on a hook by the door.

'I understand you are leaving early tomorrow,' he said. 'Do you yet know your destination?'

'Father says we have been allocated a house in Lincster.'

'That's only four miles away,' said Gaise, surprised.

'I know,' she said, her good mood fading as she recalled the reason for her visit. 'It is one of the matters I wished to discuss with you.'

'It makes no sense.'

'My father is frightened, General Macon. I have never seen him frightened before. It is most unsettling. He is talking of leaving the army. Even of going to our estates near Stone. I spoke to him this afternoon and ... your name just happened to come up. He warned me not to become fond of you. My impression was that he believes something is going to happen here.'

'I think so,' he said, with a sigh. 'All powder and supplies have been removed, and this afternoon they even tried to remove our mounts. We are isolated here. If Luden Macks were to attack we'd be sorely tested.'

'I don't believe Luden Macks is the problem, general.'

He looked at her and said nothing. She found herself reddening under his gaze. 'I know my father well, and what I see in him is not just fear. I think he is ashamed. You have powerful enemies, general. I think they mean to bring you harm.'

'The thought has crossed my mind,' he admitted, with a wry smile. 'They have tried to kill me twice now. I'm sure a third attempt will come in due course.'

'Then why do you stay?'

'A good question, lady. Honour. Duty. I am a king's man. I have pledged myself and my men to his service. I cannot just ride away. That would make me an oath-breaker and bring shame upon my family.'

'Shame upon the Moidart? Now that is a novel idea.'

'He and I have never been close,' he said, a touch of ice in his voice. 'Yet still he is my father and I will not hear him slighted.'

'My apologies, sir.'

His expression softened and he smiled. 'I have heard the stories, Cordelia. I even lived some of them. My father is a harsh man – aye, and cruel. I wish I could know of one good deed to set on the side of righteousness. I don't. It is my hope that I am not like him, and that I never will be.'

'I do not think you are like him,' she said, rising from her chair. 'I do not think you are like any man I have ever met.'

'I hope that is a compliment.'

She moved in close to him. 'Have you ever been kissed, general?'

'No.'

'Then I think I shall kiss you, Gaise Macon. Unless of course you object.'

He shook his head, and she smiled at the panic in his eyes. Then she took his hand and stepped towards him. Their lips met, and the moment lingered. His arm slid round her waist, drawing her more closely against him.

When at last she pulled away her heart was beating fast. She took a deep breath. 'Take care, General Macon,' she said, her voice husky.

For a moment he couldn't speak. He felt light-headed, his emotions churning. Nothing else mattered, save the sweetness of the memory of her lips upon his. 'When may I see you again?' he asked.

Reality sent a cloud across the sunshine in her mind. 'I don't know, general. I wish I could stay. But our belongings are packed and our wagon prepared. Father is waiting. '

'No,' he said, moving close. 'Not yet. Grant me one more hour.'

They kissed again, this time more slowly. Gaise felt unsteady, and drew her back to the chair. Then he sat and gently pulled her to his lap. His arms were around her, and he could feel the firmness of her body beneath the green waistcoat. For the first time in his life Gaise Macon felt all his worries and concerns melt away. All but this moment seemed insubstantial and meaningless. Wars, battles, enmities became small, inconsequential matters. He felt he had been granted the gift of a great truth. Cordelia lifted her mouth from his and kissed his cheek and his brow. Gaise sighed and closed his eyes. Then their lips met again. In those few moments the castle walls of his secret loneliness crumbled away. The cold disregard of the Moidart, and a life bereft of close physical contact, became a ghostly memory of the past. This was the present, and it was joyous.

In full ceremonial dress of floor length crimson cloak and tunic emblazoned with the Tree of Life, Winter Kay – his head masked by a black full-faced helmet – strode through the corridors of Baracum Castle's east wing. Behind him came six other Redeemers similarly clad. Two of them were dragging a small, slender man dressed in a nightshirt of heavy white silk. All the Redeemers carried swords. Blood dripped from the blades.

Winter Kay did not look down on the bodies, which lay sprawled in the corridor. He walked on, down the circular steps to the eastern dining hall, and through it to the hidden panel before the broad staircase leading to the lower levels.

Here other Redeemers were waiting. Silently they fell in step behind their lord. Two Redeemers were waiting at the arched double doors leading to a second staircase. As Winter Kay approached they dragged open the doors.

In the Redeemer Hall below – the walls decked with blood red banners – places had been set at table. Crystal goblets of red wine stood in rows, awaiting the assembly.

Winter Kay took his place at the head of the table. Lifting the black visor of his helmet he raised a goblet. Then he waited as the crimson-garbed warriors took their places. 'The will of the Orb,' he said, his words echoing in the vaulted room.

'The will of the Orb,' they repeated. Then each drained the wine.

Winter Kay raised his hand and gestured to the two Redeemers holding the prisoner. The little man was dragged forward. He tripped and fell to his knees. 'Lift him,' commanded Winter Kay. 'A king should not be made to kneel.'

The little man drew himself up. There was a deep bruise on the side of his face, and blood from his broken nose had stained his pale, wispy moustache. The fourteenth king of the Varlish people looked into the face of Winter Kay. 'Not made to kneel?' he said, his voice shaking with anger. 'He can be dragged from his bed, and brought to a place of murder, but not made to kneel? You are a monster, Winterbourne. Foul and treacherous.'

'Ah, my liege,' said Winter Kay, his words echoing with regret, 'I, and these gallant men around us, have served the nation well and loyally. We continue so to do. Who was it that plunged the Varlish people into civil war? Who was it that made a covenant with Luden Macks, offering greater powers to the people's assembly – and then broke his word and had Macks sentenced to death? Not I, majesty. Indeed tonight this tragic war ends. Tonight Luden Macks will be dead – or his power destroyed.'

The king looked around at the Redeemers, who had once more pulled down the black visors. Each one was embossed with a bearded, demonic face, so that all the warriors looked identical. 'Well might you all cover your faces,' said the king. 'Cowards will always find something to hide behind.' He swung back to Winter Kay. 'As to you, your talent for self-deceit is colossal. You blame me for the arrest of Luden Macks. Was it not you who supplied the information that he was plotting against me? Was it not you who railed against the Covenanters, calling them traitors?'

'They were traitors – and you made them so with your vanity and your stupidity,' said Winter Kay. 'And now it is time for you to pay for your crimes.'

'I should have listened to Buckman,' said the king. 'He warned me you were a wretch.'

'And there is the problem,' said Winter Kay. 'The epitaph for an idiot king. I should have listened. You did not. Now your day is over, your house is ruined. It is time to join your wife and children.'

All colour drained from the king's face. 'You killed . . . ? Sweet heaven . . .'

'I see the full effect of your actions has finally found its way into your thick skull. Yes, my liege, your wife and your two sons had to suffer for your sins. Their deaths were swift and relatively painless. Yours will not be. Your death – and the flow of royal blood – will enhance an object of great holiness. Through it we shall rebuild this land and enter an age of golden hope and true fulfilment.'

Winter Kay gestured once more to the Redeemers alongside the king. Taking his arms they dragged him to the rear of the hall. Broken by the news of his family's fate he did not, at first, struggle. Not until they laid him on a blood-encrusted length of timber and

231

a third Redeemer stepped into view bearing an iron mallet and several iron spikes.

He screamed as the first of the spikes was hammered through his wrist.

For Winter Kay the sound was eerily musical. He felt his body relax, and his mind free itself of burdens. The screams continued as other spikes plunged home. Then the timber was hoisted into place. Unlike the unfortunate Lord Ferson the king was crucified upside down, his head only a few feet from the marble floor.

Someone laughed then. Angry that the ritual should be marred by such behaviour Winter Kay swung round to see the cause of the amusement. The king's white nightshirt had slipped down over his head. Winter Kay strode to the victim and drew a knife, cutting away the garment, which he hurled to one side.

Returning to the table he opened the black box which had been set at his place, and removed the velvet-covered skull. Holding it lovingly in his hands he walked back to the king and gently laid the skull on the ground beneath his head.

'Now it begins, my liege,' he said, softly, as he sliced open the flesh of the king's throat – carefully avoiding cutting deeply into the main arteries. Blood ran over the monarch's face and into his hair, then dripped and splashed onto the skull beneath.

Winter Kay stood and raised the knife high. 'The New Age begins, my brothers,' he said. 'Let us pray.'

# CHAPTER ELEVEN

THE WYRD OF THE WISHING TREE WOODS ROSE FROM HER CHAIR AT
the bedside of Call Jace. The once powerful Rigante leader was
sleeping fitfully. Saliva drooled from his now twisted mouth. On
the other side of the bed Chara Ring reached out and stroked her
father's face. Then she looked up at the Wyrd, her eyes questioning. The Wyrd shook her head, and gestured for Chara to follow
her from the room.

'There must be something you can do. Some magic,' said Chara.
'I cannot bear to see him like this.'

'The damage to his brain is permanent, Chara. I cannot restore
it. He will not survive more than a few days. Already his spirit is
weakening – as if he knows he will be naught but a cripple.'

'Are there not herbs to aid him?' persisted Chara. 'I know you
never liked him. He told me that. He said you thought him to be
too much like the Varlish.'

'Whisht, child! If I was at the bedside of the dying Moidart I
would heal him if I could. I was not given this gift so that I could
make judgements about who to save. Also – despite the fact that
you are right about my not liking him – I do love him. I love all the
Rigante people. If I could restore his health I would, child. That I
promise you.'

Chara looked into her green eyes, then sighed. 'I am sorry,' she said. 'That was wrong of me. It is just . . . he was so powerful. It seemed to me that nothing could ever lay him low.'

'Aye, he was a man of great strength, and great appetites. Those appetites laid him low. His liver has all but been destroyed by the quantities of uisge he has consumed. Even had the stroke not paralysed him he would not have seen out the year. I am truly sorry, Chara.'

'I'll sit with him awhile,' said Chara, sadly. 'There are things I want to say. Can he hear me?'

'I think that he will.'

Chara turned away and re-entered the bedroom, quietly closing the door. The Wyrd drew her shawl around her slender shoulders and walked out to the gallery steps and down into the wide hall below. Scores of clansmen were waiting there, but by the door she saw the hulking figure of Draig Cochland. She moved towards him, and noted that he looked away, embarrassed.

'How are you faring, Draig?' she asked him.

'I am well, Dweller. You?'

'I have known better days. What are your plans?'

'Chara has offered me a job at Ironlatch. A job.' He laughed nervously. 'I have never had a job.'

'Perhaps it will suit you.'

'Aye, and perhaps not.'

'What is troubling you?'

'Who said I was troubled?'

'Do not play games with me, Draig Cochland. I am the Dweller by the Lake. I know these things.'

'I don't feel right here, Dweller. Like a spare prick at a wedding, if you take my meaning.'

'Delicately put.'

'What? Oh. I didn't mean to offend.'

'You don't offend me, Draig. What you have done has made me proud. You should be proud too.'

'Yes, well, I'm not. If I could do it all again I wouldn't. I'd have my brother with me and we'd be safe and warm back home.'

'I think you are wrong, Draig. If you did have your wish granted you would set out alone. Regret your wasted life of stealing and whoring, by all means. Do not allow yourself to regret the one

234

great action of your life. You are a hero, Draig. Not many men can say that. Three lives will be lived out because of your deeds.'

He reddened and shuffled his feet. 'How is the great Jace?' he asked.

'Dying.'

'Nah, he'll pull through. He's tough. He's Call Jace.'

'He is a man, Draig. Death has called for him.'

'Seems like the whole world is changing,' he muttered. 'Nothing is as it was.'

'There's truth in that,' she replied, moving away, and out into the night. Rayster was standing in the moonlight, his long cloak fluttering in the breeze. He seemed to the Wyrd to radiate loneliness. He turned as she approached.

'How long?' he asked.

'A day. Perhaps two.'

'Was he my father, Dweller? I often wondered. I felt close to the man.'

'No. He was not your father, Rayster. Why are you not inside with the others?'

'I prefer my own company at such a time. How is Chara taking it?'

'Badly. There is no other way.'

'First Jaim and now Call Jace. It seems all the great highlanders are leaving us.'

'You are one of the great highlanders, Rayster. Kaelin Ring is another. Then there is little Feargol, who killed the bear. If he lives he will be great too.' They stood in silence for a while, staring at the clouds drifting over the mountains. 'The nights are getting warmer,' she noted.

'Aye. It will be good to see the sunshine and watch the flowers grow.'

Reaching out she took his hand. 'If ever you decide you need to know about your parents just speak to me.'

He shrugged. 'What does it matter, Dweller? I am who I am. I am Rigante and that counts for much.'

'The *desire* to be Rigante is what counts,' she said.

Hundreds of miles to the south-east the first drop of the king's blood splashed to the yellow bone of the skull.

The Wyrd staggered back and cried out. Rayster rushed to her side, supporting her just as she began to fall. 'Are you ill?' he asked.

'Move away from me,' she whispered, her eyes wide and staring towards the south. She began to tremble. Rayster moved back a pace, worried now. 'Further back,' she said, waving her arm at him.

As he watched her Rayster saw the wind begin to billow her white hair. Her shawl fluttered out, then blew away from her, flipping in the air. Yet where Rayster stood there was no wind, merely a slight, cooling breeze. The Dweller leaned into the gale all around her, and cried out in a language Rayster had never heard. Then she toppled to her knees and fell. Rayster stayed back no longer. Running in he knelt by her, lifting her unconscious body from the cold ground.

Inside the great round house someone shouted. Rayster carried the Dweller inside, and saw men running up the stairs. He thought at first that Call Jace had died. Laying the Dweller upon a long, leather-covered couch he touched her neck, feeling for a pulse. Reassured by the steady beat under his fingers he left her there, and followed the men upstairs. Several women were standing in the doorway of a bedroom. Rayster eased his way through the crowd. Little Feargol Ustal was sitting on the floor. A large bed had been upended and was resting against the wall. Rugs were scattered everywhere and a blanket was hanging from a ceiling rafter. Rayster moved into the room.

'What happened, little man?' he asked.

Feargol looked up at him. 'The man with the antlers came,' said Feargol, tears in his eyes. 'He brought a storm with him.'

Rayster knelt by the boy. There was a deep bruise on his cheek-bone, and a small cut on his brow. He was trembling, and Rayster took him into his arms, lifting him from the floor.

Moving back through the crowd Rayster saw the fear in their eyes. 'The boy is possessed,' he heard someone say.

Ignoring the comment Rayster carried Feargol downstairs. The Dweller was conscious now. Rayster took the boy to her.

'What is happening here, Dweller?' asked the clansman.

'Darkness and death,' answered the Wyrd.

*

Taybard Jaekel always enjoyed night duty. It was cold and lonely, but it meant freedom from the social interactions of the day. His thoughts could roam, his mind relax. It wasn't that Taybard did not enjoy the company of friends like Banny Achbain and Kammel Bard, or even that he disliked sitting in taverns with his comrades. It was just that the night was so tranquil.

He had hunkered down in the small garden outside Gaise Macon's cottage, his cloak – and an extra blanket – round his shoulders, and his thoughts were all of home. Much had changed for the young rifleman in the last four years, and at times he looked back on the wildness of his youth as if viewing the life of someone else entirely. He had been loud then, and arrogant, looking down on highlanders and seeing himself as a Varlish, proud and un-conquered. It was such a grand nonsense. Almost all of the Varlish in Old Hills had highland blood. The pure blood folk of Eldacre town referred to them contemptuously as 'kilted Varlish'.

Taybard found himself once again thinking about Chara Ward – the only girl he had ever loved. She had been murdered. Her killers had been found slain and mutilated some days later. One of the men had been a friend of Taybard's named Luss Campion. Even now it was incomprehensible to Taybard. Luss had grown up with Chara, children together, playing in the meadows behind the shop of Apothecary Ramus.

No-one ever discovered who killed Campion and his uncle, the vile Jek Bindoe. Many thought it to be Jaim Grymauch, the one-eyed highland warrior. Taybard knew this was not so. Jaim might well have killed them – but he would not have mutilated them afterwards.

At times like this Taybard would imagine what life might have been like had he and Chara married. They would have had children by now. Perhaps a girl and a boy. The boy would be like me, thought Taybard. Only I would not let him become loud and arrogant. Taybard sighed. Even had they married, where would they have lived? He had no skill and would have sought work as a labourer. They would have ended up in rat-infested rented rooms in Eldacre.

Taybard pushed himself to his feet and strolled out to the gate.

There was no movement on the roads, and even the wild dogs were silent tonight. Taybard recalled that several of them had been killed yesterday as meat grew scarce. At some point during this war I guess I'll find out what dog tastes like, he thought. He glanced across to the low wall. Kammel Bard was lying on the snow fast asleep, his blankets drawn up tightly under his chin.

If Lanfer Gosten or Captain Mulgrave were to come by Kammel would face a flogging for sleeping on duty. This did not seem to worry Kammel. He was a man of little imagination, who believed the whole world was more stupid than he. The world would be in a harsh and dreadful state were that to prove the case, thought Taybard, with a wry smile. Kammel's Emburley rifle was beside him. He had at least thought to place it under the blankets with him, but had then turned over in his sleep, exposing the weapon to the elements. Taybard walked over and retrieved it. There was snow on the flash pan cover, but the barrel was clear. With nothing else to do Taybard returned to the doorway, cleaned out the flash pan and recharged it with fresh powder. Then he laid the rifle against the inner wall of the small porch.

He had spent the last two days on scouting trips and had seen a large number of troop movements. It seemed odd to him that so many men were on the move during a truce, but then the army rarely seemed to operate on lines of logic that Taybard could understand.

He was just starting to wonder about what role he would have in life when the war was over when he saw Lanfer Gosten running down the street, another man behind him. Taybard left the porch and ran across to the sleeping Kammel, nudging him with his boot. Kammel grunted and opened his bleary eyes. 'What the hell?'

'Lanfer is coming.'

Kammel rolled to his knees as the burly sergeant arrived at the wall. He was breathing heavily. 'This man says he has urgent news for you and the general,' said Lanfer, casting a hard glance at the soldier beside him. 'Wouldn't tell me a damned thing.'

'I need to talk to the Grey Ghost,' said Jakon Gallowglass. 'And it better be pretty quick or we'll all be dead.'

*

Gaise Macon listened in silence as Jakon Gallowglass reported the surprise attack that was planned. The soldier had sneaked away into the trees as the column advanced through woods not three miles from Shelding. He had then run all the way here. Gaise thanked him, then ordered Lanfer Gosten to rouse the men from their billets. He also sent Taybard Jaekel to summon Mulgrave.

Alone now once more with Cordelia Lowen he stepped in close and raised her hand to his lips. 'I am sorry,' he said. 'The hour you granted me has put you in peril.'

'It was worth it, Gaise Macon.'

'You must go now.'

'I'll not leave Shelding without you.'

He drew her into a swift embrace, then kissed her brow. 'Go,' he said. 'Wherever you are I will find you.' Opening the door, he called out to a young soldier to accompany Cordelia to her home, and watched her walk away. She looked back, and waved. Gaise responded, then moved back inside the house.

The situation was grave. Macy, with two thousand men, cavalry and infantry, would be at the outskirts of Shelding within the hour. Gaise scanned the scouting reports received over the last two days. With the news of Winterbourne's treachery the reports now made complete sense. Two columns of artillery had been reported moving north of Shelding. One had veered to the west. The other remained beyond the northern woods. This meant that should any of the Eldacre men break clear of Macy's surprise attack from south and east they would run directly into cannon fire and be ripped to pieces.

Mulgrave arrived and Gaise swiftly explained about the coming attack.

'Why would Winterbourne sacrifice six hundred loyal men merely to kill you, sir? What sane man would do such a thing?'

'His sanity does not concern me now,' said Gaise. 'The question is: how do we survive this night? Macy will send his musketeers in from the east. He knows the men are billeted throughout the town and will expect no organized resistance.' Gaise opened a rough-drawn map of the area, spreading it out on his desk. 'The cavalry will likely come in from the south, over the bridge, seeking to find me here. They will leave two routes of apparent escape open, north and west. Both these areas will have musketeers in hiding, and cannon loaded with grapeshot.'

'A neat trap, sir.'

'Aye. Neat is the word. Macy has three hundred musketeers, fifteen hundred cavalry and two hundred heavy infantry, mostly pikemen, though some also have pistol and sword.'

'What do you plan, sir?'

'I plan to see how swiftly Macy can think and re-organize his *neat* attack. I want you to take the riflemen and musketeers to the eastern edge of Shelding. As the enemy approaches hit them with volley fire. Since this will be unexpected it is likely they will fall back towards the woods to regroup. Then they will charge. Hit them again. If they keep coming fall back to the old depot buildings.'

'Where will you be?'

'South. I'll find Macy and his cavalry. Scatter them. Then I'll charge the musketeers confronting you.'

Mulgrave smiled grimly. '*If* the cavalry is to the south you will be outnumbered three to one, and the King's Second Lancers are veterans.'

'I know. If Macy is skilled we may not get out of this alive.'

'He is not as skilled as you, my lord.'

'We will see.' Gaise moved towards the door. 'I'll either see you at the eastern end of town, or in the Void.'

'The eastern end of town would get my vote,' said Mulgrave. 'Take care, sir.'

'Care? Oh no. This is a time for recklessness.'

'For the Stormrider,' said Mulgrave.

This time Gaise did smile. Then he left the cottage. Mulgrave heard him call out orders to Lanfer Gosten.

Jakon Gallowglass crouched behind a low, dry stone wall, two muskets close by, and a smell reminiscent of old pea soup radiating from the armpits of the borrowed Eldacre tunic he now wore. He was not a happy man. Beside him Taybard Jaekel was priming a musket, which he then leaned against the wall beside his Emburley rifle.

'I thought maybe we'd be leaving this place,' muttered Gallowglass.

'Don't look like it,' observed Taybard, his eyes scanning the tree line some three hundred paces away. This section of wall was no more than forty feet long, bordering the garden of the mayor's house. Fifty of the Eldacre musketeers were hidden here. Across the roadway were three houses. There was little cover there and Mulgrave had ordered carts and wagons to be drawn up. Beyond these was a long ditch, originally built to prevent cattle from wandering through the vegetable gardens behind the three houses. More musketeers were hunkered down in the ditch, under the command of Lanfer Gosten. All the Eldacre men had been ordered to stay low.

'I thought maybe I'd go north with you,' said Gallowglass. 'Maybe take a break from the war. Maybe even settle down up there.'

'That's a lot of maybes.'

Gallowglass raised his head and peered over the wall, gauging the distance from here to the trees. A running man could cover it in just over a minute. Laden with musket or pike it would be perhaps two minutes. Certainly no more than that. Any time now, with the dawn breaking, some five hundred soldiers would be charging across that area, with maybe fifteen hundred cavalry. Cavalry would cover the ground in a third of the time. He tried to figure the odds. The Eldacre Company had around a hundred musketeers, half of them issued with two weapons. Most good musketeers could load and fire around three times in a minute. The mental arithmetic made his brain hurt. Whichever way he looked at it there was no chance of a hundred musketeers and less than half that number of riflemen holding back a determined charge – even if the cavalry were occupied elsewhere. The Eldacre men could perhaps take out around half of the attackers – and then only if they were all as skilled as Taybard Jaekel. How likely was that? Gallowglass swore softly.

'You ain't thanked me yet,' he said.

'Grey Ghost thanked you,' said Taybard. 'Heard him say it. That why you did it? For thanks?'

'Reckoned I owed you my life. Didn't expect to die for it, though. Can you smell this tunic from there?'

'I can. Pretty ripe.'

'Didn't expect to die in no stinking tunic. And it's too big.'

'It belongs to Kammel Bard. He's the big fellow over there,' said Taybard, pointing to where Kammel was sleeping again.

'He's welcome to it. Reckon if I took it off it's ripe enough to walk back to him by itself. If I don't die here he can have it back.'

'You usually talk a lot about whores. I never liked it, but I'd prefer it right about now to talk of dying.'

'I ain't scared of dying, Jaekel,' muttered Gallowglass. 'It's just that the odds favour it, I reckon.'

'Look on the bright side. You could have been about to walk out over that open ground with my rifle aimed at you.'

'Not likely. If I hadn't warned you there would have been no-one here to stop us.'

'True,' agreed Taybard. 'Having regrets?'

'Damn right I'm having regrets. I don't even know why this is happening. Were you all thinking of joining Luden Macks?'

'Not as I know of.'

'Makes no sense to me. And where the hell has the Grey Ghost gone?'

Taybard shrugged. 'No idea.'

'Well, that's comforting. I'm going to feel damned foolish if he's riding off north and leaving us behind.'

'He wouldn't do that, Jakon.'

'Well, you know him better than me,' said Gallowglass, doubtfully.

'Hardly know him at all. What I do know is he's always the first to lead a charge and he don't put us through nothing he won't tackle himself. Expect he's gone out to fight on ground of his choosing. What's Macy like as a commander?'

'How would I know?' replied Gallowglass. 'Hardly ever see him. Wish I hadn't seen him in that damned wood. His brother's a real turd. *That* I do know. Now *him* I'd like to get in my sights.' Gallowglass suddenly chuckled. 'Actually I'm not so good with a musket, so I'd prefer him to be in *your* sights. Do you ever miss, Jaekel?'

'Once or twice. Not since I've had the Emburley.'

'Well, I'll point him out to you if the cavalry come. What are the whores like in Shelding?'

Taybard Jaekel smiled. 'That's more like it, Gallowglass.'

The sound of distant gunfire came to them. Taybard glanced to the south. 'Expect their cavalry have just found out why he's called the Grey Ghost,' he said, licking his thumb and touching it to the sight of his Emburley.

Crouching low, the officer Mulgrave came alongside them. 'They're in sight,' he said. 'Wait for the command. Pass it along.'

Gallowglass resisted the urge to peer over the wall. His heart was beating faster now, though he could feel the beginnings of calm in his mind.

It was just another fight, he told himself, taking up his musket.

The first thin rays of the new dawn were shining above the eastern mountains, and the air was cold and clean, as Mulgrave watched the advancing enemy leave the sanctuary of the trees. Hidden behind a wagon the white-haired swordsman took a deep breath and scanned the line of red-coated musketeers. They were moving forward slowly, in open formation, their muskets fitted with the newly designed bayonets. Mulgrave kept his face calm. He knew the men would be watching him. More and more of the enemy moved into sight. The formation – each man more than ten feet from his nearest companion – would lessen the effects of the volley fire.

Did they know then that the Eldacre men were ready?

With practised eye Mulgrave swiftly counted the advancing line. Nearly five hundred men were now in sight, and moving out over the open land. To the extreme right came a group of Lancers. When Mulgrave first saw them his heart skipped a beat. If Gaise was wrong and the full force of the enemy were to strike here the Eldacre men would be overrun in moments. His tension was eased when he realized there were only thirty riders.

Everything depended now on the discipline of the men of both sides.

The first volley would need to be timed to perfection. Too soon and the distance would leach power from the shots and cause the enemy to charge, too late and the distance between the advancing line and the defenders would be less than the distance back to the trees. This would inspire the musketeers to continue their attack.

Mulgrave stared hard at the enemy. Did they know what they were walking into?

He focused on a group at the centre of the wide line. They were advancing warily, but he saw several of them swing their heads to talk to comrades. This calmed him. An advance against a position that was known to be defended tended to make men feel isolated. There was little conversation.

As the first of the units reached a hundred paces from the woods – a third of the distance to the defensive wall – Mulgrave shouted an order. 'Make ready!' he called. All along the wall men reared up. Muskets and rifles bristled over the stone. Mulgrave held his breath. If one idiot were to fire early it would cause a reaction. Others would follow suit and the full effect of the volley would be heavily diluted.

No-one fired.

The advancing line faltered. The men immediately behind the front carried on walking, compressing the open formation.

'Fire!' bellowed Mulgrave. Lead shot tore into the infantry, hurling men from their feet. Grey smoke billowed over the defensive wall like sudden mist, and the stink of black powder filled the air.

'Second units prepare!' shouted Mulgrave.

The fifty men issued with second muskets brought them to bear, while the other men swiftly and smoothly reloaded their weapons.

'Fire!'

Another volley ripped into the centre of the approaching infantry.

Some of the enemy began pulling back, but others stood their ground. One of their officers tried to assemble the men to return fire. He was barking out orders, and they were obeying. 'Jaekel!' yelled Mulgrave. Taybard Jaekel glanced over. Mulgrave pointed towards the officer. The young, sandy-haired rifleman nodded, licked his thumb and applied it to the sight of his Emburley.

Mulgrave swung to his right. Lanfer Gosten and the men in the long ditch were waiting for his command. 'Gosten, hold fire until we see what the Lancers plan.'

'Yes sir.'

A single shot came from Taybard Jaekel's rifle. Mulgrave saw the officer crumple and fall, his sabre spinning from his hand.

'Prepare to volley!' shouted Mulgrave.

244

Once more the muskets came into sight. A ragged volley came from the attackers. Most of the shots struck the wall, or screamed by the defenders. But several men were hit.

'Fire!'

Instinctively the Eldacre men concentrated their weapons on the group struggling to reload their muskets. They were scythed down. Beyond them the musketeers began to withdraw in good order towards the woods. On the right, however, the thirty Lancers heeled their mounts and charged.

It was a gallant and reckless move – the kind Gaise Macon may well have made. If the Lancers broke through the infantry would gain fresh heart and charge again. They had timed the move well – between volleys. But their officer should have noted that on the third volley no fire had come from the ditch.

They galloped forward, lances levelled, the new dawn sun glinting on their brocaded blue tunics. 'Ready Gosten!' shouted Mulgrave.

The fifty Eldacre men reared up. Muskets thundered. Twenty of the advancing riders were hammered from their saddles. Four other horses went down, pitching their riders to the ground. The remaining six Lancers ducked low and continued forward.

Several shots screamed into them. Another four went down. Mulgrave climbed to the wagon and drew his pistol. One of the two surviving Lancers swung his horse and tried to flee. Three shots struck him in the back. Slumping over his saddle he rode back towards the trees for a little way, then tumbled from his mount.

The last of the Lancers rode at the defences, his huge chestnut gelding clearing the wall with a graceful leap. The rider headed directly for Mulgrave. It was Konran Macy, the officer who had tried to remove the Eldacre horses.

'Give it up, sir,' said Mulgrave, his pistol levelled. 'There is no need to die today, and you can achieve nothing.'

'I can kill you, you treacherous cur.'

'You have been misled, sir. No-one here is a traitor. No-one here planned to quit the army, nor join Luden Macks. You have been lied to.'

Macy dismounted, thrust his lance into the ground, and drew his cavalry sabre. 'Do you have the nerve to fight me, sir?' he asked. 'Or are you a coward as well as a traitor?'

Mulgrave uncocked his pistol and thrust it into his belt. Then he leapt down from the wagon and drew his own blade. Macy slapped the rump of his horse. The beast moved away from the two men. The Lancer advanced.

'You are making a second mistake, captain,' said Mulgrave. 'You are being used in a private feud between Winterbourne and Gaise Macon. There are no traitors here.'

Macy attacked. Mulgrave parried and swayed away. Their sabres clashed. Macy launched a furious assault, hacking and slashing, seeking to overcome Mulgrave by brute force. Mulgrave swayed and moved, blocking and parrying, always in balance.

'Damn it, sir, can you not see you are outclassed?' said Mulgrave. 'Put up your sword.'

'They are coming again, sir!' called out Lanfer Gosten.

Macy took this moment to attack. His sabre lanced out towards Mulgrave's heart. Mulgrave blocked the lunge with ease, rolling his blade over and round Macy's weapon. The point of Mulgrave's sabre entered Macy's throat, ripping through the jugular. The officer stumbled to his knees, then pitched to the earth. Mulgrave stepped across his body and ran back to the defensive wall.

The enemy was charging. Two more volleys – which was all the defenders had time for – would not stop them now.

As Gaise Macon left the cottage and walked across to where his cavalrymen were preparing their mounts his mind was calm. There would be – hopefully – time for anger later, when the danger was past. Of all the lessons he had learned during this ghastly war this was the most important. A leader needed a cool mind in battle. As he walked he pictured the route south of Shelding. Fighting an enemy who outnumbered you three to one required several key elements for success. First there was surprise. This was vital. Men needed time to gear themselves for fighting. A sudden onslaught could lead to the most seasoned troops buckling and fleeing the field. Luden Macks, in his famous book on cavalry warfare, had called it the Consideration Effect. In short this maintained that many men would willingly risk death for a cause they believed in, and would fight relentlessly given time to consider the reasons for battle. Others less principled would fight if they knew that to refuse would mean vicious punishment or death. Hence the discipline of the army. Take orders and do your duty, for if you do not we will hang you for a coward. Given time to consider most men would also convince themselves that *they* would not die. Take away that time and the mind would revert to a simple animal state involving self-preservation at all costs.

The second key element was to leave an obvious line of escape open to the enemy. If in their panic they saw no means of escape then self-preservation would cause them to fight rather than to run.

Third there was the battleground itself. For surprise there would have to be cover, and in this area it would need to be trees and undergrowth. This posed its own problems for a cavalry leader. To operate with full effectiveness a cavalry unit needed some open ground.

Finally there was the question of motivating the men. Although the general needed to have a cool mind, the soldiers under him should have fire in their bellies, and a determination to succeed against any odds.

Gaise thought all these problems through as he walked to the town square. Men were still arriving, moving to their horses and saddling them. Gaise walked to his own mount, a tall grey gelding. Someone had already saddled him. Gaise mounted the gelding and sat quietly as his riders prepared.

The moon was bright in a cloudless sky, and the men continued their preparations in silence. Hew Galliott, a nephew of Galliott the Borderer, stepped into the saddle and guided his horse alongside Gaise.

'What is happening, sir?' he asked.

Gaise called out to the men. 'Gather round, lads.' The four hundred and fifty riders rode their horses into a circle around him and waited. 'We have been betrayed by the southerners,' said Gaise. 'All through this war we have suffered their jealousies – aye, and their envy. Northern scum, they called us. They gave us the hardest tasks, and when we performed them with distinction, still they looked down on us.' There was a murmur of agreement from the riders. 'Did we let it stop us from our duty? Did we?'

'No,' chorused the cavalry.

'Now they have decided to kill us all. Don't ask me why, lads. As we speak General Macy is leading the Second against us, seeking to find and slay us in our beds. I'll be honest with you, as I always have been. Our escape routes are blocked to the north and the west by hidden cannon. This leaves east and south. As we know the east has some rough country, ideal for infantry. My belief is that Macy will send his musketeers and pikemen from that area. Our own musketeers are waiting for them. To the south will be Macy himself and his Lancers. I for one will not wait to be slaughtered here. I will ride out and smite Macy and his men and scatter them to the winds. We have little time for discussion on this matter, but any man here who wishes to avoid this action has my leave to try to find his way home as best he can.'

He sat silently, eyes scanning the group. No-one spoke. For a moment he wondered if he had over-gilded his words. Tension was heavy in him, and he wished that Mulgrave were here, or even Lanfer Gosten. It was tempting to break the silence, but he held back and waited. Finally Hew Galliott spoke.

'When we have thrashed the Lancers,' he said, 'will we be going home?'

'Aye, Hew, we will bid farewell to the curs and head north.'

Hew Galliott swung in the saddle. 'We are going home,' he called out. 'We scatter the bastards and then we go home!'

A ragged cheer went up. 'Very well then,' shouted Gaise Macon. 'Make sure your pistols are primed and your sabres ready. In formation of twos, follow me.'

Back through the town they rode, and over the humpbacked bridge, passing the church with its crooked spire. Gaise called Galliott to him, and another man who had performed well and coolly in previous battles, Able Pearce. Able was popular among the Eldacre men, not just for his bravery, but because he was the son of the bootmaker Gillam Pearce, who had been murdered four years ago for speaking up in defence of Maev Ring when she was accused of witchcraft. This put the Pearce family at the centre of the legend of Jaim Grymauch, giving Able and his mother celebrity status back in Eldacre.

248

Gaise told Galliott and Pearce his plan of attack. They would strike the enemy on the road a mile south of Shelding, where it dipped into the woods. There would be good cover on both sides. Galliott would take two hundred men and take to the western woods, Gaise would attack from the eastern side. Able Pearce would have a hundred men in reserve, and swing out to the south, coming in either against the enemy rear, or facing them as they fled.

'Questions?' asked Gaise.

'Macy has over a thousand Lancers,' said Pearce. 'They'll be well strung out. That section of wooded road you speak of is only around six hundred yards long at the dip. It's likely there'll still be several hundred men yet to reach it when you attack.'

'True. However, Macy and his senior officers will be with the lead column. We hit them first and the rest will be leaderless when you come in from the rear.'

'Won't be able to completely close the trap, sir,' observed Galliott. 'Once we're in among them they'll be able to flee back up the slopes and away to the south, past Able and his men.'

'That's what I want. Once they are in full retreat, with no senior officers, they will pose no threat to us. Once that is achieved we ride back to relieve Mulgrave and the others.'

'We are going to take heavy losses,' said Able. 'The Second are fine fighters. They'll not break easy. We'll have wounded, and, once we are on the run, no surgeons and no hospital tents.'

'Aye, it is grim, lads. No denying it. But we'll hit them hard and fast. Hew, find a rider to scout ahead. Tell him to avoid being seen. It would be best if he wore a heavy coat over his tunic, just in case.'

'Yes, sir.' Galliott did not immediately turn away, and Gaise saw he looked troubled.

'What is it, Hew?'

'I don't get it, sir. Why would they want to kill us all?'

'I don't pretend to understand the workings of the evil mind,' said Gaise. 'Lord Winterbourne has twice tried to have me killed. I know not why. Now he has decided to achieve that murder by slaughtering the Eldacre Company. One day, if the Source is willing, I may have the opportunity of asking him the cause of his hatred.'

'He's a Redeemer,' said Able Pearce. 'Vile whoresons all of them.

They don't need a reason for evil. It's just what they are. It's the same with the Knights of the Sacrifice. I hate them all.'

'Send out the scout, Hew,' said Gaise. Hew Galliott turned his horse and moved back down the column.

'You are wrong, Able,' said Gaise, softly. 'They will have reasons. To them they will even sound like good reasons. I never yet met an evil man who thought himself evil. My father – a man as vile as any Redeemer – would laugh at being called evil. He would probably speak of dark deeds achieving a greater good.'

'My father wouldn't,' said Able Pearce. 'He was a bootmaker, and a gentle man. He never harmed anyone in his life. I used to curse the day Alterith Shaddler came to him, and prevailed upon him to stand up in defence of Maev Ring. My mother still does.'

'What changed your mind?'

'Oh, I still regret it, sir. I miss him dreadfully. I was in Varingas when it happened. I did not find out for a month. Why did I change my mind? Hard one to answer. He always taught me to stand up for what was right under my own conscience, no matter what the consequences. He did exactly that. I regret it – but it fills me with pride. I used to think he was a weak, little man. His death showed me how wrong I was. He was a great man. I pray I will do no less when my time comes.'

'I think blood runs true in your family, Able.'

'I hope so, sir.'

'Ride back and pick your men. Then we'll plan more as we ride.'

Able swung his horse and Gaise rode on alone.

Barin Macy rode at the head of the column. His mind was troubled, and he could not shake off the depression that had left him sleepless for the past two nights. Everything about this coming action was wrong. He knew it. Had known it from the start. If Macon was truly planning to defect then Eris Velroy would not have asked for a meeting in a deserted wood at night. Orders would have come directly from Winterbourne. The Eldacre Company was an elite fighting force. Macon was a dashing general, reckless and brave.

Macy had met him on a number of occasions. He liked him. There was about him a curious naiveté, which seemed odd when set against his tactical acumen. No, this action was about politics. Winterbourne hated Macon and wanted him dead. Hundreds of good, loyal men were going to die because of this hatred.

And you are party to it, Macy told himself as he rode.

Yet what choice did he have? Refusal would have resulted in his own death, or banishment. Winterbourne would then have given this task to another commander. The result would be the same. Macon and his men would be dead.

As he rode towards the woods Macy found this argument to be limp and worthless.

A rider came galloping along the line of the column. Drawing up alongside Macy he saluted. 'A message, sir,' he said, handing Macy a sealed letter. 'I was told it was for you alone, sir.' Macy thanked him. With another salute the rider swung his mount and galloped away.

Macy stared down at the seal. In the moonlight he could just make out that it was from Winterbourne. The writing above the seal was small and neat. So small, in fact, that Macy had trouble in the dim light even making out that it was his name upon it. Dawn was less than half an hour away now, and Macy tucked the letter into his tunic.

Velroy had said that the Redeemers would enter the town following the raid. That would mean citizens being tortured and burned. Macy sighed. He enjoyed army life, and when he had first joined the king's army had believed in the cause. His thoughts had been of glory, bravery and comradeship. Macy had even allowed himself the fantasy that he too could achieve the kind of fame once enjoyed by Luden Macks.

Instead he had witnessed the horrors of mutilated corpses, and listened to the agonized screams of hideously wounded men. He had learned there were no absolutes in war. No glorious heroes facing vile villains. Just men – thousands of men – all fighting and dying for what they believed in.

Until now.

Vile villains. Did they come more vile than Winterbourne and his Redeemers?

Macy hoped that Konran and the foot soldiers would have taken the town by the time he arrived. He hoped that Gaise Macon would have ridden away, escaping the cannon and the slaughter.

'Avoid evil, my son,' his father used to say. 'It carries the seeds of its own destruction.'

The column rode on, into the shadowed woods.

Some two hundred yards along the road Barin Macy drew rein. The light was increasing now. He held up his arm for the column to halt. Then he drew the letter from his tunic.

The message was short: *Macon knows of your plan. He intends to waylay you in the woods. Keep away from the road.*

Macy read the message twice, then slowly folded the parchment and replaced it in his tunic. His heart was beating faster now as he swung to look at the ground on either side of the road, as it sloped upwards into the tree line. His mouth was dry. The woods were silent, save for the sound of creaking leather and the snorting of the horses.

Then the air was filled with thunder and screaming shot.

Horses and men went down in their scores. Macy felt a blow to his back and slumped forward over his mount's neck. Struggling back to a sitting position he tried to pull a pistol from the scabbard on his pommel. Another shot struck him and he tumbled to the ground.

Horsemen came into sight, charging down the slope. Some of the Lancers managed to draw weapons and fire, but they were swiftly cut down. Others spurred their mounts and sought to gallop back down the trail.

Macy managed to crawl to the side of the road. He hauled himself to a sitting position, his back against a fallen tree. Then he watched as the men of the Eldacre Company tore into the shocked and terrified Lancers. There was no anger in Macy now. He felt calm. A neutral observer watching a drama. He noted the discipline of the attack, and its sheer ferocity. He saw with appreciation that a line of escape had been left open. Many of the Lancers were now spurring their mounts up the slope in a desperate bid to be away from the terror. Then he saw Gaise Macon, his golden hair shining in the new dawn light.

Glorious heroes, thought Macy. And vile villains.

He felt suddenly thirsty, and his mind shifted to the old well back at the manor house. He and Mirna loved that well. She always claimed that the water was magical. He smiled at the memory. When the war was over he would rejoin

Mirna and the children, and never leave again.

The fighting moved away from him, and the rising sun cleared a section of trees, the light falling upon him. It was a wonderful feeling. He tilted his head to enjoy it. A shadow fell across him. Opening his eyes he saw Gaise Macon step down from his mount and walk towards him.

'Good morning to you,' said Macy.

'And to you, general. Your men are scattered or dead. I have no time to deal with your wounded.'

'No, I expect not. Beware if you head west or north, Macon. There are cannon hidden.'

'I know. We are not traitors,' said Gaise Macon.

'I worked that out. To my shame I came anyway.' Macy reached for the letter in his tunic, and winced. Pain was beginning to radiate from his chest and lower back. He handed the letter to Gaise Macon, who read it swiftly. Macy spoke again. 'Velroy told me the Redeemers can *see* events at great distance. They are probably watching us now.'

Gaise Macon gently opened the offier's tunic, and examined the wounds. He said nothing.

'It is going to be a nice day,' said Macy, tilting his head towards the sun. He saw Mirna at the well. He was about to ask her to draw him up some water.

Then he was falling.

Down and down into darkness.

He had no idea the well was so deep.

Gaise Macon saw him die. 'You were a good man, Macy,' he said. Returning to his grey Gaise stepped into the saddle.

The Lancers were fleeing now in disorder and many of the Eldacre men were returning to the wood. From the distance came the sounds of a musket volley. Gaise felt a sudden sadness swamp him. Then Cordelia Lowen's face appeared in his mind. I will survive this, he thought. I will save my men and take them – and Cordelia – north. Away from this war. There was a parcel of land to the east of the Moidart's Winter House. Gaise had always loved it. I will build a house for us there, he decided.

Then, gathering his men, the Grey Ghost rode back towards Shelding.

# CHAPTER TWELVE

AT FIRST GLANCE JAKON GALLOWGLASS DID NOT LOOK LIKE A SOLDIER. He was thin and round-shouldered, and generally moved with a gangling gait, appearing clumsy and lacking in co-ordination. His uniforms were always ill fitting, for his right arm was two inches longer than his left. This, and his concave chest and sloping shoulders, made him entirely unsuited to the needs of fashion. He was also, as his officers would say continually, disgracefully unkempt, with little understanding of discipline. He had been flogged eleven times during his five years of service. In short, all the reports on Gallowglass stated that he was a bad soldier. He had only one redeeming feature. Jakon Gallowglass was a fighter, who didn't know when to quit.

It was a skill he needed in all its vicious glory now as he ran back through the streets of Shelding. The enemy had broken through on the right, and the fighting had moved into the back streets. Several of the citizens had tried to run for the transient safety of the meadows. They were shot down by the advancing musketeers.

Jakon Gallowglass ran round a corner, directly into three advancing musketeers. His own musket was empty, but he lashed it across the face of the first man, knocking him from his feet. Dragging his knife from its scabbard he rammed it into the chest of the second man. The third tried to impale him with his bayonet.

Letting go of his knife Jakon slid to his right, dragging the stabbed man with him. The bayonet plunged into the wounded man. Jakon leapt at the musketeer, cracking a head butt against the man's nose. He fell back with a cry of pain. Jakon shoulder-charged him from his feet and ran on. Several shots came close, one spattering stone chips from the wall beside him.

'You don't hear the shot that kills you,' he remembered someone saying.

Oh yes, he thought, as he ducked into an alleyway. So how does anyone know that then?

Weaponless now he moved swiftly down the alley, then paused at the far end, risking a glance out onto the wider street beyond. Two musketeers came alongside him. Jakon kicked the first in the knee then grappled with the second, seeking to wrench his musket from his hands. The man was strong. Jakon tried a head butt. The man swayed away. Jakon kneed him in the groin. He grunted with pain, but held on to his musket. The first man was climbing to his feet. He swore at Jakon and advanced with his bayonet poised to strike. Jakon dragged the man he was fighting around, so that he was between Jakon's body and the bayonet. A shot rang out. The first musketeer arched backwards, then dropped his weapon. The death of his comrade seemed to stun the man Jakon was grappling with. He tried to pull away. Jakon thrust his head forward, this time successfully butting the man on the bridge of his nose. With a strangled cry he fell towards Jakon, who twisted round, hurling him from his feet. Even before his assailant had hit the ground Jakon had run to the dead musketeer and swept up his weapon. The second man, blood leaking from his smashed nose, feebly brought up his own musket. Jakon thrust it aside and lanced the bayonet through the man's tunic. He fell without a sound.

Spinning on his heel Jakon saw Taybard Jaekel calmly reloading his Emburley. Bringing it to his shoulder he took aim. Jakon glanced back along the street. Five enemy musketeers had come into sight some forty paces away. Jaekel's rifle boomed and one of the men went down. The others charged. Taybard took off down the alleyway opposite where Jakon stood. Jakon needed no invitation to sprint across the road and follow him. Shots screamed around him.

He saw Taybard scramble over a low wall and ran to join him. Once more the Eldacre man was reloading. Jakon checked the flash pan of his stolen musket. It was primed.

'Ready?' asked Taybard coolly.

'Why not?' responded Jakon.

Both men reared up together. The four remaining musketeers were running down the alleyway. Jakon's shot took one of them in the face. Taybard shot another through the heart. The two survivors kept coming. Taybard laid down his rifle, and drew a pistol from the back of his belt. Cocking it he fired swiftly, the shot exploding the right eye socket of the closest man.

Jakon clambered over the wall and ran at the last musketeer, shrieking at the top of his voice. The man paused, turned, and ran for his life.

Jakon Gallowglass chuckled and swung back to where Taybard had been standing. Only he wasn't there any more. Jakon caught a glimpse of him moving past several wagons at the rear of the old supply depot.

The sound of musket fire was coming from all around now. Jakon set off after Taybard, catching up with him at the edge of a building overlooking the town square. Here there was hand to hand fighting. Jakon saw the officer, Mulgrave, and around sixty Eldacre men battling with swords against the bayonets of the enemy. Taybard reloaded the Emburley. Jakon – though not as swiftly – added powder, ball and paper wadding to his musket.

Mulgrave went down and rolled, coming up like an acrobat to plunge his sabre into the chest of a musketeer. A second man ran at the officer. Taybard downed him. Jakon fired into the crowd of enemy musketeers, then charged, screaming at the top of his voice. The noise was shrill.

More shots rang out from surrounding buildings. Enemy musketeers fell. Jakon stabbed a man. The bayonet broke in the musketeer's body. Taking the musket by the barrel Jakon wielded it like a club, smashing left and right. Lanfer Gosten and twenty more Eldacre men charged in and the town square seethed with fighting men, some grappling, some holding to their bayonets, some with daggers, and others fighting with fists and feet. It was hard and brutal, and there was no give on either side.

Then came the thunder of hoofbeats on the stone road, and Gaise Macon and his cavalry rode into the town. No more than eighty of the attacking musketeers were still alive and fighting, and at the arrival of the horsemen a lull fell. The fifty surviving Eldacre men paused and stood staring with weary malevolence at the enemy.

'Put up your weapons,' said Gaise Macon. 'No harm will come to you. You have my promise on it. Your general is dead, your cavalry in retreat.'

A bearded officer, his face bloody from a sabre cut, stepped towards where Gaise Macon sat his horse.

'There will be no escape for traitors, General Macon,' he said.

'I agree with you,' Jakon heard Gaise reply. 'The sad truth is that there are no traitors here. You have been lied to, lieutenant. There was never any intention of joining Luden Macks. You have my word on that too. There is no victory here. Only defeat for all of us. Good men have died here for no cause that I can understand. You talk of treachery. What must I call it when, while doing my duty for my king, I am attacked by forces in our own army? I tell you this – and I speak from the heart – I wish I was the traitor you believe me to be. Then there would at least be some merit in this action of yours. At least these poor dead souls all around us would not have died in vain. Gather your men, lieutenant. Leave your weapons behind. They will be here when you return.'

'What of my wounded, sir?'

'The townsfolk will tend to them as best they can. My wounded I will take with me, for they would be treated far more harshly, I fear, when Winterbourne sends in his Redeemers.'

'And will you now join Luden Macks?'

'No, lieutenant. I shall take my men home to the north. I may have been forced to become an outlaw, but I'll not fight willingly against the king or his men. Lay down your weapons and depart this place.'

'We will do that, general. I thank you for your chivalry.'

Gaise swung his horse. Mulgrave moved across to him. 'I'm sorry, sir,' he said, 'but there's something you must see.'

The swordsman moved away across the square. Gaise rode after him, and Jakon Gallowglass, curious now, followed them both.

Gaise dismounted and walked alongside Mulgrave to the house beside the supply depot. The two men entered it, and Jakon Gallowglass eased himself up to the doorway. He glanced inside. There were two bodies there, a man and a woman. The man was wearing a bright red tunic, the woman a travelling dress of green wool edged with satin. In her hand was a small pistol.

Gaise Macon knelt by the woman's body and lifted her hand to his lips, bowing his head. Mulgrave stepped in and placed his hand on the general's shoulder.

'I am so sorry, sir,' he said.

'I asked her to give me an hour, Mulgrave. It cost her her life.'

Jakon Gallowglass saw the Grey Ghost begin to weep. Quietly he moved back from the doorway and out into the street. He found Taybard Jaekel sitting on the wall of a well, cleaning his Emburley.

'Well, we survived,' said Gallowglass.

'Some of us. Kammel Bard won't be needing his tunic back. My friend Banny died in a back street. Told him to stick with me. He did and he died anyway.' Taybard let out a sigh, and then went back to polishing the ornate hammer of his Emburley. All around them were the wounded and the dead of both sides.

'I'm sorry about your friends,' said Jakon.

He could see that Taybard was suffering, and he wanted to put his hand on his shoulder the way Mulgrave had for the Grey Ghost. But he couldn't. Instead he stood and walked away. It was then that he realized the tunic no longer stank.

'Now there's a thing,' he said aloud.


The Pinance was a handsome man, tall and broad-shouldered, his features rugged. He was a fine rider, and was enjoying immensely the feeling of power as he rode his favourite black stallion, and gazed at his marching army.

He had longed for this moment for some twenty-five years. He and the Moidart had never been friends. Their parents and their ancestors had ruled adjoining lands for centuries, and there were always squabbles and ill feeling. The hatred the Pinance felt for the Moidart was not, however, born of ancestral disputes. It came to life the day Rayena Tremain had married the Moidart. Even thinking about it now – on this day of looming triumph – caused his stomach to tighten.

Though he would never admit it to others, Rayena Tremain had been the love of the Pinance's life. He had adored her to the point of worship, and had come to believe that she felt the same.

Looking back from the vastness of his fifty years the Pinance knew now that Rayena had been a feckless and unreliable woman, given to small acts of spite, and larger acts of betrayal. But back then she had been a goddess, and the centre of his life. Unfortunately for him, the Moidart's lands and his tax revenues were far in excess of those enjoyed by the Pinance and his family, and she had chosen her husband on this basis. And so the gorgeous Rayena had become the mistress of Eldacre Castle.

Two years later she was dead – slain, it was claimed, by assassins seeking to kill the Moidart. What nonsense.

By then many of the northern noblemen had heard of her disgusting affair with a clan chieftain, and had wondered why the Moidart did not put her aside. When the news came that she was dead the Pinance knew in his heart that the Moidart had killed her. He had voiced these feelings to his father, who had dismissed the idea. 'The Moidart himself was stabbed and is close to death. No, my son, put the thought from your mind.'

In the years that followed the Pinance had gathered information about the attack. None of the guards had seen the attackers. Not a single servant had glimpsed men running from the manor house. All they saw was the strangled Rayena and the stabbed Moidart. One piece of information, from a surgeon who attended the stricken earl, brought the pieces of the story together. He said there was blood on the right hand of the murdered woman, though there were no cuts to her flesh. The Pinance had guessed the truth then. The Moidart was not attacked by assailants. He was stabbed by his wife as he murdered her.

Now, twenty-five years later, he would pay for this sickening crime. He would pay for robbing the Pinance of his one true chance at happiness.

Five thousand musketeers were marching at the head of the column, flanked by outriding scouts seeking signs of enemy defensive lines. There were none. As the Pinance had expected, the

Moidart had drawn back into Eldacre Castle, secure in the knowledge that the Pinance had no cannon as yet. They were coming, however, and within days he would have the Moidart in chains.

Rarely had the Pinance experienced such sweetness of anticipation.

Twelve thousand men now marched under his command, and soon he would be the most powerful earl in the north. It was a shame they would have to breach the walls of Eldacre, for it was a fine castle, and would have made an excellent seat of government. I will have it rebuilt, he thought.

A horseman cantered his mount along the column, and drew in alongside the Pinance. The earl felt his good mood begin to evaporate as he glanced at the red-cloaked Redeemer. He did not like the man.

'The Moidart has left Eldacre,' said Sir Sperring Dale.

The Pinance glanced at the man's thin face. 'He is coming to meet us on the field?'

'No, my lord. He is fleeing to the north with five thousand men.'

The Pinance was amazed. 'You said he would hold Eldacre. You said that Eldacre was the key to the north and he would not give it up.'

'Indeed I did, my lord,' answered Sir Sperring. 'It was the logical course of action. We have been watching him, and we were led to believe this was his plan. However, he has hired a vile and demonic creature who casts evil ward spells which prevent our mystics from seeing within the castle. This creature has obviously witnessed the power of your forces, and has prevailed upon the Moidart to withdraw. Our belief is that he intends to seek aid from the Rigante.'

'Then Eldacre Castle is mine without a fight?' The Pinance laughed. 'I hate the man, but I have never before seen him as a fool or a coward.'

'He is not a military man, my lord. He is a schemer, skilled in the art of politics and treachery.'

'It seems to me that those two beasts are one and the same,' said the Pinance.

'Perhaps so,' agreed Sir Sperring. 'Yet there is some small merit in the retreat. Had he attempted to hold the castle we ourselves could have sent men north to engage in dialogue with the Rigante.'

'For what purpose?'

'Much as they may be despicable barbarians, and lacking in all civilized virtues, they are also fighting men, numbering close to five thousand. Better to assuage any fears they might have than to allow them to link with the Moidart and double his force.'

'The clan would never fight for the man,' said the Pinance. 'Sweet heaven, he has hanged, tortured and murdered them for twenty years and more.'

'Aye, he has been a rock for the Varlish people. It is shameful that such a man has become an enemy to our race.'

The Pinance glanced at the Redeemer, seeking some indication that he was making a small joke. He was not. His expression, as always, was one of earnest seriousness.

As the army closed on Eldacre town the Pinance, with his five senior officers, rode to the head of the column. He still could not quite believe that there would be no fight. They passed through the village of Old Hills and down onto the main road. Citizens came out to watch them, their eyes curious. Some of the children even waved at the soldiers, who grinned and waved back.

A tall, spindly man in a black frock coat emerged from a shop and stood staring at the marching soldiers. 'He should be taken now and hanged,' said Sir Sperring Dale.

'Who is he?' asked the Pinance, staring hard at the man.

'Alterith Shaddler. A traitor and a defamer.'

'Ah yes, the schoolteacher who defended the woman accused of witchcraft. I have heard of him.'

'There is evil in him. I can feel it.'

'I am not in the mood for a hanging today, Sir Sperring. Once we are established in Eldacre you can bring a troop back here and deal with him then.'

'Thank you, my lord. A wise decision.'

Much of the snow on the hills had melted away, and the sky was bright and clear, the sunshine warm. There were clouds building to the east, and it was likely that by evening there would be rain. It was a comfort to the Pinance that tonight he would sleep in the ancestral home of his retreating rival.

They reached the castle two hours after noon, and the Pinance left the junior officers in charge of billeting the men. Many of the soldiers were moved to the deserted barrack buildings. Others pitched their tents on the open fields beneath the southern walls.

The Pinance entered Eldacre Castle with two squads of twenty soldiers each. Sir Sperring Dale remained outside. 'I will enter when our people have found a way to remove the foul spells. They are a pain to me even at this distance.'

It took more than an hour for the soldiers to search the building. There was no-one here. Not a servant, not a stable boy. Even the dungeons were empty.

The Pinance ordered food and drink to be brought to the main hall, where he and his senior staff settled down at a long table. Three of the generals with him were relatives; cousins, reliable men with little imagination or ambition. The fourth was his nephew, Daril, a large clumsy boy with little wit. To be honest, thought the Pinance, I wouldn't trust any of them to fight a battle. Which is why he had acquired the services of Colonel Garan Beck. The man was low born, and therefore could not be offered the most senior rank, but he was a skilful soldier.

'There'll be no fighting then, uncle,' said Daril, disappointment etched in his broad, flat features.

'Not today, Daril. Tomorrow you can take a troop out towards the north and see how far the enemy has run. For today we will rest and enjoy the fruits of our first victory. After we have eaten we will take a little tour of the castle.'

'You are in a good mood, uncle.'

'Indeed I am. My enemy has fled before me. I am sitting in his chair, as lord of his castle. From today his tax revenues will be mine, and all of his belongings and lands. My mood is golden, Daril.'

The golden mood lasted less than an hour.


Apothecary Ramus closed the door of his shop, clipped a padlock in place, and then walked slowly down the cobbled street, a small package in his hands. It was a little lighter in the evenings now that spring was approaching, and the weather was definitely improving.

He wandered on, stopping to watch the new lambs in the field, snuggled down with their mothers. Several people called out to him, and he smiled politely, or bowed.

It had been a strange day. Almost everyone who had come to his small shop had wanted to talk about the coming of the Pinance and his army, and the departure of the Moidart. Ramus had no understanding of military matters, but he was glad the Moidart had gone. Ramus had no wish to gaze down upon a battlefield, or walk among the mutilated and the dead.

He remembered his father's words, said so long ago now, but still apposite. 'All wars are started by angry old men, but they are fought by young men who die for reasons that are beyond them. In the end the same old men sit around tables and the war ends. Nothing is achieved. Nothing is gained. New faces move into old castles and the sons of the dead build families ready to feed new battleground graveyards.'

Ramus had tried to ignore the southern war. People spoke of it when they came to his shop, and he gave the appearance of listening politely. But he let the words roll over him. He concentrated on the preparing of medicines, the drying and mixing of herbs, the sunshine on the hills, and the condition of his patients. For the last few days he had enjoyed immensely the new lambs. New life, experiencing the sun and the wind, scampering about the fields on spindly legs. The lambs raised Ramus's spirits.

He walked on, stopping at the house of Tomas Cantinas, the tanner. He tapped at the door. It was opened by Kellae, the youngest daughter, who called back to her mother that there was a man outside. 'What's your name?' asked the child.

'I am Ramus.'

'He says he is Ramus,' she called out.

The tanner's wife, Lyda, came from the kitchen. Ramus bowed. 'How is he today?'

'He's sleeping better, apothecary, but the weight is dropping away from him.'

And from you, thought Ramus, looking at her sunken features and red-rimmed eyes. 'I have some more herbs. They will dampen the pain and enable him to sleep.'

'Won't cure him, though, will they?'

'No. Nothing will cure him now. I have written instructions on how to administer the herbs.'

'I have no coin, apothecary,' she said, reddening.

'Pay me when you can,' he told her. 'How are you sleeping?'

Lyda forced a smile. 'Not well. The nights are the worst for him. He cries out.'

'I will bring a sedative potion tomorrow. Good night to you.' Ramus stepped back into the street, and the door closed. He sighed. Life was hard in these highlands, but death was harder. Tomas Cantinas had six children, a small business, and cancer in his bowel. His oldest son was only fourteen and would not be able to carry on the business. Ramus decided that tomorrow he would visit the local butcher, and prevail upon him to supply meat for the family.

He walked on to his house. There was light shining through the leaded lower windows, and smoke drifting up from the chimney. He opened the door. His housekeeper, Shula Achbain, came out to greet him, helping him remove his heavy black topcoat.

'Sit you down by the fire,' she said. 'I'll fetch you a glass of mulled wine.'

Murmuring thanks the little apothecary sank gratefully into his favourite armchair. Shula was a good housekeeper. Several years ago she had worked for Maev Ring, but before that she had been a herb gatherer for Ramus. Her life had been harsh. She had fallen in love with a highlander at a time when such couplings were frowned upon. Frowned upon? Ramus smiled. Shula had become a pariah to her own Varlish people. When her husband left her she and her son, Banny, had all but starved to death.

Shula returned and handed him a goblet of warmed, mulled wine. He sipped it. 'Excellent,' he said. 'Have you heard from Banny?'

'He doesn't write much, sir. He is in a town called Shelding, and there is a truce. So that is good.'

'Perhaps the war is ending at last.'

'Aye, that would be wonderful. I miss him so.' She walked to the coat rail and lifted her shawl clear. 'There is a stew upon the stove, sir, and fresh made bread in the pantry.'

'Thank you, Shula. Goodnight to you.'

Once alone Ramus settled down in his chair and dozed for a while. He found himself thinking of the Moidart. He would miss him, and their meetings to discuss painting. He had even begun to dabble himself – not attempting the awesome landscapes so enjoyed by the Moidart, but more simple compositions of flowers and herbs. They were not good, but he had noticed a small improvement during the past year. He had shown none of them to the Moidart.

After a while he grew hungry, and was about to fetch his stew when he heard the sound of horses' hooves upon the street outside. Then came a hammering at his door.

Ramus opened it. Several soldiers were standing there.

'Apothecary Ramus?'

'Yes. Is someone ill?'

'You will come with us.'

'I am finished for the day, gentlemen.' The soldier struck him in the face. Ramus fell backwards, colliding with the coat rail.

'You'll do as you're damned well told,' said the man, stepping into the house and dragging Ramus to his feet. 'You are in trouble, little man. Don't make things worse by annoying me further.'

Half stunned, Ramus was hauled from the house and lifted to the saddle of a tall horse. One of the soldiers took the reins and Ramus clung to the pommel as the cavalrymen rode at speed from Old Hills.

His head was pounding as he rode, his mind confused. '*You are in trouble, little man.*' How could he be in trouble? He had never offended anyone. Nor would he seek to, for that would be bad manners. There had to be a mistake somewhere.

The horses cantered on, down the hill road and into Eldacre town, past the billeted troops and into the castle itself. Here Ramus was hauled from the saddle and led inside. He was taken up the stairs and along a corridor. Then the soldier leading him paused and rapped at a door.

'Yes?' came the voice of the Pinance. The man sounded angry, thought Ramus.

The soldier pushed open the door and pulled Ramus inside. 'As you ordered, my lord. This is the apothecary.'

'I know who he is. We have met before. Well, what have you to say for yourself, apothecary?'

'I am afraid I don't understand you, my lord.'

The Pinance stepped forward. He was carrying a riding crop. It

265

lashed across Ramus's face. The pain was instant and excruciating. 'I am angry enough. It would not be wise to further incense me.'

'I am sorry, my lord. I don't know what you want me to say.'

'Are you an idiot? Look around you.'

Ramus blinked. He did not need to look around. A half-finished painting stood on an easel. It was a lake scene, with awesome mountains in the background. 'Yes, my lord? It is the Moidart's studio. This is where he paints.'

'You *are* an idiot. You fooled me, you laughed at me, and now you don't know why you are here.'

'Fooled you, my lord?' Ramus was mystified. 'In what way?' The Pinance raised his crop again. Ramus shrank back, automatically lifting his arm to protect his face.

'In what way?' repeated the Pinance angrily, slashing the crop across Ramus's forearm. The apothecary cried out in pain. 'In what way? Did you not know that we were sworn enemies?'

'Yes, my lord.'

'Yet you tricked me into buying one of his daubs?'

'No, my lord. You ordered me to speak to the artist. You recall? You came to my house and saw my painting. I told you the artist did not want his name revealed. When you said you desired a painting I came to the Moidart and told him. He created something beautiful for you. It was not a daub.'

'I expect the Moidart found it most amusing.'

'I think he did, my lord, but he found cause to regret it.'

'Do enlighten me.'

'You paid seventy-five pounds for it. Within a year his paintings were fetching double that. This year the value has doubled again. I think it irked him that your painting was now worth four times what you paid.'

'I don't care what it is worth. When I return home I shall take great pleasure in slashing it to shreds with my sabre.'

'Why?' asked Ramus.

The crop lashed out again and again. Ramus fell to his knees, his hands over his head. The crop brought blood from his wrist and he cried out.

The Pinance stepped back. 'Do not question me, little man. Your life hangs in the balance. What was your relationship with the Moidart?'

'He is my friend,' said Ramus.

Suddenly the Pinance laughed. 'Your friend? The Moidart has no friends. He is a serpent, cold-blooded and vile. Get up.' Ramus struggled to his feet. There was blood upon his face and hands. 'How can you talk of friendship with a monster? Did you know that he killed his own wife? The man has no soul.'

'I disagree, my lord.'

'By the Source, you are an impudent wretch. Have you not yet had enough of my crop?'

'I have, my lord. It frightens me. You frighten me.'

'Then why do you persist in annoying me?'

'I thought you wanted to hear the truth.'

'So you can prove he has a soul?'

'No, my lord.'

'Then what truth can you offer me?'

'His wounds, my lord. Many years ago he sustained a wound to his lower belly. It never healed. Then he was burned saving his son from a terrible fire. Those burns have never healed. There is no reason for them not to heal. I have given him many herbal lotions that would, in all other men, encourage healing. They don't heal because he does not *want* them to heal. They are his punishment against himself. A man with no soul would not punish himself so.'

'Perhaps they are a punishment from on high – from the Source Himself. Have you thought of that?'

'No, my lord, but it seems to me that if the Source chose to punish all evil men in such a way I would have seen it before. There is no shortage of evil in the world. Mostly, however, evil appears to prosper.'

'Are you, by chance, suggesting that I am evil?'

'No, my lord. I have never heard it said that you are evil. You are merely powerful.'

'Have you heard it said that the Moidart is evil?'

'Yes, my lord.'

'Yet you say he is your friend. A man should choose his friends with care. You obviously have not. I shall assume that the Moidart also holds you in some regard. So tomorrow I shall watch you hang, and

I will derive great pleasure from it.' The Pinance turned to the soldier who had brought Ramus to the castle. 'Take him away and find some dark and gloomy place for him.' He swung back to Ramus. 'There you can think about friendship and evil and souls.'

The Pinance had difficulty sleeping. This was rare. Normally he would lay his head upon the pillow and slip away into a dreamless state and wake refreshed. Tonight, however, he had suffered nightmares. In one he had been drowning in a lake, while a sea creature sank its fangs into his leg. He had awoken in a cold sweat, suffering from cramp in his left leg. In another he had been running through a wood, pursued by something he dared not look back at. Again he had woken with a start, and drunk a little wine.

Perhaps, he thought, the Redeemer had been right to avoid the castle. It was likely that evil spells were affecting his sleep.

The third dream was the worst. He felt a light tapping against his forehead and opened his eyes to see the Moidart sitting at his bedside, his gaunt features lit by a lamp on the table beside the bed.

Something floated before his eyes, and he realized it was a dagger blade. Closing his eyes again he sought the refuge of sleep. The dagger tapped his cheek.

'Go away,' said the Pinance, groggily.

The dagger point pierced his cheek. The pain was real and he jerked awake, causing the blade to sink a little deeper.

'There!' said the Moidart. 'Are we awake now, cousin?'

The dagger slid over his face until the point rested on his throat. 'How did you . . . ?'

'I never left, cousin. My little army did. I stayed behind with a few loyal men. You really haven't seen the best of Eldacre Castle, you know. My ancestors had all sorts of hidden passageways built, hideaway rooms, secret stairwells. Some of them are a trifle cramped. It was quite uncomfortable in places.'

'Why did you not just kill me in my sleep?'

'One should not lightly set about the task of murdering a nobleman, cousin. One wouldn't want a death that lacked dignity. My grandmother used to say that a man murdered in his sleep would wander in the Void not even knowing he was dead. A lost soul, if

268

you like. I wouldn't want your soul lost. I mean – unlike me – I would suppose you have one.'

The Pinance swallowed hard. 'You were there when I spoke to the apothecary?'

'Yes. Interesting little man, isn't he? It really surprised me when he said he was my friend. I have to own I was a little touched by that. I suppose that growing old is mellowing me. With you it seems to have increased your stupidity. Once you'd hung him what would you have done the next time you had the pox?'

'Just kill me and be done with, damn you!'

'Gently, cousin. Would you rob me of so sweet a moment? So tell me, would you really have gone home and destroyed my painting?'

'In a heartbeat.'

'You liked it, though, didn't you? You bragged of it to your friends. You were the first nobleman to purchase a work of art from the unknown painter. You it was who discovered the secret of his genius. Happy moments.'

Flat on his back, the dagger point resting on his jugular, the Pinance was helpless. There was no way he could roll free or strike out before the blade plunged home. 'Yes, I liked it,' he admitted, trying to buy a little more time. 'I often used to sit beneath it, staring up and wondering about the artist. I do not understand how a man so steeped in evil could create such a work.'

'Baffling, isn't it?' agreed the Moidart. 'Well, it's been nice to chat, but I have so much to do.'

'Wait!' said the Pinance, desperation in his voice. The dagger lanced through his jugular. Blood spurted across the pillow. The Pinance struggled to rise, to lash out, but all strength seeped away.

Just before dawn the Moidart's army marched quietly back into Eldacre. There was no fanfare, no blare of trumpets, and no attempt to attack the enemy. They marched to an area south of the castle, some little distance from the billeted invaders, and began to pitch their own tents.

A few soldiers wandered over to watch them, and stood faintly bemused. 'Is the war over then?' one of them called.

'Must be, I suppose,' came the answer.

No fighting broke out, and not a musket was raised. Other

enemy soldiers gathered, then an officer walked over. 'What is going on here?' he asked one of the men.

'Eldacre boys have come back, sir. War's over.'

The officer, as bemused as his soldiers, strolled to where Galliott the Borderer, a colonel now, was organizing the pitching of tents.

'You, sir! Do you have news?'

'No,' replied Galliott. 'I was instructed to move my men here. Is there a problem?'

'A problem?' The officer suddenly chuckled. 'I was led to understand we were here to fight an enemy. You are that enemy. Yet here we are talking. It would be helpful to know what is going on.'

'True,' said Galliott. 'Troops are always the last to be told.'

'Isn't that the truth?'

'I am told that the Moidart will address the men shortly,' said Galliott.

'The Moidart? He has made peace with the Pinance?'

Galliott shrugged. 'I know little more than you, captain. And now, if you will excuse me, I must see these tents pitched and my men fed.'

'Of course. If you hear anything would you be kind enough to relay it to me?'

'I will,' promised Galliott.

The officer wandered away, and roused several of his comrades to discuss the situation.

As the dawn light seeped over the eastern mountains a group of men came from Eldacre Castle, carrying a trestle table and its supports. They moved to an area close to the nearest tents of the soldiers of the Pinance and set up the trestle. Other men brought a high-backed chair which they placed behind it. By now hundreds of the Pinance's men had been awakened, and were standing around in groups. Many of the Eldacre men moved among them, chatting and discussing events.

Then the Moidart appeared. Dressed in a tunic shirt of black leather which shone like satin, grey leggings and black riding boots he strolled out from the castle unarmed. Behind him came a huge man, bearing a heavy sack upon his shoulder. The Moidart walked to the trestle table and gestured for the giant to lay the sack upon it.

'Gather round, if you please,' said the Moidart. 'Officers to the front. Eldacre men give way and allow our friends from the south to come close.' He waited as the men shuffled forward, then climbed to stand upon the high-backed chair. 'I am the Moidart,' he said. 'Appointed by the king as Lord of the North. I will keep my comments short, so that you can all discuss them later with your comrades at the barracks and billeted in the town. Firstly, let me address the point most soldiers care about: wages. How much are you promised?' He pointed to an officer at the front. It was the same man who had earlier spoken to Galliott.

'Three chaillings a month for officers, one for musketeers, two for cavalry, sir.'

'Has any payment been received so far?'

'No, sir.'

'Then I shall see to it that every man receives his first month's wage in full tomorrow.'

'Thank you, sir.'

'The correct address is *my lord*. Make that error again and I shall have your tongue cut out.'

'Yes . . . my lord. I am sorry, my lord.'

'Now, to move on,' said the Moidart, ignoring the hapless man. 'The Pinance has no more need for an army, but I do. Any man who wishes to join with me should remain here after I am gone and give his name to Colonel Galliott and the other officers who will attend him. Any questions?'

'Yes, my lord,' called out another captain. 'Why does the Pinance not need his army?'

The Moidart smiled and signalled the giant. The man delved into the sack and drew out the head of the Pinance, holding it high. 'Be so kind as to move among the men, Huntsekker,' he said. 'Let them all see.'

Huntsekker walked through the silent crowd, the head held aloft. The movement caused blood to begin to seep from the severed arteries. There was not a sound from the gathered men as Huntsekker moved on.

'Your attention, if you please,' called out the Moidart. 'I have much to do and cannot spend all day on this matter. All of you will, as I promised, receive your first month's wages tomorrow. Thereafter, those who choose to join me will be paid on the first

271

day of every month. Those who do not wish to remain in my employ are free to return home, without their weapons, of course. I would imagine that those with wives and children in the lands of the Pinance would not relish remaining in Eldacre. There will be a meeting of officers in the castle this afternoon an hour before dusk, to find replacements for the men whose heads remain in the sack. I shall now leave you to your breakfast, gentlemen. Any further questions will be answered by Colonel Galliott.' With that the Moidart stepped down from the chair and walked back to the castle, Huntsekker beside him, still carrying the head of the Pinance.

For a while no-one spoke or moved. They stood and watched as the Lord of the North returned to his castle. Then Galliott stepped up to the table.

'Gentlemen, your attention please. Would the senior officers attend me? We need to discuss the logistics of this situation.'

An hour later Huntsekker strolled the southern battlements, Aran Powdermill beside him.

'Can you believe it?' asked Huntsekker, shaking his head. 'I was convinced they would run for their muskets and blow us away. My heart was in my mouth when he told that officer to call him my lord, and when he said he'd have his tongue cut out . . . well! The man has balls of brass, I'll say that.'

'Soldiers like strong leaders,' said Powdermill, gloomily. Huntsekker glanced at him.

'Why so melancholy? We've damn near trebled the size of the army and our immediate enemies are dead. I'd say that was a victory to be thankful for.'

'I'll be *thankful* just to be alive two months from now.' Powdermill leaned his slender frame against the battlements and stared down at the mass of soldiers below. There were now some fifteen tables set out, and lines of men had formed before each of them. 'Galliott is a good organizer,' he said.

'Aye, he's solid,' agreed Huntsekker. 'So you think it was just the strength of the Moidart's leadership that won the day?'

'No. Not just that. He's a canny man. Soldiers *do* like strong leaders – but they are also pragmatic. The first thing he mentioned was the wages. Dead men don't pay wages. Once they saw the

Pinance's head they knew there was only one man going to do that. After all, most of them are mercenaries. If they're paid on time, and they can get strong drink and loose women they'll stay. And if they get victories. One defeat and you'll see this little army bleed away in days.'

'You *are* in a sour mood.'

'Aye, I am. Do you fear death, Huntsekker?'

The big man tugged at the twin silver spikes of his beard. 'Don't think about it overmuch.'

'Well, I thought I feared death worse than anything else. Now I'm not so sure.'

'Is this about the dream you had?'

'It *wasn't* a dream,' snapped Powdermill. 'It was a *vision*. I saw a city, and a man wearing a crown of antlers. No, not a man exactly. I don't know what he was. But I sensed his power, Huntsekker. It was colossal. This was someone – some *thing* – that could rule the living and the dead.'

'Makes no sense to me.'

'Nor me – but it wasn't a dream. I felt terror such as I never thought to experience.'

'Well, there's no terror here and now. The sky is blue. We are both alive and we have an army. I'm satisfied with that, for the moment. Now aren't you supposed to be going into a trance, or whatever you do? The Moidart wants to know what is happening with his son.'

'I'm too frightened, Huntsekker. I can avoid these Redeemers, or spit castaway spells at them. But what if the man with the antlers is waiting for me? He'll tear my soul to shreds.'

Huntsekker heaved his huge bulk onto the battlements. 'Look at it this way, Aran. There *may* be a man with antlers waiting for you. On the other hand there *is* the Moidart. He won't rip your soul from your body. He will, however, rip your body. That's a certainty.'

'Greed got me into this,' said Powdermill, mournfully. 'I swear to the Source that if I get out of it alive I'll never give in to greed again.'

Huntsekker laughed. 'We are what we are, little man. We won't change. Now set to and *see* something we can take to the Moidart.'

# CHAPTER THIRTEEN

GALLIOTT THE BORDERER STOOD UP FROM THE TABLE AND MADE WAY for Sergeant Packard to replace him. The fingers of his right hand were inkstained and his wrist ached from the hours of unaccustomed writing. The ledgers he had purchased from Wincer's Store were all full now, and the names of newly enlisted men were being written on spare sheets of paper.

And this was only the beginning. The new soldiers would have to be assigned to officers, billeted, fed, and paid. The logistical nightmare was making Galliott's head spin. He had sent riders into Eldacre to gather clerks, who would hopefully have access to a supply of new ledgers, and who would then take the responsibility of gathering names and information. It was all very well acquiring an army, but the organization of it was a massive headache.

Galliott moved away from the table. As he walked towards the castle several of the former Pinance's officers approached him, firing questions for which he had – as yet – no answer.

'All will be made plain when the Moidart meets you this afternoon,' he said, keeping his voice calm, his manner assured.

Once clear of them he entered the castle, and made his way to his own office on the first floor. Possibly twelve thousand new men now had to be absorbed into the Moidart's force. The Pinance had offered a chailling a month for musketeers, two for cavalry and three for officers. This was a third higher than the Moidart paid his own men. Therefore, to prevent mutiny and desertion all the Moidart's soldiers would need to have their wages raised. Seventeen thousand soldiers – averaging say a chailling and a half per month – would cost the Eldacre treasury what? Sitting at his desk Galliott dipped his quill pen into an ink jar and began to write figures on a sheet of paper. Seventeen thousand multiplied by one and a half made 25,500 chaillings. Dividing this by twenty to arrive at pounds Galliott discovered that the treasury would need 1,275 pounds a month merely for wages. Adding in the cost of feeding the men would raise it by . . . Angrily he tossed aside the pen.

The treasury contained just over two thousand pounds. Taxes would raise the figure by roughly four hundred pounds each quarter. The last quarter's revenues had just been gathered, so it would be twelve weeks before any new funds were available.

It didn't take a mathematician to know that the Moidart could not afford an army of this size. He had promised the Pinance's men they would be paid their first month's wage tomorrow. That would come close to emptying the treasury; in a month's time there would be nothing left to pay them.

Galliott had nothing but admiration for the Moidart's plan to defeat the Pinance. It was masterly. Yet its achievement had caused massive problems.

Picking up his quill, he worked on for half an hour, producing estimates. Then Sergeant Packard tapped at his door, entered and saluted. Packard was a big man, a twelve year veteran, solid and reliable. He was tough and brighter than his bluff, everyman manner would indicate. 'Clerks is here, sir. The lines are getting shorter.'

'What's the mood like down there?'

'Most of the soldiers are fine. They had no love for the Pinance. There's been some talk, though. A couple of my boys heard some Pinancers muttering about revenge.'

'That's inevitable.'

'I didn't have 'em rooted out, sir. Thought it might cause problems.'

'That was wise. Most of the dissenters will leave.'

'How we going to pay all these men?' asked Packard.

'Good question. I am sure it is one the Moidart has considered.'

'Yes, he's a clever man,' said Packard. 'How did he know they wouldn't fire on us the moment we marched up to the castle?'

'I don't think he did *know*,' said Galliott. 'It was a calculated risk. We didn't come in with muskets ready. We just marched slowly to the walls and began to erect tents. There was nothing threatening in our movements. If it had been the other way round would you have opened fire on the men pitching their tents?'

'I guess not. I'd have thought the generals had patched up a treaty or something.'

'There you are then. Any word on the Redeemer?'

'No, sir. Looks like he slipped away.'

'The Moidart won't be pleased with that.' Galliott pushed himself to his feet and scratched at his unshaved chin. He hadn't slept now for twenty-eight hours. He felt bone weary.

'You look all in, sir.'

'Thank you for pointing that out,' said Galliott. 'I need to see the Moidart. You keep an eye on the clerks, and make sure all the ledgers and papers are secure.'

'Yes sir. What will happen now, sir?'

'In what way, sergeant?'

'Well, we've killed the Pinance and his generals, and we've got most of his troops. So who is there to come against us? I mean the king is fighting Luden Macks. They won't be able to send a big army against us.'

'I'll remember to make your concerns known to the Moidart,' said Galliott.

The Great Hall at Eldacre Castle was rarely used. Once a year, on the Day of the Veiled Lady, its high, vaulted ceiling would echo to the sounds of music and laughter as hundreds of invited guests from Eldacre and surrounding areas came to enjoy the Moidart's hospitality. The Moidart himself, who loathed such occasions, would appear at the start, greet a few of the most important guests, and then leave the gathering to the revellers.

Now two hundred and seven officers were gathered there. There was no seating, and the three huge fireplaces were empty of coal or wood. Lanterns had been lit, and hung on brackets around the walls, the flickering light reflecting from the marble statues set in the many alcoves. The floor had been decorated with a giant Fawn in Brambles mosaic, the family crest of the Moidart.

The attending officers formed a number of groups. The forty-one Eldacre men gravitated towards Galliott at the eastern side of the hall. The Pinancers remained separate. There was a feeling of tension in the air, and Galliott was only too aware that no order had been given to disarm the newcomers. All of them wore swords and daggers, and many had pistols tucked into their belts.

There were stairs leading to a gallery at the northern end of the hall, and it was from these that the Moidart made his entrance. An immediate hush fell over the crowd, and Galliott cast nervous glances at the waiting men, dreading that one of them would pull a pistol.

The Moidart, resplendent now in a grey satin shirt edged with black silk, grey leggings and riding boots, raised his arm. 'Gather round,' he said. 'We have much to discuss.'

The officers edged forward. Galliott, his mouth dry, his heart beating wildly, moved to the front and left and stood watching the officers, his hand on the pistol in his belt.

The Moidart seemed unconcerned with thoughts of danger. His cold, hawk eyes scanned the men. 'First, I have news from the south, gentlemen. The king is dead, murdered by those he trusted.' Galliott's fear of assassination melted away. The news was stunning. No-one spoke, and the Moidart allowed his words to hang in the air. 'You will hear in the days to come,' he said, after a few moments, 'that the king was murdered by Luden Macks in a treacherous attack. This is not true. The king was slain by Lord Winterbourne. He was hung on a stake, his throat cut in a Redeemer ritual. His death was painful and slow. His children and his wife were also murdered.'

Galliott stared at the faces all around him. The silence held an almost unbearable tension. 'Luden Macks is also dead,' continued the Moidart. 'Having signed a truce he believed that both sides would hold to the old notions of chivalry and honour. Lord Winterbourne's troops attacked his camp. Macks was killed while trying to lead a counter charge. His men were scattered or slain.

Those of his generals taken alive have been burned at the stake. Winter Kay and his Redeemers now rule the south.'

Once more he paused for a moment. 'This leaves us with hard decisions to make. The Pinance was misled by the Redeemers. He was told that I was a traitor to the king. Most of you will have heard this also. It is why he marched you all into my lands. He was tricked, lied to and deceived. He died for it. You are alive. It is my hope that you are king's men, and that you will wish to see him avenged. It may be that some of you harbour Covenant loyalties. If so you may wish to see Luden Macks avenged. Others may desire to flee this coming war. By heaven, that is understandable. I wish I could flee it myself. Does any man here wish to leave now?'

No-one spoke, though the officers turned and glanced at one another. 'You need have no fear, gentlemen. There will be no treachery. Two hundred or so men have already departed for the territory of the Pinance. Any here who wish to leave may do so without fear of harm.'

'Might I ask what your intentions are, my lord?' asked a captain. He was the man who had spoken to Galliott earlier. He was young, no more than twenty years old, his hair fair, his eyes a soft brown. He did not look like a fighter, thought Galliott.

'My intentions, young man, are to fight. Winter Kay will bring his armies north.'

'Aye, my lord, I expect he will. He will outnumber us greatly and will also bring cannon.'

'Indeed so. What is your point?'

'The Pinance had ordered cannon, ready for the breaching of this castle. Those cannon will even now be on their way. It would be wise to send troops to intercept them before they hear of events at Eldacre and turn back.'

'An excellent thought,' agreed the Moidart. 'Now we must turn our attention to the structure of our forces. We have here some two hundred junior officers. Outside these walls we have seventeen thousand men. I will need four generals from among you, and twenty senior officers with the rank of colonel. In normal circumstances I would know each of you well, and have taken measure of your strengths and your weaknesses. I know few of you well, and most of you not at all. What I do believe, however, is that *you* know the men in this hall who would make the best generals and colonels. Therefore you will choose twenty-four from among your number. The twenty-four will then choose the four who will become generals. The four will report to me with Colonel Galliott in two hours. Are there any further questions?'

Galliott could see that there were, but no-one spoke. 'Very well,' said the Moidart. 'I shall leave you, gentlemen, to your deliberations. Choose wisely. Do not consider voting for reasons of advancement, or future reward. Your lives will rest on the choices you make today.' He paused, then pointed at the young captain who had spoken earlier. 'You, sir, what is your name?'

'Bendegit Law,' replied the captain.

'Well, Bendegit Law, I am promoting you to the rank of colonel. How many men will you need to take the cannon and bring them to Eldacre?'

'Two hundred should be sufficient, sir. Cavalry, of course.'

'Choose your men and leave as soon as you have cast your vote.'

'Yes, my lord.'

Without another word the Moidart turned and walked up the stairs.

As soon as he had gone the hubbub began. Galliott moved to the far wall and sat down on the floor, his back resting against the marble base of a statue. For a blessed few moments he dozed. Then an officer approached him. 'How best do you think we should conduct this election, sir?' he asked.

Galliott allowed himself the fantasy of drawing his pistol and shooting the man in the head. Then he wearily pushed himself to his feet.

Galliott was not the only weary man in the castle. Huntsekker felt the weight of his years as he walked along the corridor. His left elbow was aching, a sure sign that rain was on the way, and his heart was heavy. He had not lied to Powdermill about being relieved that the Moidart's plan had succeeded. What he had not said was how tired he was of killing. He had spent the whole of yesterday hidden with the Moidart in the secret passageways of Eldacre Castle, waiting for nightfall. When that came they had

279

sat quietly in the darkness. Once the enemy generals had taken to their beds Huntsekker had emerged. He had killed most of them in their sleep, but the Pinance's nephew had awoken just as Huntsekker's knife was poised above his throat. He had struggled, grabbing Huntsekker's wrist. Then he had begged. 'I have children!' he wailed. Huntsekker had killed him anyway.

How many was that, he wondered? How many men have I killed for the Moidart? He had lost count years ago.

Would they all be waiting for him in the Void?

Huntsekker shivered and plodded on towards the Moidart's rooms. His mind reeled with weariness and shame, which was why he forgot to knock at the Moidart's door. Instead he lifted the latch and pushed open the door, stepping inside.

The Moidart, bare-chested, was standing by his desk applying a pale unguent to his upper body. Huntsekker stood in stunned amazement. The Moidart's back was covered with angry scar tissue, the flesh twisted and puckered. There was blood seeping from a fist-sized lesion over his right hip. The nobleman was engrossed in his actions and failed to see Huntsekker, who silently stepped back outside, drawing the door closed. Then he rapped on it with his knuckles.

'Who is it?' came the commanding voice.

'It is I, my lord. Huntsekker.'

'Wait!'

Huntsekker crossed the corridor and sat on a wooden bench. The wounds looked almost fresh, and the pain from them would be ghastly. He could also tell that they extended to the man's chest, for that was where the Moidart was applying the balm. How in the name of heaven did the man carry on with his life?

'Come!' called the Moidart.

Huntsekker entered the room. The Moidart had put on a grey silk robe, and was now sitting behind his desk. The jar of unguent cream remained. Huntsekker saw that it was almost empty.

'Is Powdermill recovered?' asked the Moidart.

'Aye, my lord. Though his fear is growing. Good news, though, about the Lord Gaise escaping the trap.'

'He is not safe yet. They will send men after him. I need you to go north. At speed.'

Huntsekker's heart sank again. Who was he to kill now? 'Yes, my lord.'

'There is a woman there, named Maev Ring.'

'I do not kill women,' said Huntsekker, the words tumbling out before he could stop them.

'Kill women? What are you talking about?'

Huntsekker rubbed at his tired eyes. 'Forgive me, my lord.' He sighed. 'I am getting tired of death and I misunderstood.'

'I want you to go to her with a letter from me. I want you to tell her of the situation here and impress upon her the need for unity of purpose. She could be vital, Huntsekker.'

'In what way, my lord?'

'She is rich, and as a highlander unable to bank her wealth probably has a great deal of gold and silver hidden. My letter will request . . .' Suddenly the Moidart shook his head. 'In days not so long gone by I would have confiscated her wealth and had her hanged. Still, no point harping on about lost golden times. My letter will request a loan.'

'Why send me, my lord? Surely I am more vital here. There will still be those among the Pinancers who will wish to see their lord avenged.'

'I don't doubt it. However, you are the man for this task, Huntsekker. She trusts you. You will assure her that my word is good, and that every chailling will be repaid – with interest.'

But will it, wondered Huntsekker?

He noticed the Moidart's hawk eyes staring at him intently. 'Do you doubt my word, Harvester?'

'I have served you faithfully, my lord, and I have always been loyal. Do you doubt me?'

'Not so far,' answered the Moidart, carefully.

'Then I shall be frank. I helped Maev Ring because of Grymauch. He was a good and heroic man. I promised him that no harm would come to her while I lived. That is not a promise I will break. I am not a forgiving man and will destroy any who seek to harm her.'

'You are getting soft in your old age, Huntsekker. Time was when you would have had the wit to keep that information to yourself. It does not matter in this case. I too have a regard for

Maev Ring, and you have my promise that I will not, now or ever, seek to cause her harm.'

'Thank you, my lord.'

'You liked Grymauch?'

'I did, my lord. He was . . . colourful.'

'Which is why you lied about the escape of Chain Shada? You said you were attacked from behind, whereas the reality is that it was Jaim Grymauch who rescued the fighter. Your man, Boillard Seeton, was killed by you to prevent him from giving me his name.'

'So, Mulgrave came to you after all. That surprises me, my lord.'

'Life is full of surprises, Huntsekker. It seems no-one wanted Grymauch punished. No, it was not Mulgrave. It was a highlander arrested for stealing. He tried to barter for his life by telling a story about how, on the night Chain Shada crossed the bridge, he was seen in the company of Grymauch.'

'How did you know about Seeton?' asked Huntsekker.

'I know *you*, Harvester. Had someone else killed your man you would have moved mountains to find the killer. Since you did not, then you had to have killed him yourself.'

'You are a surprising man, my lord. Why did you not have me hanged?'

'Ah well,' said the Moidart, with a smile, 'perhaps it was because – unlike you – I am a forgiving man.' The smile faded. 'Which reminds me. Go and find the apothecary. He is in one of the dungeons. Get him out and tell him I need some more balms.'

The body of the great outlaw leader, Call Jace, was buried on a hillside overlooking the Round House. There were oaks growing there, and in the summer their leaves would shade the resting place.

More than two thousand Rigante gathered for the ceremony, which was led by the old warrior Arik Ironlatch. He spoke movingly of Call Jace's achievements, holding the Rigante together through the darkest days of Varlish dominance. While the southern clans around Eldacre had been forced to endure endless humiliations, through Call Jace's courage and cunning the harsh laws were never fully enforced in the north.

Ironlatch spoke for some time, recalling anecdotes of Call Jace's life, many of them amusing, and there was laughter in the crowd.

At the graveside stood Jace's son, Bael, a tall, redheaded warrior, his handsome face set in an expression of grim sorrow. He did not sob, for that would be unmanly, but he could not stop the tears that fell to his cheeks. Beside him was his sister Chara, and her husband Kaelin Ring. Chara took Bael's hand as the Dweller stepped forward to speak the words of farewell.

*'Seek the circle, find the light,*
*Say farewell to flesh and bone.*
*Walk the grey path,*
*Watch the swan's flight,*
*Let your heart light*
*Bring you home.'*

Then the body of Call Jace, shrouded in a Rigante banner, was lowered into the grave. Rayster stood just back from the main group, his heart heavy. The slender young clansman Fada Talis leaned in to him. 'Will you attend the Gathering?' he whispered. Rayster shrugged and said nothing.

After the Battle of the Pass four years before Call Jace and Kaelin Ring had changed the nature of the Rigante fighting machine. Before that the highlanders merely gathered at the place of battle and charged the enemy. This system had worked well through the centuries, when the enemy's tactics had been largely similar. Modern warfare with cannon and shell, musket and rifle, pike and lance required greater tactical awareness. Jace and Kaelin had re-organized the militia army, creating captains and officers, and specialist units working together with discipline. Rayster was one such officer, in command of three hundred men. As such he had attended all the meetings held to discuss martial business. The Gathering, however, was a different matter. Clan chieftains and under-chieftains would select the new leader. Was he now to be regarded as a clan chieftain? Rayster doubted it. He had no name.

Truth be told he did not greatly care. The choice would be between Bael and Kaelin Ring. Both were good, strong men. As a peacetime leader Bael, with his fine mind and keen eye for detail, would ensure the Rigante prospered. If war was coming – as the Dweller believed – then Bael would be less effective than Kaelin

Ring, though not by much. Bael was his father's son. He had courage and intelligence and he had fought well at the Battle of the Pass. Rayster would not be unduly troubled should either man be elected leader.

As the immediate family members began to fill the grave Rayster found himself watching the Dweller. She seemed more frail than before, her face pale, her eyes dark-rimmed. He saw her walk over to Chara Ring, who was crying openly. They spoke for a moment and Chara nodded, then leaned in and kissed the Dweller on the cheek. Rayster stepped forward. Chara looked up at him. 'I can't believe it,' she said.

Rayster hugged her close and kissed her brow. 'A good man gone,' he said.

Later, as the crowd streamed back towards the Round House and the settlement, the Dweller came alongside Rayster and Fada Talis. Fada moved away from them, allowing them privacy.

'You will be at the Gathering, Rayster,' said the Dweller.

'I've not been invited,' he said.

'I need you there. No-one will stop you.'

He looked into her eyes. 'You seem . . . different,' he said, softly. 'Are you ill?'

'Aye, I am sick – sick with terror. And I am angry and hurt and confused. I feel lost, Rayster. As never before.'

Rayster took her hand. 'You are not lost, Dweller. You are among your own people. You are loved here.'

She tugged on his hand and led him away from the departing crowd, back up the hill. On the brow there were two standing stones, and other fallen, broken columns. Some of the stones were carved with symbols no clansman could now decipher. The Wyrd sat down upon a fallen stone. Rayster joined her. 'Can one evil ever cancel out another?' she asked him.

'I don't know, Dweller. I do not think of these things.'

'Do you believe the Rigante should ally with the Moidart?'

'There has been much talk of this,' said Rayster. 'Kaelin Ring believes the enemy to come are evil men. He says they have sought your death. We should resist evil men.'

'The Moidart is an evil man.'

'Yes.'

'So the Rigante should partner with evil to defeat evil?'

'I am not the man to debate this with. I keep to myself, Dweller, and I live my life by my own lights. I am Rigante. I am proud to be Rigante. Yet not all that we have done has been good. When Call Jace began to exert his authority over the Black Mountains people were killed. Some of them were good people. Call said he regretted their deaths, but that the future of the clan was paramount. I suppose he would have said that the small evil of his deeds led to a greater good for the Rigante.'

'He did say that,' admitted the Dweller. 'He was wrong.'

'I cannot judge that, Dweller. If the clan decides to fight along-side the Moidart I will fight. For I am a clansman. It seems to me, though, that evil in men is never a constant. If it was, then there would be no hope of redemption, no opportunity to change. Draig Cochland's deeds would see him branded as evil, and yet he defended Chara and the children.'

'Draig's sins are as nothing compared to the Moidart,' said the Dweller. 'The man murdered his own wife. He has tortured and slain without mercy for thirty years. He is only fighting now because the enemy tried to have him killed. Given the opportunity he would ally with them in a heartbeat and betray us all.'

'Then you believe Kaelin is wrong? That we should not be drawn into this war?'

The Dweller closed her eyes. 'No. That is why I am lost, Rayster. The enemy *must* be overcome. He is a Destroyer the like of which the world has not seen in almost two thousand years. If he succeeds . . .' Her words tailed away.

'A Destroyer?' queried Rayster. 'This Winter Kay?'

'No, he is merely a servant. You will hear of the true evil at the Gathering.'

They sat in silence for a while. Then the Dweller took a deep breath. Turning towards him she reached up and touched the oval brass cloak brooch he wore. It was unadorned, save for an empty circle at the centre. All other clansmen had their family name engraved within the circle. 'Why did you not accept Ironlatch's offer of adoption, Rayster? You would have had a name. You could have stood for the leadership.'

'I am content with who I am, Dweller. Rayster No-name.' He

grinned at her. 'When I was a child I wanted a name. I wanted the name to be mine, though. My true name. Not something gifted to me. Ironlatch has sons and daughters. They carry his name and his blood. That is as it should be. I have long since ceased to stare into the faces of the older men of the clan, wondering which of them fathered me. It is enough that I am Rigante.'

'You are the *best* of the Rigante,' she told him. 'You make me proud.'

He smiled. 'When I was young I used to think that you were my mother. You always seemed to care for me so. You always visited and spoke to me when you were in the north. I wish that it were so.'

Her eyes misted, and she took hold of his hand. 'I wish that too. If ever I had a son I would want him to be just like you.' She brushed away the tears forming and stood. 'Now we must attend the Gathering.'

The thirty chieftains and sub-chieftains of the Black Rigante filed into the long room, moving to their places at the massive oval table. Arik Ironlatch stood behind the empty Leader's Chair at the head of the table. Bael took his traditional seat to the right. Potter Highstone sat beside him. Arik called out to Kaelin Ring to take his seat to the left.

When all were seated Arik Ironlatch tilted the Leader's Chair forward against the table and remained standing. Just as he was about to speak the door opened and the tall figure of Rayster entered, followed by the Dweller by the Lake. For a moment only, Arik looked embarrassed. But he said nothing. Rayster strolled over to the far wall and stood quietly, seemingly at ease.

'You wish to address the gathering, Dweller?' asked Ironlatch, after a pause.

'Aye, clansman, I do,' said the white-haired Wicca woman. 'You need to know the enemy you face.'

'I think we do,' said Ironlatch. 'Kaelin Ring tells us that Varlish from the south will soon invade our lands.'

'Would that were the only truth,' she told him. 'Sit yourself, man. Your arthritic knee will not tolerate standing for so long. I saw you favouring it at the funeral.'

'It would not be seemly to sit in Call's chair. Not today,' he said. 'I'll stand.'

'Very well. I have invited Rayster to attend this Gathering. The clan denies a vote to a man with no name, but he needs to hear what is said, and offer his advice to the chieftains. Are there any here who wish to dispute my invitation?'

'Rayster is welcome anywhere,' said Korrin Talis. 'He is my friend and a true clansman.' Others murmured agreement.

'That is good,' said the Dweller. 'They are, I fear, the only good words you will hear tonight. It is true that a southern Varlish army will be marching on the highlands. This in itself is grim news, for there are more attackers by far than defenders to face them. Even so, if this was merely an extension of the Varlish war I would advise the Rigante to stand back from it. Wars among the Varlish are not our concern.'

'I agree with that,' muttered Potter Highstone, leaning back in his chair.

'I'm with you on that, Badger,' agreed Korrin Talis.

'Yet this is no longer a war among the Varlish,' said the Dweller. 'Something infinitely more powerful – more evil – is at work. Before I explain it further we need to look back on our own history. Our legends tell us that we are the Children of the Seidh, that the Rigante were blessed by the Old Ones, and named as Guardians of the Land. Older legends talk of wars among the Seidh. Some among the gods believed that mankind would prove the salvation of the universe, in that they alone of all the animals could create earth magic, which is at the heart of all life. Others believed mankind were a plague, that they devoured the magic faster than it could be created, and would ultimately destroy life itself. These opposing views led to conflict. The eldest and strongest of the Seidh, the great Lord Cernunnos, was chosen to test mankind. He took human form and became a king. A mighty king. A dread lord. The world was plunged into terrible wars, vast numbers of people perished. The excesses of Cernunnos were colossal. Human sacrifice, mass murder, the creation of were creatures, part man, part wolf or bear. You know the legends.'

'We are not talking of legends, Dweller,' said Arik Ironlatch. 'We are talking of Varlish armies.'

'Have patience, clansman,' she said. 'Cernunnos ruled for hundreds of years. In that time he took human wives and raised many sons. One of those sons, Rigantis, rose against him. A colossal war took place. In the end Rigantis stormed the castle of his father and beheaded him. The reign of Cernunnos ended. He was the only Seidh ever to suffer death, as far as we know. Rigantis tossed away the crown, returning conquered lands to conquered peoples. He stayed in the north and raised his own sons, at last forming the Rigante clan. These are our legends. These legends are known to every Rigante child.

'And here is the hard fact: they are not legends at all. Cernunnos lived. Cernunnos reigned. Cernunnos was beheaded. But he did not die. The body was burned in holy fire, the bones reduced to ash. But not the skull. Cernunnos was a Seidh, and the Seidh took the skull. They placed it in a box of black iron, and covered it with ward spells. It was hidden then from the eyes of men. For centuries. I have not tried to follow the events all the way from that day to this, but what I do know is that the skull was found five hundred years ago. The men who found it called themselves the *Dezhem Bek*, the Ravenous Ravens. They brought the world to the brink of ruin before they were overthrown. They called the skull the Orb of Kranos, and claimed it healed wounds and offered visions. The skull disappears from history at that time, but some two hundred years later it was brought to the town of Shelsans, across the narrow sea. Priests there understood its potential for evil. They tried to destroy it, but no-one now knows how to make the holy fire. The skull was impervious to blows. They could not smash it, nor grind it. So they hid it below ground.

'It was in Shelsans that Winter Kay found the skull. Unlike the original *Dezhem Bek* he did not merely use its latent power. He fed it. He fed it with blood. A few days ago he killed the king, and allowed his blood to flow over the ancient bone. This was an error of tragic proportions. As every man here knows the king's grand-father was from the north. He had Rigante ancestors. Traces of that Rigante heritage were in the king's blood. The first Rigante were born of Cernunnos and a human wife. In effect a living part of Cernunnos – the blood of one of his descendants – was applied to the dead bone of his skull. What was before merely a relic with some latent earth magic clinging to it is now fully sentient. It hungers for life, for power. It seeks a return to the flesh. It desires to walk upon the earth, and rule as it once did. Should that happen then the war in the south will seem little more than a child's game in a meadow.'

She fell silent and approached the table. Jugs of water and goblets had been laid there. The Dweller filled a goblet and sipped the contents.

Korrin Talis was the first to speak. 'You are saying that the Seidh have returned, Dweller. Is that not what we have been praying for these last eight centuries? Have you yourself not spoken of such a miracle?'

'Aye, I have,' she admitted. 'I dreamed, as the old often do, of a return to a golden age. I thought the wisdom of the Seidh would help us restore the land. What I now understand is that their wisdom was what led them to leave us in the first place.'

'You believe then,' said Potter Highstone, 'that Cernunnos is evil?'

She shook her head. 'He transcends evil, Badger. If an ant were able to think as we do, would he not see as evil the child who stamped on him? Would the bull about to be slain for the Beltine Feast see as good and kindly the Rigante who cut his throat? Cernunnos is evil in our terms. He will bring destruction and terror on a scale not seen for millennia. He will do this because he can, and because it brings him closer to his goal: the destruction of all human life.'

'How can a skull be returned to life?' asked Arik Ironlatch.

'He is Seidh,' the Dweller replied. 'I do not understand all their powers. What I do know is that he will need to be brought into the north, to the lands he once ruled. Perhaps he needs the blood of the Rigante to regenerate himself. I do not know. What I do know is that we must oppose him. We must stop him, as Rigantis once stopped him.'

'That is all very well, Dweller,' said Bael, 'but can it be done?' In his late twenties Bael had put on weight, and looked much like his father, Call Jace. He had a strong jaw, and deep set eyes, and his manner radiated authority.

'It is not a question of whether it *can* be done,' answered the Dweller. 'Merely that it must be attempted.'

'I don't understand,' he told her. 'If we can't win, then what is the point of sacrificing ourselves?'

'We are the Rigante, Bael. We have always stood against evil. It is our fate and our destiny. We are the Children of the Seidh, the Guardians of the Land. You think Connavar would not have fought Cernunnos? You think Bane would have turned his back on the fight because he could not win? Jaim Grymauch could not win when he marched into the cathedral square to rescue Maev Ring. Fifty soldiers against one clansman? He did not know that the crowd would grab and hold the guards. He went to that square because he had to, because he was Rigante.'

Bael shook his head. 'I do not dispute that we are a brave and noble people. I believe that in my soul. Cernunnos, however, is a Seidh, and we have always worshipped the Seidh. He is also, Dweller, by your own account, the Father of the Rigante. He made us. What if you are wrong? What if he wishes to come north to lead us again? Perhaps the golden age you spoke of will be found in his service.'

'Aye, he would promise that,' said the Dweller. 'Perhaps for some around this table it would even prove to be true. You could become the new *Dezhem Bek*. Long-lived, free of disease, your every wish made reality. Gold trickling through your fingers, beautiful women obeying your every whim. Does it sound good, Bael?'

'Of course.'

'You think evil corrupts men by saying come with me and I will turn you into a merciless killer, and damn your soul for eternity? Who would agree to such a bargain? Evil corrupts, Bael, by promising us what we *want*, and telling us that it is *good*. Evil talks of the end justifying the means. It speaks of distant goals – aye, and of golden ages. It seduces, Bael. It does not threaten. Not at first. So how do we judge the merits of Cernunnos? We look at the realities. His first reign was one of blood and terror, and mass destruction. And what since? The first *Dezhem Bek* were killers, plunging the world into war. The next? Winter Kay and his Redeemers, torturing, burning, wiping out whole villages, slaying men, women and children. These are the followers of Cernunnos.'

'With respect, Dweller,' said Bael, 'we have only your word that any of this . . . history . . . is true.'

His words stunned the Dweller. She looked at him and could find nothing to say.

'You think the Dweller would lie?' put in Rayster, his face ashen. 'You will withdraw that, Bael. Instantly!'

'I am not saying anything of the kind,' snapped Bael. 'What I am saying is that one woman's view of world history is not necessarily accurate. She was not there during the time of Cernunnos, nor at the coming of these *Dezhem Bek*. These are men who have sought to use the skull for their own ends. It does not make the skull evil, any more than a sword is evil. It is the man who wields it.'

'I trust the Dweller,' said Arik Ironlatch. 'If she says we must fight, then we must fight.'

'I agree,' said Rayster.

'I am with Bael on this,' said Korrin Talis. 'What do you say, Kaelin?'

Kaelin Ring pushed back his chair and stood. Having arrived only this morning he was still wearing his travelling clothes, a jerkin of gleaming black leather, buckskin trews and boots. He had shaved off his beard, and the sabre scar on his cheek showed clearly. His dark eyes scanned the men in the room, coming at last to Bael. 'For years,' he said, 'the Wyrd – or as you call her, the Dweller – warned your father of a great evil coming from the south. Your father believed her. That is why we have spent four years training our men. Now the evil is upon us. I am not interested in ancient legends, and I have no time to debate the nature of evil, or the desires of dead gods. What I *know* is that an army will march on the north. Either we support the Moidart, or we do not. Either we fight as a clan, or we do not. I have spoken to the Wyrd, and I believe her. Therefore I will fight.'

'You are not the clan leader,' said Bael. 'You cannot choose whether we fight or stand.'

'I did not say *we*, Bael. I said *I* would fight. I will fight because it is right to do so. The Redeemers – or their minions – have killed Finbarr Ustal and his family. They cut down Senlic Carpenter. They have tried to kill my wife, and my child. They are my blood enemies now, regardless of any other consideration.'

'They are not mine,' said Bael.

'They would have been your father's,' snapped Kaelin.

Bael lurched to his feet. 'That is not true! My father also believed the Dweller. She told him the enemy was the Moidart. Now she tells us we should fight *alongside* the Moidart. What next, Ravenheart? I respect the Dweller. She has worked tirelessly for our clan, both here and in the south. But she is not infallible. She has already been proved wrong once. Why not twice?'

'You are twisting the facts, Bael,' retorted Kaelin. 'The Dweller *knew* that evil was coming. She assumed it would emanate from the Moidart. That was a natural assumption. She was not wrong, though. That evil *is* upon us.'

Arik Ironlatch moved alongside Kaelin. 'Sit down, lad. We are getting ahead of ourselves. Only one man can say whether the clan will go to war. That man is the elected clan chief. So let us do what we are here for and elect a leader.' He swung towards the Dweller. 'Lady, you have spoken your piece and we have listened to your words. It is time now for us to move on.' He turned to Rayster. 'And since we are to vote, and Rayster has no vote, he must also leave. I wish that it were not so. In fact, I repeat now my offer to formally adopt Rayster and give him my name. Should he accept then his vote will be cast with the other chieftains' here.'

Rayster bowed to the old warrior. 'You do me great honour, Arik. I would have been proud to be your son. I am not, though. So I will leave, and follow loyally whoever is elected. May I offer one thought before I go?'

'You may,' said Ironlatch.

Rayster looked at Kaelin and Bael. 'There is anger now between you,' he said softly. 'This saddens me, for you are both fine men. I was there when you fought your duel, when Bael put that handsome scar upon your face, Kaelin. I was there when you later shook hands and became brothers. You *are* brothers. You care for one another, and for the clan. Do not let anything come between you. We are all Rigante, even when our views differ.'

With that he walked from the room. The Dweller followed him. Inside all was silent for a moment.

'Four names have been put forward,' said Arik Ironlatch. 'Bael Jace, Kaelin Ring, Korrin Talis and myself. I withdraw on the grounds of age, though I thank those who considered me. Thirty men were entitled to vote. Twelve cast their vote for Kaelin Ring, twelve for Bael, four for myself, and two for Korrin. As is our way these votes were cast in secret. Now, however, we need a show of hands.'

'I wish to stand down,' said Korrin Talis.

'So be it. How many here wish to vote for Bael Jace?'

'Wait!' said Kaelin Ring, once more rising to his feet. 'I have already said that it is my intention to travel south and fight the enemy. If Bael will agree to the Rigante's entering this war then I withdraw also. If not I stand.'

Bael looked at Kaelin in surprise, then switched his gaze to Arik Ironlatch. 'What say you, Bael Jace?' asked Arik.

Bael took a deep breath, and scanned the group. He knew the men who had voted for him, and those who had voted for Kaelin. The question was: how many votes could he expect from the remaining six who had wished to see either Korrin or Arik lead the clan? Potter Highstone would have been one who voted for Korrin. The other would have been Korrin himself. Both these votes should come to me, thought Bael, though Potter had always spoken highly of Kaelin Ring. Damn, but there was no way to know! The likelihood was that Bael's destiny would be decided by a casting vote. Bael met Kaelin's steady gaze. His expression was unreadable.

Bael had two choices: take the risk that he had enough votes, or accept the leadership with the understanding that the Rigante would go to war.

Like his father before him Bael Jace was a pragmatist. Rising from his seat he moved to stand beside the Leader's Chair. 'I accept Kaelin Ring's terms. And since there are no other candidates I take my father's seat.' Pulling back the chair he sat down. 'And, before we talk of the war coming to Eldacre, would someone fetch Rayster. His wisdom will be needed here.'

# CHAPTER FOURTEEN

HAVING CHECKED ON THE SENTRIES MULGRAVE SAT QUIETLY BY THE camp fire. Around him some of the men were sleeping, others sitting in small groups, speaking in hushed voices. Gaise Macon had wandered away into the woods alone. Mulgrave was glad of this, for he did not wish to talk to him at the moment. He would not know what to say.

After the battle at Shelding Gaise had led the survivors east and then north, bypassing the enemy's artillery force. They had made good progress, despite the fact that more than forty of the men were wounded. Three had died on the journey so far. It was likely several more would succumb.

Gaise had sent outriders to scout ahead. One of these had returned on the second day of travel with news of a small column of musketeers, with some fifty cavalry, moving to the north-east. Gaise had made no attempt to avoid them. As soon as the report was received he took two hundred men and rode at speed to intercept. The fight had been brief and bloody. Gaise outmanoeuvred the cavalry and led a lightning charge against the startled musketeers. They managed one ragged volley before the Eldacre men tore into them. They were cut to pieces. Many tried to surrender, but Gaise had ordered that no prisoners be taken, and they were killed where they stood, most of them with hands raised.

Then Gaise had turned his attention to the cavalry. They sought to flee, and rode straight into the ambush Gaise had laid. Taybard Jaekel, Jakon Gallowglass, and fifty other musketeers concentrated their fire on the horsemen. The fight was over in a matter of minutes. One officer was taken alive, a young man, tall and well featured. He was in the custody of Lanfer Gosten.

Gaise rode up, Mulgrave alongside him. 'We caught this one, sir,' said Lanfer.

'Was there something about my order that you did not understand, Gosten?' asked Gaise Macon coldly.

'Sir?'

'I said no prisoners.'

'Yes, sir, but . . .'

Gaise Macon drew a pistol from the scabbard on his saddle and cocked it. The young officer saw the move. He made as if to speak. The pistol came up and the shot boomed in the morning air. The officer staggered back, his face a mask of blood, then toppled to the earth.

'Move among the bodies,' said Gaise Macon, as coldly as before. 'Strip them of all that could prove useful. Be prepared to move on within the hour.' Swinging his horse he rode away from the stunned men. Mulgrave did not follow him.

'I'm sorry, sir,' said Lanfer Gosten. 'I didn't think . . .'

'Don't apologize, Lanfer,' said Mulgrave. 'You did nothing wrong. Now follow your orders and search the dead.'

'Yes, sir. What's wrong with him?'

Mulgrave did not reply.

They made another twenty miles before dusk, acquiring supplies from a small village. Gaise paid in coin for the food. Mulgrave avoided him for most of the journey, but as they came towards the woods in which they were to make camp he rode his horse alongside the young warrior. 'That was not a noble deed, sir,' he said.

'Tomorrow we will cut to the north-west, then follow the line of the river. There are settlements along the way. We will need to leave the worst of the wounded. They are slowing us down.'

'Put aside your anger, my lord.'

'You are not my priest, Mulgrave.'

'No, sir, I am your friend.'

'Then be a friend. I need no lectures on nobility. Not today.' Gaise spurred his grey gelding and cantered on ahead.

Now as he sat by the fire Mulgrave was worried. He believed – hoped would probably be more accurate – that the murder of Cordelia Lowen had temporarily unhinged the young noble. Yet was that true? Gaise had spoken to him in the past of his fear of becoming like his father; of the constant need to hold back the demons in his soul. Had those demons now been unleashed?

Mulgrave had been raised in Shelsans. There he had learned of the strange duality that, by turn, enhanced or diminished the souls of men. 'All people are capable of great love and great hate,' his father had said. 'We are all, in spiritual terms, both angelic and demonic, constantly at war with ourselves. To understand this is to overcome it. Do not seek to justify hateful thoughts. Merely accept them as part of the flaws of humanity, and move beyond them.' His father had been a gentle, loving man. When the Knights of the Sacrifice butchered the people of Shelsans Mulgrave had been filled with the desire to visit the same destruction upon them and their families. Yet he had not. He had held – as far as he was able – to the path his father laid out.

I should never have come to this war, he thought. It has corrupted my soul.

His thoughts turned to Ermal Standfast. The little priest had fled Shelding because he had known the horror that was to come there. He had fled in terror. Many men would brand him a coward and despise him for it. Mulgrave did not. If all men were like Ermal then there would be no wars, no soul-blinding hatred, no acts of murderous revenge. He sighed. And there would be no heroism, no unselfish acts of courage, no strength to face the grim harshness of life. If all men were like Ermal, who then would leap into a raging torrent to rescue a child, or walk into a plague house to tend to the sick and the dying?

Taybard Jaekel moved alongside him, handing him a tin cup containing hot tisane. 'Thank you,' said Mulgrave.

The soldier nodded and moved away. Mulgrave drank the tisane, then stood and walked around the campsite, moving among the wounded men. They had lost more than a hundred in Shelding.

Forty others had died today. Less than five hundred remained, and many of these bore wounds.

A horseman came riding up the slope. Mulgrave stepped out to meet him. It was Able Pearce, a young man from Eldacre, the son of a shoemaker, Mulgrave recalled. Pearce slid from the saddle.

'Any sign of the enemy?' asked Mulgrave.

'No, sir. I rode into a village and went into a tavern. The talk there was of Luden Macks having killed the king.'

'What?'

'The word is that Luden Macks broke the truce and sent a small force to Baracum. The king and his entire family were killed. Lord Winterbourne led his forces against Luden Macks and killed him in revenge.'

'That is nonsense.'

Able Pearce shrugged. 'They got the story from soldiers who had passed through.'

'Get some rest, Pearce. I'll find the general and pass on what you have said.'

'Should mean the war is over, sir, shouldn't it?'

'Not for us, I fear. Lord Winterbourne wants us dead.'

'I'm sick of this war,' said Pearce. 'Today made me sicker, though. I don't like seeing men shot down who are surrendering. It's not right.'

'Get some rest,' repeated Mulgrave.

Pearce led his horse towards the picket line and Mulgrave strolled back past the camp fires and on into the woods. He found Gaise Macon sitting on the crest of a hill, his eyes focused on the north.

Gaise glanced up as he saw Mulgrave approach. 'What news?' he asked.

'The king is dead, with all his family. So is Luden Macks.'

'It does not surprise me. Winterbourne had this planned from the start. It all makes sense now. The nation is rent by civil war, torn and bankrupted by the vanity of a king and the rebellion of a lord. The king's popularity plummets, as does the reputation of Luden Macks as the champion of the common man. People grow sick of the endless carnage. They cry out for anyone who can bring an end to it. Winterbourne prolonged this war, Mulgrave. It could have been won years ago. He prolonged it because it served his purpose. Had he killed the king two years ago there would have been uproar. Had he defeated Macks the king would have been restored to the crown and Winterbourne become again merely another rich lord. Now he has the country – and the crown, should he desire it. He has it all. And no-one is powerful enough to stand against him.'

'The word is that Macks broke the truce and killed the king,' said Mulgrave.

'A splendid touch. Winter Kay the noble avenger. That is a move that would please the Moidart himself.'

'I expect it would,' agreed Mulgrave. 'As I expect he would have applauded had he seen you shoot an unarmed prisoner in the face.'

Gaise Macon took a deep breath before answering. When he spoke his voice betrayed his anger. 'You push the bounds of friendship too far, Mulgrave.'

'No, sir, I do not. *You* push them too far when you make me an accessory to murder.'

Gaise Macon gave a harsh laugh. 'One man dies and it is murder. A thousand die and it is war. What next, Mulgrave? Do we argue about how many angels can dance on the head of a pin?' Gaise rose smoothly to his feet. 'I behaved as a noble should. I stayed in Shelding when every instinct bade me take my men and desert. I risked death because I felt it was honourable so to do. Yet there is no honour here, Mulgrave. Winter Kay and his Redeemers are murderous vermin. Honour is just a word to them, a noisy sound with no meaning. And because I held to notions of honour Cordelia is dead. She kissed me, Mulgrave. She opened my heart. She reached in and comforted my soul.' His words tailed away, and Mulgrave saw he was struggling with his emotions. Gaise swung away and stared out to the north.

'So what is it that you desire now, my lord?' asked Mulgrave, softly.

'Oh, the answer to that is simple enough, my friend.' He glanced up. 'I expect that we are being observed still, so my words will reach the right ears. I will not rest until Winter Kay and all his Redeemers are dead. I will find each of them, no matter how long it takes. They will all die.'

'The officer today was not a Redeemer. He was a young man obeying his orders.'

Gaise sighed, and Mulgrave saw his shoulders relax and the tension flow out of him. His curiously coloured eyes, though, glittered with hatred.

'When we get to Eldacre you should leave my service. Where I travel from this moment on there will be blood and death. Those who stand against me will be destroyed, or I will be destroyed. No quarter will be asked for, and none will be given. Every Redeemer will perish, as will every man who rides or marches under their banner. Those who supply feed for their horses, or water. Those who obey their orders. I will hunt them down and kill them like vermin.'

'What then will separate you from Winter Kay? Will you meet evil with evil?'

'Yes,' said Gaise Macon.

When the glowing image of Kranos had appeared two days previously, floating above the skull and the dying king, the Redeemers had sat awestruck, their faces shining with religious zeal. All of them had experienced the surge of power radiating from the figure. It had flowed over them, lifting their spirits, strengthening their bodies.

Not so Winter Kay. He had stood in stunned surprise as the golden light formed into the shape of a man, golden-haired and wondrously handsome. In that moment Winter Kay had felt a truly terrible fear. Like all fanatics and zealots he had never in his life experienced self-doubt. Single-minded and ambitious, he had plotted and planned for years to become king. The Orb of Kranos had merely been a tool towards that end.

The moment that the figure appeared Winter Kay saw all the certainties he had held to so strongly melting away like morning mist in the sunshine. And when it spoke his heart had missed a beat. 'On the day of my resurrection you will be blessed, my children.'

Then, as swiftly as it had formed, the image faded.

The underground chamber was silent, and Winter Kay felt all eyes upon him. 'The will of the Orb be done,' he managed to say.

Then he had walked back to the blood-drenched skull, covered it with the black velvet cloth and replaced it in the iron box. He had stood there for some moments, staring into the open, dead eyes of the king. Not one of the Redeemers had moved or spoken. Winter Kay's mouth was dry.

He swung back to face his followers. 'Go, my brothers,' he said, surprised that his voice remained as commanding as ever despite the dryness of his throat and the trembling in his limbs. 'We will meet here in three days and I will explain to you then the mystery you have witnessed.'

Carrying the iron box Winter Kay strode from the room. In fact he wanted to run. Close to panic he climbed the stairs, making his way to his own apartments. Locking the door he slumped down on a couch, and placed the black box on the low table before it.

He felt dizzy and faintly nauseous. Instinctively he reached for the lid of the box. Always before when he had felt less than powerful he would place his hand on the skull and receive an instant burst of energy. Now he felt nervous and fearful, and merely sat staring at the box. The palms of his hands were damp with sweat, and he wiped them on his leggings.

'Why do you fear me?' came a voice inside his mind.

Winter Kay jerked and surged to his feet, his heart hammering wildly.

'Be calm, mortal. No harm will befall you.'

'Who are you?' demanded Winter Kay, his voice no longer commanding, but querulous and frightened.

The soft sound of laughter filled his mind. 'The will of the Orb be done. I liked that. You *know* who I am, Winter Kay. You have visited me many times. Sadly my blood does not flow in your veins, and your conscious mind has been unable to retain the memories. It will be different now that I am stronger.'

'How is it that you can now . . . speak to me?'

'The wretch you sacrificed for me had traces of my blood in his veins. But I asked why you were frightened.'

'I fear nothing!'

'Well said. I prefer it when my servants show spirit.'

'I am no man's servant.'

'Indeed not. All men will serve you, Winter Kay. Me they will

300

merely worship. Take my skull from that cursed box. Do it now.'

'No. I will not.'

'Oh, mortal, you disappoint me, and that is not wise. Without me you will have no throne. Your enemies will gather and tear you down. Without me you will live a normal human lifespan. What would that give you – even were you to defeat your enemies? Twenty more years perhaps?' The laughter came again. 'No, Winter Kay, you will release me from this iron chamber, for I offer immortality. And only I can protect you from the man with the golden eye.'

'I need no such protection,' said Winter Kay. 'That man will be dead tomorrow as the dawn comes.'

'You speak of Gaise Macon? We will see. I have waited centuries, mortal. I can wait a while longer. Though I will tell you now that when next you come to me I will punish you for your disobedience. It will be painful, Winter Kay. But then I will forgive you, and you will serve me loyally.'

Winter Kay did not sleep that night. Instead he entered a trance state and sent his spirit soaring out over the town of Shelding. There he saw the traitor telling Gaise Macon of the iron ring encircling him. He watched with silent fury as Macon gathered his riders and headed south.

Returning to his body Winter Kay wrote a hasty note to Macy, sealed it, and sent a rider galloping to intercept the cavalry column.

Late the following morning came news of the utter defeat of Luden Macks. The general had tried one desperate counter attack, and had been shot down as he rode with his troops. The Covenanters were now scattered and demoralized. Cavalry were hunting down the fleeing troops.

Winter Kay's joy at this news was short-lived. Sir Sperring Dale had contacted Eris Velroy and relayed the grotesque events at Eldacre Castle. The Moidart had killed the Pinance and his generals, and had appropriated his army. Seventeen thousand rebels were now at large in the north. Worse was to follow.

Gaise Macon had escaped the trap and killed Macy.

Winter Kay returned to his rooms and stood staring down at the black box. With trembling hands he opened the lid, and lifted out the velvet-covered skull. The cloth clung to the bone as he tried to remove it. Congealing blood had made it sticky. Winter Kay wrenched it clear, hurling the cloth to the floor. With the skull in his hands he sat down on the couch.

'I need your help,' he whispered.

'Of course, my servant,' came the answer. 'But first the pain I promised you.'

Fire blazed through Winter Kay's slender frame. His head arched back and he tried to scream. No sound came forth, and the agony grew. He began to shake. A huge vein began to swell and throb at the centre of his brow, and the muscles of his upper body spasmed into a fierce cramp. It was as if needles of fire were being pushed into his skin, rasping against his bones. And then it was gone. Winter Kay sagged back against the couch.

'And now I forgive you, Winter Kay, for your impertinence. Here is a reward for your previous loyalty.'

This time Winter Kay did manage to cry out. Joy flooded his mind, and he experienced a feeling of ecstasy unparalleled by any event in his life. All his tensions and fears disappeared, replaced by an immense sense of well-being. Then this too faded, leaving him dazed and weak.

'Will you disobey me again, Winter Kay?'

'No, my lord. Never.'


In the days following the murder of the unarmed officer Mulgrave spoke little with Gaise Macon. The journey was fraught with danger, and no-one but Gaise knew which direction they would take following night camp. He had said to Mulgrave that they would journey north-west, but at dawn he led them north-east. Mulgrave understood this. Gaise was aware that the Redeemers could spy on them. This information was not relayed to the men, who became confused by the switching of trails, and the seemingly bewildering routes Gaise chose.

Able Pearce rode alongside Mulgrave as dusk approached on the fifth day of travel. 'The men are worried about the Grey Ghost,' he said.

'He knows what he is doing, Pearce. Trust me on that.'

'I do, sir. But he's changed. There's talk he was in love with the general's daughter.'

'Not a subject we should be discussing. Let me merely say her death has hit him hard. So have the deaths of the Eldacre men he led south.'

'I don't understand any of this,' said Able. 'Why did our own troops think we were going to desert?'

'They were lied to. I can offer little more than that. Lord Winterbourne wishes to see the Lord Gaise killed. Why? I cannot understand it myself.'

'He was the one who wanted to take those civilians away from us after Nollenby,' put in Able. 'He was going to kill them, but the Lord Gaise refused him.'

'That's him. Winter Kay.'

'Is that what this is all about, do you think, sir?'

'Perhaps. No point trying to make sense of it, Pearce. Any more than trying to find logic amid the madness and stupidity of this war. Forget the reasons for his hatred. Concentrate only on staying alive. If we survive this nightmare that will be the time to wonder how we were drawn into it in the first place.'

'A lot of my friends were killed back in Shelding. Good men. I grew up with most of them. We attended school together. I'd like this to be over soon.'

'You'll get no argument from me on that.'

Gaise Macon chose a campsite on a sparsely wooded hilltop, with good views to the south and west. Scouts were sent out. Mulgrave chose the picket area for the mounts. The horses were tired, their strength also sapped by the limited amount of feed time during the past five days. A supply of grain and a solid day of rest would help, Mulgrave knew. There was little chance of that.

By nightfall the cook fires were lit and the four hundred or so men of the Eldacre Company settled down to enjoy their sparse rations. Mulgrave went in search of Gaise Macon. He found him on the hilltop, once more staring out towards the north. The black hound, Soldier, was lying on the ground, his head resting on the general's boot.

'There it is, Mulgrave,' he said, pointing to a distant snow-clad peak. 'Caer Druagh. It is good to see it again. Tomorrow we should – if the Source is willing – reach the abandoned settlement of Three Streams. Did you know Connavar the King was born there?'

'Yes, sir, so I understand. Close to the Wishing Tree woods.'

'Yes, I was thinking of camping the men there tomorrow. I'd love to walk under those trees. So much history.'

'The people who dwell in that area still refrain from entering the Wishing Tree woods,' said Mulgrave.

'They think the old dark gods will eat their children, do they?'

'No, sir. They avoid them out of respect. To the Rigante the Wishing Tree woods are special. It was there that Connavar lifted the magical fawn from the brambles, and was given his Seidh knife. It was there that Connavar and his son found the last of the gods, the Morrigu, and carried her to a secret gateway to heaven.'

'You know the Keltoi fables well, Mulgrave. I doubt there were gods and magical blades back then. Storytellers love to embellish tales of heroism with mystical touches.'

'I expect you are right. I shall go back and wait for the scouts to report. Shall I have food sent up to you?'

Gaise looked at him closely. 'Have I lost your friendship?'

'No,' said Mulgrave, sadly. 'Though I wish you had.'

In the moonlight Kaelin Ring and Rayster walked with the Wyrd, entering the woods above Shrine Hollow, and gazing down over Sorrow Bird Lake. The waters were still, the night sky clear and bright with shimmering stars. The Wyrd had not spoken much on the long walk from the Round House, though she had bidden Kaelin and Rayster to join her.

The two warriors followed her down to the narrow beach, where her small boat lay.

When she reached it she turned to them. 'You are the best of the Rigante,' she said. 'Remember that. When all around you reeks with evil deeds, hold to the Rigante way.' She gazed at them both fondly. Kaelin Ring, dark-eyed and sombre, a man of passion constantly seeking to control his turbulent nature, and Rayster, fair-haired and blue-eyed, modest and calm, yet possessing a quiet courage that would stand tall against a tidal wave of evil. They were night and day, the sun and the moon of the Rigante.

'Will you be coming south with us?' asked Rayster. She shook her head, and reached up to stroke his face. 'My talents are not for war and death. But my thoughts will be with you, clansman.'

'Why did you want us here tonight, Wyrd?' said Kaelin.

She sighed. 'Look around you. Soak in these mountains, the silence and the beauty of the lake. Draw in the air, fresh and cold from the peaks, and scented now with the early flowers of spring. This is the *land*. As it should be. Carry it with you in your hearts.'

'You wanted us to fight the evil, Wyrd,' said Kaelin, 'and yet now you seem sad that Bael has agreed to send us south.'

'Of course I am sad, clansman. The Rigante are dear to me. They mean more to me than life. Now many will die.' Her head drooped and she swung away to stare at the lake. 'Bael was right, you know. I have been wrong. I sensed there was danger and I believed it to be the Moidart. It hurts me to my soul to know that Rigante will fight alongside the man. He is detestable to me. Were he merely a Varlish lord I could despise him for his cruelty and his malice. But he is not. He is of the blood of Connavar and Bane, just as you are, Ravenheart. That makes his evil all the worse in my eyes. Now this monster is to be a champion for the Rigante.' She shook her head and fell silent. Then she turned back to them. 'I asked you here not just so that you could feel the peace and beauty of this sacred land. You are about to enter a war. It is often said that war brings out the best and the worst in men. This war will be vile, and even the strongest will be changed by it. War makes beasts of men. The Rigante must not become beasts. The magic of this land is weak enough. War will drain it further. The more it is drained, the more dreadful will be the deeds of the warriors. The coming horror will stain the souls of all who take part in it. The worms of hatred and malice will gnaw at your minds. You will see evil deeds, and you will feel what you believe to be righteous rage swelling in your hearts. Such righteous rage is a lie. See it for what it is. A deceiver, a trick to allow us to become as vile as those we fight. If the Source wills that you both survive these coming days, try to ensure that you will return here with no shame upon your souls. Be Rigante and follow your hearts.'

'Where will you be, Dweller?'

'Tomorrow I will be far away. The day after that I will be here once more, ready to take Feargol to a place of destiny.'

'Will he be safe there?' asked Kaelin.

'No, Ravenheart. For those blessed with his gift there is no safety to be found in the world.'

'When will he be brought back?'

'He will not be coming back. Fear not. He is to be raised and tutored by a friend of mine, the man who taught me the Way. He will grow to manhood in a land full of magic, where the people hold to the spirits of the earth. It is a wonderful land, Ravenheart. Feargol's destiny is to help preserve it.'

'Are the Varlish there?' asked Rayster.

'Not yet, but they will find it. They will seek to dig in its earth for minerals and metals, to tear up the land for timber and wealth. It is their way. However, that is not a problem for this day. Our problem is the Seidh lord and his minions.'

'You think we can beat them?' asked Kaelin.

'We must, Ravenheart.'

'How can men defeat a Seidh god?'

'As long as he does not return to the flesh he is merely a force of small magic. If ever he walks the earth he will be unstoppable. With a wave of his hand he could destroy armies. His body would be impervious to weapons of base metal. Swords would not cut him, musket balls would not pierce his flesh.'

'And this is why he is being brought to the north,' said Kaelin, 'to return to the flesh?'

'Yes. We are his blood line. The Rigante are fashioned from his life blood.'

'So by killing us he will regain his own life?' asked Rayster.

'I do not understand the process of his resurrection,' said the Wyrd. 'Perhaps Rigante blood will strengthen him, perhaps there is a secret place here in the north where he can draw upon the magic. All we can do is to defeat the armies that defend him. Then perhaps we can find a way to destroy the skull.'

'If he is impervious to weapons how was it that he was beheaded in the first place?' asked Rayster.

'Weapons of base metal cannot harm him. His son, Rigantis, was said to have used a golden sword to kill him. Rigantis was half Seidh, and therefore found a way to breach his father's magical defences. I have tried to walk the ancient paths and see the truth behind the fables. It is too far for me. I asked my friend Riamfada to make the journey, but even he – he who is spirit – could not pierce the mists of time. All we can know for certain is that Cernunnos must be prevented from resurrection.'

'And to do this we must fight alongside the Moidart,' said Rayster. 'It does not sit well with me. Can the man be trusted?'

'No,' said the Wyrd. 'He would switch sides in a moment if he thought there was profit in it. You can, however, trust the son. There is a darkness growing in him, but he will not betray you. Of that I am sure.'

'I have a question about him,' said Kaelin.

'I know what it is – and do not ask it at this time,' said the Wyrd. 'Do your best to keep him alive, Ravenheart. The Stormrider is vital. He must survive.'

'Why?'

'I wish I knew. The many paths of the future are closed to me. Cernunnos and the Stormrider are linked in some way that I cannot yet fathom. I may know more tomorrow when I meet him.'

Maev Ring was kneading dough in the kitchen when Draig Cochland tapped at the door and entered. She glanced up, irritation in her eyes. Maev was not happy that this thief had been offered a role at Ironlatch by Chara.

'There is a man coming,' he said. 'I don't like the look of him.'

This made Maev smile. A man that Draig Cochland didn't like the look of? This was something to see. Wiping her hands on a cloth she followed the big highlander out through the main room and into the yard beyond. Riding towards the gate of the farm was Huntsekker the Harvester. His massive form looked out of place on a horse.

'Do you know him?' asked Draig Cochland.

'He is the Harvester.'

Cochland swore softly and Maev could hear the fear in his voice. 'He'll not harm you,' he said. 'I have my sword.'

She glanced at him. 'You will protect me, Cochland?'

'Aye. As best I can.' He made to step forward, but Maev took hold of his arm.

'It is all right, Draig. The man is a friend.'

His shoulders sagged with relief. 'Thank the Source for that,' he said. 'I thought I was dead for sure.'

Huntsekker dismounted, and opened the gate. 'Good afternoon to you, Maev Ring,' he said.

Maev told Draig to take Huntsekker's horse, then led the Harvester into the house. He sat down at the pine table.

'I hate riding,' he said. 'Never mastered the rhythms of it.'

'You look tired,' she said. 'I'll fetch you some food and drink.'

For a little while she busied herself in the kitchen, washing the flour from her hands and arms, then cutting Huntsekker some fresh baked bread and a hunk of cheese. She carried this out to him, then poured him a goblet of red wine. He sipped it appreciatively.

Maev sat down opposite him. She felt ill at ease in his presence. In a curious way he reminded her of Jaim Grymauch. He radiated the same feeling of awesome strength. Yet there the resemblance ended. Where Jaim was like an amiable bear Huntsekker was far more cold and deadly. Even so his presence made her aware of her own femininity.

'What brings you so far north?' she asked.

'The Moidart sent me. With a letter.' Reaching into the pocket of his long bearskin coat he handed her the package. Maev broke the seal and read the contents of the single sheet. She shook her head and smiled.

'He wants to borrow money from *me*? How bizarre.'

'The man is in trouble,' said Huntsekker.

'And I should care? This is the man who killed my brother. This is the butcher of the highlands.'

'Aye, I know. Didn't kill Jaim though.'

'What?'

'He knew it was Jaim who rescued Chain Shada from me. Told me that himself. He knew I lied to him about it. Yet he did nothing.'

'Why?'

'Damned if I know, Maev. He's a strange man.' Huntsekker tugged at the twin spikes of his silver beard. 'There's an army coming against us. We killed the Pinance and we have his men with us. Even so we'll be outnumbered maybe three – four – to one. There's not enough money in the treasury to pay the army for more than a few weeks.'

'So he wants me to finance his war? Does he think I have two thousand pounds lying around my farm?'

'He thinks you have twelve thousand hidden close by.'

Maev was shocked, though she did not show it. The Moidart was wrong – but only by a few hundred pounds. 'What is your view, Huntsekker?'

'About your wealth? I don't know. I don't much care. You're a canny woman, Maev. Every business you touch turns to gold. Never known anyone with such a talent.'

'I meant about the Moidart's request.'

He drained his wine. 'I don't know. I've served the man for too many years. I don't like him. I don't think anyone likes him. Save maybe the apothecary.'

'So he didn't ask you to kill me if I refused?'

Huntsekker looked up, his eyes angry. 'No, he did not. If he did I would have killed him where he sat. You heard me make my promise to Jaim. No harm would come to you while I lived. I don't make promises lightly, Maev Ring.'

'So why did he send you? Why not Galliott? Why not a troop of men to torture me into telling where my wealth might – or might not – be buried?'

'He thought you would trust me, I guess. No reason why you should.'

'He is a clever man,' said Maev. 'I do trust you, Huntsekker. You know why? Because my Jaim liked you. He was a flawed man, but a great one. He let you live. I railed at him for that. I thought it was stupid. I thought you would go straight to the Moidart and that Jaim would be arrested and hanged. Jaim was right, though. You were worth his trust. You are worth mine. If you believe I should loan the Moidart this money, then I will do so.'

'Gods, woman, don't put this on me!'

'Shall I do it, Huntsekker? Will he betray me?'

Huntsekker let out a long sigh. 'If he does I'll kill him for it.'

'Very well. I will lend him the money. And I will come south with you to see that it is wisely spent.'

'What? He said nothing about bringing you south!'

'You said yourself that you have never known anyone with my talents. He will need to feed his army, to purchase powder and shot, swords and pistols. He will need supplies of all kinds. In short he will need a quartermaster. Together we will bring him the coin for his army, but he will need more. There is not a businessman in Eldacre or the surrounding lands who does not know that my word is good. I shall organize the supplies, and ensure that my investment is returned with interest.'

'He'll never agree!'

'On the contrary, Huntsekker. It is what he is hoping for.'

All was silent at the centre of the Wishing Tree woods. The ancient standing stones – only three of them upright now – cast long moon shadows across the hilltop. Other pillars lay cracked and broken on the ground, the meaning of the runic symbols carved into the golden stone long forgotten. A black beetle scurried across the surface of one fallen stone, its tiny legs powering it over a written wisdom it would never know.

A brief moment of bright light shone between two of the standing stones. Then a small woman appeared. She staggered, then righted herself.

The Wyrd stood very still, allowing the faint nausea to seep from her system. Then she looked round at the silent trees. Her legs felt unsteady and she sat upon a stone and saw the small beetle. It moved swiftly into the shadows, away from her gaze. She took a deep breath. A headache was beginning now, and her mouth was dry.

A glowing sphere of light formed close by, and, for a moment, her heart lifted, for she believed it to be Riamfada, and his presence always comforted her. Then the light swelled and took the shape of a man's head, crowned with antlers. The face was handsome, the eyes keen and sparkling with intelligence. He smiled at her.

'The Gateways always made my stomach uneasy,' he said, 'when I took human form.'

'If you have come to kill me, do it,' she said. 'I have no wish to speak with you.'

'Sadly I do not have the power as yet to wither away your flesh, Caretha.' The light swelled further, shaping itself into the full figure of a tall man. 'I remember when these woods were but a tiny part of a huge forest. It was here that I first learned how to breathe air, and to run.'

'What do you want, Cernunnos?'

'From you? Nothing. I merely felt the power of the Gateway and was curious to know what had activated it. I had some small hope that it would be one of my old friends, perhaps the Morrigu.'

'They have all gone now. As you should be gone.'

'I expect they left in despair,' he said. 'One day I shall find them again. I will encourage them to come back and see the world as it ought to be.'

'And how is that?'

'Without humans in it.'

The Wyrd sat quietly, trying to gather her thoughts. 'Who then will you rule? Who will dance and die at your bidding? Where will you find your pleasures?'

'You think it pleases me to see humans die?'

'Oh yes.'

'I expect you are right. A child stamping on ants, you said. Would that it were so simple. These woods once pulsed with magic. The land was fertile beyond belief. Now the earth is merely dirt, and the trees struggle to exist. Where has the magic gone, Caretha?'

'I don't want to talk to you. You represent everything I detest.'

'Not so! I represent everything you have longed for. You have watched man desecrate the land. You have prayed for the return of the Seidh to protect it. Now I am here.'

The Wyrd felt her anger swell, but fought to control it. 'You are worse than any man could ever be. Your rule saw only torment, war and death.'

'You humans are so short-lived. It is why you can only ever see the moment. For you it is all that exists. Man is the destroyer, Caretha. Man devours the magic. Man consumes the life force of the world. His hatred and his pettiness, his lusts and his greeds. When I first knew man he was a creature who had just learned to stand upright. He spoke in grunts. And yet we who were spirit saw in him vast potential. He was capable of great love. We watched him, and we saw also – to our amazement – that he could add to the magic of the world. The Seidh could not. We were born of the magic, and could manipulate it. We could not create it. Imagine the excitement among us, Caretha. Here was a creature with the

311

potential to reshape the universe. Were we jealous of it? We were not. We sought to guide it, to help it evolve. Soon – well, in your terms a few hundred thousand years – we began to see problems develop. Yes, man could make magic. He could also drain it. Hatred, envy, and lust dissipated the power. Some of the Seidh knew then that man was the great enemy of the universe. I was not among them. I still believed he could achieve greatness. The Morrigu and I, and some others, took on fleshly forms and moved among the humans. We found people like you, Caretha. We inspired you. We gave you gifts of talent and power. We struggled for aeons to help you. But we could not overcome the one great flaw in the plan. A single human like you can spend her entire life creating magic, but one vile man, with one vile act, can consume it in an instant. The experiment failed. Some like the Morrigu refused to see it. She watched man destroy a thousand worlds across the vastness of the universe, and yet still had hope that on one he could achieve the potential she longed for. This one. Now she too is gone. Look around you, Caretha. Where is her legacy? Famine and death, war and destruction. Brooding hatreds fester in the souls of men, and the Wishing Tree woods have no magic in them.'

'There are still places of magic,' she said.

'Of course there are. It will take more than a few generations of mankind to destroy it utterly. Have you seen Uzamatte?'

Her heart sank. 'Yes. It is wonderful.'

'Once the Wishing Tree woods were like that.'

'There are people living around Uzamatte who feed the magic,' she said. 'They do not drain it.'

'Ah, Caretha, if only all people were like you. One day soon the people on this side of the ocean will journey across the mighty sea. They will discover the wonders of the lands there and they will seek to settle them. This is not prophecy. This has happened on other worlds, whose histories mirror this one almost perfectly. The new settlers will arrive. They will begin to die. The people who dwell in that land will take pity on these poor travellers. They will bring them food. They will show them love. In return, as the centuries pass, that love will be repaid by murder and death and betrayal. These newcomers will spread, and they will, in a few hundred years, devour the magic that has taken a million years to create.

They will rip up the earth, and tear down the trees. They will create poisons to pollute the rivers. This is the human way, Caretha. Mankind is what it is. It does what it does. Mankind is a plague.'

'Then why do you wish to return, Cernunnos?'

'Why, to destroy man, of course. To eradicate him from the planet. I will help him to play his vile games, to develop his weapons, to perfect his murderous nature. Then the world can be at peace.'

'You cannot destroy all of mankind through war,' she said.

'Oh, but you can. Man is capable – given time – of creating weapons that can obliterate nations. I shall merely increase the speed of such invention.'

'Why do you tell me this, Cernunnos?'

'Perhaps even a god does not like being misunderstood.'

'I do not misunderstand you. You deceive yourself. You and the Seidh took a creature with enormous potential, and you began to mould it in your own image. *You* created man as he is. If we are a plague then we are a plague of *your* making. And I do not believe the Morrigu left here in despair at humans. I believe she left because, as you said, the Seidh could not create magic. They too devoured it. They too, therefore, were parasites. So spare me your specious reasons for becoming a part of the hatred that curses us. You are not a god, Cernunnos. You are just another sad, tormented creature consumed by rage and a need to justify your actions. The Rigante will stop you. And better than that, we will find a way to preserve our world and rebuild the magic. We will conquer our demons.'

Cernunnos laughed then, and there was no malice in the sound. 'Spoken as I would expect by someone with my blood in her veins. Go then, Caretha. Seek out young Gaise Macon. In him you will find all that I have said to be true. Hatred consumes him. Even if he could defeat me – which he cannot – you would all lose eventually. The only way he can win is to become more vile than that which he faces. He knows this.'

'I pray to the Source of All Things that you are wrong.'

Once again he laughed, and this time there was an edge of bitterness. 'I too once prayed to that paralysed and senile force. No more. Fare thee well, kinswoman. Fight your valiant, losing battle.

If all were indeed like you there would be no need for what is to come.'

The light faded. The Wyrd struggled to her feet. Then despair, like a mountain upon her heart, overcame her and she sank back to the stone.

Once more a light formed. This time a sense of peace came with it, and with the peace tears flowed.

'Did you hear?' she asked.

'Yes,' said the voice of Riamfada, in her mind.

'Everything he said had the resonance of truth, Riamfada. We have proved to be a plague upon the world.'

'Man is a complex creature, Caretha. You also spoke the truth. We were shaped by the Seidh for their own purposes.'

'He said Uzamatte would be destroyed, its magic devoured in a few short centuries.'

'That is why we are taking Feargol to that land. We will do what we can to protect it. Go home now. Go back to Sorrow Bird.'

'I need to speak with the Stormrider.'

'Now is not the time. His darkness would burden you. I will speak with him. I will take him to the cave. It is fitting, after all, when you think on it.'

'Do not let him be evil, Riamfada,' said the Wyrd. 'I had such hopes for him.'

'Hold to them. There are two wars now, the one being waged with sword and cannon upon the land, and the second being fought within the emotional valleys of the Stormrider's soul. You and I cannot take part in either. Go home and prepare Feargol.'

She nodded. 'If he is evil, will you still give him the gift?'

'It is his destiny to receive it.'

'I feel so lost, Riamfada,' she said. Once more the tears began to fall.

'You are not lost. I am here with you.' In that moment she felt a great warmth settle over her, as if she were a child again, safe in the arms of her mother. She remembered the small hut they shared, and the little fireplace, fashioned of stone. One night, when the child Caretha had endured a bad dream, her mother had carried her out and sat her on the rug in front of the fire. On a baking tray were a dozen biscuits, scented with cinnamon. Her mother had held her close, and given her a biscuit. It was still warm from the oven.

Caretha had never felt so loved as in that moment. It was a time to treasure.

The warmth left her. Riamfada had gone and she knew was alone again. Then a scent of cinnamon came to her. She looked down. There on the stone beside her was a perfectly round, golden biscuit. She took it up and bit into it. Then she smiled.

'Thank you, Riamfada,' she whispered.

# CHAPTER FIFTEEN

GAISE MACON SLEPT FITFULLY. HE AWOKE IN HIS TENT JUST BEFORE THE dawn. Fragmented shards of his dreams clung momentarily to his conscious mind: Cordelia Lowen leaning in to kiss him, her lips cold and blue, her eyes lifeless.

He shivered and sat up.

Pushing back his blankets, he climbed to his feet. Soldier stirred beside him, raising his large head and yawning, showing his teeth. Gaise stepped over him and left the tent. Some of the soldiers had built cook fires, but most were still sleeping on the bare earth, huddled close to the ruins, seeking some shelter from the night winds.

Gaise wondered what this community had been like in the days of Connavar. It was said there was a forge, where the king's Iron Wolves had first received their armour. Ruathain had lived here, and Bendegit Bran. At the centre of the ruins lay the massive stump of an oak. Eldest Tree it was called when it lived. It was at the heart of many Rigante festivals. The Varlish had cut it down two hundred years ago in an effort to stamp out clan culture. It was around this time that the romances had been published declaring Connavar to have been a Varlish prince, who had travelled to the far north to lead the barbarous people there.

Gaise wandered to a rickety bridge spanning one of the three streams. He gazed around the ruins, and scanned the surrounding hills. Connavar had walked these same hills, with his brothers Braefar the traitor and Bendegit Bran. It was here that he had met his first love. Gaise could not remember her name, but he recalled that she was the mother of the battle king, Bane. So much history had been seen by these hills.

On one of them Connavar had fought the bear, to save his crippled friend, Riamfada.

Gaise wished he had studied the tales more closely. As a child he had listened in awe to the stories of Seidh gods and magic, and later, as a young boy, had read the mystical adventures of the man who had come to be known as Conn of the Vars, who had slept with a goddess and sired a demigod called Bane. Alterith Shaddler had stripped away the gloss of legend, offering a historical perspective, based on the folk tales of the Rigante.

A cool breeze whispered across the bridge. Gaise wandered back through the camp.

Mulgrave was sleeping by the remains of a low wall. Gaise felt a stab of remorse as he recalled the sorrow in his friend's eyes. For all his skills Mulgrave was not a man made for battles and wars. There was only one way to deal with an enemy as evil as Winter Kay. Kill him, and all who serve him. Wipe them and their memory from the face of the earth. Anger roiled in Gaise Macon's heart as he saw again the still, lifeless form of Cordelia Lowen. He had not even been able to stay and bury her. He had left her body alongside her father and led his men from Shelding.

What a fool I was, he thought, allowing my head to be filled with thoughts of honour and chivalry. The Moidart would never have allowed himself to be trapped as he was. He would have moved his men out at first sign of Winter Kay's treachery, not sat like some sacrificial lamb awaiting the slaughter.

Cordelia had tried to tell him to leave, but he would not listen. Had he done so she would now be alive, as would the two hundred Eldacre men who had trusted him to lead them. Would Connavar have sat waiting to be murdered? Would Bane have talked of honour and good faith?

Gaise walked over to the picket line and saddled his gelding. Lanfer Gosten approached him. 'Scouts report no troops any- where, sir,' he said.

'Take Soldier and give him some food. I'll be back soon,' said Gaise.

Gosten hooked his fingers into the hound's collar. 'Yes, sir. Might I enquire where you're going?'

'The Wishing Tree woods. I've always had a hankering to see them.'

'Yes, sir.'

Gaise rode off. He could hear Soldier barking and wanting to follow. He glanced back. Lanfer Gosten was struggling to hold on to the hound. Once Gaise topped the rise the barking ceased. The gelding stumbled as they moved onto the downward slope. Gaise slowed him from a canter to a walk. The horse was weary, his movements sluggish. 'You'll be able to rest soon, boy,' said Gaise, patting the gelding's sleek grey neck. There were only a few patches of snow now on the higher hills, and the rising sun shone with the warmth of spring.

*'Scouts report no troops anywhere, sir.'*

They will be coming soon, thought Gaise. Winter Kay will bring his army north.

He reined in the gelding and swung back to look down on Three Streams. On one of these hills Bane had fought a battle against Varlish raiders. He had been aided, according to some accounts, by outlaws, and had saved Connavar's mother, Meria.

Gaise had always enjoyed stories of Bane and his father Connavar. Their uneasy relationship mirrored that of Gaise and the Moidart. It had moved Gaise to tears when he had read how Bane returned and became reconciled with his father at the point of Connavar's death. As a child he had longed to be reconciled with the Moidart. He would have given ten years of his life just to have the man smile and hug him. It was not to be. The Moidart had been constant in his contempt.

Pushing thoughts of his father from his mind Gaise rode towards the woods. It surprised him that they looked just like every other stand of trees: oak, sycamore, birch and beech. There was nothing mystical about them. What did you expect, he asked himself? Fire breathing dragons? Unicorns? A Seidh maiden, dressed in white?

As he approached the woods a young man stepped from the shadows of the trees. He was fair-haired and dressed in a long, grey, threadbare coat. His leggings and boots were of cheap cloth and leather. He appeared to be carrying no weapon. Gaise scanned the trees behind him.

'Good morning,' said the young man.

'And to you. You live near here?'

'No. Not any more. Once I lived here.'

'In these woods?'

'For a time. I was born in Three Streams.'

'There has not been a settlement here in a hundred or so years.'

'I know,' said the man, 'sad, isn't it? Such good land.'

'What is your business here now?' asked Gaise.

'I was waiting for you, Stormrider. I have a gift for you.'

Gaise backed his horse away and drew a pistol from its scabbard on the pommel of his saddle. 'How kind of you, stranger,' he said, coldly. 'But I have no need of gifts. How is it that you know my Rigante name?'

'This is not a trap, Gaise Macon. The Wyrd would have been here, but I have come in her place. Be at ease, I am no danger to you.'

'I have learned the hard way that what men say and what they do are often wildly different. Stand up and turn round. Let me see that you are carrying no weapons.'

The young man did as he was bid, opening his coat to show no knives or pistols were hidden upon his person. 'Who are you?' asked Gaise.

'I am Riamfada.'

Gaise laughed. 'You look well for your age, swordsmith.'

'I was never a swordsmith. I made jewellery, brooches and pins, a few rings. Only after I died did I learn the skill of bladecraft. But I only made one sword, Gaise Macon. Just the one. I made it for my friend, Connavar.'

Once more Gaise scanned the trees for sign of any men concealed there. Then he looked back at the young man, and relaxed. 'You are an amusing fellow. But if you wish to play the part of Seidh legend you should have dressed up a little more. Perhaps an old-fashioned conical hat, or a patchwork cloak. Now will you get to the point. What is it you want of me?'

'There was only one patchwork cloak, and I did not wear it. As

I said, I have a gift for you. It is within the woods. Do you have the nerve to accompany me?'

'Nerve, fellow? Are you going to tell me it is still haunted by the Seidh?'

'No, Gaise Macon, it is not haunted. The Seidh no longer walk here. I have not walked here in centuries. It seems to me to be a sad place now. The magic is all but gone. Will you leave your horse and walk with me?'

'There is a price on my head, and my soldiers rely on me. I would be a fool to walk into a shadowed wood alone with a stranger. Especially a deranged stranger who pretends to be dead. Do I look foolish to you?'

'You look like a man carrying many sorrows, Stormrider. But no, you do not look foolish. There is no-one here to harm you, but I understand your concern.'

'What is the gift?'

'Come and see,' said the young man. Gaise chuckled and dismounted, tethering the gelding's reins to a bush.

'You don't object if I bring my pistol?'

'Not at all.'

The young man walked off into the trees. Gaise followed him. The ground was soft underfoot. Gaise paused suddenly. The man ahead was leaving no footprints.

'Wait!' called Gaise. The young man turned. 'You make no mark upon the earth.'

'That is because I am long dead and the form you see is merely an illusion. I can become solid, but it takes energy and effort and serves no real purpose. If it would make you happier I could conjure a conical cap.'

'You are a ghost?'

'I suppose that I am, in a manner of speaking. Does this disturb you?'

'I have to admit that it does,' said Gaise. 'Are you truly Riamfada?'

'Truly.'

'And you knew the great king?'

'I knew him. He taught me to swim.'

'To swim? I had heard that you were a cripple.'

320

'My legs did not function. Conn used to carry me to the Riguan Falls. I found that I could propel myself along in the water with my arms. It was the most marvellous sensation. I have never forgotten it. Conn was a good man. No-one else bothered with a sickly cripple.'

'Is he here too, in this place?'

'I don't believe so. But then I do not know a great deal about the afterworld of spirit. He could be, I suppose.'

Riamfada walked on. Gaise followed him. The spirit paused and pointed to a dense section of undergrowth. 'It was in there that Conn freed the fawn from the brambles. It was that deed which endeared him to the Morrigu. A frightened boy in a magical wood, and yet he paused to help what he believed to be a terrified fawn.'

'I feel I must be dreaming this,' said Gaise.

'Come, we must travel a little further.' Riamfada moved on, coming at last to a sheer cliff face. He kept walking and disappeared into the solid rock. Gaise waited. 'Walk through, Stormrider,' he heard Riamfada say. 'It is only another illusion.'

Gaise stretched out his hand. No cold stone met his fingers. Taking a deep breath he stepped forward, and found himself standing in a narrow cave. Two ancient lanterns flickered into life and light. Riamfada was standing by the far wall. Leaning against it was an old-fashioned sword, the kind once carried by knights into battle. The long blade was slightly curved, and shone like the brightest silver. Keltoi runes were engraved along its length. The hilt was a mixture of gold, silver and ebony; the black quillons shaped like oak leaves, the golden fist guard embossed with the head of a bear. There was a round silver pommel, bearing a beautiful carving of a fawn trapped in brambles.

Gaise stepped closer, kneeling down to examine the weapon. It was stunningly beautiful. 'This is the only sword I ever made,' said Riamfada. 'I am not fond of weapons of death. This is your gift, Stormrider.'

Gaise rose to his feet and backed away. 'It would not be fitting. I am not Rigante. I am the son of a Varlish lord, a conqueror. This should go to someone like Kaelin Ring or Call Jace.'

'It is the Sword in the Storm, Gaise Macon. Who else should carry it but the Stormrider?'

'It is a Rigante treasure. I have no right to take it.'

'You have Rigante blood, through your father. You are of the line of Connavar. And who has a greater right to offer this gift than the being who crafted it?'

'I could not use it, Riamfada. It is huge and cumbersome, and not suited to modern cavalry warfare.'

'Try it, Gaise.'

Reluctantly Gaise Macon reached for the hilt. It was far too large for his hand, yet, as his fingers curled around it the hilt seemed to shrink. He raised the blade. It was remarkably light. Gaise blinked. The black quillons narrowed, the golden fist guard swirled around his hand. The blade shivered in the light, becoming more slender. Within a few heartbeats Gaise found himself holding a cavalry sabre. The fist guard no longer showed the image of a bear. Now it showed a rearing horse, surrounded by golden clouds.

Riamfada gestured towards Gaise's own sabre, which lifted from the scabbard and floated to the floor. 'Sheathe your blade, Stormrider.'

Gaise did so. It fitted perfectly. 'It will cut through all armour and never require sharpening. The blade will not dull or dent, and while you carry it no Redeemer spirit will be able to see you. You will still be discernible to human eyes, but you will be invisible to those who seek to spy on you with spirit eyes. The runes upon the blade are old and powerful. Ward spells they were once called. No demonic force can harm you while this blade is by your side. And now you should go. The Moidart has need of you, and there is much to do before Winter Kay brings his army north.'

'Will you help us in this war?'

'No. I will be taking a child to a distant place. I will be raising him there, and teaching him the wonders of a beautiful land. Then I too will depart this earth, and seek out the realms of spirit.'

'You will die?'

Riamfada smiled. 'I have already died, Gaise. My spirit was taken by the Seidh, who gave me new life. I am not immortal, though, and my time is now short. I have no regrets. I have seen wonders indescribable, and known people whose lives made my heart sing. Some, like Conn, were warriors, others have been mystics and poets, farmers and labourers. One was a schoolteacher. These people and their lives have inspired me. Perhaps when I leave this world I will see them again. Perhaps not. But you and I will not meet again in this world, Gaise Macon. I wish you well.'

The world shimmered and went dark. Gaise Macon staggered and almost fell. Reaching out, he grabbed at the trunk of a tree to steady himself. The grey gelding whinnied in surprise at the sudden movement. Gaise blinked. He was standing again at the edge of the Wishing Tree woods. There was no cave, no bramble thicket, and no mysterious stranger.

'Damn, it was a dream after all,' he said aloud. 'I am more tired than I thought.' He drew the sabre idly from its scabbard.

The Keltoi runes shone, and the golden fist guard gleamed bright in the morning light.

Sheathing the blade once more Gaise stepped into the saddle. 'My thanks to you, Riamfada,' he called out. There was no answer, though it seemed the breeze picked up, rustling in the branches above him. With a wave he turned his horse and rode back to Three Streams.

Apothecary Ramus sat outside the Moidart's offices as a seemingly endless stream of people exited and entered the rooms. He had never seen such relentless activity within the castle. On the ride to Eldacre he had seen thousands of soldiers, some marching in column, others engaged in manoeuvres. Wagons and carts clogged the roads, most bringing in supplies, but some carrying frightened families towards the north. Rumours abounded. The king had decided to move his capital north and Eldacre was to be the centre of the war. The king was dead and the Moidart had declared war upon his killers. Everyone, however, knew that the Pinance was dead, and that his head had been held up before his own troops. This act of savagery had – much to the surprise of the apothecary – impressed a great number of people.

'Ah, you don't mess with our Moidart,' the baker had said proudly, when Ramus bought his daily loaf of bread. Others in the bakery had agreed.

'Canny man,' someone added. 'Pinance bit off more than he could chew when he came north.'

'Never much of a brain on him,' said the baker.

'No, but the Moidart used his head,' said the other, to general laughter. It baffled Ramus that such an act could produce levity.

The apothecary had known nothing of the Moidart's coup. He had waited in the dank, dark dungeon for a full night and a day, cold and terrified. When the door finally opened and light flooded in he had screamed with terror. 'Whisht, man!' snapped Huntsekker. 'You're free.'

'Free?'

'Aye. Come on out and stop your wailing. I have a pounding headache and the noise is making me irritable.'

Ramus had tottered out. He was offered no food or transport, and had trudged back to Old Hills, arriving at his home just over two hours later. Not a word from the Moidart. It was on the way home that he had passed a group of soldiers, two of whom he knew. They told him of the murder of the Pinance, and how the Moidart had acquired a new army.

It was then he learned that the coup had taken place before the dawn. Yet he had been left in the dungeon almost to dusk. Ramus had slept then for almost fourteen hours. After that he tried to re-establish his routines. He drank camomile tisanes to calm his nerves, and went back to the preparation of tinctures and creams, salves and balms.

Alterith Shaddler, the schoolmaster, came into the shop complaining of a toothache. Ramus examined him and pointed out that the tooth needed to be pulled. He saw the fear in Alterith's eyes. 'I am not good with pain, apothecary. Is there not some other remedy?'

Aye, thought Ramus, you'd not have suffered this pain had the Pinance lived. Rumour has it that you were due to hang alongside me. 'No,' he said. 'I am sorry. I can give you something to dull the pain, but it will get worse. Better to have it pulled today. I can do it for you immediately.'

'I'll think on it,' said Shaddler.

'Do not take too long.'

After three days Ramus was beginning to feel like his old self. Then came the summons from the Moidart.

Ramus sat quietly, his bag of balms upon his lap. Colonel

Galliott came by, but he did not speak. The man looked terribly tired. He seemed to have aged ten years since Ramus last saw him. He was followed by a slender young man with fair hair. Ramus heard him announced by the Moidart's servant as Bendegit Law.

Time dragged on. Ramus was thirsty, and he stopped a passing servant and requested something to drink. 'I'll send someone,' said the man. Then he rushed off. No-one came.

After three hours the bustle around him slowed down. Servants moved along the hallway, lighting lanterns. Ramus saw the man he had asked for water, and repeated his request. 'I'll get it now, apothecary,' he said, apologetically. This time he did come back. Ramus thanked him and drank deeply.

He heard his name called and moved to the door. Another servant opened it and announced him. Ramus stepped inside. The Moidart was sitting at a desk, upon which was a mass of papers. He leaned back in his chair, his hooded eyes focusing on the new-comer. 'Did you bring the balms?'

'Yes, my lord.'

'Well, don't just stand there. I do not have all day. Bring them to me.'

Ramus moved forward and laid his bag upon the desk. Opening it he produced three jars, wax-sealed. Upon each was a hand-painted label with carefully written instructions. The Moidart lifted one. 'You only make these for me, do you not?'

'Yes, my lord.'

'And you have been doing so for years.'

'Yes, my lord.'

'It puzzles me why you write the instructions so carefully upon each jar. After all this time I know how to apply the balms.'

'Yes, my lord.'

'You are sounding like a parrot bird,' said the Moidart. 'Sit down, Ramus. Relax. No-one is going to hang you today.'

'Is the war coming to Eldacre, my lord?' asked Ramus, as he settled into the chair.

'I fear it is. A more stupid and wasteful business there never was. Fields will not be planted, food will run low, tax revenues will dry up – save from the makers of swords and munitions.'

'And many will lose their lives.'

'Yes. Productive men will cease to be productive. So how are you faring after your brush with death?'

'I am fine, my lord. And you?'

'In pain. But then I am always in pain. There is no time to paint now, and I miss it. There is a ruined church on the high hills close to the Winter House. In the late afternoon the sunlight upon it is most pleasing. I had thought to recreate it on canvas.'

'I would like to see that, my lord.'

'My son is coming home. He escaped the treachery, fought his way clear.'

'That must have been a great relief to you.'

'Aye. I need a good cavalry general now. That will be all, apothecary.'

'Yes, my lord,' said Ramus, clambering to his feet.

'I fear I will paint no more, so there will be no further need for you to attend the castle. I shall send riders to collect the balms in future.'

'I am sorry to hear that, my lord. Perhaps when the war is over you will feel differently.'

But the Moidart had returned his attention to the papers on his desk and did not answer.

Huntsekker disliked riding, but at this moment he would far sooner have been on horseback. Instead he was driving a four horse wagon along a narrow road, Maev Ring sitting beside him. In the back of the wagon, hidden under sacks of grain, lay eight large wooden boxes, each containing two hundred and fifty pounds in silver chaillings. Under Maev Ring's direction Huntsekker had dug them up the previous night. It had taken all his strength to haul them from the earth. Each one weighed as much as a full grown man.

Huntsekker was a powerful man, but by the time he had hauled the boxes from the small wood to the farmhouse and loaded them onto the wagon he was exhausted. Once back inside the house he sank gratefully into a chair, his hands and arms still trembling from the effort of heaving the last of the boxes to the wagon floor. 'Smaller chests would have been wise, I think,' he told Maev.

'My Jaim had no problem carrying them out there,' she observed.

326

'I'll wager he grumbled worse than I did,' said Huntsekker. 'Jaim Grymauch was never too fond of physical labour – until it came to stealing bulls.'

Maev Ring suddenly laughed. Her face became instantly more youthful, highlighting for Huntsekker the beauty she must once have possessed. Hell, man, he thought, she's beautiful enough as she is now!

'You are correct,' said Maev, with a smile. 'He complained bitterly and swore it had ruined his back.'

'Why did you bury it?' he asked.

'A highland woman with so much coin? What would she spend it on, Huntsekker? I have acquired many business interests in my life. Each has cost me a great deal of coin, and yet each has then supplied ten times the outlay in profit. I seem to make money far faster than I can spend it.'

'You make that sound like a complaint. Most men would give their left arms for such a talent.'

'Yes, that is exactly the kind of thinking that shows why they do not possess it in the first place. One doesn't become rich by risking one's limbs. The problem with men is that they bring obsessive pride into their undertakings. Often it blinds them to their own shortcomings. Making money is easy. If I were Varlish I would own a palace, and the king would probably have made me a duchess. As a Rigante I am not allowed to use a bank, nor to own large parcels of land. So I bury my wealth. Since Jaim died I have used smaller boxes.'

'Shame we didn't dig those up,' muttered Huntsekker.

'We will leave soon after first light,' she said. 'You may sleep in Kaelin's room. It is at the top of the stairs on the left.'

Huntsekker had not slept well. His dreams had been all of Maev Ring, and her smile, and he awoke discomfited and uneasy. Now, as they sat close together on the wagon's driving seat, he could smell the scent of her hair.

'You are not a talkative man,' she observed.

'Not unless I have something to say.'

'I recall you were married once.'

'Twice. First wife left me while I was in the army. Second wife died. Sixteen years ago now. Selma. Good girl.'

'You were still young then. Why did you not remarry?'

'Why didn't you?' he countered.

'I wish I had,' she said.

'To Grymauch?'

'Of course to Grymauch,' she snapped. 'What a stupid question.'

'Wouldn't have worked,' he said.

'Would you care to explain that?' she asked coldly.

'No. Don't think I would.'

'Well, that is truly irritating.'

'No more than you should expect from a stupid man,' he retorted.

'I didn't say you were stupid. I said the question was stupid. There is a difference. If I offended you I apologize.'

The wagon reached a slight rise. Huntsekker flicked the reins across the backs of the team. 'It's not important,' he said. 'I can be as stupid as the next man. I never pretended to be clever. Neither did Jaim.'

'I never understood why you liked him. He stole your bull and he prevented you from killing Chain Shada. I would have thought you would have hated him.'

'I don't hate anyone. Never have. And I couldn't really tell you why I liked him. Everyone did, though. Galliott often talks of him. He took it hard when his musketeers shot Jaim down. He'd spent two days trying to find Jaim, to arrest him and prevent him making an appearance.'

'Yes, people liked him,' said Maev. 'They soon forget, though. Parsha Willets said she loved him. Didn't stop her marrying that cloth merchant two years after Jaim was dead.'

'Damn, but you are a hard woman,' said Huntsekker. 'I used to see Parsha Willets. Damn fine whore. Always gave a man his chailling's worth.'

'Thank you for sharing that.'

Huntsekker ignored the sarcasm. 'I saw her two nights after Jaim's death. Went to her house. We sat and talked for a little. I could see she wasn't in the mood for business. Her eyes had a kind of faraway look. She'd been drinking and crying. She didn't say much at first, but I sat there quiet and she started to talk. A lot of it flew by me. Love and such. Then she started to slur her words.

All the colour had gone from her face. When she passed out I knew it wasn't just a drunken stupor. I went and got the apothecary. Nice little man. He got to her, managed to rouse her a little, forced her to drink something. Then she vomited. I carried her up to her bed. The apothecary sat with her for a while. I waited downstairs. When he came down he took the goblet she'd been using, dipped his finger into the dregs and tasted it. He told me the name of the stuff, but I've forgotten it now. Anyways it was poison when taken in large doses. Parsha Willets tried to kill herself. As far as her marrying the cloth man – well, good for her. Whoring's no trade for a woman of her age. I'll bet Jaim would have said the same.'

Maev was silent for a moment. 'I never had any ill feeling towards Parsha. In some ways I envied her. Not her life, you understand. Merely the fact that she and Jaim . . . had something I did not. It was kind of you to help her as you did.'

'And that surprises you?'

'Why would it not? Kindness is not a trait one would associate with someone in your chosen profession.'

'A farmer, you mean?'

'You know very well what I mean, Harvester. You kill for the Moidart. I don't doubt it was you who wrung the neck of that vile bishop after the trial.'

'Some tasks are more pleasurable than others,' he admitted.

It began to rain, and Maev busied herself raising a canvas hood above the driving platform. The wind rippled at it, and the hissing and splattering of raindrops made conversation difficult. This was a blessed relief to Huntsekker.

Sadly the rain did not last long. Huntsekker was beginning to dread the night camp. 'So how did you become a hunter of men?' she asked.

'I forget. It was a long time ago.'

'Do you enjoy it?'

'Sometimes. It makes a break from the monotony of farm life. Most of the men I've hunted have been killers themselves, or thieves, or rapists.'

'And that justifies your calling?'

'I don't have to justify myself to anyone.'

'Then what are you doing now?'

'By heaven, woman, given the choice between continuing this conversation and having a wasps' nest in my ear I'd choose the latter.'

Her laughter rang out. 'You are easily nettled, Harvester. Are you usually so short-tempered?'

Huntsekker did not reply. Three men had moved into sight on the road ahead, and were waiting for them. One of the men carried a musket, the other two had pistols in their belts. 'Good evening to you,' said the man with the musket, as Huntsekker hauled on the reins.

'And to you, friend. Now move aside, for I'd not want the wagon wheel to run over your foot.'

'Nice wagon,' said the man. 'Well made. What are you carrying?'

'I'm going to repeat my order to you, boy, on the off chance that you are either deaf or stupid. Move aside.'

'Not very friendly, are you, old man? That's a big mistake out here.' He swung the musket from his shoulder. As he did so Huntsekker produced a pistol from inside his bearskin coat. Cocking it he pointed it at the man's head and pulled the trigger. The musket man flew backwards, landing in a heap. One of the others pulled the pistol from his belt. Huntsekker was about to leap from the wagon when a shot came from his left, making him jerk. The second man shouted in pain as a pistol ball slammed into his shoulder. His own weapon fell from his fingers. The third man slowly raised his hands. Huntsekker glanced to his left. Maev Ring was holding two small pistols. Smoke still curled from the barrel of one of them.

Huntsekker looked hard at the men. 'Is our business here concluded?' he asked.

Both men nodded.

'Good. Hand me the pistols and the musket.'

The uninjured young man did so. Huntsekker threw them into the back of the wagon. 'Best take your friend to the nearest surgeon,' he said. 'That ball will have pushed cloth and dirt into the wound. Likely he'll come down with gangrene.' Flicking the reins he drove the wagon past the two surviving robbers. The wheels crunched over the body of the musket man.

'How on earth were you planning to defeat three armed men with one pistol?' asked Maev.

330

'I figured if I shot the first you'd tongue lash the others to death.' He watched as Maev placed the pistols back in the leather bag at her feet.

'It's a wonder to me you've survived so long in your chosen profession,' she said. Huntsekker tugged at the spikes of his beard. 'I've noticed you do that a lot when you are nervous,' she pointed out.

It was going to be a long ride to Eldacre.

Winter Kay had always been a man of restless energy, with an ability to drive himself harder than his colleagues. Since the death of the king this talent had increased to a level which astounded his officers. He rarely slept, keeping a team of riders on hand around the clock to deliver messages to senior officers and distant army groups.

Within three days of the assassination the Redeemers had control of the capital, and all major ports. The last vestiges of the defeated Covenant army were hunted down, many of their supporters in the south arrested and summarily hanged. Redeemer forces across the land established military law, and the power of Winter Kay closed around the nation like a fist of iron.

At Baracum he reorganized the army, in preparation for the march on the north. With all secure behind him Winter Kay would be able to lead sixty thousand men on the march. Sir Sperring Dale had arrived from Eldacre, and his reports showed that the Moidart now had around eighteen thousand men, including new recruits. Redeemer seer scouts also reported some two thousand Rigante moving south to join him.

Winter Kay involved himself in all aspects of the current campaign, from supply of foods and necessary equipment to training and recruitment of officers. Strategy meetings were called often, and Winter Kay spent hours scanning written reports detailing the minutiae of preparation. With his senior officers he studied maps of the north, calling for population estimates and supply routes for the rebels.

'This,' he told his staff, 'will be a war of annihilation. The north will be laid bare. Not a single rebel is to be spared. We will lay waste to his lands and ensure no future rebellion ever returns to haunt us. Choose your men with care. Weed out those with weaker dispositions. The men who march north must be like wolves, savage and uncompromising.'

He radiated confidence, and seemed unperturbed by the news that Gaise Macon could no longer be seen by his seer scouts. 'He has acquired a demonic amulet or some such,' he said. 'It will avail him nothing.' Attempts to kill the spirit of the vile little magicker aiding the Moidart had also met with no success, though Winter Kay now knew his identity. Aran Powdermill, a demon worshipper and mystic.

Powdermill did not have the talent to penetrate the seer ring around Baracum, and his spirit always fled swiftly when discovered. He was a nuisance, nothing more, though his use of ward spells around Eldacre meant that the Moidart could meet with his generals in secret. This was of only limited use, as the same men would then have to relay his orders to their own officers outside the walls, and these orders were observed and reported back to Winter Kay.

The attack on the north could not proceed for another five weeks, while supplies were gathered. Winter Kay used the time wisely, strengthening his hold on the nation. He had himself declared Protector General of the realm, and issued edicts and proclamations, promising the restoration of the Great Council and changes to the law once the enemy had been defeated. Attempts were being made, he announced, to find the true heir to the murdered king, and when this was completed a golden age of peace and harmony would be restored. A nation sick to its soul of war greeted the news with joy.

Other reports were sent out, telling of the atrocities committed by the vile Moidart and his treacherous son, Gaise Macon. Macon had been part of the force who murdered the king. His capture was of paramount importance and a reward of two thousand pounds in gold was announced for any man, or men, who brought his head to Winter Kay.

In Eldacre Galliott the Borderer was on the verge of exhaustion. The problem facing the army of the Moidart was a simple one. It would begin to starve in less than two weeks. The food required to maintain the strength of eighteen thousand men was just not available in Eldacre, so soon after a harsh winter.

Galliott had sent out skirmishers to scour the countryside and buy cattle where they could, and the main warehouses in Eldacre had been commandeered – much to the chagrin of the owners. A rationing system had been speedily introduced. This had already caused ill feeling among the residents of Eldacre. That ill feeling would grow substantially worse when the food ran out.

Eldacre had been one of the main suppliers of cattle, grain and oats to the king's army. Many merchants had become rich on the profits, but this meant that only the bare minimum of supplies was warehoused in the north. It was shipped immediately south where it earned twice what it would in Eldacre itself. This avaricious pursuit of wealth had backfired alarmingly now that the north itself needed feeding. There were no substantial stock piles. Food was still being imported through the three coastal towns in the east, and some was due to be brought to Eldacre within the next month. Too little and too late.

If the army was to be fed, then the people would starve. If the army starved the people would be enslaved or murdered.

Galliott was close to his wits' end when Maev Ring arrived. He was summoned to the Moidart's office. As he entered he stumbled and righted himself. Maev Ring was sitting opposite the Moidart. Galliott saw the concern in her face as she looked at him. 'Are you well, captain?'

'It is colonel now,' said the Moidart, 'and he is simply tired.'

'Yes,' mumbled Galliott, 'tired.'

'Madam Ring is to take charge of supply,' said the Moidart. 'Find her a suitable office and apartments. She is to have the rank of quartermaster general.'

'A woman?' said Galliott.

'Very observant, colonel. She is indeed a woman. Were you in some doubt of this?'

'No, my lord. I meant . . . there has never been a woman with army rank.'

'As far as I know,' said the Moidart, 'there has never been an army which selected its own officers. I have discovered that I am an innovative man. By my reckoning the question of supply will prove crucial within the next three weeks. It is vital therefore that we have a quartermaster who will ensure that no disasters occur. I suggest you find General Ring an office, brief her on the situation, then get some rest. You look like a walking corpse.'

'Yes, my lord.' Galliott led Maev Ring back to his own office. Papers littered the desk. Some had fallen to the floor.

'Talk me through the actions you have taken so far,' said Maev Ring.

Galliott yawned and tried to bring his thoughts to order. He outlined the rationing programme, told her of the skirmishers, and the attempts to purchase cattle and meat.

'I have two thousand cattle being herded towards Eldacre,' said Maev Ring. 'It is also the lambing season, so meat will not be in short supply. We will issue promissory notes to farmers for their produce, these notes to be redeemed for coin upon request. Grain is a greater problem, but we will surmount it. Get me a list of Eldacre's most prominent exporters. I will need to speak to each of them.'

'I have already spoken to them. There are no stocks.'

'Where there is wealth there is a way, Galliott. You spoke to them as a soldier seeking to appropriate their goods and thus reduce their profits. I will speak to them as a businesswoman and promise them riches. You will find thereafter there is at least three times the amount of food available.'

Moving to the desk she lifted one of the papers lying there and scanned it. 'Go and get some rest, colonel. I shall remain here and look over your paperwork. Come back in three hours and we will begin to make plans.'


Gaise Macon's arrival in Eldacre caused a flurry of excitement. He rode in with his weary men, left Mulgrave to see to their billets and travelled on to the castle, a black hound running alongside his horse.

Citizens and soldiers paused to watch him as he rode past, a handsome young man with golden hair, riding a tall grey gelding. In a well cut cavalry jacket of dark grey silk, thigh length boots over pale grey leggings, he looked every inch a cavalryman. Glancing neither to right nor left, he did not acknowledge the occasional cheer that went up from those who recognized him.

Inside the castle walls he dismounted, leaving the gelding in the care of a groom. Then he strode into the castle, the black hound at his side. The beast padded alongside him, casting baleful looks at any who came close to the general.

Gaise climbed the stairs and walked to his father's offices, pushing open the door. The Moidart looked up, then stood, his face expressionless. 'You took your time coming home,' he said, moving round the desk. As he approached Gaise the black hound bared its teeth in a snarl. The Moidart glanced down at it, then flicked his fingers. 'Sit!' he commanded. The dog sank to its haunches instantly.

'I understand you have now acquired the Pinance's army.'

'Indeed.'

'Have you sent forces into the Pinance's land?'

'No. Not as yet.'

'It is necessary, one to acquire a fresh line of supply, and two to offer us a second line of defence. It should be done today. There are far too many troops sitting around here doing nothing. How many men do we have?'

'Just under eighteen thousand, though I expect the Rigante to send a force.'

'Winter Kay will have more than fifty thousand when he comes. Twenty thousand cavalry, twenty-five thousand musketeers and pikemen, and some two hundred cannons.'

'I quake in my boots,' said the Moidart. 'A glass of wine?'

'Aye, that would be welcome.'

'I take it that Shelding was hard on you. You seem to have acquired a touch of steel in your personality. I am most happy to see it.'

'A touch of steel?' said Gaise, coldly. 'Nicely put. But wholly incorrect. I always had a touch of steel. You were just blind to it, as you were blind to everything else I ever did. It used to concern me that you held no affection for your son. It used to worry me, and make me think I had done something to offend you. Now it concerns me not at all. You do not like me, Father, and I detest you and everything you have failed to stand for. That said, we now face a common enemy. I will lead your forces. In public I will acquiesce to your wishes, but you will merely be the figurehead. In reality I am now in control here.'

'Ah, so you are now the Moidart?'

'Something I would never wish to be. No, sir, I am the soldier. I understand war, and I know how to fight it. You have a problem with any of this?'

The Moidart moved to a cabinet by the western wall and filled two goblets with wine. He passed one to Gaise. Once more the dog growled. 'Fine beast,' he said.

'I would be obliged if you did not shoot it.'

'Ah, that accident still rankles with you. I did not intend to kill your dog, Gaise. I value a good dog, and Soldier was one of the best. However, that is the past. Do I have a problem with you running the army? No, of course not. As you say, you are the warrior – the Grey Ghost, I understand. Very colourful. You will inspire the men and give them confidence. Is Mulgrave still with you?'

'For the time being. He has a desire to leave my service.'

'Why?'

'He is soft-hearted.'

'Yes, I noticed that when he was in my employ. Not a natural killer. Sit down.' The Moidart returned to his chair. Gaise sat opposite him. 'How did you see this war developing?'

Gaise sipped his wine, then placed the goblet on the desk top. 'Winter Kay is an able general. He will know through his Redeemers how many men we have. It will be important to him to split our forces. Therefore he will probably send three columns into our lands. One will move along the east coast, closing off our supply routes from the sea. A second will come in from the west, across the lands of the Pinance. The main thrust will come directly from the south and be directed at Eldacre. This will be more slow-moving, since it will have the artillery. The other forces will, I suspect, consist of cavalry detachments and musketeer support. We will need to oppose them, and this will involve weakening our defences here. He is also likely to send a raiding force ahead of the three columns, trying to draw us out. The object of the raiding force will be to terrify the non-combatants and drain the morale of the citizenry.'

'Winter Kay does seem an able fellow,' said the Moidart. 'I am surprised it took him so long to defeat the Covenanters.'

'He had no wish to defeat them. It suited his purposes for the war to be prolonged. The king's popularity plummeted, which meant that by the time Winterbourne killed him the people were ready for a change, and will not mourn him.'

'A *very* able fellow. One could almost admire him.'

'I am sure the two of you would have become the best of friends,' said Gaise. 'I was almost touched when I learned you had become his enemy after he tried to have me killed.'

The Moidart smiled. 'Much as I would like to bask in the sunshine of your appreciation, I should point out that I became his enemy after he tried to have *me* killed. However, that is by the by. You will need to meet the staff officers. I will have them gather in the main hall this evening. In the meantime I shall order a force to march into the lands of the Pinance. How many should we send?'

'Two thousand is all we can spare at present,' said Gaise, 'but it should be sufficient in the short term. How capable are the generals under your command?'

'I have no idea at all,' answered the Moidart. 'They chose themselves. The only man I know well is Galliott. He is a fine organizer, but I fear he is no war leader. The others are Pinancers.'

Gaise considered the problem. 'Galliott's nephew, Hew, has served with me. He is a brave and skilful cavalryman. I shall promote him and put him in command of the force. He can choose his own junior officers. The majority of the men should be from Eldacre. There will be too many desertions if we allow the Pinancers to head back to their own lands.'

'Agreed,' said the Moidart. Gaise rose to leave. 'An unusual sword,' added the Moidart, as sunlight glinted upon the golden fist guard. 'Where did you get it?'

'From a dead man.'

'May I see it?' Gaise drew the gleaming sabre and passed it hilt first to the Moidart. 'This dead man appears to have had our family crest engraved upon the pommel. It is a handsome piece. What is the meaning of the rearing horse in the clouds?'

'It stands for Stormrider.'

The Moidart looked nonplussed.

'It is my Rigante soul-name.'

'Quaint and yet poetic. Perhaps I should acquire one.'

'I think, by definition, a soul-name requires a soul, Father.'

The Moidart laughed aloud. 'You are the second man in a matter of days to remind me of my lack in this regard.' He returned the sabre. 'And now you had better seek out Hew Galliott. I will arrange for a meeting of staff officers.'

Gaise Macon sheathed the sabre and walked from the room. The hound padded after him.

The Moidart stood for a moment, his expression thoughtful. 'I do have a soul-name,' he whispered.

Jakon Gallowglass was content. He had survived the attack on Shelding and the subsequent flight north. He had eaten a meal in the shadow of Eldacre Castle, and had discovered the whereabouts of a lively whore, with whom he had spent his last chailling. She had apologized for keeping him waiting while she serviced her previous customer. Jakon had not minded. The theatrical moans and cries he had heard only heightened his own anticipation.

Sated and happy Jakon Gallowglass wandered through the night dark streets of Eldacre town, heading back towards the hundreds of tents pitched to the west of the castle. He was idly wondering when the next wage would be paid when he saw a column of dark-garbed men loping down from the hills.

As they came closer he studied them. All of them wore black leather jerkins, beneath pale blue and green cloaks. They carried short, heavy sabres. Many had muskets, and all wore pistols in their belts. Long knives were thrust into scabbards at their sides. Gallowglass was a fighting man, and he knew fighting men. These were special. They were lean and hard-eyed, their movements smooth, sure and confident. Old Tamor had called it 'the look of eagles'. Gallowglass fully understood the phrase when he saw the warriors move towards the castle.

Colonel Galliott came out to meet them. He seemed uneasy as he approached them. Gallowglass sat on a low wall and cast his eyes back along the column. There was no banter among the men. He saw several of them glance towards him, and felt the coldness in their stares.

One of the warriors emerged from the column to meet Galliott. They did not shake hands, but they spoke quietly. Gallowglass stared at the man. He was powerfully built and dark-haired. He carried no musket, but two silver pistols were thrust into his belt. The two men talked for some time, then Galliott pointed to an area some distance from the tents, alongside a stream. The dark-haired warrior spoke to another man, who led the column away. Gallowglass saw them spread out and begin to make camp. Then Galliott and the leader walked into the castle.

Gallowglass considered wandering over to where the newcomers were gathering. He decided against it. They didn't look very welcoming. Instead he walked back to the line of tents, trying to recall which one he was sharing with Taybard Jaekel and Lanfer Gosten. Most of the flaps were drawn shut. Gallowglass opened several and peered inside before moving on. Just when he had decided to crawl into the next damned tent that had a space he saw Taybard emerge some twenty yards further along. Gallowglass waved and strolled over to him.

'Found the whore,' he said. 'Mighty fine she was.'

'I need to piss,' said Taybard.

'Me too.'

Together they walked back to the castle wall and emptied their bladders. 'How do you feel about being home?' asked Jakon.

'I'm not home,' said Taybard.

'What are you talking about?' responded Gallowglass, tying the front of his leggings. 'This is where you come from, isn't it?'

'Yes. This is where I come from.'

Taybard moved away. Gallowglass watched him go. The man had not been the same since Shelding. The deaths of Kammel Bard and Banny Achbain had changed him in a way Gallowglass did not understand. People died in war. That was a fact of life. Indeed most of the men Gallowglass had known at the start of the war were now in the ground. Old Tamor had been the first to go, his face blown off. They had identified him by a red birth mark on the back of his neck. His death had saddened Gallowglass, but it hadn't turned him weird.

He saw that Taybard had not gone back to the tent, and caught sight of him wandering along the line of the wall. Gallowglass ran after him. 'Wait up,' he said. 'Where you headed?'

'Just walking.'

'You want to walk alone?'

'I don't care.'

'Not like you to leave your rifle behind.'

'No. Hanging offence to lose your rifle.'

'What the hell is wrong with you, Jaekel? Are you drunk?'

Taybard suddenly sat on the ground. 'I'm not drunk,' he said. 'I just want to go home.'

'You *are* home.'

'We marched past my house yesterday. Only it didn't seem like my house. Nothing is the same, Gallowglass. Old Hills, Eldacre, the Five Fields . . . it's all changed.'

'New buildings, you mean?'

'No, they're all the same. But they're not home any more. They're just buildings. I want to go home. I want things to be as they were. I want to see Banny, and hear him making jokes. I want to hear Kammel complaining about everything.'

'They are dead, Jaekel. You are not.'

'I know they are dead. I know things will never be the same. I just thought that when I came home I would be free of . . . I don't know what I thought.'

'You should get some sleep. Sleep is good. You haven't slept much since Shelding.'

'I think I'll walk a bit.' Taybard rose to his feet and wandered off. Gallowglass followed him. They approached the area where the newcomers were camped. Fires had been lit, and groups of men were sitting around. Taybard Jaekel ignored them and kept walking.

'This is a Rigante camp,' said someone. 'You Varlish can stay clear of it.'

'I'm Rigante,' said Taybard Jaekel. 'She told me that. She said . . .'

'I don't care what she said,' snapped the man, surging to his feet. 'Get your stinking carcass away from us.'

Gallowglass moved in. 'Rigante is it?' he said. 'Well watch yourself, Rigante, or I'll rip off your head and piss in the hole.'

'The Wyrd said I was of the line of Fiallach,' said Taybard Jaekel tonelessly. 'He was a general, you know. He served Connavar the King. Don't know much about him. The books don't say. Don't know who I am really. Don't know anything any more.' A silence fell on the scene. Jaekel just stood there, lost in dark and gloomy thoughts.

A tall, fair-haired man stepped forward and approached Gallowglass. 'What is wrong with your friend?' he asked.

'Too much death, I reckon.'

The man who had first insulted them moved alongside Taybard. He was tall and sharp-featured, his dark hair close cropped and receding, leaving a pointed widow's peak at the centre of his brow. 'Drink this,' he said, offering Taybard a small, leather-covered flask. Taybard drank deeply. 'Sit you down,' the man went on, no anger now in his voice. 'I'll tell you of Fiallach and his Iron Wolves. Then you'll know who you are and where you came from.'

Taybard sat obediently and the men seated themselves in a circle around him. Gallowglass stood by, forgotten, but he listened as the tale of Fiallach unfolded. It was a story well told, of a rough and arrogant man who had, at first, sought to kill Connavar, but then had served him faithfully unto death. All the while the story was unfolding the Rigante plied Taybard Jaekel with their flasks. When it came to Fiallach's death in battle Taybard began to weep. The man closest to him told him to lie down. Taybard did so. Within moments he was asleep. Someone covered him with a blanket. Gallowglass remained where he was, unsure of what to do. The storyteller rose silently. The others followed his lead, then moved away from the sleeping man.

Then the storyteller moved past Gallowglass, gesturing for him to follow. Once they were a little way from Taybard the Rigante looked into Gallowglass's eyes. 'So, you'll rip my head from my shoulders, will you?'

'And piss in the hole,' said Gallowglass.

The man laughed. 'Is there Rigante in you too, by any chance?'

'If there is no-one ever told me. What were you getting him to drink?'

'Uisge. He'll sleep well, and wake with a head that feels it's been fired from a cannon.'

'Why did you do that for him?'

'The man was hurting, and the Wyrd said he was Rigante. The Wyrd is known to us as the Dweller by the Lake. If she says he is

Rigante he is Rigante. We look after our own. I am Korrin Talis. You?'

'Jakon Gallowglass.'

'Leave your friend with us. We'll give him breakfast and send him back to you.'

'I'd like to stay with him.'

'But you can't,' said Talis, with a wolfish grin, 'for you are a stinking Varlish, and if you disobey me I'll be forced to rip off your balls and make you wear them as a necklace.'

Gallowglass laughed aloud. 'Goodnight to you, Korrin Talis.'

'And to you, Jakon Gallowglass.'

# CHAPTER SIXTEEN

KAELIN RING FOLLOWED GALLIOTT INTO THE CASTLE, AND UP THE WIDE
stairwell. He paused at the top and stared at the picture of a beautiful young woman, standing alongside a tall grey horse. The horse
was stylized, its head far too small, but the woman was extra-
ordinarily lifelike. 'The Moidart's grandmother,' said Galliott.
'Beautiful, wasn't she?'

'Aye. She looks familiar to me.'

'Gaise Macon has the same odd coloured eyes. You have met
him, have you not?'

'Once.'

'Well, I'm glad to say he is back. Heaven knows we'll need his
skills. Come on now, best not to keep the Moidart waiting.'

Kaelin's lips tightened, but he said nothing, and followed
Galliott to the Moidart's apartments.

Inside were two men: the Moidart, dressed in a shirt of white
satin, the breast embroidered with the Fawn in Brambles crest of
his house, dark leggings and boots, and Gaise Macon. He wore a
grey cavalryman's jacket, with split sleeves. It was well cut, though
showed signs of wear. There was an old bloodstain on the right
sleeve.

Galliott bowed to the Moidart and left. Kaelin walked into the
room. The Moidart remained seated, but Gaise Macon rose and

moved towards Kaelin, his hand outstretched. He was leaner than when Kaelin had first seen him, back in Old Hills. Gaise Macon had stopped Taybard Jaekel from plunging a knife into Kaelin's unprotected body. It seemed so long ago now.

Kaelin Ring shook the proffered hand. 'Good to see you again, Ring,' said Gaise Macon.

'I see you have brought less than two hundred men,' said the Moidart.

'Eighteen hundred more are following. They will be here in three days.'

'Ah, that is better news,' said the Moidart. 'I was not aware that you two had met.'

'A long time ago, Father. As I recall, Master Ring has a fine left hook. He was taught, so he told me at the time, by the champion, Jaim Grymauch. You might recall he was the highlander who defeated the Varlish champion.'

'I do recall,' said the Moidart, rising from his chair. 'And now I will leave you to become better acquainted. There will be a meeting of staff officers tomorrow at first light. You will be most welcome to attend, Master Ring.'

Kaelin noticed Gaise Macon looked surprised by the announcement. 'With respect, Father, I thought you would wish to speak to Master Ring about his troops.'

'Not at this time. You and he should converse. You will find you have much in common. Good night to you, Master Ring.'

Kaelin nodded.

'Oh, by the way, your aunt Maev is now a general in my army. Novel, don't you think?'

Kaelin made no attempt to disguise his shock. 'A general?'

'She is in charge of supplies,' said Gaise Macon. 'My father has developed an odd sense of humour.'

'Indeed I have,' said the Moidart. 'Life, I have discovered, is almost always so tragic that it becomes amusing. However, in this case, the appointment was not made lightly. As one of my generals she will have powers that a quartermaster could not call upon. I will see you at the briefing, Master Ring. When you have finished here, Gaise, join me and Powdermill in the upper apartment.'

After he had left Kaelin looked hard at the blond-haired

cavalryman, seeking any sign of resemblance to himself. Having never known his own father, nor seen a painted likeness, Kaelin had no point of reference to make comparisons. They were around the same height, but there any similarity ended. Kaelin was square-jawed, his dark eyes deep set. Gaise Macon looked like the nobleman he was, fine ascetic bone structure and an aquiline nose.

'Is there something about me that troubles you?' asked Gaise.

'No.'

'You seem to be staring rather.'

'You don't look much like your father,' said Kaelin.

'Something to be thankful for. You say there will be two thousand Rigante?'

'Within three days.'

'I am not sure how best to use them. Modern army warfare requires discipline and an understanding of the structures of command. You follow?'

'Oh, I am sure I can keep up – if you speak slowly and clearly.'

'I am not trying to insult your men, Ring.'

'Best not, Macon.'

Gaise rubbed his hand across his face, then moved to where a flagon of wine stood on a cabinet. 'We seem to be heading in different directions, my friend. Would you like a glass of wine?'

'No.'

'I know the Rigante are fine fighters. I know they crushed an army of my father's a few years back. I have no doubts whatever concerning their skill in combat. What I am saying is that unless there is discipline they will be cut to pieces. This will not be a war won by a single charge. We will need to co-ordinate our attacks and seek common objectives. We do this by developing a plan of action and relying on every unit to follow its orders implicitly.'

'I understand that,' said Kaelin. 'So do my men.'

'The plan, for instance, may call for the Rigante to attack suddenly, and then fall back in apparent disarray, leading the enemy to think they have won. This will draw the enemy forward into a trap. I need to be able to rely on you to follow my orders to the letter.'

'You don't put a saddle on a war hound,' said Kaelin Ring.

'Meaning?'

'I'll take that wine now, if I may?'

'Of course,' said Gaise Macon, filling a goblet and passing it to the clansman. Kaelin sipped it.

'It's good – though a little young.' He put down the goblet. 'My meaning is simple. The Rigante are fighting men, hard and relentless. The men I bring are the best of the best. Every one of them has courage and tenacity. They will cut their way through any force the enemy can offer. Give us ground to hold and we will defend it to the death. You'll have no worries about the Rigante fleeing the field. We will stand. But we are not army men. Your clever plans, your flanking movements, your deceptions will need to be carried out by those trained in that kind of warfare. From what I understand you have twelve thousand men enlisted from the army of the Pinance. Professional soldiers. They will fight for you only so long as they believe you can win, and only so long as their wages are met. You have over five thousand Eldacre men, who will stand fast – at least for a while – because they are fighting for their own land and have nowhere to run. And you have the Rigante. You do not know it yet, but the Rigante are the best hope you have. We can either be the hammer or the anvil. Nothing in between. Use us wisely.'

'Outnumbered three – maybe four – to one I will need to use all the men wisely,' said Gaise. 'Have you any thoughts on the coming invasion?'

'I think they'll send an advance force, trying to draw us out. If I was Winter Kay I'd then send two columns east and west of Eldacre. The biggest problem, though, is those damned Redeemers and their talent for observing us. Galliott says they can't *see* us when we are inside the castle. We need to be able to extend that protection over our forces as they move. Otherwise it won't matter how prettily you plan; they'll know everything we are about to do.'

'My thoughts exactly. It is something we are working on. That's why my father is with Powdermill. He is a magicker of sorts. However, we can talk about that tomorrow. My father has appointed generals. I would appreciate your view on them after the meeting.'

'You think he has appointed unwisely?'

'I doubt it. Much as I loathe the man he is a shrewd judge.'

346

Kaelin chuckled. 'Not an easy man to like, though it surprises me that you feel the same. The Moidart murdered my father. I have reason to hate him. What reason do you have?'

'My reasons are my own – and I don't wish that to sound offensive to you, Kaelin. I thank you for bringing the Rigante to Eldacre. Will the Wyrd be joining us here? She could be of great help against the Redeemers.'

'No. We asked her to come with us. She says her talents are not for war and death.'

Gaise shook his head, and, for a moment, showed irritation. 'According to what we now know, we are facing the spirit of a Seidh god. Do you find it strange that the unholy can use all their powers to destroy, while the holy cannot?'

Kaelin shrugged. 'Perhaps that is what makes them holy.'

'I wonder. The Wyrd has helped me, and advised me. This is because I am the Stormrider, and she relies upon me to save the day. She relies upon me to fight. And you. And the Rigante. So is she not a part of the war already? We can go out and kill and sully our souls for her and her dreams. But she will not sully herself. Can you make sense of it?'

'I don't try,' said Kaelin. 'I am not holy. I know she is pledged not to use her power to harm others. That is good enough for me.'

'I am not holy either, Kaelin Ring. If I had the power I would kill them all in an instant.'

Kaelin looked into the man's oddly coloured eyes. It seemed to him then that, just for a moment, there was the glint of insanity there.


'Explain it again,' said the Moidart.

Aran Powdermill's patience snapped. 'To what purpose? I cannot teach you the principles of magic in a single night.' Tiredness had made him bold, but even as he spoke, his stomach turned. 'Forgive me,' he said swiftly, 'I meant no offence.'

'Calm yourself, Powdermill. You are rather valuable to me at present. Small discourtesies can be forgiven. Best not to make a habit of them, however.' The Moidart paced the small room. 'The ward spells you have placed on the castle keep out the Redeemers, but they need to be constantly recast.'

'Yes, my lord. A spell is like a living thing. It is born, it ages and grows weak, then it fades.'

'What is the source of its energy?'

'In this instance I am, my lord. This is why I am so drained.'

'And you replenish this magic merely by rest?'

'Not exactly, my lord.'

The door opened and Gaise Macon entered. He nodded to Powdermill, then moved to the fireplace and held his hands out to the flames. 'You never did like the cold,' said the Moidart.

'It does not bother me now,' replied Gaise. 'Are we any closer to an answer?'

'Not at present. Powdermill was just explaining about the casting of spells. Go on, Master Powdermill.'

'I can use my energies and talents for small spells. I have never been able to hold the shape of the larger spells.'

'The shape?' asked Gaise.

'This is not easy to explain, my lord. Think of a juggler, tossing three balls in the air. His dexterity is better than most men's. What he does is amusing and clever. Now imagine five balls. This man is very talented. The concentration required to keep all the balls in the air is matched only by his extraordinary co-ordination. My ward spells are five ball tricks. To create a greater spell, covering, say, the whole of Eldacre, would be like a man juggling a hundred balls in the air at the same time. I do not possess that degree of talent. I cannot hold all the incantation words in my head at the same time, nor balance the rhythms of the Words of Power.'

'Something is missing here,' said the Moidart.

'Missing, my lord?'

'This replenishing of energies. You cast a spell. It lives for a while then it dies. You replace it. You say the spells come from your talent.'

'Yes, my lord.'

'But the Redeemers do not possess your talents?'

'No. They use the power of the Seidh skull.'

'An external source that they can draw upon.'

'Indeed, my lord.'

'But you do not use such a source. Your talent is from within.'

'Yes, my lord.'

348

'You were born with this talent for manipulating the magic that is all around us?'

'Yes.'

The Moidart looked at him closely. 'And you use nothing to enhance it?'

Powdermill could not meet the Moidart's hawk-eyed gaze. 'I have an amulet that was blessed by the Veiled Lady. This adds to my talent.'

'Put aside your fears, Powdermill, I shall not steal it from you. Let me ask you this: if you had the Orb of Kranos would your powers increase?'

'Yes, my lord.'

'Would you then be able to create a ward spell to cover the whole of Eldacre?'

'I don't know, my lord. But I would certainly be able to perform greater spells than I can at this moment.'

'The cathedral is full of holy ornaments,' said the Moidart. 'Perhaps one of them could be useful.'

'No, my lord,' said Powdermill, glumly. 'I have been to the cathedral. There is nothing there but forgeries and fakes. I went to Varingas once, to see the Blessed Veil. When I reached out with my talent I knew it was merely a piece of gauze. The image of the face was created by carefully applying iron oxides to the cloth. Items imbued with genuine magic are rare.'

'What I still do not understand,' said the Moidart, 'is the central principle. Magic, you tell me, is like a living thing. How is it that the magic in your amulet does not fade as your spells do?'

'There are only theories to answer that, my lord,' said Powdermill. 'The one I feel is closest to the truth concerns the nature of magic. It is born in some way through sunlight and its effect on living things. My amulet was blessed by the Veiled Lady. This made it a vessel of magic. You have seen the weird pieces of iron that attract other pieces of iron?'

'I have seen magnets,' said the Moidart.

'I believe the amulet operates in a similar fashion, drawing magic to it from out of the air, from sunlight. I do not know how the process works. I do know that it regenerates itself. In some places it will regenerate more swiftly. Forests, for example, seem to give it greater power.'

'Have you tried blood?' asked the Moidart.

'I once sacrificed a chicken, but I almost destroyed the amulet in the process. This is not a piece that requires sacrifice, my lord.'

'Pity.'

'Yes, my lord.'

'So, it seems that we can find no way to combat these Redeemers outside the castle?'

'I know of no way to accomplish that, my lord.'

'All you need,' said Gaise Macon, 'is a strong source of magic?'

Both men turned towards the golden-haired warrior. 'Yes, my lord,' said Powdermill.

'Something of the Seidh?'

'Indeed, sir.'

Gaise Macon drew the Sword in the Storm and laid it on the table. 'Use your talent to examine this, Master Powdermill.'

Aran Powdermill looked quizzically at Gaise. 'It is a modern sabre.'

'Use your talent, man.'

Aran took a deep breath and closed his eyes. Then he reached out. His hand lightly touched the golden hilt. He stiffened and drew in a deep breath.

'This is the sword of Connavar,' he said. 'Sweet heaven, how did you come by it?'

'A dead man gave it to him, apparently,' said the Moidart.

'A dead man named Riamfada. Can you use the magic, Master Powdermill?'

'I need time to prepare, my lord. This is . . . this is remarkable. Priceless.'

'Forget the monetary value,' snapped the Moidart. 'Can you cast a spell with it?'

'Oh, my lord, I can,' said Powdermill.

Mulgrave was wandering in a green meadow under starlight. He had no idea how he had arrived there, or indeed where he was.

He thought he could hear running water, and realized he was thirsty. The sound was coming from somewhere to his left.

Walking on a little he saw an old mill, its wheel slowly turning as the river pushed against its blades. It was very like the mill back in Shelsans, where his father had worked. On some summer afternoons Mulgrave would run along the river bank, bringing the food his mother had prepared for Father. He would emerge from the warehouse alongside the mill, and sit in silence, breaking bread with his son. Even now the memories of those quiet days filled Mulgrave with a mixture of sadness and great joy.

He walked on towards the river bank, half hoping his father would be there. Instead he saw the white-haired woman he had dreamed of so often lately. A pale blue and green shawl was wrapped around her shoulders. She turned towards him, beckoning him to sit beside her. 'Can you speak now?' he asked her.

'I could always speak, Mulgrave. You could not hear.' Raising her hand she tapped a finger to his chest. 'The little amulet Ermal Standfast gave you contains earth magic. Not much – but enough to allow a Rigante to make contact with a foreigner.' She said it with a soft smile.

'Is Ermal safe?'

'Of course. Men like Ermal are always safe. They run and hide when danger threatens.'

'Good for him. I wish I could run and hide from it all. I hate what I see now, and I despise what I have become.'

'Love often carries us along roads we would not wish to travel,' she said. 'Love is a burden sometimes. Yet it is still to be treasured.'

Mulgrave picked up a stone and threw it out over the river. 'I see myself in him,' he said. 'After the massacre I was raised for a while by a cold-hearted couple who used me badly. I don't know why, but after I escaped them I found it hard to trust anyone. When I met Gaise I saw the same secret sorrow in his eyes. I wanted him to find the happiness that was lost to me. I wanted to see him with a wife and family. To know the joys of life. Instead he is following a darker path.'

'He has unchained the bear,' said the Wyrd sadly. 'It is a curse of his bloodline. Great men they can be, but there is inside them a terrible beast. While they control it they are heroes. When it controls them they become . . . the Moidart, and villains like him.' She sighed. 'I have no right to criticize them. Not any more.'

'Have you killed people?' he asked.

'Not directly. I urged the Rigante to march to Eldacre. Many of them will be slain. Perhaps all of them. I have taken the first tottering steps on the road to damnation. Do you believe that committing a small evil to prevent a greater evil is justified?'

'I don't know,' said Mulgrave. 'I remember once thinking it would have been a good thing if the Moidart had been strangled at birth. Now he is fighting against evil. I don't know what any of it means. I just wish I wasn't part of it.'

'I know,' whispered the Wyrd. 'I once dreamed of bringing back the Seidh to guide the world, to renew its magic. I would then spend my life healing and encouraging people to do good. When I died I would leave the world a better place than it was before me. Now I have encouraged a people I love to take part in a war to *stop* the Seidh coming back. To shoot and stab and kill. Perhaps Cernunnos is right. Perhaps we are a race not worth saving.'

They sat in silence for a while, watching the sunlight gleaming on the water, and listening to the slow splashing of the millwheel blades as they turned.

'Are you a seer, lady? Can you see the future?'

'Glimpses only, swordsman. I have known for twenty years that Gaise Macon would hold our destiny in his hands. I knew the future of the Rigante would depend upon it. I did not know how, or why it would come to pass. I guessed – wrongly – that the Moidart would be the evil force. Now I see something else. I see you, Mulgrave. Gaise Macon will ask a service of you. It will break your heart.'

'My heart is already broken. I shall refuse him. I want nothing more to do with his evil.'

'It will not be evil which inspires him to seek you. I see him in the vision wearing a patchwork cloak. This signifies that his Rigante heritage will be in the ascendant. Not the beast which now rules him.'

'What will he ask me?'

'I do not know. But he will ask it here. By this stream. Where he cannot be overheard. I will arrange it, for that is my destiny.'

*

For four days the new generals and colonels met with Gaise Macon and the Moidart, discussing battle strategies. Gaise conducted further meetings, getting to know the men, and making judgements about their talents. Mostly they were solid officers, with a good understanding of strategy and logistics. Three were exceptional. Kaelin Ring had a fine mind, and, despite appearing outspoken, showed a subtle and perceptive understanding of human nature. Bendegit Law, the only officer appointed directly by the Moidart, had already proved himself by acquiring fifty cannon in a bloodless raid to the east. He was a natural leader, well liked by his men. Garan Beck was a career soldier, who had served in three wars across the seas, and had been hired by the Pinance to train his infantry. Without a trace of noble blood he had never till now held any rank higher than colonel. Bluff and powerfully built, the middle-aged general talked little during the meetings, but when he did speak his words were direct, cutting to the heart of the problems they faced.

When the broader meetings were over Gaise would discuss them with the Moidart. Much as he disliked the man he found his observations to be razor sharp.

'Beck can be relied upon,' said the Moidart, as they sat in the high office, the windows open to the northern stars. 'He feels no need to prove himself and will do nothing reckless. My advice would be to appoint him as your number two.'

'I agree. I need to be heading south tomorrow. I'll leave Beck in charge of training here. Who do you see as leading the eastern force? Galliott?'

'No,' said the Moidart. 'Galliott is not equipped to be a battle commander. He is a peacetime officer, with a fine understanding of bureaucracy. He does not have the mind of a warrior.'

'Kaelin Ring and his Rigante?'

'He would be fine,' said the Moidart, 'but I doubt you really want to send them.'

'Ring says they are the best of the best,' said Gaise. 'Do you agree with that?'

The Moidart leaned back in his chair. 'I abhor the Rigante. Always have. They could have conquered the world. Finest fighting men I have ever seen. Their biggest problem is they are not ever *prepared* for war. Battles, yes. They will fight like demons. Then they want to go home, and plant their crops and tend to their cattle. In this instance, though, Ring is right. They are the best we have. In my view they should be central to our plans.'

'Who then for the east?' asked Gaise.

The Moidart looked at him for a moment. 'Is the responsibility beginning to weigh on you, boy?'

'I am not a boy, Father. Not any more. But, yes, I feel the weight of responsibility. Is that unnatural?'

'Not at all. Now you seek to offload some of that weight. You cannot. It pleased me when you stood up to me and said that I would be the figurehead. That is as it should be. The young lion stretching his muscles. Now you must discover whether you have the stamina and the power to sustain leadership. To do that you must accept that it is lonely on the top of the mountain. You may ask for advice. You may listen to the plans of others. But yours is the final decision. Yours is the only word that counts. Success and glory, defeat and death, will be laid at your door. So now, tell me what you think of your other generals.'

Gaise took a deep breath. He wanted to argue, to rail at his father. His emotions were in turmoil. Instead he rose to his feet and began to pace the room. 'They are solid but unimaginative.'

'Do you need dashing and reckless in the east?'

'No,' said Gaise. 'The east cannot be held for long.'

'Then what do you need?'

'I need a man who can maintain an organized and spirited withdrawal, keeping the men in good order while holding up the enemy advance.'

'Someone who will not panic.'

'Of course.' Gaise suddenly relaxed. 'I need Beck for the east,' he said.

'Good choice.'

'Why then did you agree when I said I would keep Beck in Eldacre?'

'You are the leader, Gaise. Men always tend to agree with the leader. It is the nature of things.'

'This is not a game, Father.'

'Of course it is – the oldest game in the world. You have proved yourself in battle, leading men in cavalry charges. This game is different. This game is unlikely to be won by a single, heroic charge. This will be like the wolf pack hunting the stag. This will be about planning, movement, wearing down the enemy, bringing him to bay at exactly the point he is at his weakest. This will be about subtlety and deception. Winter Kay is an excellent strategist. He thinks he is the wolf. He is right. We are the stag. To win you must make *him* the stag.'

Gaise walked to the window, and stared out at the moonlit mountains. 'You realize this is the longest conversation we have ever had?'

'I am not much of a talker. This is no time to be maudlin.'

Gaise laughed. 'Maudlin? Oh, Father. You have no idea. You talk brilliantly of strategies and leadership. You understand men and what motivates them. Do you have the remotest idea of what motivates me?'

'No – and nor do I care to,' snapped the Moidart, rising.

'Why did you risk yourself for me that night?' asked Gaise.

The Moidart stiffened. 'What are you talking about?'

'The manor was ablaze. Those who could had escaped into the night. You were one of them. When you heard no-one had brought me out you ran back into that blazing building. You found me in my crib. You covered me with a blanket and you ran through the flames and smoke. When you leapt from that upper window your clothes were on fire. The only wound I received was this small burn on my face. You almost died. Why did you do that for me, when you so obviously despised me?'

The Moidart walked to the door, and opened it. He glanced back. 'I am *The Hawk in the Willow*,' he said.

Then he was gone.


Three days south of Eldacre, Kaelin Ring and seven hundred Rigante made camp on a high ridge overlooking a long, wooded valley. No fires were lit, and Kaelin gathered his senior men together. Among them were Rayster, Korrin Talis and Potter Highstone.

Earlier that day they had seen the advance columns of Varlish cavalry, and their outriding scouts. The Rigante, as ordered by Gaise Macon, kept out of sight, fading back into the woods and allowing the enemy to pass unhindered.

A force of several thousand men were heading north, complete with supply wagons and twenty cannon – almost exactly as Aran Powdermill had predicted. They were not, Kaelin was encouraged to know, reinforced by Knights of the Sacrifice, but were made up from elements of the King's Fourth and Fifth Armies. Many of the foot soldiers of the Fourth had been recruited from prisons. They were known as hardy, brutal fighters. Some of the atrocities committed upon Covenant towns had been laid at their door. The cavalry were a mixture, some battle-hardened veterans, others recruits from the south. The force was led by a Redeemer Knight named Sperring Dale. Gaise Macon's generals all knew the man. He had ridden into Eldacre with the Pinance, but had fled swiftly after the Pinance was slain. None liked him, and none knew whether he was a talented officer. All they knew was that his conversation generally revolved around punishment and death for the enemies of the cause. It was said he had supervised the massacre at Barstead, when women and children had been burned alive. However, no-one asked him, and it was just as likely to be mere rumour.

Kaelin Ring had been unusually tense for two days now. He did not doubt the Rigante could stand against the enemy. What concerned him was whether the enemy could still *see* into the lands of the north. Gaise Macon had assured him that a mighty ward spell had been cast; that they were safe from observation. 'How do we know?' asked Kaelin.

'Aran Powdermill says it is so. I believe him.'

'I do not even know him. We could march out from here and be massacred before we realize the error.'

'True,' said Gaise, with a smile. 'There is, as they say, only one way to find out.'

So here they were, upon a ridge to the south of the invaders. Kaelin's orders were to follow hard on the heels of the advance force until they reached the abandoned settlement at Three Streams thirty miles north. It was here that Gaise intended to fall upon them. The Rigante would then surprise them by attacking from the rear.

'They seem to have passed us by without incident,' said Korrin Talis. 'And look. They are making camp.'

'Aye, but we'll stay wary. Let's move back off this ridge and find two campsites. Rayster, I want you to scout to the south. Potter, you stay here and keep an eye on their camp.'

'They've already passed us by, Kaelin,' said Rayster. 'What am I to watch for?'

'As best I could I counted the men moving north. I reckon they have around four thousand. This Powdermill the Stormrider believes in said there were six thousand. So where are the other two?'

'This would not be a good place to be caught between two armies,' said Korrin. 'Not with just seven hundred of us.'

As the night wore on the Rigante lay on the cold earth, sleeping lightly. Kaelin dozed for a while, but could not relax into sleep. Just before dawn he roused Korrin Talis and ordered the men to make ready to march.

As the Rigante roused themselves Kaelin saw Rayster come running into the camp. 'Fifteen hundred men are moving towards us, Kaelin. They are no more than half a mile south.'

'Order all weapons loaded,' Kaelin told Korrin Talis. 'And send someone to relieve Potter.' Then, followed by Rayster, he ran back through the trees. Just before they reached the ridge Rayster ran alongside him. 'Look!' he said, pointing ahead through the gloom. Moving across the floor of the valley below were three lines of armed men. Dressed in the grey tunics of the King's Fourth, their muskets were held ready, bayonets fixed to the barrels. They were advancing in attack formation, and heading for the trees.

In that moment something moved to Kaelin's left.

The trap was well sprung, the four dark-garbed knifemen moving in swiftly. The victims should have been stunned into inaction by the speed of it. Most men would have been. Even most Rigante men. Rayster ducked to his right, Kaelin to his left. One knifeman went down as Rayster's fist slammed into his jaw. Kaelin grabbed another man's knife arm and swung him into one of his comrades. Rayster managed to draw his sabre, which plunged through a man's chest, causing a grunt of pain. Kaelin, with no space to draw his sword, pulled his hunting knife clear, slashing it across the face of a charging man. The blade sliced down over his jawbone, cutting deep into the jugular. As the attacker fell the man behind him sprinted for the safety of open ground. Rayster dropped his sabre, drew his hunting knife and hurled it. The blade took the man at the base of the skull. He stumbled and fell. Rayster ran to him, driving the knife deeper before ripping it clear.

The first man Rayster had punched tried to struggle to his feet. Kaelin moved in and cut his throat.

The advancing men below had reached the foot of the ridge. 'Let's move,' said Kaelin. Rayster gathered up his sabre and followed Kaelin back through the trees.

There was little time for any elaborate battle plans and Kaelin's mind was racing as he sped back to the main body of the Rigante. Calling Korrin Talis to him he swiftly outlined what he had seen. Fifteen hundred men were marching up the ridge to the south.

Four Rigante emerged from the trees to the south and loped to where Kaelin, Rayster and Korrin were talking. One of them was Korrin's brother, Fada. 'Potter is dead,' he said. 'Throat cut. They sent assassins into the woods. The whole of their army is marching on us from the north.'

They were caught in a vice.

'We need to head east,' said Korrin. 'There's open ground there. We could make it around them and scatter. Meet up later with Macon at Wishing Tree.'

'Did you see any cavalry?' Kaelin asked Fada.

'No. Just infantry.'

'The cavalry will be east of us, waiting for just such a move. They'll hammer into us as we make the break. West is no option. That will take us down onto the valley floor, with nowhere to escape to. No. We have to fight.'

'Then fight it is,' said Korrin.

'Take half the men north and hold the slope,' said Kaelin. 'I'll deal with those in the south, then come to your aid.'

'Three hundred and fifty against four thousand. Well, don't take your time, cousin. Those odds are steep – even for the Rigante.'

Kaelin ran back among the clansmen. 'Every second man follow me!' he shouted, then headed back towards the south. By the time the Rigante reached the crest of the ridge the enemy musketeers were halfway up.

'Volley line!' yelled Kaelin. The Rigante instantly spread out along the crest and, kneeling, brought their own muskets to bear.

'Fire!' A murderous volley tore into the advancing ranks. The front line was scythed down, but the second returned fire, then charged up the slope. Coolly the Rigante reloaded, then sent a second volley into them. 'Down muskets!' yelled Kaelin. 'Charge!'

With a terrifying battle cry the Rigante drew their sabres and pistols and hurled themselves down the slope into the startled musketeers. They had been told they outnumbered the enemy, and they had expected their attack to be a surprise. Now they themselves were being attacked. At point blank range the Rigante fired their pistols into the enemy. Then they tore into them with sabres and knives. The Varlish musketeers were tough men, but they had never faced a foe as savage and remorseless as the Rigante.

Even so, they tried to hold to their formation and fight back. They had the advantage of superior numbers, and they were armed with bayoneted muskets. But they had advanced in skirmish lines and were not closely ordered. The Rigante tore into them. Even those clansmen stabbed by the bayonets lashed out, killing the wielders, and, bleeding heavily, rushed forward to kill again and again until they were cut down.

Kaelin Ring, with sword and hunting knife, cut his way through the first line. Sidestepping a bayonet lunge he stabbed the musketeer in the chest with his knife, then spun to slice his sabre across the throat of another. Rayster was close by, hacking and slashing with two sabres.

Panic spread through the musketeers like windblown flames through dry brush. They turned and fled, throwing aside their muskets. The Rigante surged after them, cutting them down in their scores.

Kaelin Ring lifted the horn at his side and blew it three times. The Rigante halted and loped back to where he stood. 'Our comrades need us,' he said. 'Let the rest go. Reload your weapons.'

As they ran back up to the crest of the ridge Kaelin looked back. Of the fifteen hundred musketeers who had made the charge less than two hundred had escaped. The slope was littered with the dead and the dying. Many Rigante were among them.

Back at the north end of the woods Korrin Talis had fallen back, and the enemy were into the trees and pursuing the clansmen. Kaelin's men swarmed into the fray. For a while the battle ebbed and flowed, but the sheer ferocity of the Rigante began to tell. They drove the enemy back from the trees and out onto open ground. The fighting was fierce, hand to hand, toe to toe. On the valley floor below the enemy cavalry rode in from the east and began to advance up the slope. The foot soldiers fell back, streaming through the lines of advancing Lancers.

Then came the sound of trumpets.

A column of green-clad musketeers emerged from the northern woods, and spread out in a fighting line, before charging into the unprotected enemy camp.

The Lancers reined in their mounts and gazed back. Then they swung their mounts and galloped to face the new enemy. As they did so Gaise Macon and two thousand cavalry came hurtling into sight. The Eldacre musketeers sent a volley into the Lancers. Gaise Macon's cavalry ripped into their flank. The Lancers' formation broke and they were soon engulfed.

At first Kaelin felt a wave of exultation flow through him. Then his expression darkened. Rayster came alongside. There was blood all over his shirt. 'Are you hurt?' asked Kaelin.

'It's not my blood,' said Rayster.

'Get some men together to gather the wounded and prepare the dead for burial.'

'Mighty strange that they should show up,' said Rayster. 'They should have been thirty miles away.'

'Aye, I was thinking the same thing.'

Down below the Varlish tried to break and run, but they did not get far. Kaelin watched Gaise gallop in among them, his bright sabre flashing in the morning sunlight. Within minutes the battle had become a rout, the rout a massacre.

Kaelin swung away from it and walked back into the trees. Korrin Talis was sitting on a fallen tree. He had two shallow wounds, one to his left arm and a second in his right thigh. Kaelin sat down beside him. Korrin swore softly. 'Fada is dead, Kaelin. He was a good lad. Mother's favourite. It will hit her hard. He was beside me. A ball took him in the temple. And I shall miss Badger. He taught me to fish when I was a youngster. Lake salmon. He'd catch them with his hands.'

'We lost many today, my friend.'

Kaelin moved back towards the wounded. For an hour he wandered among the Rigante. They had lost one hundred and eighty-two men, with another two hundred and thirty-seven wounded. Most of the wounded would recover, but perhaps another twenty would die. Two hundred Rigante had virtually given their lives this day. Kaelin fought to control his anger.

Towards midday Gaise Macon came riding up to the ridge. He stepped down from his grey gelding and approached Kaelin. 'You were right, Kaelin,' he said, with a bright smile. 'Your men are the best of the best. By heaven, you damn near cut them to pieces without our help.'

'I lost two hundred. Would you care to tell me why?'

Gaise Macon's smile faded. 'This is war. Men die. But we won a great victory.'

'There was no ward spell. They *knew* where we were. You let me lead my people into a trap.'

'There *is* a ward spell, but it does not extend far beyond Wishing Tree. And, yes, I let you walk into the trap. I took you at your word, Kaelin. You said to use the Rigante wisely. I did that. No-one else could have held this position as you did. As a result we have all but wiped out their advance force. We have a victory – and that will give backbone to the men.'

'You could have told me.'

'No. Think on it. Had I done so you would have acted differently. You would have deployed your men in a stronger defensive perimeter. The reason they fell for *my* trap was that they believed – as you did – in my stated strategy. You understand?'

'Oh, yes, Stormrider, I understand. You tricked the enemy and tricked me and you won. Now you understand this: if you ever seek to trick the Rigante again I will kill you, and then I will take my men back to the north.'

'You have my word that it will not happen again,' said Gaise Macon.

'Your *word*, Varlish, is dog shit on my boot heel.'

With that he strode away to supervise the burial of the Rigante dead. Towards the afternoon Kaelin stretched himself out on the ground and slept for a while. He was awoken by Rayster. 'What is it?' he asked sleepily.

'Something you should see,' answered the clansman.

Kaelin rolled to his feet and followed Rayster to the top of the crest. Many of the Rigante had gathered there and were watching something below. Kaelin eased his way through the mass of men.

Long stakes had been hammered into the earth of the valley floor, hundreds of them. The heads of dead Varlish soldiers had been rammed atop them. And the bloody work was continuing.

'Like a forest of death,' said Korrin Talis. 'Why are they doing it?'

'To frighten the soldiers who are following,' said Kaelin. 'They will come here with their huge army, and they will see the rotting heads of their comrades. It will tell them that this is going to be a fierce and deadly war, with no quarter.'

'It is appalling,' said Rayster. 'Makes me ashamed to be part of it.'

'There's no humanity in these Varlish,' said Korrin Talis.

They watched as a wagon trundled along the trail below, carrying more stakes, and more heads. Kaelin turned away. 'Let's bury our dead and head back for Eldacre,' he said.

# CHAPTER SEVENTEEN

AT DUSK GAISE MACON SENT OUT ORDERS FOR THE HUNTING PARTIES to cease looking for Varlish stragglers and to return to the captured enemy camp. He should have been exultant, for the victory had been nothing short of spectacular. Four thousand eight hundred enemy dead, the acquisition of four thousand muskets, fifteen supply wagons and twenty unused cannon. There were also tents, tools, sabres, knives, pistols – all of which would be helpful to the cause.

The only small note of annoyance had come with the escape of Sperring Dale and a group of his officers. They had not taken part in the attack, and had galloped from the camp at first sight of the Eldacre counter attack. But this was not what sat heavy upon the heart of Gaise Macon.

'*Your word, Varlish, is dog shit on my boot heel.*'

Gaise tried to push the memory from his tired mind. He could not. How would *he* have felt had the same trick been used on him by – say – Sir Winter Kay during the civil war? Yet what else could he have done to gain such a victory? Had he fought in a more noble way he might still have won, but his losses would have been far higher. Many more Rigante would now be dead and buried.

The Moidart was right. Leadership was lonely. All around him now were happy, contented men. Victors. More than that, they looked to him now as a conqueror. He was the Grey Ghost, unbeaten and invincible.

He had also learned that two of his other new generals, Ganley Konin and Ordis Mantilan, could be relied upon to follow orders well. Konin's cavalry had performed excellently, while Mantilan's musketeers had shown nerve in the initial charge of the enemy Lancers.

He wondered about the Moidart's luck. He had chosen none of these men, and yet Beck, Konin and Mantilan – none of whom had ever commanded such large units – were proving to be invaluable.

What would Mulgrave have made of it? Sadness touched him at the thought of his friend. Mulgrave was back in Eldacre. They had not spoken since arriving home. Gaise missed him terribly.

Sitting now in the tent occupied so recently by Sperring Dale Gaise lit a lantern and idly searched through the belongings left behind by the Redeemer. Spare shirts and leggings, a crimson cloak, and a small selection of books. One was a book of verse, another the gospel of Persis Albitane. This last made Gaise smile. What did a murderous savage like Sperring Dale gain from reading the words of a man of peace and love? Did he find it humorous?

An image appeared in his mind and a sweet voice rose up from his memory. '*I think I shall kiss you, Gaise Macon.*' He groaned and pushed himself to his feet. The more he struggled to forget Cordelia Lowen, the more hurt he felt when her face came unbidden to his mind. Had he loved her? In truth he did not know. Now he would never know.

A shadow fell across the tent flap. Gaise glanced up. 'Who is it?' he called.

'Powdermill, my lord. May I enter?'

'Come in.'

The little man ducked under the flap and grinned, showing gold teeth. 'They're still running south. No other force is in sight.'

'Good. You have done well, Master Powdermill.'

'It'll be weeks now before any other armies come north.'

'Yes. Was there something else you wanted?'

Powdermill shifted uneasily. His eyes flicked towards the golden-hilted sabre. 'I just wanted to . . . touch the sword again, my lord.'

'Feel free,' Gaise told him. Powdermill moved across the tent to where the scabbarded sabre lay. He crouched down and gently placed his hand upon the hilt.

'It is a wondrous piece. Wondrous,' he whispered. Gaise saw there were tears in his eyes.

'What do you feel when you touch it?' he asked.

Powdermill sighed, then straightened. He turned towards Gaise. 'It is not what I feel, my lord, but what I see. Connavar was not as big as legends say. He was the same height as Kaelin Ring and yourself. He was not godlike. He was a man. He made mistakes. He had fears and doubts. He carried a great burden for most of his life. He loved two women. One died because he broke a promise. He was warned by the Seidh never to break his word or terrible harm would befall someone he loved. Connavar bragged that he had never broken his word and never would. But he did.'

'What promise did he break?'

'He told his wife he would be home to take her riding. Instead he spent time with his first love. His wife rode off without him – and was murdered.'

'I have never heard that tale.'

'Connavar was filled with remorse and a terrible fury. He rode alone into the village from which the murderers came, and he killed everyone, every man, woman and child. Then he burned the village to the ground.'

'And all this you know from touching the sword?'

'Yes, my lord, and so much more.'

'I feel nothing when I hold it, save that it is light and yet perfectly balanced.'

'You are not a seer, my lord. Sometimes it is a blessing, sometimes a curse. The sword is a blessing. It was made by a man with great love in his heart.'

'Riamfada.'

'Yes, my lord.'

'Did you see Connavar fight and kill the bear?'

'I saw him fight it, my lord. He did not kill it. Ruathain his stepfather killed it. Connavar could never kill the bear. It was with him always.'

'The bear was with him?' asked Gaise, mystified.

'In a way, my lord. The bear represented Connavar's darkest

side. He could never quite overcome it, though he battled it hard for most of his life. He never forgave himself for the death of his wife, but his greatest regret was murdering the villagers. The bear was on him then.'

'I understand the bear,' said Gaise Macon. 'Sometimes it is necessary.'

'If you say so, my lord.'

'Any time you want to touch the sword you may come to me, Master Powdermill. I would like to learn more of Connavar.'

'Thank you, my lord.' Powdermill bowed and left the tent.

For several hours Gaise busied himself with the needs of his force, meeting with Ganley Konin and Ordis Mantilan. The wounded were to be taken back to Eldacre in the morning, but Gaise and his force would head north-west into the lands of the former Pinance, there to link with Hew Galliott and his men and discuss the defences.

It would also be an opportunity to survey the possible battle sites in that area, and see how the new power structure sat with the communities there. The Pinance, like the Moidart, was not well loved by his people, but even so they would need to be reassured concerning their safety. It was important that they did not view themselves as a conquered people.

When Konin and Mantilan departed Gaise tried to sleep, but his mind was filled with the problems and potential problems of this coming war. In the dark of the night he rose from his blankets and relit the lantern. Then he sat for a while reading the small book of verse he had found among Sperring Dale's possessions. The wind rippled the canvas walls of his tent, and the lantern flickered, making his eyes tired. Gaise put down the book and yawned.

Suddenly there was silence. Utter and total. No breeze billowed the canvas, no sound came from the camp outside. Not a horse whinnied, not a bough creaked. The lantern no longer flickered. Gaise rose from his folding canvas chair and stared at the flame. It sat proud and unmoving.

Moving to the tent flap Gaise lifted it and stared out at the camp. Everything was as it should be. Men were sleeping, sentries stood quietly, the picketed horses were asleep on their feet. No, not as it should be, thought Gaise. The sentries were statue still. Nothing moved. He stepped out into the night and approached a sentry, walking in front of the man. The sentry's eyes stared ahead. They did not flicker as Gaise peered into his face.

'The death heads were a fine idea,' said a voice. Gaise spun. He was not wearing his sabre, but he drew his knife. 'No need for that, kinsman.' A tall man was standing some twenty feet from him. His hair was golden and long. He was dressed in an old-fashioned knee length tunic of pale green, embroidered with gold thread. His feet and legs were bare.

'Who are you?' demanded Gaise.

'I am your ancestor, Stormrider. Look upon me. Can you not see the resemblance?' Gaise looked into the man's eyes. One was emerald green, the other tawny gold.

'You are Connavar?'

The man laughed. 'No. He was yet another of my children. I am Cernunnos, the father of the Rigante. My children did well today. Fighters all of them.'

'This is some trick,' said Gaise. 'You are the enemy.'

'No, Gaise. I am *with* the enemy. Since I do not as yet have a body I have little choice as to who carries me and where.'

'What do you want with me?'

'I want to be your friend, Gaise. You are important to me. You are a part of my destiny. You just do not know it yet. Let us sit and talk. I will answer all your questions. If you wish you may summon the little mage. He will hear what I say and will vouch for my honesty.'

'I will judge that myself,' said Gaise.

'Good. I always did prefer one to one conversation.' A small fire sprang up and the golden-haired man sat down before it. Gaise sheathed his knife and joined him.

'You give power to the Redeemers. Is that not true?'

'Absolutely true. I enable them to use their puny minds with greater focus.'

'Why?'

'Do you know how long I have languished in an iron box? Thousands of years. Alone with my thoughts. Winter Kay found me. I tried to communicate with him, but it was largely useless. There is no Rigante in the man. It is easier now since he killed the unfortunate king, and allowed his blood to touch the decaying bone of my skull.'

'And now you are leading him north to destroy us?'

'Now he is *bringing* me north. He is the one who will be destroyed. If you allow me to help you.'

'Why would you wish to?'

'The north is my home, Stormrider. I once had a palace there, though it drowned beneath a lake aeons ago when the ice melted. I sired the Rigante. I took human wives and one of them bore Rigantis, my beloved son. Ah, but I joyed in his strength and courage. The Rigante owe their name and their clan to my son. But I am what makes them – and you – special. You have traces of my blood. Seidh blood. You are touched by magic. I want to be among my own people, Gaise.'

'To rule them.'

'Of course to rule them. I am a god. Can you imagine a ruler better qualified?'

'And what if they don't want to be ruled by you?'

'Ah, but they will. All men desire strong leaders. There are none stronger. I am their father. I gave them life. I can give them immortality. Those I choose to walk beside me will live for almost as long as I do.'

'You are offering me immortality to serve you.'

'Sadly no, Gaise. You have a different purpose. I wish that it could be altered, but, as I said, it is a part of destiny. You are the vessel which will allow my return to the flesh. I will, in short, become you.'

'And I die?'

'Yes.'

'You don't make serving you sound very attractive.'

'I promised you the truth, Stormrider. I will not *take* your life. You will give it freely. You will take my skull in your hands and you will ask me to return.'

'Why would I do that?'

'To win, Gaise Macon. To save the lives of those you love. To destroy the enemy utterly. When you accept the skull you will be a god for a few hours. You will have all the powers I once possessed. In that time you can do as you will.'

'Why would you give me that time?'

'I will have no choice. It will take me some hours to fully control your body, to fill it with the essence of my being. But in those hours you will be a Seidh, Gaise Macon. That will be my gift to you. Until then be assured that I will not show the Redeemers how to pierce the ward spell Powdermill has cast. This war will be fought between men. You have my promise on that. And now I shall leave you to rest. Rest is most important for a human. The mind needs to be sharp.' The golden figure rose. 'The Rigante made me proud today,' he said.

'What happened to this beloved son of yours?' asked Gaise.

'He chose life as a man and died after three hundred and twenty-two years.'

Gaise heard the sorrow in his voice. 'You were close, then?'

'We were until he cut off my head. The boy was misguided. It is a familiar tale, Gaise, and one which you will understand more than most. Fathers and sons, squabbles and conflicts. The laws of nature cannot be avoided – even by the gods. Ah, but that reminds me. You asked your father a question back in Eldacre. He gave an elliptical answer.'

'*You* can pierce our ward spells?'

'Of course. They are tiny. The Redeemers cannot, so put aside your fears. I do not share with them what I observe. You asked your father why he carried you from the flames. Would you like to know why?'

'No.'

'It also explains why he and you have never found that bond of love you so desperately needed as a child.'

'Tell me,' said Gaise.

'Your mother had an affair with a clansman. Kaelin Ring's father, Lanovar. He was golden-haired, and had one eye of gold and one of green. When you were born and the Moidart saw your eyes he believed you to be the result of his wife's infidelity. He would have had you killed, save for one small doubt.'

'My great-grandmother had the same eyes.'

'Exactly. So he has lived in torment ever since, never knowing if you are the only son he will ever have, or if you are the son of the man who cuckolded him. But when the flames engulfed the manor house he acted as a father should. Heroically. Instinctively. Like a Rigante.'

'Is he my father?'

'Do you really wish to know?'

Gaise hesitated, then he sighed. 'No,' he said.

'Farewell, Stormrider. When next we meet I will give you what you ask for. Though first you will receive a visit from the Wyrd. Delightful woman. If I were but a thousand years younger and alive . . . ah, well. She will bring you something of mine. Keep it safe for when you need it.'

'Why would the Wyrd do anything for you?'

'Because she must, Stormrider. Win or lose, this is her destiny also.'

The spirit disappeared.

The month that followed saw frenzied activity on both sides of the border. In the north the Moidart recruited men, leaving Galliott and Mulgrave to oversee the training. In the south Winter Kay began gathering three armies, each more than twenty thousand strong. The massacre of Sperring Dale's force had galvanized the Redeemers, and stories of the atrocities committed by the 'foul northern barbarians' spread through the land. Winter Kay was now leading a holy war of vengeance upon the evil men who had killed the king.

He sent a second advance column against the lands of the Pinance. They were turned back by Gaise Macon. Four hundred Varlish prisoners were taken. All but one were hanged and then beheaded. The survivor was placed in a wagon loaded with the heads of his comrades and sent back to the south. Other skirmishes followed. The fighting was brutal and vicious. No prisoners were taken by either side.

News of Gaise Macon's excesses were the talk of the northern army. The middle-aged general Garan Beck made a special journey from the east to see the Moidart. The two men were strikingly different in appearance. The Moidart, slim and fine-boned, his clothes immaculately tailored from the finest cloth, and Beck, round-shouldered and stocky, his broad, flat face and large hands betraying his peasant stock. He wore now a ready made uniform jacket in pale green, bearing the Fawn in Brambles crest. The sleeves were slightly too short. Despite the oddness of his appearance he still radiated a sense of physical power and purpose.

'I'm a plain speaking man, my lord,' he said, 'and this butchery turns my stomach.'

'It sends a powerful message, Beck.'

'Indeed it does, my lord, but – putting aside the restraints of civilized behaviour – it is also bad soldiering. An enemy who knows he can surrender and be well treated is the more likely to surrender when faced with disaster. If they know that certain death awaits them they will fight all the harder.'

'What of our own troops, General Beck? How do they view my son?'

'Close to adoration, my lord.'

'So – as you say, apart from considerations of civilized behaviour – our morale is high?'

'Yes, my lord.'

'These are perilous times, general. Within a month we may all be dead. My son is taking harsh measures. Like you I would prefer to be more humane in my dealings with the enemy. For, in the end, enemies must become friends. In this case our enemy is particularly vicious. He has already proved this by murdering his own king. You are also aware of the butchery that took place during the civil war in towns like Barstead. The truth is, we are short of food and men. Prisoners would need to be fed and guarded. Every prisoner taken would sap our meagre resources.'

Garan Beck sighed. 'Aye, my lord, there is truth in that. Even so it sits badly with me.'

'You can always leave my service, general. I would hate to lose you but you must follow your conscience.'

The general shook his head. 'You are the first nobleman to give me the chance to prove myself in the highest rank. You ignored my lack of noble blood. I need to repay that debt to you, my lord. I will do so. You have my loyalty, and I will die for this cause if necessary.'

'Well said, general. Now get yourself some rest before returning east. You are looking tired.'

After he had gone Huntsekker appeared from behind the

hidden panel. 'You still want him killed tonight, my lord?' he asked.

'No, I have changed my mind.'

'I am glad. I like the man.'

'What odd times these are, Huntsekker. Did you hear him declare his loyalty?'

'Yes, my lord.'

'Damn, but he meant it. Every word.'

'I believe you are right.' Huntsekker suddenly chuckled.

'What is so funny, Harvester?'

'I have walked the city these last weeks, running errands for Maev Ring. I have spoken to a lot of people. You have always been feared, my lord. And always respected. Did you know that you are now popular? The people like you. They speak of you with affection.'

'I have become a likeable fellow,' said the Moidart. 'How annoying.'

'I can see that it would cause a man grief,' said Huntsekker.

'Good heavens, Harvester, was that a joke?'

'A small one, my lord.'

'Try to avoid them. How is Maev Ring?'

'Irritating. She has increased the supplies fourfold, and those who do not succumb to her charming manner and promise of riches get visits from me. I am not to threaten them, she says. Merely deliver letters from her requesting greater co-operation. Of course, she says I should take my scythe with me.'

'Clever woman. I rather admire her. You should marry her, Harvester. You need a wife.'

Huntsekker was aghast. 'The woman has a tongue on her that could cut through steel. You know she is now looking after that murderous hound your son brought back? It behaves like a little puppy around her. One word and it sits. A flick of her fingers and it crouches down. Never seen the like. I don't know if the hound loves her or is terrified by her. I suspect the latter.'

'You could marry in the cathedral. I could give the bride away.'

Huntsekker shook his head and stared hard at the Moidart. 'There is a change in you, my lord. It is very unsettling.'

'Perhaps I am mellowing with age.'

372

The next two weeks brought a lull in the fighting. No new forces attacked the lands of the Pinance and the news from the east was routine. Supplies were reaching the coastal cities and Garan Beck had arranged convoys to Eldacre. Gaise Macon rode his two thousand cavalry south again, but encountered no enemy troops.

The attack when it came was sudden and deadly. Thirty thousand soldiers poured in to the east, cutting through Garan Beck's defensive lines. He pulled back expertly and re-formed, but the fighting was fierce and he was forced further and further back towards Eldacre. Gaise Macon sent Kaelin Ring and the Rigante to support Beck, and waited. A second army, spearheaded by the dreaded Knights of the Sacrifice, thrust like a lance into the lands of the Pinance. Hew Galliott tried to counter attack, but his troops were surrounded and all but annihilated. Hew himself was taken and publicly disembowelled. Gaise Macon led a series of lightning raids on the knights, temporarily halting their advance. Then he too pulled back to re-form.

Two thousand more Rigante, led by Bael Jace, arrived in Eldacre to support the army. These the Moidart sent west to join with Gaise Macon and his cavalry. The generals Konin and Mantilan remained in Eldacre with six thousand men, plus Bendegit Law and his fifty cannon.

For three days battles raged to the east and west. Beck and Ring's Rigante took a heavy toll on the enemy, but could not prevent them inching ever nearer to the city. In the west Gaise Macon fought desperately to prevent the knights from advancing.

Then came the news that a third army, led by Winter Kay himself, was heading up from the south. Twenty thousand men and two hundred cannon.

'I think we should make plans to leave Eldacre,' said Huntsekker, as he and the Moidart walked the battlements of the castle.

'I disagree,' said the Moidart. 'There is nothing north of us now. The Rigante are here, fighting with us. Running would only accelerate the inevitable. You may leave, Huntsekker. I shall stay. I may even fight.'

'You have arthritis in your right arm, my lord. I doubt you could wield a sword for long.'

'Then I shall take a selection of pistols. This is my land, Huntsekker. Damned if I'll flee like a wretch.'

Then a surprising event occurred. Winter Kay's southern army suddenly ceased its advance. Scouts reported that it had stopped at the Wishing Tree woods, and remained camped there for two days.

Winter Kay had awoken with a throbbing headache and a feeling of nausea. He had sat up long into the night holding the skull in his lap while reading reports from his generals. Eris Velroy was making slow progress in the east and taking heavy losses. He kept trying to draw the enemy into a major pitched battle, but Garan Beck was proving a wily adversary. Then there were the damned clansmen. Velroy had finally broken through and was in the act of encirclement when the Rigante charged, ripping through his ranks. Velroy had fallen back and summoned heavy cavalry. By the time they arrived the Rigante had melted away into the woods. Of the original thirty thousand men he had led east only around twelve thousand were able to fight. The enemy had suffered too. By Velroy's estimation they had lost around half their men. This left between four and five thousand. Not enough to prevent him advancing, but more than enough to take a terrible toll on the attackers. In the west the Knights of the Sacrifice were faring little better. True, they had taken the castle of the Pinance, but Gaise Macon had won several small victories, and the main force was pinned down some thirty miles from Eldacre. Gaise Macon's cavalry, split into fast-moving strike units, raided behind the lines on one day, and on the flanks the next. Losses among the knights were also substantial. Yet day by day both armies were moving ever closer to Eldacre.

The plan was essentially simple. The three armies would converge on the city, closing in like a mailed fist, crushing the life from the defenders. The attacks from east and west would draw away men from the centre, and then Winter Kay would strike like a lance, leading his Redeemers on a sudden, deadly thrust to the castle. On this day Winter Kay's twenty thousand were due to march to within twenty miles of Eldacre.

Only they did not march.

Winter Kay had rolled from his pallet bed and sat up. His head was aching terribly, and his mouth was dry. He felt exhausted, drained of energy. It was then that he realized he was fully clothed, and his muddy boots had stained the blankets. He stared down at the boots. It was inconceivable that he would have slept like this. He clearly recalled undressing some hours before dawn.

He rubbed at his temples in a firm, circular motion. The veins were like wire under his fingers. A water jug was placed on a folding table. Lifting it he drank deeply. The water tasted sour and metallic. There was only one sure way to clear his head. Rising from the bed he walked to where the iron box lay, and opened the lid. The shock that struck him was like a blow to the belly. His body convulsed.

The iron box was empty.

Winter Kay spun round, his eyes scanning the tent. There was no sign of the skull.

The pain in his head forgotten he stumbled to the tent entrance and dragged back the flap. Two Redeemers stood guard outside.

'Who has been in here?' yelled Winter Kay. Both men stood transfixed. Never had Winter Kay appeared so distressed before his men. 'Answer me, damn you!'

'No-one, my lord,' said the first. 'We've been on guard ever since you came back.'

'Came back?'

'Yes, my lord. From your ride.'

'What are you talking about? What ride?'

'The men glanced at one another. Then the second Redeemer spoke. 'Just before dawn, my lord, you told me to saddle your horse. Then you rode off to the north.'

'Liar!' screamed Winter Kay. His fist hammered into the man's face, hurling him from his feet. Dragging a knife from its sheath he knelt over the fallen Redeemer. 'Give me the truth or you die now!'

'It is the truth, lord!' The knife point plunged through the man's right eye. Blood spurted and he writhed under Winter Kay's grip. The knife tore into the man's brain and he twitched once and then was still. Winter Kay tore the knife loose and swung on the first man, who was backing away, horrified.

'The truth – or you die too!'

'What do you want me to say, my lord? I'll say anything you want!'

375

'Just the truth!'

'He told you the truth. You called for a horse and rode out. Everyone saw you. The captain asked if you wanted guards to ride with you, but you ignored him.'

Winter Kay stood very still. The knife dropped from his fingers. 'What was I carrying?'

'A black sack, my lord. Velvet, I think. It's true, I swear it.'

'Did I have it when I came back?'

'I don't recall . . . Wait! No, sir, you did not. I remember helping you down from the saddle. You seemed weary and we wondered if you were ill.'

'Fetch me a horse, and find someone who knows how to track,' said Winter Kay.

Two hours later Winter Kay and a footsoldier entered the Wishing Tree woods. The undergrowth was heavy and Winter Kay needed to dismount and tether his horse. He followed the man deeper into the woods, down a long slope and up to an ancient site of broken standing stones.

The tracker knelt and examined the soft earth around the stones. 'You came here, my lord. You were met by someone with small feet. Likely a woman, though it may have been a child. Then you turned back.'

'Where did the woman go?'

The tracker took an age walking around the rim of the hill. 'There are no fresh tracks at all leading away from the hilltop, my lord, save yours.'

'Check again.'

The nervous man did so, and returned with the same story.

'Are you telling me there was someone here who did not leave?'

'No, my lord. She left all right. She just didn't leave a sign. Must have picked her way with care over firm ground. It'll take me time to find anything.'

'How long?'

'Could be most of a day.'

'You need more men?'

'No, my lord. They'd only churn up the ground and make it even more difficult.'

'You find where she went. Your life depends on it.'

'Yes, my lord.'

Winter Kay walked away from the man. For a while he became lost among the old trees, but at last he found his horse and rode back to the camp. The body of the Redeemer had been taken away, and two new guards awaited him. Both looked nervous.

All day the army waited. By dusk the tracker had still not returned and Winter Kay rode out with four men, and another tracker, to find him.

The second tracker walked around the hill top, kneeling to study the ground. After an hour, with darkness approaching, he returned to Winter Kay.

'I found his trail, my lord. He ran off towards the east.'

'What other tracks did you find?'

'None, my lord. There's a woman's footprints in the circle of stone, but none leading to them or away from them.'

Sick at heart Winter Kay once more returned to camp. For the first time in many years he did not know what to do. Panic tugged at his mind. That night he sat in his tent, trembling and frightened, refusing to meet with his officers.

The Orb was gone. Soon it would be in the hands of his enemies. They would wield its power against him.

In his panic his first thought was to order the armies to withdraw from the north, to move away from danger. But what good would that do? Gaise Macon would gather men, and, with the power of the Orb, come south against him. No, his only hope was to win this war swiftly, before his enemies learned how to manipulate the magic. He felt calmer now. Kranos would not allow himself to be used by such wretches. The Redeemers were the true followers. Kranos loved them and would protect them.

'He will protect *me*,' said Winter Kay aloud. Closing his eyes he prayed, 'Lord, show me the way. Help me in my hour of need.'

All was silence.

Winter Kay sat alone.

Somewhere in the night he fell asleep, and in that sleep he saw again his forgotten ride to the Wishing Tree woods, and the long walk to the standing stones. A small woman in a pale blue and green shawl was waiting there, her hair silver white in the moonlight.

377

'Give it to me,' she said.

He had handed her the velvet sack. She had shuddered as she took it. Winter Kay watched her walk back to the standing stones. A bright light blazed and she was gone.

He awoke with a cry and scrambled to his feet. Scrabbling in a pack by the tent wall he produced papers, a quill pen and a cork-stoppered jar of ink. Then he wrote messages to his generals and called for riders.

There was no time now for an encircling action. That could take some weeks. He would gather all his troops together and smash through to Eldacre in one ferocious battle. The enemy would be slaughtered, and Winter Kay would once more possess the skull.

With the army split there was no way for Gaise Macon to accurately gauge the losses suffered by the Eldacre forces during the last five days, but it was fair to assume they were heavy. Of the force Gaise led in the west more than a third had died, and half of the remainder carried some wounds. They were also close to exhaustion.

The enemy had taken more fearsome losses. Even so they still outnumbered his men here by more than three to one. Even with his daring – and occasionally reckless – attacks Gaise knew that such attrition would soon render his force useless.

Earlier they had routed a section of heavy cavalry, only to be driven back by a charge from the Knights of the Sacrifice. Gaise had wheeled his men and cut away to the left. His musketeers had then sent volley after volley into the attackers, forcing them to withdraw. Any other force would have fled the field. Not the knights. They swung their heavy chargers and pulled back in good order. Gaise estimated the enemy had lost around six hundred men in that one encounter, but he had lost two hundred and seventy. Such odds still favoured the Varlish.

Camped now on high ground, his remaining twelve cannon trained on a narrow open section of grassland between two stands of trees, Gaise Macon sent out scouts to report on the enemy's movements. There was almost no need. Their plan was obvious and strikingly effective. Slowly and steadily they pushed ever nearer Eldacre, inexorably forcing Gaise back. The same was happening in the east. Within a few weeks at most only the town itself would offer shelter. Cavalry would be useless and the forces of the Moidart would be contained within the castle. Unable to get supplies they would be starved into submission.

It was galling in the extreme. Gaise had enough men to inflict terrible damage on the enemy, but not enough to ensure a victory.

News had also come in that Winter Kay and a further force of twenty thousand were marching from the south. Konin and Mantilan would not be able to stop them for long.

Lanfer Gosten approached where Gaise was standing alongside a cannon. 'Another twelve, sir,' he said. 'Not so bad.'

'It will get worse, Lanfer,' said Gaise. Twelve deserters a night would not damage his ability to fight, but soon the army would begin to haemorrhage. The more they were forced back, the more desertions would escalate.

'I expect the enemy are losing men too,' offered Lanfer.

'Aye,' agreed Gaise.

'If they didn't have them damned knights we'd crack 'em,' said Lanfer.

'But they do have those *damned* knights,' replied Gaise. 'And great fighters they are.'

'We're not doing so bad against 'em, though, sir.'

Gaise placed his hand on the older man's shoulder. 'No, my friend, we have done ourselves proud. We will continue to do so.'

Moving to the picket line Gaise saddled a chestnut gelding. His grey had been killed under him two days ago. He rode down the slope to the left and into the camp of Bael Jace and his Rigante. They had fought coolly and well since their arrival, and were the match of anything the enemy could offer, including the knights. They had lost eight hundred of their two thousand, and each man now carried two muskets, as well as pistols, knives and sabres.

Bael Jace strode out to greet him. There were no smiles or handshakes when Gaise dismounted. Jace had a bandage around his temples, and blood had leaked down, staining the right side of his face.

'What news?' asked the Rigante leader.

'None yet. I just wanted to see how you were faring.'

'We are fine, Stormrider. Never better.'

'We'll draw back tomorrow. There is a good defensive site around four miles east, a high ridge and before it a killing ground.'

'Whatever you say.'

'I want you and your men to guard the left flank as we pull back. That's where the attack will come from. I'll keep the cavalry in reserve to come to your aid.'

'I saw a few of your men running away to the east tonight. They had thrown away their muskets.'

'A shame you didn't stop them.'

'Not my problem, Stormrider. If a man wants to leave he is free to do so.'

'I note that no Rigante has left.'

'I wouldn't stop them if they wanted to. They are fighting a war they cannot win.'

Gaise was irritated, but he struggled not to show it. 'There is always a chance of victory, no matter what the odds.'

'Oh, that's true,' said Jace, 'but in this case our fate is in the hands of the enemy. I may not be the strategist my father was, but I know what I know. The only way we can win is if the enemy makes a big, big mistake. As matters stand we are killing two of them for every one of us. Since they outnumber us more than three to one you don't need to be a scholar to know that when we are all dead they'll still have a few thousand men left.'

'Are there any more Rigante to call upon?'

'Aye, there are a thousand warriors back home, Stormrider – and that's where they'll stay. I'll not see the clan wiped out down here. There are enough left there to man the high passes, and I doubt the enemy will want to march north after the pounding we've given them here.'

Gaise considered his words. There was wisdom in them. 'We would never have held out this long without you and the Rigante. I want you to know that I am grateful.'

'Don't be. We didn't come for you. We came because the Wyrd said we should. I don't care if Eldacre falls. I don't care if your head and the Moidart's end up on stakes. You are the enemy of my people. It grieves me to see men die in your cause.'

Gaise said nothing for a moment. Then: 'I have Rigante blood,

Bael, and I value the clan highly. You know this. That is why you call me by my Rigante soul-name.'

'Aye – and that is why I despise you. You are a brilliant fighter, Gaise Macon. I've seen few better. You are fearless and you lead men well. *That* is your Rigante heritage. That is what would make me proud. Yet you slay without compunction or compassion, and you cut off the heads of fighting men and plant them like a forest of death. You murder men who put up their hands and you soak yourself in blood. *That* is your Varlish heritage. To see a Varlish do these things is bad enough. But we expect it from them. To see a man with Rigante blood do it is sickening beyond belief.'

Something deep, dark and cold touched Gaise Macon in that moment. There was no anger. He looked at the red-headed clansman and felt his body relax. 'Eight hundred years ago Bane led the Rigante to the city of Stone. They defeated the armies. The world was theirs, to do with as they pleased. Rigante codes and laws, notions of honour and courage, could have been imposed on all the peoples. Instead Bane brought the clans back across the sea to the Druagh mountains. The Rigante did not want to rule. The honest truth, Jace, is that they did not have the stomach for it. History shows us one harsh and iron fact: those who do not rule are themselves ruled. Once the Keltoi roamed the lands, strong and free. Now you are a tiny, conquered people, holding to a few rocks in the far north. If I want lessons in how to be defeated I will come to you, Jace.'

Stepping into the saddle, Gaise steered the chestnut from the Rigante camp and rode back up to the ridge. He saw one of his scouts galloping across the open ground below. Remaining on his horse Gaise waited for the man. He was young and fair-haired, and his horse was lathered and weary by the time it reached the crest.

'They have pulled back, my lord. They are heading south-east.'

'What?'

'It is true. In full formation, with all supply wagons.'

Gaise sat very still. Was this a trick? Were they seeking to outflank him? It made no sense. The three-pronged attack assured them of victory. Why would they change plans so suddenly? 'Get a fresh horse and follow them,' he told the man. 'Keep well back. I will send other riders to join you. Every hour one of you will come back to report. You understand?'

'Yes, my lord. You think they are retreating? Have we won?'

'Time will tell.'

# CHAPTER EIGHTEEN

KAELIN RING DUCKED AS HE RAN THOUGH THE CANNON-BLASTED RUINS of the village. Enemy snipers were hidden in the woods to the north-east, and some of them were highly skilled. Dropping to his knees Kaelin crawled along the shelter of a low wall, then sprinted across a short section of open ground.

No shots were fired.

Garan Beck and his senior officers were within the ruins of a church. The stained glass windows had been blasted away, and fragments of coloured glass littered the nave. Musketeers had set up firing platforms by the windows, and at the far end of the church a surgeon and his orderlies were tending close to a hundred wounded men.

Kaelin approached Beck. The general had lost weight, and the skin of his face was sagging now, adding years to his features. His dark hair was also showing a white line from the temples and up over his brow. Kaelin realized he had previously dyed his hair in a bid to appear younger. Idly he wondered how old Beck really was. The general glanced up as Kaelin entered.

'Ah, Ring,' he said. 'We were discussing where to fall back to, and when. They have a cavalry force which has punched a breach in our lines. The Source only knows where they are now.'

'Mostly dead, the rest scattered,' said Kaelin. 'We trapped them in a wood to the south.'

'That's a damned relief.' Beck spread a map over the altar table. 'As far as I can see there is no adequate defensive ground between here and Eldacre. It is mostly flatland. Once we pull back we'll be at the mercy of any fast-riding column.' Kaelin rubbed at the wound in his left shoulder. The bayonet had stabbed deep. He could no longer feel any sensation in the fingertips of his left hand, and movement was painful. The bleeding had taken an age to stop, and a deep bruise had extended down over his chest and under his armpit. 'I hope you keep checking that,' said Beck. 'Don't want it to go bad.'

'I smear it with honey every morning,' said Kaelin. 'It will be fine. Go on.'

'My best estimate is that we have around six thousand fighting men left. If we are to withdraw successfully we'll need a tough rearguard to keep them off our backs.'

'My Rigante.'

'Only if you are willing, Ring. It's likely to be a murderously tough assignment, and your Rigante have already performed miracles here. I've seen fighting men for most of my life, and I've never known the equal of you clansmen. If you feel you have done enough then I'll stay myself with a division of musketeers.'

Kaelin gave a broad smile. 'I like you, general,' he said. 'Damned if I don't! We'll be your rearguard.'

'If we had a few thousand more men I'd try to hold this line. It's the best defensive site I've seen in years. However, if we stay we'll be encircled and cut off from supply.'

'What is your plan?'

'There is heavy cloud. We'll pull back in the deepest darkness, and as quietly as possible. You and your Rigante will stay until tomorrow night, and fend them off. Twenty-four hours should see us clear.'

'And then what?' enquired Kaelin. 'Supplies from the east are already lost to us. The western line is barely holding. You think we can win by withdrawing?'

Beck shook his head. 'No. We just survive a little longer.'

'What about the badly wounded?'

'I'll take as many as I can, but we lack the wagons. Many will have to be left behind.'

'To be slaughtered,' pointed out Kaelin.

'Aye, that's the reverse side of the coin. It is all very well for Macon to stick heads on poles, but it only encourages the enemy to behave in a similar fashion. That said, we are facing Redeemers and their lackeys, and they are not known for compassion either.' Beck sighed. 'I don't like asking you to undertake this assignment, Ring. I'll be honest, the chances of you getting out alive are very slim.'

'Perhaps, general,' said Kaelin, 'but I have nine hundred fighting Rigante here. I'd bet them against five thousand of the enemy.'

'So would I. Unhappily there are around fifteen thousand of them. Do you have enough powder and shot?'

'Plenty. Not much food, though.'

'I'll leave what I can. Just twenty-four hours, Ring, then you and your men should break out and scatter. Go home would be my advice.'

'Take care, general,' said Kaelin, reaching out and gripping the man's hand.

'You too, Ring. It was a rare pleasure to lead the Rigante.'

Kaelin moved to the doorway, braced himself, then ran across the open ground, dropping flat behind the low wall. The impact caused his shoulder to burn, and he felt the warmth of fresh blood oozing from the wound. Ignoring the pain he pushed on, reaching the abandoned buildings beyond the marketplace. Rayster was there, with around fifty men.

'What is happening?' asked the clansman.

'The army is pulling back to Eldacre.'

'About time,' said Rayster.

'We stay and act as rearguard for twenty-four hours.'

'They'll be long hours,' said Rayster dryly.

Korrin Talis squirmed across open ground and joined them. 'They seem to have pulled back their snipers,' he said.

'I noticed,' said Kaelin. 'Let's not get complacent, though. We need to spread out more. Tomorrow we are going to need to look like a much larger force.'

'If we spread too thin we'll not be able to concentrate firepower,' said Rayster.

'Once the concerted attacks begin tell the men to fall back to the church and outlying buildings. We'll make a last stand there.'

'Maybe the Stormrider will come galloping to the rescue again,' said Korrin.

'Not this time. Go and speak to the men. Tell them that if any wish to leave they can. We all have families back home. They should at least be offered the chance to return to them.'

'I'll do that,' said Korrin, 'but no-one will leave, Kaelin.'

'I know.' Suddenly he laughed. 'If anyone had ever told me I'd be risking my life so that Varlish soldiers could make a withdrawal I'd have laughed in his face.'

'Some of those boys are fine lads,' said Korrin, 'Varlish or no. And I like Beck. I'll bet there's a touch of clan in him somewhere.'

Korrin moved away to spread the word among the men. Rayster remained with Kaelin. 'How is the shoulder?'

'Painful.'

'You were lucky. I thought for a moment he had speared your heart.'

'Came close.' Kaelin grinned. 'Lucky for me that Eldacre lad was close by.'

'Aye, it was luck. Let's hope it holds. I'd like to see Sorrow Bird again. I love that lake.'

'It's a beautiful spot right enough.'

Kaelin settled down on his back. The hard ground felt soft as a feather bed, and he lay there thinking about the man who had saved him.

Enemy musketeers had almost broken through. The Rigante rushed in, and with the aid of some Eldacre men turned them back. As the enemy were retreating one of the musketeers had run at Kaelin, his bayonet lancing into the clansman's shoulder. Kaelin had fallen. The musketeer loomed above him, his blood-drenched blade poised to strike through Kaelin's heart. A young Eldacre volunteer had leapt at him, knocking him from his feet. A shot sounded. The Eldacre man spun and then toppled to the ground. The enemy musketeer rose again. Kaelin pulled his Emburley from his belt and shot him in the head. Then he scrambled to the Eldacre man. He had been hit just under the breastbone. There was little blood and his face had gone grey. Rayster appeared alongside. He patted the dying young man's shoulder. 'I thank you for your courage,' said Kaelin.

'I've got a wife and youngsters,' whispered the man. 'Will I live?'

'No, lad,' said Rayster. 'You are mortally hit.'

'I'll burn then,' he said. 'The Source will burn me.'

'You'll not burn,' said Kaelin. 'A brave young man like you, fighting for your homeland. Nonsense.'

'I've done . . . bad things.'

'We all have,' Rayster told him. 'But today you gave your life to save a man you didn't know. That will count.'

'I know him. He's Kaelin Ring. I saw him once – back in Black Mountain.'

'I used to go there often,' said Kaelin. 'Were you in barracks there?'

'Yes, but I saw you walking with your wife. I was with my family. I waved to you. You remember? By the stream?'

'Yes,' said Kaelin, though truth to tell he did not. 'Tell me your name, and if I live I shall find your family and tell them what you did here today.' The man whispered his name, and then reached up and gripped Kaelin's arm. Pain from the bayonet wound flared, but he showed no sign of it.

'I will burn for what I did,' said the man, tears in his eyes. 'Tell her I was drunk. Tell her that I am sorry. Tell her . . .' He sagged back. A tremor went through him and he died. Kaelin eased the dead fingers from his arm. He was still pondering the young man's death when he fell asleep.

Rayster woke him with the dawn. Kaelin sat up. 'Have we not withdrawn?' he said. 'I heard no wagons.'

'There has been no movement,' said Rayster. 'Obviously Beck changed his mind. Maybe the enemy have moved behind us.' The clansman glanced across towards the church. 'Now there is an idiot!' he said, pointing towards an officer walking across the open ground. The man seemed to have no care. He waved at Kaelin as he approached.

'Get down!' shouted Kaelin.

The man grinned and walked over to where the two Rigante lay. Then he crouched down. 'The enemy have pulled back,' he said. 'Our scouts report they are moving south-west. The woods are empty. No snipers. No infantry. No cannon.'

'Where is Beck?'

'The general sent me to find you. He is at the church. Faith, sir, but it's a miracle, is it not?'

Kaelin did not answer. Moving swiftly he dashed across the open ground and made his way to the church. Beck stepped out into the morning sunlight just as he approached. A troop of Eldacre cavalry were riding up towards the wooded slope beyond.

'Is this some strategy of theirs to cut us off?' asked Kaelin.

'It can't be,' said Beck. 'They've surrendered good ground and pulled out. By heading south-west they've also freed the eastern supply lines. None of it makes military sense.'

'What do we do?'

'Hold our lines until we get orders from Eldacre. The Source just smiled upon us, Kaelin Ring. I don't know why, and I don't care. Perhaps the Moidart is a religious man.'

'If he is it's not a religion I'd choose to follow.'

On the second day following the surprise withdrawal of the southern armies the Moidart summoned his generals back to Eldacre for a strategy meeting. Scouts had reported the enemy armies were converging on a point some forty miles south of the town and regrouping. The force was estimated to be close to forty-five thousand strong, considerably less than even the Moidart had dared hope.

Even so, the defenders were still heavily outnumbered.

The meeting was held in the Moidart's east-facing apartments. The sun was shining brightly in a clear blue sky, its light streaming through the high arched windows. Around the table sat Garan Beck, Gaise Macon, Kaelin Ring, Ganley Konin and Ordis Mantilan. Bael Jace and Bendegit Law were scouting to the south.

Ganley Konin was the first to speak. A slim, well spoken man, he had been a cleric in Varingas for twenty years, and had only become a soldier upon the outbreak of the civil war, purchasing his commission in a cavalry unit. He had proved to have a fine eye for ground and had been promoted steadily to the rank of colonel. An argument with the doomed Lord Ferson had seen him transferred north into the army of the Pinance. 'It seems to me, sirs, that we have a respite. No more than that. There is no indication that the enemy intends to withdraw south. It is my view he will advance in full force upon the town.'

'I agree,' said Garan Beck. 'What I don't understand is why. His plan was working. We could not have held out for more than a few weeks.'

'I believe I have the answer to that,' said the Moidart. 'Our seer, Powdermill, reports that there is no longer any indication of Redeemer spirit activity. He thought at first that the Orb of Kranos had been overused, and was in need of replenishment. That, however, is not the case. The Orb is no longer with the Redeemers. In short, Winter Kay is without any special powers now. He has panicked, and drawn his army around him like a wall.'

'Then now is the time to strike him,' said Kaelin Ring.

'Given a few thousand more men I would agree with you, lad,' said Garan Beck. 'The truth is we simply do not have the manpower to launch an attack as swiftly as it would be required. As far as I can tell we have around eleven thousand men fit enough to fight, and another two thousand recruits who don't know one end of a musket from the other. Given another week we might add more, and train those we have. I don't believe we will have another week.'

Ordis Mantilan spoke next. A commander of musketeers for twenty years, he was a short, stout man, with a shock of tightly curled greying hair. 'I'd like to know two things,' he said. 'First, how did Lord Winterbourne lose the Orb of Kranos, and, more important, where is it? If it is as powerful as has been claimed we could surely use it ourselves.'

'I have it,' said Gaise Macon. The room was suddenly silent. All eyes were on the young general. 'It cannot – must not – be used. To do so would unleash an evil upon the world far in excess of anything Winterbourne would bring.'

'Then why did they not unleash it?' asked the Moidart.

'They couldn't. We could. The skull is the last remnant of a Seidh lord named Cernunnos. He seeks a return to life.'

'It is a magical relic, no more,' said the Moidart. 'Winter Kay used its power. So should we.'

'It is more than a relic, Father. Believe me. The spirit of Cernunnos lives. I have spoken with it. I have also listened to the

Wyrd, who brought the skull to me. Cernunnos transcends evil. He cannot be allowed to return.'

'She gave you the skull?'

'Yes, Father.'

'How did she acquire it?'

'Winter Kay gave it to her at the Wishing Tree woods.'

The Moidart shook his head. 'Perhaps you can tell us why he would have done something so monumentally stupid?'

'Cernunnos possessed him. He forced him to it. The god needs Rigante blood to live again. That is why he seduced Winter Kay into coming north.'

Slowly and carefully Gaise explained all that the Wyrd had told him of the history of Cernunnos. How he had once plunged the world into war, and of how his own son, Rigantis, had beheaded him with a golden sword. The officers listened in silence. When Gaise had finished Kaelin Ring spoke. 'I do not know anything of Cernunnos,' he said. 'I do know the Wyrd. When she speaks it is the truth. If she says this god cannot be allowed to live, then he cannot be allowed to live.'

'I was not talking about him being allowed to live,' said the Moidart. 'Winter Kay found a way to use the magic. Why can we not do the same?'

'For the answer to that,' said Ganley Konin, 'perhaps we should look at Winter Kay. Look at the work of his Redeemers. Treachery, murder, massacre, burnings. They are vile men and their deeds shame us all. Would we become as black-hearted as they?'

The Moidart interrupted him. 'We don't have time for theological debates, or philosophical discussion on the nature of evil,' he said. 'Men have been killing each other for centuries without need to blame skulls or relics. However, since my son is adamant about the need to avoid using this weapon let us move on to more practical matters. How do we, with thirteen thousand men, set out to defeat the enemy?'

For another hour the debate raged, and when it ended there was no clear plan. Gaise had said little during the discussions. As the officers left, the Moidart called out to his son to remain. When they were alone he poured him a goblet of wine. 'What is it you didn't say?' he asked.

'What do you mean?'

'Damn it, boy, you are the war leader here. You made that plain when you returned. Yet you have just sat in near silence while lesser men wittered about impossible plans and ludicrous tactics. What is it? Tell me.'

Gaise looked at his father, and took a deep breath. 'Cernunnos wants *me*. He needs *me* to take the skull and in some way accept it into myself. He will then have my body, and will have returned.'

'Why you?'

Gaise was silent for a moment. 'I looked into his face, Father. He and I have the same eyes. We are like . . . brothers. Perhaps that is why.'

'This talk of evil and good is beginning to bore me to tears,' said the Moidart. 'You say the skull cannot be destroyed. So, if they defeat us they will have the skull anyway. If this creature is truly some ancient god then he will find some other man with Rigante blood. It is inevitable.' The Moidart poured himself a second goblet of wine. 'Though why someone with the powers of a god would want to rule men is another matter. I would have thought there were better ways for a god to spend his time.'

'He wants to eradicate mankind, Father. He believes we are a plague upon the earth, that we are – and will remain – savage and unbridled, and that, given time, we will destroy not only ourselves but the world.'

'I am beginning to warm to him,' said the Moidart. 'I often feel the same way myself. So where is the Wyrd now? We could use her help.'

'She has returned north. She wants no more to do with wars and death. I fear I have disappointed her.'

'Life is full of disappointment. Can I see the skull?'

'No, Father. You would seek to make a pact with Cernunnos. It is your nature. Therefore I have hidden it.'

'In that case, Gaise, you had better find a plan to defeat the enemy.'

For the next two days there was great activity on the outskirts of Eldacre. Gaise Macon had chosen the battleground, a low line of hills stretching for a half mile east and west of a level area of grassland. Huge stakes were cut, sharpened and driven into the earth on the slopes of the hills to deter cavalry charges. Pits were dug and camouflaged to hide cannon, and weary soldiers with spade and shovel prepared long trenches to conceal musketeers. Workers were also pressganged from the citizenry of Eldacre, though little pressure was needed. Most offered their services willingly.

Fearful of the coming battle and its outcome, hundreds of families packed their belongings into wagons and set off for the relative peace of the northlands.

Gaise worked tirelessly, overseeing the construction of fortified defences, and the placement of cannon. While riding along the line he caught sight of Mulgrave, working alongside Kaelin Ring. They and a group of Rigante were filling canvas sacks with earth, tying them and creating a low wall at the centre of the open ground between the hills.

He saw Mulgrave glance up at him. Then his old friend merely looked away, without acknowledgement. Saddened, Gaise swung his horse and rode carefully up the hill, negotiating the forest of stakes placed there.

General Beck was standing with the young Bendegit Law. They were estimating cannon range, and directing soldiers in the placement of small white stakes at various places along what would be the enemy's line of advance.

Gaise dismounted. Twenty cannon were set here, some twelve feet apart. 'When their cannon are drawn up we'll be outranged,' said Beck. 'These are eight pounders. Maybe two hundred and fifty yards at best. The knights have fifteen pounders. Big bastards. They can pour down shot from almost half a mile. They'll range them on that hill,' he added, pointing to the south.

'The scouts report they have over a hundred cannon,' said Gaise, 'but I don't know how many of those fifteen pounders they can bring up. I spiked sixteen of them in the west.'

'Shame you couldn't have captured them, sir,' said Beck.

'Damn, but I should have thought of that,' said Gaise.

Beck looked embarrassed. 'Forgive me, sir. I know it was a lightning raid, and you had no opportunity to do more than spike them. I spoke without thinking.'

'It is all right, Beck,' said Gaise. 'I wish I *could* have taken them. They were fine pieces, beautifully wrought. But we barely had time to hammer the iron spikes home before the knights counter attacked.' He paused. 'You and your men are going to come under heavy fire,' he said. 'When it begins pull most of your men back from the slopes. When the cannons cease, and the attack starts, re-form.'

In the afternoon the Moidart paid a visit to the fortifications. Some of the soldiers cheered as he arrived on a splendid white mare. The Moidart ignored them and spent time talking with Beck.

Gaise, weary after two days of constant work and planning, rode back to where his own men were camped. Lanfer Gosten took his mount and Gaise made his way to his tent, where he lay down for a few hours' sleep.

Towards dusk Lanfer woke him, offering him a copper cup of warm tisane. Gaise sipped it gratefully. 'Have the scouts reported?' he asked.

'Yes, sir. The enemy is on the move. We should sight them to-morrow. Oh, and a group of Rigante captured some soldiers. They are questioning them now.'

'When they have told what they know see they are put to death,' said Gaise.

'Yes, sir.'

Gaise walked from his tent. His eyes felt gritty. There was a stream close by and he wandered to it, crouching down and splashing his face with cold water. Then he called for a mount and rode back to where Ordis Mantilan and his musketeers were camped behind the line of eastern hills. For a while he spoke with Mantilan, discussing the likely attack plans of the enemy. Walking to the top of the fortified rise he stared out to the south. Mantilan joined him.

'My guess is they'll come at us from two sides,' said Mantilan. 'Going to be hard to hold them for long. I'd be happier with six more cannon, set out on the eastern slopes.'

'If we had six more you'd be welcome to them,' said Gaise. 'You'll have Bael Jace and his Rigante in reserve. Do not call them in until the situation is desperate.'

Mantilan chuckled. 'I have to say that Bael Jace makes me uncomfortable,' he said, running his fingers through his curly hair.

'I always feel he is staring at my head and longing to separate it from my shoulders.'

'He doesn't like the Varlish,' said Gaise. 'But he'll fight.'

'Oh, I know that, sir. Those Rigante are a terrifying bunch. If they scare the enemy half as much as they scare me we could actually win.'

'That's a good thought.' Gaise stared out over the battle site. There were six hundred yards of open ground to the southern hills. He pictured the enemy formations. They would form up on the hills, set up cannon, and begin a barrage. Then the infantry would attack on two fronts. The heavy cavalry would ignore the staked hill fortifications and ride through the centre. Gaise had placed a two-hundred-yard wall of earth bags there, packed to a height of four feet, behind which musketeers would defend the open ground. This area too would be within cannon range.

The first stars began to twinkle in the new night sky. Gaise rode back to his camp and ate a meal of thin stew and bread. Lanfer Gosten approached him. Gaise looked into the older man's face and saw the concern there.

'What is it, Lanfer?'

'I couldn't obey your orders, sir.'

'What?'

'The Rigante refused to surrender their prisoners to us.'

The three prisoners were all young men, wearing the red coats and yellow sashes of the King's Third Infantry. One was little more than a boy, and he sat trembling, wide eyes staring at the powerful men of the Rigante who had gathered round the camp fire. They had been told to sit where they were and await events.

All three knew what the 'events' would lead to. They had been among the first to see the forest of heads as they entered the northlands. Crows had pecked out the eyes, and stripped flesh from the cheekbones. Many carrion birds were waddling on the ground between the stakes, their bellies full of flesh.

The youngest of the prisoners, thirteen-year-old Slipper Wainwright, had begun to cry. He had not wanted to go on patrol through the woods. He had been filled with a sense of foreboding that he now took to have been a premonition. When the Rigante had come upon them – seemingly out of nowhere – the ten-man patrol had not even been able to fire a shot. Seven men were dead in a matter of heartbeats. The youngster, and the two men sitting alongside him, had thrown down their weapons and put their hands in the air.

The Rigante leader, a ferocious killer with a scar on his right cheek, had stepped in close. Slipper thought he was going to die right there, and had squeezed shut his eyes. Nothing happened.

He and the other two men had been hauled away, back through the trees and along a narrow trail. After an hour they emerged into this camp. Then the man with the scar had questioned them about their unit, and their division. He had asked for the names of officers, and wanted to know how skilful they were. So many questions that the boy could not answer. How could he know how good the officers were? He had only joined the regiment five days prior to the invasion. He had lied about his age and signed up in Baracum because food was running short and his family could not afford to eat. The signing on payment had been two chaillings, which he had given to his mother. Slipper told all this to the killer, who listened without comment.

Then another group of men had arrived in the camp. An older man, with a kind face, dressed in a pale green tunic jacket, bearing a Fawn in Brambles motif upon the breast.

'You are to hand over the prisoners to me,' he said. 'Upon the orders of Gaise Macon.'

The boy felt a surge of hope. He would have given anything to be away from these harsh, deadly men.

'We like their company,' said Scarface.

'We have our orders, General Ring.'

'And your orders are to take these boys away and kill them. Not today, Master Gosten. You can satisfy your bloodlust tomorrow when the battle starts. There'll be no killing here.'

'I don't have bloodlust,' said Gosten. 'I just have orders, sir.'

'Some orders should never be obeyed. Not ever. You think when you come before the Source of All Things He will accept such an excuse for murder?'

'Probably not, sir. I don't suppose He'll have much use for any

395

of us warriors. I'll report back to General Macon. I wish that would be the end of it, but I doubt it.'

The soldiers in green marched away. Scarface said nothing to the boy or his comrades, but another man brought them food. He was tall and slim, his hair prematurely white. 'Stay calm, lads. I am Captain Mulgrave and you are with the Rigante. No harm will come to you.'

'Is that true, sir?' asked the boy. 'We was told you murdered all prisoners. Cut off their heads and stuck them on poles. We seen 'em.'

The officer nodded gravely. 'I know, but that man there is Kaelin Ring. His men call him Ravenheart. He will not let anyone take you for execution. Neither would any one of his men. Deadly fighters they may be, but you can trust me on this: they are not murderers. Eat and rest, and do as you are told.'

'We will, sir.'

'What is your name, boy?'

'Slipper, sir. I mean Brene. Brene Wainwright.'

'You seem unsure,' said the man, with a smile.

'Slipper's what I've always been called. Come from my first day at school. My mother made me some shoes, but they weren't very good. Soles was all shiny and I slipped and slid all over the place.'

'Make sure your comrades understand this also, Slipper. Do not run, whatever happens. Just sit here quietly.' With that he rose and moved away to talk to the Ravenheart.

It was two hours later, the night sky ablaze with stars, when horsemen rode towards the camp. The boy looked round and saw the kind-faced man was back, and riding ahead of him was a golden-haired horseman. Other riders followed them.

The Ravenheart walked out to meet them, and a number of Rigante went with him. All were carrying their muskets.

'Hand over your prisoners,' said the golden-haired man.

'Men who come to do murder are not welcome in my camp, Stormrider.'

The horseman angled his mount past the Ravenheart. He looked at Slipper and reached for one of the pistols in the pommel scabbard of his saddle. Slipper knew then that he was going to die. The man's face was hard, his expression one of undiluted hatred.

Slipper could not take his eyes from him. He felt his stomach lurch. The man's pistol slid clear of the scabbard. Slipper wanted to get up and run, but his body was frozen in terror.

'Fire that and I'll kill you,' said the Ravenheart, pulling a long-barrelled silver pistol from his belt, cocking it and pointing it at the rider.

The golden-haired man swung his horse and glared down at the scarred man. 'You would risk everything we have fought for – everything your men have died for – to save these scum?'

'Why not? You are. And I fear we have very different definitions of scum.'

The horsemen who had arrived with the golden-haired rider had also now drawn pistols. The Rigante raised their muskets. Slipper sat open mouthed, unable to fully comprehend what was happening. Why were these men ready to fight over three of the enemy?

Captain Mulgrave moved forward to stand alongside the Ravenheart. 'So, we have come full circle it seems. As I recall it was not so long ago that I stood alongside another noble young man. Winter Kay rode into his camp and demanded prisoners to be executed. He refused. That made me proud. By heaven, Gaise, I never thought to see the day when you would become an animal like Winterbourne. There is no difference between you now. It sickens me to my soul to see it.'

'What is sickening,' said Gaise, 'is to see how swiftly you forget. Winter Kay had our men murdered. He had Cordelia murdered. Men like these ripped her life from her.'

'Do not bring her into this,' Mulgrave told him. 'Her death did not make you a murderer. You just gave in to the darkness. You unchained the bear and now it chains you. Look at where you are, Gaise. Look at the men around you. Lanfer Gosten back there is sickened by this. You have blackened his soul as well as your own. And I see Taybard Jaekel there. Not a man who joys in killing. What are you doing to these good men? What kind of devils are you trying to create?'

'I am trying to win a war against evil men. Can you not see that?'

'And you will win it by slaughtering three boys?'

Slipper saw the golden-haired man look directly at him once more. He blinked. The man had strange eyes. One was almost golden. Mulgrave walked across to stand beside Slipper. 'He is thirteen, Gaise. He joined the army because his family were starving. He was given two chaillings, which he passed on to his mother. His name is Slipper. Tell us all how we will win by killing children.'

The rider seemed to sag in his saddle and the tension went out of him. Without another word he turned his horse and rode from the camp.

Mulgrave walked back to the prisoners. 'Get some sleep. Tomorrow you will either be released by us or rescued by your comrades. You are probably the luckiest men in the area. You won't have to die tomorrow.'

'Thank you for what you said to him, sir,' said Slipper.

'What I said to him broke my heart, boy,' answered Mulgrave.

During the night the various divisions of the Eldacre army took up their positions. Kaelin Ring and eight hundred Rigante moved stealthily forward to the line of earth bags guarding the open ground between the hills. There had already been some skirmishes with outriding scouts from the enemy, and Rayster had taken a ball through his left elbow. He had been moved back to Eldacre with close to twenty other Rigante who had been caught in a crossfire.

Kaelin settled his back against the earth bag wall and glanced at the line of bushes some three hundred feet away. Korrin Talis moved alongside him. 'I don't think Rayster will have use of that arm,' he said.

'Bad wound,' agreed Kaelin.

'You think this plan will work?'

'Even if it does it will not be enough,' said Kaelin.

A troop of musketeers and riflemen began to march up the slope to their left. Korrin Talis saw Taybard Jaekel and waved. 'I didn't know you knew him,' said Kaelin.

'Descended from Fiallach, according to the Dweller.'

Kaelin smiled. 'And that is why he was in the camp when I returned from meeting the Moidart?'

'He came in with Gallowglass. He was in a sad state, Kaelin. We made him feel at home.'

'By getting him drunk?'

'Drunk is good. I wish I was drunk now. There's not a drop of uisge left in Eldacre. I tried their ale. I'd sooner drink horse piss in future.'

Kaelin glanced up at the night sky. There were heavy clouds gathering in the east. 'It'll blow over,' said Korrin. Kaelin chuckled. 'I'll never know how you can predict the weather so well.'

'That's because you were raised among the soft Varlish, Ravenheart. Didn't get a chance to develop a feel for the land. The cloud is fast-moving. It'll be wet on the eastern coast tomorrow.'

Kaelin glanced along the earth wall. The Rigante warriors were mostly asleep now. 'I think I'll join them,' said Korrin, stretching himself out and drawing his cloak over his two muskets. Within moments he too was breathing deeply. Then he began to snore.

The wound in Kaelin's shoulder was throbbing again, the fingers of his left hand twitching. He rubbed at the fingertips and leaned his head against the earth bags. Sleep would not come. He found himself thinking back. He had spent his childhood close to these hills. It was less than an hour to the old schoolhouse where Alterith Shaddler had, on many occasions, beaten him with a cane. Back then he had longed to be a warrior. His plan was to one day kill Shaddler. Jaim had warned him against such thoughts. The one-eyed clansman had been right. Shaddler had risked his life to defend Maev Ring in the witchcraft trial. Life, Kaelin realized, had a curious talent for reversal. In those days the great enemy had been the evil Moidart. Now, as the man himself had cynically predicted, the Moidart was a hero. And Kaelin Ring, the son of the man he had murdered, was risking his life in the Moidart's service. Who could have foreseen it? Even the Wyrd – who he had always believed to be the well of all wisdom – had been amazed at the events of the past months.

And earlier this night Kaelin had pointed a pistol at a man who might well be his brother. He would have used it too. He would have shot Gaise Macon from the saddle.

For three unknown Varlish soldiers.

Kaelin sighed. It was all madness. He found himself longing to be back at Ironlatch, holding Chara in his arms, watching little Jaim play in the meadow. Thinking of his son made him remember yet again the man whose name he carried. He wondered what Jaim

Grymauch would have made of this war. Then he smiled. If Jaim had been here he would even now be stretched out and fast asleep, just like Korrin Talis. Jaim was not a man who worried overmuch about matters outside his realm of control. He lived for the day, and gloried in every breath he took.

Turning and easing himself up Kaelin glanced over the top of the makeshift wall. On the southern hills he could see the enemy cannon being brought into place. There were already some forty in view. There would be more coming.

The whole of the valley was strangely peaceful, the moonlight pure silver. Within a few hours the air would be filled with screeching shells and the screams of dying men.

'Sleep, you fool,' Kaelin told himself. 'You'll need all your strength soon.'


On the western slope Taybard Jaekel was sitting in a narrow trench, Jakon Gallowglass beside him. The trenches had been the idea of General Beck. Once the cannon fire began the vast majority of the men on the hill tops would retire back into the relative safety of the low ground. A few would remain, keeping a watch for enemy advances. The trenches were for them. Taybard failed to see how a narrow hole scraped in the mud would keep him safe, but there was little point in questioning the orders of a general.

Taybard was feeling ill at ease. His Emburley rifle was clean and ready, a new flint locked into the hammer. The forty lead balls in the pouch at his side had been fashioned by Taybard himself, and rubbed down with sanded paper to remove any hint of imperfection. He could feel the weight of the pouch. Tomorrow, if he survived the full day, it was likely that at least thirty more souls would be added to his ever lengthening death list. In large part Taybard would have loved to be able to toss the rifle aside and say to Gallowglass: 'That's it, my killing days are over.' He would walk from the battlefield and not look back.

His heart yearned for him to do just that. But that would mean leaving Lanfer and Jakon, and the Grey Ghost, to do his fighting for him. Caught between the desire for escape and the demands of loyalty Taybard Jaekel felt lost.

'Are you all right, Jaekel?' asked Gallowglass.

'Will you stop asking me that?' Ever since the night at the Rigante camp Gallowglass had hovered around him like a mother hen. 'I'm fine. Steady as a rock.'

'Good to have the Rigante so close,' said Gallowglass. 'Can't see anyone cutting a swath through them bastards.'

'I wish I knew how they did it,' said Taybard.

'Did what? Fight? Born to it, I guess.'

'No, I didn't mean that. I meant how do they kill so savagely and yet retain so much . . . nobility. I was so proud of them when they refused to let us kill those prisoners.'

'Crazy if you ask me. I mean, where's the sense in it? Kill them in battle or kill them in camp. We're still killers. Would it have been sensible for Kaelin Ring to shoot the Grey Ghost over three men he didn't know? The war could have been lost as a result. No. He should have just let the prisoners be taken.'

'I disagree – though I can't offer any proper reason as to why,' said Taybard. 'I just know in my heart it was right.'

'You are an odd one for a soldier,' said Gallowglass. 'I don't see where right comes into it. The duty of a soldier is to kill the enemy. Those men were the enemy. End of story. It's not about right. It's about rules. The rules of war say prisoners should be treated with respect.'

'But that rule was made because it was right.'

'I have enough trouble carrying musket, powder and shot. I don't need to carry any more burdens, thank you very much. Tomorrow I'll kill every whoreson who comes at me from the south. Then, when we've won, I'm going to find the best whore in Eldacre.'

'Has it occurred to you, Jakon, that we might not win, and that even if we do you may die in the battle?'

'No, I won't,' replied Gallowglass. 'I thought I would die in Shelding. I was convinced of it. Having survived *that* it is my belief I will survive anything they throw at us, and then some. If we lose I'll take off into the hills and wait. When things have quietened down I'll sneak back into Eldacre and find the best whore in town.'

Taybard relaxed and smiled. 'It doesn't really matter to you, does it, whether evil or good wins this battle?'

'Not as long as—'

'—there are still whores around,' chimed in Taybard.

'Exactly.'

A rider on a white mare cantered into sight in the valley below. Gallowglass peered down at him. 'Is that the Moidart?' he asked.

'Yes,' said Taybard.

'I missed him earlier, but they said he had a beautiful white horse. Looks a bit skittish for a war mount.'

'I doubt the Moidart will take part in the battle,' said Taybard. 'He's not young any more.'

The Moidart continued to canter across the valley floor, skirting the line of bushes behind the ramparts where the Rigante were stationed, and on behind the western hills to where the original Eldacre Company were camped. Gaise Macon and General Beck were sitting by the stream discussing the coming battle when the Moidart rode up and dismounted.

Beck rose and bowed. 'You may continue, gentlemen,' said the Moidart, joining them.

'We had all but concluded our business, Father,' put in Gaise swiftly. 'There is nothing more to be done now save fight.'

'I have decided to attend the battle,' said the Moidart.

'That would be most unwise, Father,' objected Gaise. 'The plans are set, and everyone knows their place.'

'Would I be wrong in assuming that the heaviest attacks will be against Beck's ridge?'

'That is what we expect,' agreed Gaise.

The Moidart turned to Beck. 'Would it lift or demoralize the men if I were to place myself among them?'

'It would lift them, my lord.'

'Then that is my role. I am not a soldier, Beck, and will make no attempt to issue orders, nor countermand any that you may give.'

'I would be honoured to have you with us, my lord, but I fear for your safety.'

'I have been shot at before. I will join you just before the dawn. Now, will you allow me a few words in private with my son?'

'Of course, my lord. Good night to you,' said Beck, bowing and then departing.

'Why are you doing this, Father?' asked Gaise.

'Because it is sensible. You are a fine cavalry general, Gaise, but you are too reckless and daring. The likelihood is that you will be cut down tomorrow leading a charge. Without you there will be no central focus. Beck, Mantilan and the others will begin to act independently. The spirit of the defenders will start to wilt. The reality is that your brilliance has made you *too* important. If I am with Beck I will become a rallying centre.' He shrugged. 'It may make little difference. Time will tell.'

Gaise shook his head. 'You lied to Beck. You *are* a soldier, and one as naturally gifted as any I have known.'

'It is in the blood, Gaise. Varlish and Rigante, warriors both. Our ancestors have fought wars since time immemorial. And won them. More than that we have built societies and held them together. We are the rulers, Gaise. We are the mighty. Remember that tomorrow.'

'Do your best to stay alive, Father.'

The Moidart smiled. 'I do not care one way or the other. My time is almost over. If we win – and since no-one can hear us I'd say we have less than one chance in twenty – I shall stand down as Moidart, and pass on the mantle to you.'

'Why? What would you do?'

'Picture the mountains,' said the Moidart.

'What does that mean?'

'It means a lot to me,' replied his father, walking back to the white mare and stepping into the saddle. 'Do your best tomorrow, boy. I shall be watching you with a critical eye.'

'No change there,' said Gaise, and realized there was no bitterness in the words.


Aran Powdermill did not see himself as a traitor. He did not serve the Moidart out of loyalty. He had been hired to perform a service, and then pressganged into continuing that service. Indeed, had he chosen to exercise his rights as a free man and leave the Moidart had made it clear that Huntsekker would come after him and take his head. No, there was no question of treachery here. Quite the opposite, Powdermill decided. He was the victim of treachery, in that the Moidart had tricked him, and not allowed him to leave.

Added to which Powdermill would not be taking this action had the Moidart and his son not made such a stupid decision. Gaise

403

had the skull, probably the greatest magical relic in known history. How could they not seek to use it? They would be killed now, the enemy triumphant, and the skull once more in the hands of Winter Kay. It was inevitable.

Why then should Aran himself not find a way to profit from the disaster?

It all made perfect sense.

He recalled his last conversation with the Moidart, late the previous afternoon.

'The skull is hidden somewhere in the castle. Can you locate it?'

'No, my lord,' lied Powdermill. 'The Lord Gaise has the Sword in the Storm. It blinds my talents. But has he not said it is too dangerous to use?'

'Nothing is too dangerous to use,' said the Moidart. 'But if you cannot find it then that is an end to it.'

In truth Aran had not set out to lie to the Moidart. It had been a sudden impulse. Part of it was the truth. When Gaise hid the skull he had been protected by the Sword in the Storm. But as soon as he moved away Aran had *felt* the power of the skull, radiating from deep within the castle. It pulled at him, tugging at his conscious mind. Aran was a man who loved magic, and had never, until he felt the Sword in the Storm, handled any object of great power.

With the Moidart and Gaise away from the castle he took a lantern and climbed to the upper levels, locating the now unused apartments where Gaise had spent much of his youth. Powdermill hauled aside the threadbare rug beside the bed and knelt to examine the timbered flooring beneath. Drawing a slender knife he inserted the blade between two sections of board and applied pressure. The hidden section creaked open. With trembling hands he lifted the velvet sack from its hiding place. Even through the cloth he could feel the power radiating.

Now back in his own room he sat with the skull in his lap. He had expected to commune with the spirit of Cernunnos, but nothing happened. Even so, he felt his own talents swelling and growing. And with them came the realization that he had in his hands an object far more powerful than he could safely use.

His first plan had been to flee the castle and take the skull with

404

him. This was no longer an option. The raw energy it radiated could never be hidden completely by ward spells. Other magickers would sense it. Warriors would find him and seize it. He tried once more to commune with Cernunnos. Nothing. No, he realized, not quite nothing. He sensed that he was being heard, but ignored.

Closing his eyes he soared above the night dark battlefield, pausing to gaze down on the waiting men of both sides. From here he could see the formations, the two main ridges occupied by Beck and Mantilan, the infantry spread out thinly behind earth bags, or within trenches. Cavalry mounts were picketed on both flanks.

The enemy force was drawn up into three great divisions. From this great height the sheer numerical superiority of Winter Kay's forces was manifestly apparent.

This strengthened Powdermill's resolve. *He* could not safely harness the power of the skull, but if he found a way to serve it, he could still profit by it. If Cernunnos was to live again, then he would need worshippers. His spirit flew to the centre of the enemy camp. Not a single Redeemer spirit was in the air. None of these men had *natural* talent. The skull had fed them, as it was now feeding him.

Powdermill flowed through the officers' tents, seeking out Winter Kay.

He found him at last, standing on a ridge beside a huge cannon. He was staring out over the enemy fortifications. For a few moments Powdermill observed him. He was similar in look to the Moidart, the same harsh, patrician features, the same hawklike eyes. Yet Powdermill sensed a weakness in the man, shards of self-doubt and fear that were missing in the Moidart.

Focusing his newly boosted powers Powdermill spoke. Winter Kay jerked and spun. 'Who is there?'

'A servant of Kranos, my lord.'

Winter Kay stepped back, his hand upon the hilt of a slim-bladed dagger at his belt. Powdermill concentrated, allowing his spirit to glow gently in the night. 'I have what you desire to possess. I have that which was stolen from you.'

'Bring it to me. You will be rewarded handsomely.'

'It is at Castle Eldacre, my lord. I have it now in my hands.'

'This is some trick of the Moidart's to torment me.'

'Not so, my lord. I am Powdermill. I was forced into the Moidart's service, and threatened with death if I did not comply. Now I have the Orb, and I wish to serve you.'

'Why would that be?'

'There is something I want, and only you can give it to me.'

'Name it.'

'The sword of Gaise Macon. And to continue to serve the Lord Kranos.'

'You want a sword?'

'Not any sword, my lord. It is an ancient weapon, forged in a time of magic.'

'I promise you will have it. Bring me the skull.'

'I cannot *bring* it, my lord. Between Eldacre and yourself lie the forces of the Moidart. I could not find a way through alone. When the battle is won I shall be at Eldacre Castle and you will have the skull.'

'I need it *now*,' said Winter Kay. Powdermill heard the desperation in his voice.

'Here in the town there are few fighting men, my lord. The castle itself is virtually empty. Maybe twenty soldiers, older men unfit for service in the field, a dozen surgeons and helpers tending wounded men, plus Maev Ring and a few clerics. If you send a small force, skirt the battlefield, and ride directly to the castle, there will be none to stop you.'

'Maev Ring?'

'She is the Moidart's quartermaster.'

'The witch who brought about the death of my brother Gayan? *She* is at the castle?'

'Yes, my lord.'

'And all you want is Macon's sword?'

'Yes, my lord, and to serve you and Kranos. I have no wish to die, and it is my understanding that those who serve the Seidh lord will become immortal.'

'I will send a force, Powdermill. If your deeds match your words I will grant you what you wish.'

As dawn approached the guns on the southern ridge suddenly boomed, flame belching from the huge barrels. Taybard Jaekel squirmed down in his trench. Fifty yards to the south the earth erupted. Great plumes of mud and dirt billowed up. A terrible screeching filled the air. Shards of metal and clumps of earth showered down over Taybard and Jakon.

Taybard glanced back to where the Moidart – dressed in black, save for a stylized breastplate of burnished silver – was standing beside Beck. The earl calmly walked to the edge of the ridge and stared out at the pits and craters in the ground. 'They'll have their range presently,' he said.

'Aye, time to move back, my lord,' said Beck, nervously.

Beck shouted an order and the main body of the two thousand musketeers retired from the ridge. Some fifty men remained, huddled in narrow trenches. Beck moved up to where Taybard and Jakon were crouched. 'Sit it out, boys, and signal us when their infantry approaches.'

The fifty cannon in view on the southern hills boomed again. Beck dropped to his belly and squirmed alongside Jakon Gallowglass. Huge cannon balls, some of them containing explosive charges, hammered against the hillside less than thirty yards away. Taybard felt the ground beneath him tremble upon the impact. Several huge stakes flew overhead, blown from the earth. 'I doubt they'll have more than twenty rounds per cannon,' said Beck. 'Probably less.'

'Why's that?' asked Gallowglass.

'Weight. Fifteen pounds a ball, that's three hundred pounds per cannon. Fifty cannon. That's fifteen thousand pounds. Over rough ground a two horse wagon can pull—'

'We get the point, general,' said Gallowglass. 'Shouldn't you be—'

The guns thundered. The men on the ridge hunkered down. The earth exploded around them. Taybard was hurled into Beck. Mud and dirt rained down on them.

'Time for you to go, general,' said Gallowglass, spitting dirt from his mouth.

'See you in a while,' said Beck, climbing from the trench and walking back towards the rear slope.

'This is definitely not soldiering,' said Gallowglass, peering over the lip of the trench. On the far ridge he could see men reloading the cannon. Suddenly there was a distant explosion, and one of the pieces blew apart. Jakon watched the huge barrel rear up some ten feet in the air. 'Ha!' he yelled. 'Serve 'em right.'

The other cannons belched smoke and fire. Gallowglass swore and threw himself face down. This time the enemy gunners had found their range. All around the ridge top great gouts of earth plumed up. Thirty feet to the left of Taybard and Gallowglass a shell exploded in the air, sending shrapnel screaming across the ridge. Clods of earth thumped down on Taybard's back. Then something else dropped alongside his head. Glancing to his left he saw it was part of a man's hand.

Taybard grabbed it and tossed it out of the trench. Smoke and dust filled the air. He lifted his head and tried to pierce the man-made gloom. It was as if a fog had descended upon the ridge. He heard other cannon fire and winced, before realizing it was coming from the east, and was not directed at Beck's ridge. Beside him Gallowglass coughed and spat. 'See anything?' he asked.

'I can't even see the cannons now,' answered Taybard.

During the next few minutes the cannons fired four more salvoes. The silence that followed the explosions was rent by the screams of mutilated men.

By this time Taybard had taken to counting slowly between each salvo. The gunners were experts. Each time Taybard reached the count of twenty-eight the sound of distant thunder would herald another murderous assault from the sky.

'How many is that so far?' said Gallowglass, making Taybard lose count.

'Eight, I think. Nine maybe.'

Taybard saw movement to his left. A group of wide-eyed, fearful men were scrambling from their trenches. Two had thrown aside their muskets. Taybard could feel the panic spreading.

Just then the Moidart came into view. He had his hands clasped behind his back as if out on a morning stroll.

The fleeing men paused. 'Best keep your heads down,' said the Moidart, moving past them. They hesitated, then returned to their trenches. A breeze began to blow across the ridge top. The Moidart approached where Taybard and Gallowglass were hunkered down. They moved aside to make way for him. 'Not long now,' said the earl.

The breeze quickened, and the smoke and dust began to clear.

Taybard squinted through the last of the haze. On the valley floor he saw red-coated lines of men marching forward, muskets in hand. Thousands of them.

'Time to call up our boys,' said Gallowglass, scrambling from the trench.

'Not yet,' said the Moidart.

Other men had the same idea. The Moidart called out to them. 'Stay where you are! There's one more salvo coming.' Then he rose and calmly walked across the pockmarked ridge, disappearing from view.

Gallowglass stared after him, then looked back at the advancing enemy. They were within two hundred yards of the ridge now. At this point they quickened their pace. Sunlight gleamed from the bayonets on their muskets.

'I think we are going to need a little help up here,' muttered Gallowglass.

At that moment the cannon thundered again. Huge chunks were ripped from the ridge. The force of one blast caused a twelve-foot section of hillside to slide away, sending rock and earth tumbling down the slope.

'How in seven hells did he know they were going to fire one more salvo?' asked Gallowglass.

'They were hoping to catch more of us as we swarmed back up to defend the ridge,' Taybard told him, taking up his blanket-wrapped Emburley and untying the strings that held the covering in place.

Behind them two thousand musketeers scrambled over the ruined ridge, taking up pre-arranged positions in three ranks. Bendegit Law and his artillery men came over the ridge top, hauling barrels of powder. Eight of the twenty defensive cannon placed on the ridge had been smashed by the enemy salvoes. Four others were damaged. Bendegit Law directed his men with quiet efficiency. Bringing the eight surviving cannons to bear they loaded them and waited.

Taybard could see the faces of the attackers now, grim and determined as they stormed the slope. Lifting the Emburley rifle he cocked the hammer. 'Front rank forward!' bellowed General Beck.

The six hundred men of the front rank shuffled into position. 'Take aim!'

The red-garbed attackers faltered as the musketeers appeared on the ridge. Then they charged.

'Fire!'

Six hundred muskets loosed thunder into the charging men. Smoke billowed across the ridge top. 'Second rank forward!' shouted Beck. The first rank fell back to the rear to reload as the next line of musketeers stepped in to take their places. This manoeuvre was an innovation of Beck's that the men had been practising for weeks now. In most battles Taybard had seen or taken part in the object had been to deliver full ferocious volleys, then to reload. This rolling fire was far more effective.

The second rank emptied their muskets into the now faltering advance. Hundreds of enemy soldiers were down. Still they pushed on, stepping over the bodies of dead and dying.

'Third rank forward!' yelled Beck. 'Fire!'

Some of the soldiers below were starting to shoot up the slope now, and a score of Eldacre men went down.

The first of the enemy was almost at the top of the slope when Bendegit Law ordered the cannons to be fired. The blast ripped away the leading ranks of the enemy.

Taybard watched it all as if in a dream, his Emburley unfired. Smoke covered the ridge like a blanket of fog, and when the first rank volleyed again Taybard could not even see the enemy. Beside him Gallowglass was frantically reloading.

The second rank moved forward again, but this time Beck did not order them to fire.

The breeze picked up once more and the smoke cleared. The hillside was littered with red-coated bodies. The survivors were pulling back.

The Moidart approached Beck. Taybard heard what he said. 'While not wishing to appear intrusive, Beck, might it not be wise to pull back? I fear another salvo is likely soon.'

'Indeed, my lord, that is good advice.' He swung towards the men. 'By rank fall back to the base of the hill!'

The move was not quite swift enough. In the distance the huge fifteen pounders roared. The Eldacre men began to run. Two explosive charges burst in the air above them. More than a hundred musketeers went down.

Taybard and Gallowglass had not moved from their trench. Once more earth rained down upon them.

# CHAPTER NINETEEN

KAELIN RING WATCHED THE CARNAGE ON THE WESTERN RIDGE THEN returned his gaze to the open lands directly south. There was still no attack from that quarter. More columns of enemy musketeers were advancing now against the ridge, and he could see the Moidart and the defenders marching back into position.

'I wouldn't want to be up there,' said Korrin Talis.

Raising his head above the earth sacks Kaelin scanned the south. Lines of horsemen were gathering beneath the far slopes. 'Not long to wait,' said Kaelin. 'The knights are forming.'

'How many?' asked Korrin.

'Can't tell. Too much smoke. I'd expect around four thousand. Everyone knows what to do?'

'Of course they know what to do,' snapped Korrin. 'We're not idiots.'

A huge mass of enemy infantry moved out of the smoke, charging the eastern ridge, held by Mantilan. Kaelin saw the Rigante under Bael Jace rush to their aid.

'Here they come,' said Korrin. Kaelin jerked his gaze back to the south. The knights, wearing breastplates that glittered in the sunlight, were smoothly moving into formation. Their first line spread out until it covered about a quarter of a mile. Other lines formed behind them. 'Impressive bunch, aren't they?' muttered Korrin.

A distant bugle sounded and the knights advanced at the trot. When they reached three hundred yards they began to canter.

'Rigante!' bellowed Kaelin Ring. The eight hundred Rigante musketeers raised their weapons. The knights charged, the pounding hooves of their war horses making the ground tremble.

'Fire!' yelled Kaelin.

The first volley tore into the charging horsemen, smashing men from their saddles and bringing down mounts. The Rigante tossed aside the first muskets and lifted fresh weapons.

'Take aim! Fire!'

Another volley ripped into the enemy. But still they came.

'Back!' shouted Kaelin.

Leaving their muskets the Rigante began to run back towards the line of bushes a hundred paces away.

The knights galloped on, sabres gleaming. The first of the horses reached the earth ramparts and leapt over them. The Rigante were streaming back now, and the knights began to shout war cries as they bore down upon them.

As the fleeing Rigante passed the line of scrub growth they suddenly turned and re-formed, drawing pistols from their belts.

Then ten of the twenty cannon hidden in pits behind the line of bushes belched thunder and fire into the knights. The carnage was appalling. Each of the cannons had been packed with hundreds of musket balls – grapeshot Gaise Macon called it. Where there had been a division of highly disciplined charging cavalry there was now a charnel house of twisted corpses and mutilated men. Those horsemen who had survived the horror of the first cannon blasts urged their mounts on.

A second volley of cannon fire thundered. Kaelin saw men and horses flung to the ground.

Even then the knights did not retreat.

'Forward!' shouted Kaelin Ring.

The Rigante charged, scrambling over the corpses and the mutilated survivors. With pistol and sabre they surged into the horsemen. From the right came Gaise Macon and a thousand Eldacre cavalry. They hammered into the enemy's flank.

Kaelin blocked a savage downward stroke from a cavalry sabre, then leapt, grabbing the rider by his breastplate and hauling him from the saddle. As the rider fell he lost hold of his weapon and hit the ground hard. Kaelin stabbed him through the throat. The man's horse suddenly reared, its front hooves cracking against Kaelin's injured shoulder, throwing him from his feet. He scrambled up. The surviving knights had swung to face Macon's lighter armed cavalry. A little distance away Kaelin saw Gaise Macon cut a man from the saddle and spur his horse deeper into the fray. Then his horse stumbled and went down. Gaise kicked his feet from the stirrups and leapt clear. Two knights rode at him. Kaelin dragged his pistol clear of his belt and fired at the first rider. The shot punched through the centre of the knight's forehead. Gaise ran at the second, ducked under a slashing sabre, and buried his own blade through the rider's breastplate. The man sagged to the right. Gaise pitched him from the saddle. Grabbing the pommel with his left hand he vaulted to the beast's back. Then, taking the reins, he swung the captured mount and returned to the attack.

With the Rigante surging forward, and Macon's cavalry cutting their way through, the surviving knights finally broke. Swinging their mounts they galloped back for the safety of their lines.

Kaelin and the Rigante moved back across the field of the fallen and resumed their position at the earth ramparts, reloading their muskets.

Behind them the cannoneers recharged their weapons, then ran among the fallen knights, killing those who still lived. Kaelin Ring tried to close his ears to the almost inhuman shrieks of the mortally wounded. He had never felt any regard for the men of the Varlish, and was surprised that their deaths and their suffering should touch him so. He gazed out over the battlefield. It seemed to him that the dead almost outnumbered the living now.

And the dreadful day wore on.

The pain from the stump of Rayster's amputated left arm caused him to groan aloud. This display of weakness annoyed the clansman, and he gritted his teeth as the orderly continued to wrap the honey and wine soaked bandage around the cauterized stump. Sweat gleamed upon Rayster's face, and his jaw ached from where he had bitten so hard into the leather strap the surgeon had placed between his teeth. 'I can give you something to dull the pain,' said the orderly, a soft-faced man with large, friendly eyes. Rayster shook his head. He had no strength to reply. It was all he could do to stop from screaming out in his agony.

His head sank back to the pillow. For an hour he fought the pain, after refusing the narcotics offered by the orderly. In the distance he could hear the cannon fire. Finally he struggled up. All around him were wounded men, overworked orderlies moving among them.

Rayster stood, then staggered. The first orderly ran back to him. 'What do you think you are doing, man?'

'Where is my cloak?'

Sweat dripped into Rayster's eyes. Then he saw the garment in a heap on the floor by a window. The orderly gathered it up. Rayster's sword, pistol and knife were lying beneath it. 'I will look after everything for you, clansman. I promise you. No-one will steal your weapons.'

Rayster took the cloak from the man and tried to swing it round his shoulders. It was difficult with one hand – and impossible to open the Rigante cloak brooch. Rayster felt a wave of despair roll over him. He looked into the soft eyes of the orderly. 'Put my cloak on me,' he said. 'I'll not die in here.'

For a moment the man appeared to be ready to argue the point, but then he expertly settled Rayster's cloak into place, and unpinned the oval, bronze brooch. 'I have seen these before,' he said. 'Usually there is a name embossed within the eye.'

Rayster did not reply. He stood and swayed, then he leaned down and picked up his pistol, thrusting it into his belt. 'Strap on my sword belt,' he said. The orderly complied. Rayster felt suddenly faint and sat down heavily. The orderly sat beside him.

'You are a strong man,' he said, 'but you have lost much blood. You need to rest awhile, gather your strength. The body is a remarkable thing. It will heal itself, and you will learn to do everything you need, even though you have lost an arm.'

'I am not concerned about the arm,' said Rayster. 'I have comrades out there.'

'You'll be no help to them in this state.'

Reluctantly Rayster lay back. Amazingly, despite the pain, he slept for a while. When he awoke he felt stronger, though not much. Rising, he forced himself to walk among the injured. Other Rigante wounded were somewhere in the castle's west wing. Rayster located several of them. Their wounds were severe, and all of the men were unconscious, having availed themselves of the narcotic drink. The air in the wing was filled with a curious smell, making Rayster's stomach queasy. Moving to the open doorway he stepped out into a hallway beyond. It was filled with corpses, the bodies laid out in rows.

Rayster moved on. In a nearby corridor he saw a group of some twenty Rigante sitting together. Two, like him, had endured amputations. One had lost a hand, the other had a bloody bandage over the stump of his lower left leg. Most of the others had bandaged wounds to the upper body, and one had lost an eye. The man with the amputated left hand saw Rayster and called out. 'Looks like we were both lucky, eh, Rayster? Never was much use with my left.'

Rayster moved to where they sat. Weary now he sank alongside the man. 'You never were much good with your right, Connal.'

Connal Ironlatch grinned. 'Can you believe they wanted to take our weapons away? My father would flay me alive if I came home without his favourite sword.'

'Aye, he was put out when Bael told him to stay home,' said Rayster. 'Never seen him so angry.'

From outside came the thunder of horses' hooves on the stones. Then a shot sounded and a man cried out in pain.

It had been so long since Winter Kay felt genuine fear that he was almost unmanned by the experience. He had believed for years that he was a powerful man, in full control, and merely aided by the magic of the skull. The realization that the essence of his power came from Kranos, and that he was, in truth, merely ordinary, was almost more than he could bear.

He had no idea how to plan the battle against Gaise Macon, no overall sense of strategy. He looked at the land, the high ground and the slopes beyond the ridges and saw only meadows, hills and a valley. With the skull in his possession he had needed only a glance at a battlefield to note instantly the key areas to control.

Winter Kay desperately needed to regain the skull. After the spirit of Powdermill spoke to him he decided to send Eris Velroy and a hundred Redeemers to make a swift raid into Eldacre and retrieve it. Velroy was willing, but pointed out that a hundred men riding from the battlefield would alert the enemy, and probably cause them to send out a cavalry troop in pursuit. A smaller force might pass unnoticed. Winter Kay agreed. He didn't care how many men rode into Eldacre, as long as they rode out with the skull.

Then paranoia touched his soul. What if Velroy decided to keep the skull for himself? Worms of doubt burrowed into Winter Kay's mind. 'I will lead the raid myself,' he told Velroy. 'Thirty Redeemers should suffice.'

'Who then will conduct the battle, my lord?' asked Velroy.

'You will. It should hardly be taxing, my dear Velroy. We have overwhelming superiority in numbers.'

'But the battle plan?'

'You have always shown high skill in strategy, Velroy. Now is the time to display it.'

'I am honoured, my lord. I . . . I thank you for your trust in me.'

'As soon as I have the skull I shall return and we will review your actions.'

'Yes, my lord.'

That had been just before the dawn. Winter Kay and thirty Redeemers had ridden away to the south west, skirting the woods and circling into the hills above Eldacre. Here they had drawn up and dismounted. With an ornate long glass Winter Kay studied the town. There were no signs of troops.

Then came the sounds of cannon fire in the distance. The battle had begun.

Winter Kay was torn between the desire to ride down into the town and risk entering the castle, and a sudden fear that it was all a trap. He sat in the shelter of the trees, his mouth dry. The men with him were nervous. They were all on edge, for none of them had received the power of the skull in days. Worse than this, Winter Kay found himself seeing them differently. His Redeemers, he had always believed, were the elite. Powerful, single-minded men, the best that the Varlish could create. He looked at them now and saw their fear. With the strength-enhancing magic of the skull, and the mystical advantages they gained, they *had* been elite. Now, like him, they were merely frightened men.

Once more Winter Kay scanned the castle. He could see a sentry at the gates.

'Do we go in, my lord?' asked a Redeemer.

Winter Kay rose. Before he possessed the skull he had been a soldier, and a fine swordsman. He had not lacked courage then, he told himself. 'Yes. We go in.'

Mounting his horse he led the thirty men down the slope and into the town. They did not ride fast. There were some citizens on the street, but they largely ignored the riders. They had seen so many strange soldiers during the past weeks that they did not recognize the Redeemers as enemies. Winter Kay began to relax. They rode past the huge cathedral. His fears vanished then, replaced by the anger of memory. His brother Gayan had died here, killed by a highlander during the botched execution of a witch. Now that witch was sheltering in Eldacre Castle.

He would find the skull, then avenge his brother's death.

Cutting to the right the troop of riders headed for the castle. There was a mass of tents outside the walls, and Winter Kay saw a number of wounded men, some of them heavily bandaged, others with splints upon broken legs and arms. Ignoring them he steered his gelding through the gates.

An elderly sentry looked up as they rode through. He did not challenge them. Then an officer appeared from a side doorway. He was followed out by a burly soldier. The officer walked out towards the riders, his expression puzzled. 'Are you seeking the Moidart?' he asked.

'I am looking for Aran Powdermill,' Winter Kay told him.

'I am Colonel Galliott. Perhaps I can assist you. Are you with Konin's detachment?'

'No, colonel,' said Winter Kay. 'I am Lord Winterbourne.'

The officer grabbed for the pistol in his belt. Winter Kay already had his hand upon the butt of his own pistol. He drew it swiftly, cocked it and fired. The ball took Galliott in the chest. He fell back with a cry, dragging his own pistol clear, and shot back. A rider to Winter Kay's right took the ball in the face and was hurled from his mount. The burly soldier who had emerged with Galliott drew his sabre and rushed at Winter Kay. A Redeemer spurred his horse between them and shot the man in the throat at point blank range.

Another shot rang out. A Redeemer cried out in pain and slumped over his saddle. The elderly sentry had discharged his musket behind them. Several of the Redeemers shot him. Winter Kay stepped down from his mount. Leaving nineteen men to secure the courtyard he took nine men with him and ran into the main castle building. Two servants came into sight. Seeing armed men they turned to flee. Winter Kay chased the first and caught him by the arm. 'Where is Aran Powdermill?' he shouted.

The servant pointed up the main stairway. 'On the first floor. Fourth room on your left, sir.'

'And Maev Ring?'

'Also on the first floor, but to the right, at the end of the corridor.'

Winter Kay pushed the man aside and moved up the stairs. As he climbed he shouted: 'Powdermill, where are you?'

At the top he saw a door open, and a small man with two gold teeth step out. The man blinked in surprise, then waved Winter Kay forward. Followed by his Redeemers Winter Kay ran down the corridor.

'I didn't expect you to come yourself, my lord,' said Powdermill.

Winter Kay ignored him and entered the small room. He almost groaned with pleasure when he saw the velvet sack upon a walnut table. Pushing Powdermill aside he stepped forward and opened the sack, laying his hands reverently upon the ancient bone. Fresh energy poured into him, and a great sense of calm descended. Kneeling before the skull he kissed it. His head cleared. Then he rose and faced Powdermill. 'You have been true to your word, Master Powdermill. You may serve me, and you will receive Gaise Macon's sword. Now take me to Maev Ring.'

Huntsekker was annoyed as he paced the weapons gallery. He had planned to leave Eldacre this morning, to take Maev Ring back to the north. She had agreed to go, but had claimed to need time to settle her new affairs here. She had letters she needed to write. Letters, for heaven's sake! The world was coming apart and she needed to write letters.

After they were written they would need to be delivered. It was nonsense. They would hitch up the wagon and go riding around the town, and all the while the enemy would be drawing nearer.

I should just leave, Huntsekker told himself. Head off to my farm. Forget the woman.

It was this comforting thought that caused his annoyance. Because despite the eminent good sense of such a plan he couldn't do it. In all the great tales of heroism Huntsekker had learned as a young boy the hero never left the maiden in distress. The fact that here was a harridan in distress did not, he feared, alter the basic concept.

Huntsekker tried to quell his growing anger by examining the ancient weapons here. There were some beautiful swords and knives on display. They had been in the Moidart's family for generations. Long swords carried by knights, and designed to be used from horseback, blade heavy so that they slashed down with greater force; glaves with massive blades, forged to smash plate armour. It was just such a blade that Jaim Grymauch carried into the cathedral that day. Huntsekker's favourite, however, was the ornate short sword that had been discovered in the tomb of a Stone general. Wonderful piece, with a hilt of carved ivory and a blade of gleaming iron, burnished like silver. Short swords were infinitely more deadly in a pitched battle. When Huntsekker had been a soldier he had bought a hunting knife with a blade almost a foot in length. That purchase had saved his life on four occasions.

He strolled the gallery, idly glancing at the pikes and lances, breastplates and suits of armour. Then he saw the blank section where once hung the narrow silver breastplate which the Moidart's grandfather had worn in the First Clan War. Huntsekker sighed. It was this piece that the Moidart had donned last night, before riding out to the battle site.

Huntsekker had not been remotely tempted to ride with him. Nor had the Moidart requested it. There had been no long good-byes, no words of friendship, no valedictory statements. The Moidart had instructed Huntsekker to buckle the breastplate for him, then selected four pistols.

'I have no more need for you at present, Huntsekker.'

'Then I'll go home, my lord.'

420

'Take Maev Ring with you. I'll have your payment sent on to you after the battle,' said the Moidart, with just the trace of a smile.

'Thank you, my lord. Most kind.'

Then he had gone.

Huntsekker stood now, in his full length bearskin coat, loaded pistols in his belt, and waited for a fierce-tongued woman to finish writing her letters.

*I could just go and drag her from her office.* He chuckled at the thought.

Gunshots sounded from the courtyard. Huntsekker spun. Then he swore and began to run.

As the shots boomed in the courtyard Maev Ring opened the drawer of her desk and pulled out a small pistol, tucking it into a hidden pocket in her heavy grey travelling skirt. Rising from her seat she donned her dark green shawl and stepped out into the corridor. The black hound, Soldier, padded after her.

She heard the sound of running men. A voice shouted: 'Where is Aran Powdermill?' Then she heard her own name. Why would anyone be looking for her? The Moidart had come to her last night, urging her to leave the castle this morning. Perhaps he had sent men to escort her. It seemed unlikely. There were no men to spare, though Galliott was still at the castle.

Moving across the corridor into an empty room she made her way to a window and looked down. There was a group of red-cloaked men there, some mounted, some on foot, pistols in their hands. Then she saw the bodies of Galliott and Sergeant Packard.

Drawing her pistol she cocked it, then stood behind the closed door. She heard again the sounds of running men. They entered her office.

'Where is she?' someone demanded. There was no reply. Yet they did not move off. Instinctively Maev moved back from the door. It suddenly burst open. The first man through was heavy set and trident-bearded. Maev shot him in the head. He fell heavily.

Another man followed him. Soldier growled and sprang towards him, leaping and closing his fangs on the man's throat. Then more men ran in. One struck her in the face with his fist. Maev was

421

thrown back against the far wall. A boot struck her in the stomach and she doubled over. She heard a shot, and a dying howl of pain from the hound. Then a hawk-faced man grabbed her long red and silver hair, wrenching back her head. 'Justice was a long time coming, witch,' he said, 'but it is here now.'

From the corridor beyond came a scream, then two more pistol shots. A red-cloaked body hurtled into the room, crunching against the wall. More shots sounded. The man holding her swung his head to see what was going on. A Redeemer staggered backwards through the doorway, a knife in his chest. Maev saw Huntsekker follow him. The big man had blood on his face. Grabbing the Redeemer by the hair he wrenched the knife clear then slashed it across the man's throat. A heavy sabre lashed into the back of Huntsekker's head. Blood sprayed out. He half fell. Another man leapt upon him, bearing him to the floor. Huntsekker stabbed him in the groin, threw him clear, then struggled to his feet.

The man holding Maev Ring pulled a pistol from his belt and fired. Huntsekker grunted and went down. Maev slammed a fist into the man's jaw. Off balance he fell awkwardly. Scrambling to her feet Maev ran for the doorway. A Redeemer grabbed her. Spinning, she head butted him. Two others ran at her. A punch took her high in the temple. Then she was slammed against the wall of the corridor. She fell to her knees.

The hawk-faced man came out of the room in which Huntsekker lay. He was carrying a black velvet sack. Maev looked up. Aran Powdermill was standing by the opposite wall, his face ashen. On the floor were three Redeemer bodies. Through the door she could see another four alongside Huntsekker and the hound.

'You deserve to die slowly, witch,' said the hawk-faced man. 'And you shall. Bring her!'

Maev's vision was blurring and she could taste blood in her mouth. A man grabbed her by the hair, another by the arm and she was hauled upright.

More gunshots sounded from the courtyard. The two Redeemers paused, then looked at one another. Maev could see the fear in their eyes. The man holding her on the left suddenly jerked back, spinning her round.

She saw the huge, blood-drenched figure of Huntsekker. He had grabbed the Redeemer holding her and dragged him backwards. The knife in his hand plunged into the man's belly. In that instant Maev leaned forward, then threw back her head into the face of the second Redeemer. He grunted with pain and fell against the wall. Maev tore herself free of his grip. In doing so she lost her balance and stumbled to the floor. Huntsekker leapt over her, his bloody knife raised. The Redeemer, his nose smashed, his eyes streaming, failed to see the blade as it plunged into his chest. Huntsekker twisted the knife. A terrible scream echoed in the corridor.

Beyond them the man with the velvet sack turned and ran. Powdermill just stood there. Huntsekker was breathing heavily now. He sagged against the wall. Powdermill moved to him, taking his weight. The knife dropped from the Harvester's hand. Powdermill, unable to support his huge frame, was dragged down as he fell.

Maev came alongside. There was a huge cut on Huntsekker's head. She wrenched open his coat. Blood had soaked his shirt. Ripping it open she saw that he had been shot at least twice in the chest and belly. There were also stab wounds. The worst of the wounds – in his chest – was pumping blood. Maev put both her hands on it and applied pressure.

'Get a surgeon,' she told Powdermill.

The shots had ceased now in the courtyard. Powdermill nodded and sped away. Maev continued the pressure on the chest wound. She saw Huntsekker's eyes were open.

'Don't die, foolish man,' she said.

Winter Kay ran down the stairs, taking them three at a time. He almost fell but righted himself as he reached the bottom. Running to the door he wrenched it open. What he saw beyond made him blink in disbelief.

His Redeemers were dead, bodies littering the courtyard. Their killers stood around them. They were all bandaged and bloody. One man had an amputated arm. His supposedly elite Redeemers had been slain by a blood-soaked group of barbarian wounded.

Gripping the velvet sack tightly, Winter Kay walked towards one of the horses. A one-armed man moved across to block his way. He was holding a sabre. Sunlight gleamed upon the cloak brooch he wore. It was bronze and oval. A circle had been engraved at the centre. Now, in the sunlight, it shone like gold.

The words of the old priest came back to him. '*I will go gladly, Winter Kay. Which is more than can be said for you, when the one with the golden eye comes for you.*'

It was a horrifying moment. Time froze. Winter Kay knew then that Gaise Macon was never the enemy. In fact it was even worse than that. Had he not attempted to kill Macon, then the Moidart would never have been drawn into the battle. Without him there would have been no Rigante to fight. I would never even have been here, he thought.

The one-armed man came closer. Winter Kay dragged his own sabre from its scabbard. This man could not possibly defeat him. His face was grey with exhaustion and pain, and fresh blood was dripping from the amputated limb.

'Step aside, man, and live,' said Winter Kay. 'In your condition you are no match for me.'

The man did not move. Winter Kay suddenly leapt forward, his sabre lancing for the man's chest. The Rigante's blade swept up, blocking the lunge, then rolling over and round it, before plunging through Winter Kay's throat.

'No match for you, fool? I am Rigante.'

They were the last words Winter Kay heard.

The battle raged on for most of the day. By afternoon the losses on both sides were prodigious. Mantilan had held his eastern ridge until almost dusk, but then the enemy had forced their way through. Gaise Macon led his cavalry in a counter charge, but to no avail. Mantilan was killed, along with Bael Jace and more than eight hundred Rigante.

The western ridge, under Beck and the Moidart, did hold, though at the cost of three thousand men. Konin's cavalry had come to their aid, but had taken massive casualties. Konin himself was killed in the last charge.

As two divisions of enemy infantry had stormed the ridge Kaelin Ring had led his surviving five hundred fighters up its northern slope to reinforce the Moidart and Beck.

The fighting was ferocious. As the Rigante arrived the enemy had reached the crest of the ridge and were battling hand to hand with the defenders. Kaelin saw the Moidart holding his ground, two pistols in his hands. He brought up the first and discharged it. Then the second. Two men fell. Dropping the pistols the Moidart drew a sabre. A musketeer ran at him, bayonet lunging for the Moidart's belly. The nobleman swayed to his right. The bayonet lanced through his arm. His sabre cut down across the musketeer's neck, opening the jugular. Kaelin and the Rigante tore into the enemy.

On the slope below Gaise Macon charged his cavalry into enemy infantry reinforcements, scattering them.

With the dread Rigante cutting and killing on the crest of the ridge, and the cavalry below seeking to cut them off, the Varlish attack faltered. Men began to stream back down the slope, seeking to escape the slaughter. The Rigante pursued them, and the retreat became a rout.

Kaelin blew his horn three times, summoning his men back to the ridge. Then he saw the Moidart trying to pull the bayonet from his left arm. Kaelin sheathed his sabre and knife and moved to him. Taking hold of the musket he drew the blade clear. The Moidart said nothing. Gripping his bicep to staunch the blood flow he moved past Kaelin and stared out at the fleeing troops.

Gaise Macon's cavalry were harassing the enemy, but there were not enough of them to continue an assault on the enemy lines. They came under fire from reserves on the southern slopes and were forced to withdraw.

'It's a damned stalemate,' said the Moidart. 'Tomorrow it will begin again.'

As night fell Gaise Macon rode among the remnants of his army, knowing that tomorrow the enemy would overwhelm them.

He located Kaelin Ring. The surviving Rigante had positioned themselves on the slopes of the western ridge and, though exhausted, were busy digging trenches and throwing up earthworks.

Gaise dismounted. Kaelin saw him and nodded. 'It's over,' said Kaelin, softly. 'We'll not hold them tomorrow.'

'I know.'

'We could pull back, then hit them with raids as they move.'

'I have another plan.'

'Share it with me. I love listening to good plans.'

Gaise looked away. 'I am sorry, Kaelin Ring. I am sorry for all that you and your men have been through in this cause. Bael Jace told me he despised me. I understand that. At this moment I despise myself. I came to the point where I put aside all that I had once believed in. What did you do with those boys you captured?'

'I let them go.'

'Good.' Gaise looked around at the Rigante as they continued to toil. 'I remember, back when the world was not so vile, that day when your uncle took on the Varlish champion. I recall thinking that he was the most amazing man. Gorain had greater strength and more acquired skill and yet your uncle fought him to a stand-still, and beat him.'

'Grymauch was a great man,' said Kaelin.

'Aye, I know that. I thought he was unique. He wasn't. All you Rigante have the same qualities. Men to ride the river with, as the old books say.' Gaise drew his sword, reversed it and offered it to Kaelin Ring.

'I don't need a sword,' he said.

'This is the sword of Connavar, the Sword in the Storm. It must remain with the Rigante, Kaelin.'

'Connavar carried no sabre.'

'Take it and see.'

Kaelin hesitated, then reached out and wrapped his hand round the hilt. The blade shimmered, and once more the golden fist guard reshaped itself. Kaelin gazed at it in amazement. The rearing horse in the clouds had been replaced by a hound standing alongside a stag. 'This is how I got my soul-name,' whispered Kaelin. 'The hound was my father's. It was called Raven. It rescued a stag surrounded by wolves.'

'I was proud to carry it,' said Gaise Macon.

With that he returned to his mount and rode up the slope. The Moidart was waiting for him. His breastplate was dented, his arm crudely bandaged, but he bore no other wounds, despite the carnage inflicted on this ridge all day. 'Where is Beck?' asked Gaise.

'Sleeping. He's not as young as he pretends.'

'He's a good man.'

'He's solid,' agreed the Moidart. 'Did Mantilan get off the ridge?'

'No. He's dead, along with Bael Jace and eight hundred Rigante.'

'Konin is also dead,' said the Moidart. 'He had grit, that man.'

'There has been a wealth of courage on both sides today,' said Gaise, staring out over the field of corpses.

'What now, Stormrider?' asked the Moidart.

'Now we win, Father.'

'That would be pleasant – not to say miraculous.'

'We will talk of it in the morning. Is Taybard Jaekel still alive?'

'If I knew who he was I'd answer you.'

Gaise moved away among the men. He found Taybard apparently sleeping alongside the wakeful Jakon Gallowglass.

'How are you faring?' asked Gaise, crouching down.

'Can't complain,' said Gallowglass wearily. Gaise reached out to wake Taybard. 'He's dead, general. Didn't fire a shot all day. Said he wasn't going to kill anyone else. I tried to stop him but he just stood up during the last salvo. A lump of shot tore his chest open.'

Gaise looked into the dead man's face. In the moonlight he looked serene, and he seemed to be smiling. Gaise opened Taybard's shirt and tugged clear the golden musket ball in its cage of silver wire. 'He was a good lad,' said Gallowglass. 'But he'd had enough.'

'We've all had enough,' said Gaise. 'Tell me, Gallowglass, are you a good shot?'

'No, sir. Average, I'd say. I'm good with knife or sword, though.'

Gaise gathered up Taybard Jaekel's Emburley rifle and rose. As he turned he saw Mulgrave walking towards him.

And beside him was the Wyrd of the Wishing Tree wood.

Two hours later, back at Eldacre Castle, Gaise Macon retrieved the skull from the clansman, Rayster, and took it to his old rooms, high in the north tower. He had spent much of his childhood in these apartments, and despite the cold, gloomy décor they remained special in his memories. It was here that he had read many of the books supplied by Alterith Shaddler, the wonderful tales of Connavar and Bane, the legends of Stromengle, the axe-wielding

All-Father of the early Vars. Here he had devoured the great romances of the Bard King and the Star Princess. In these rooms Gaise Macon had dreamed of becoming a great and noble man.

He felt neither great nor noble as he wearily ascended the stairs. The rooms – unused now for years – were cold and smelled of damp. Heavy curtains had been left across the windows, and these were mildewed.

Gaise sat in an old armchair, removed the skull from the velvet sack and held it in his hands. Instantly fresh energy surged through him. A golden figure shimmered into being.

'You fought well, kinsman. There is nothing to reproach yourself for. No-one could have done more.'

'It was a charnel house. I have never seen so much slaughter in one day,' said Gaise.

'It is what you humans are so good at. If you spent half as much time trying to find ways to heal as you spend discovering new ways to kill you would have a great future. You had so much potential.'

'We *still* have potential, Cernunnos. There are still good and holy people. We will learn one day.'

'It would be pleasant to think you were right, Gaise. Unfortunately, for every man or woman on this planet who makes a little magic, there are a thousand who would drain it. However, that is not the issue today. What would you ask of me?'

Gaise sighed. 'What will happen when I accept the skull?'

'The power will begin to swell and grow. You will be able to heal all your wounded. You will even be able to bring back the most recent dead. At least those who were not mutilated beyond repair. I was never able to heal a man whose head was crushed, though I have restructured hearts. The brain, you see, is uniquely important. It actually takes three full days to die completely. As long as the head is still connected to the body you will be able to heal.'

'How will I do that? There are thousands of dead and wounded. I know nothing of restructuring hearts.'

'You think there is time to teach you what it took me a thousand years to understand?'

'Then speak simply,' said Gaise.

'The true nature of magic concerns harmony and balance. The body – wondrously designed – is self-healing. Bathe it in magic and

428

it will heal more swiftly. The more powerful the magic the faster the healing. You will merely supply the fuel for each body to accomplish what it can. Equally you can move among the enemy and draw away from them every vibrant spark of life. If you will it you can deprive the entire army of air, and watch them suffocate.'

'And all this power will come from this one, decaying skull?'

'No, not from the skull, Gaise. It will come to you when you absorb the skull. The greatest talent the Seidh possessed was the ability to draw magic from living things. The skull – *my* skull – when it is once more surrounded by life, will pull magic from the air, from the earth, from the trees and the rivers. You will swell with it, and feel you cannot hold any more. Then you will release it, to flow over your troops and heal them. Think of it. The dead Rigante restored to life, the crippled living brought back to full health. You will have won, Gaise.'

'*You* will have won, Cernunnos. You will return and there will be even greater bloodshed.'

'There is always a price to be paid for glory, kinsman. Your father was right, though. If you lose tomorrow – as you will without me – then someone else will discover this bone you hold. Someone else will restore me to life. Why see all your comrades die before that happens? When I return I will need followers. Many of them will become near immortal.'

'Until you have found a way to manipulate mankind into destroying itself.'

'Yes, until then. On most worlds where humanity has existed they have managed to destroy themselves without help from me. The problem is that they also brought about the destruction of the planets they lived upon. This planet is dear to me. I want to see it as it should be, a wealth of trees and clean rivers, good air and an abundance of life. I have always been partial to wolves and bears. I'd like to see wolves back among the mountains of Caer Druagh. Is that not a noble aim, Gaise Macon?'

'I am no longer a man with any right to discuss nobility of purpose. How long will I have as a god?'

'At least five hours, perhaps six.'

'Are there limits to what I can achieve?'

'There are always limits. You will not be the Source. You will not be able to change hearts and minds, as they say. You will not be able to die either, Gaise Macon. Weapons will not harm you. Shot and shell and sword will not touch your skin. Ah, I see you are looking downcast. Did you think to take me with you on the swan's path?'

'Yes,' said Gaise.

'I do so like honesty, kinsman. It may be less subtle than lies, but we all know where we stand. I saw you sitting with Mulgrave and the Wyrd. Where did your spirits fly? Uzamatte? Caer Druagh?'

'I do not know. It was a river and there was a mill. It was most peaceful. Tell me, when I take the skull will I be alone?'

'Alone? I do not understand you.'

'Will you and I share our thoughts?'

'Not if you do not wish it. I understand privacy. To be honest the thoughts of humans are rather banal. If you were forced to inhabit the body of a monkey, would you desire to share its last thoughts?'

Gaise sat quietly. 'Very well. What do I need to do?'

'Merely relax, kinsman. Hold to the skull. You will feel it begin to seep into your fingers. It will become smaller and more insubstantial. And then it will be a part of you.'

# CHAPTER TWENTY

KAELIN RING HELPED A WOUNDED MAN TO HIS FEET, AND, WITH THE
help of another soldier, carried the man down the slope to where
some six hundred other wounded soldiers were being treated.
There were many dead among them.

'Maybe the enemy will have had enough,' said the soldier helping him. 'Maybe they'll decide to call it a day and withdraw. Then
we can all go back to Eldacre, get drunk and find some whores.'

Kaelin began to walk back up the slope. The young soldier
followed. 'What do you think?'

'I don't think they'll leave,' he said.

'No, you're probably right. Guess we'll have to kill them all
then.'

At the top of the slope the Moidart was talking to Garan Beck.
Kaelin joined them as the soldier trudged away. 'Now that the
enemy have the eastern ridge they can ride cavalry around us and
cut us off,' said Beck. 'It would be better to withdraw to the castle.'

'It would only prolong the inevitable,' said the Moidart. 'The
enemy has suffered grievously. He will not know how we fare.
With luck he may send a message requesting a break in hostilities
to tend his wounded.'

'It will be dawn soon,' said Beck. 'Perhaps we should send a rider
to them.'

'No,' objected the Moidart. 'If I was Winter Kay that is what I would expect from a weaker foe. The fact that we do not request such a cessation will indicate we are ready to fight on.'

'And we are,' said Kaelin, 'but I have less than five hundred fighting men. We'll not hold the position for long.'

A soldier called out, and pointed to the north.

A rider was coming, and behind him marched several hundred men.

The Moidart moved back and narrowed his eyes.

'It is your son,' said Kaelin. 'Where in heaven's name did he find so many fresh troops?'

Kaelin ran down the slope towards the marching men, recognizing Rayster. The clansman looked fit and strong, and there was no sign of a bandage upon his recently shattered arm. Many of the newcomers were Rigante, and all were in good health.

'What happened?' Kaelin asked Rayster.

'I'm not sure I know how to tell you, my friend.' He held out his left arm and flexed the fingers. 'The elbow was destroyed and they cut off my arm yesterday.' Kaelin looked at him closely. 'No, I am not dreaming it all, Kaelin. Gaise Macon came into the hospital wing. Men began to cry out. I couldn't understand it at first. Then the stump of my arm began to throb and swell against the bandages. The pain was indescribable. I took my knife and cut the bandages clear. Within moments this . . . this new arm grew. All of us, Kaelin. He healed all of us. I have never felt better in my life.'

'Oh no,' whispered Kaelin, spinning on his heel and staring at the rider moving slowly up the slope. 'He made a pact with Cernunnos.'

'I have to tell you I do not care,' said Rayster. 'Look!'

The wounded men at the foot of the slope began to cry out. One by one they rose from the ground. Then there was shouting and laughter. It was the oddest sound ever to grace a battlefield.

Kaelin felt a growing warmth in his injured shoulder, and what had been constant pain for more than a day now began to recede.

'Even some of the dead came back to life,' said Rayster. 'The giant, Huntsekker. He was shot three times and stabbed. He had died as they were trying to staunch the bleeding. And Colonel Galliott. I saw him, Kaelin. He was shot through the heart!'

Leaving Rayster Kaelin ran back up the slope, in time to see Gaise Macon dismount and walk towards his father.

The Moidart backed away from him. 'Do not heal me!' he shouted. 'Do not! You do not know what I have done!'

Gaise Macon approached his father and placed both hands on the older man's shoulders. 'I know everything, Father. *Everything*. I know all your past evils. I even know much of what you may accomplish in the future. But now you will have to find another road to redemption, for I am taking away your pain.' The Moidart's head sagged forward. 'There is something else,' said Gaise. 'All my life you have been tormented by the fear . . .'

'I do not want to know!'

'I think you do. I am *your* son, Father. Blood of your blood.'

All across the ridge the healing continued. Men began cheering and shouting. Wounds disappeared, strength was restored.

'What happens now?' whispered the Moidart.

'I will be a god for a little while. Then I will be gone.'

'Oh, Gaise . . .' The Moidart shook his head.

Gaise Macon drew the man into an embrace. 'Farewell, Father,' he said.

Gaise turned and walked down the slope towards the earth ramparts. As he did so the corpses lying there began to stir. And not just the men. Within moments horses began to whinny, and struggle to their feet.

Gaise walked on.

Kaelin Ring ran to where the Moidart was standing. 'We have to stop him. The Dark God will return. Everything we have fought for will be worth nothing.'

The Moidart ignored him. The Wyrd of the Wishing Tree wood moved through the throng, and took Kaelin by the arm. 'All will be well,' she said. Kaelin saw there were tears in her eyes.

Gaise was still walking across the field of the fallen. All around him men were rising from the earth, both Eldacre and enemy. The southerners stood for a while, and then began walking back towards their lines. The Eldacre men scrambled up the slope.

General Konin approached the Moidart. There were three holes in the front of his blood-drenched tunic. 'There are no wounds,' he said, opening his tunic and baring his chest. 'No wounds.'

Beck took hold of his arm. 'You are back with us, my friend.'

'I was at a river. We all were. Was I dreaming?'

Distant shots sounded. The Moidart ran to the edge of the slope. Some of the southern soldiers on the eastern ridge were shooting at Gaise. He walked on unconcerned. Not a shot struck him. Then the shooting ceased, and the sound of shouts of joy echoed across the valley floor.

For a while Gaise disappeared among the enemy.

'Why is he bringing them back too?' asked Beck. 'Sweet heaven, will we have to go through this carnage yet again tomorrow?'

'The war is over,' said the Moidart. 'No-one will fight now. Not even Winter Kay.'

'He is dead, my lord,' said Rayster, moving forward from the shadows. 'I cut his head from his shoulders back in Eldacre.' Rayster told them of the raid, and then of how Gaise had come in the night and healed the sick, the dying, and even the recent dead.

As the dawn rose over the mountains they saw Gaise Macon walk from the eastern ridge and begin to move towards the enemy positions on the southern slopes. Hundreds of southern soldiers followed him. Other Eldacre men and Rigante crossed the valley floor, heading west towards where the Moidart and the others were standing. Bael Jace and Mantilan climbed to where they stood. Mantilan embraced Beck and Konin, and the three old friends moved away.

The sun climbed higher in the sky, and a fresh breeze blew over the battlefield. The air was curiously scented. To the Moidart it smelled of rose petals, to Kaelin Ring it was like dew-covered heather, to Rayster the scent was of lavender. For every man it was something different.

All around the ridge men were smiling and laughing. Others wept for joy and hugged their comrades. Taybard Jaekel opened his eyes and saw Jakon Gallowglass sitting beside him, tears in his eyes. 'I had a wonderful dream,' he said. 'I saw Banny and Kammel. I was going to cross a river, but they wouldn't let me.'

Gallowglass patted his shoulder. 'You're back now, Jaekel. Back among the living.'

The Moidart moved away from them all, and stood staring

southwards as his son climbed to the enemy position. No-one fired a weapon, and within minutes the cheering began.

Time flowed by.

At last Gaise reappeared. He strolled down the slope, his golden hair gleaming in the sunlight. He did not walk towards his own waiting men, but moved off towards a stand of trees to the west.

Just before he reached them he stopped, lifted his hands in the air, and tilted his head to the heavens.

A single shot broke the silence.

Gaise Macon could feel the growing strength of Cernunnos within him as he walked from the enemy camp. His right arm spasmed and he almost lost control of it. 'Let yourself go, kinsman,' came a voice in his mind. 'You cannot hold me back. You know that.'

'I know,' Gaise told him. He walked on. His legs were feeling heavier, and it was an effort of will to propel himself forward. He looked up. The trees were closer now, but not close enough.

'Why did you not kill your enemies?' asked Cernunnos. 'Now I will have to do it for you.'

'I wanted to show you that we can learn.'

'I always knew that a few of you humans were worthwhile, kinsman. It is just that there are not enough of you.'

Gaise tottered on. Then his legs ceased to move. He stared at the trees. 'I do have a gift for you,' he said.

'I already have your gift. Let your spirit go!'

'You have shown me how to live like a god. Now you can learn what it is to die as a man.'

Gaise raised his arms, and tilted back his head.

The silence was shattered by a single shot. Gaise grunted as the ball tore into his chest, ripping through his lungs. His body slumped to the ground. As his life faded he felt Cernunnos desperately, and unsuccessfully, trying to heal the wound.

Hidden in the trees Mulgrave stood up, took the Emburley rifle by the barrel and smashed it against the trunk of an oak. Then he slumped to the ground and began to weep.

High on the western ridge the Moidart cried out and began to run to where his son lay, arms spread out upon the grass. Thousands of men swarmed out behind him.

The body began to glow, brighter and brighter. The Moidart could not gaze upon it and shielded his eyes with his hands. A cold wind blew. The light flared out over the gathering multitude. The Moidart felt its power wash over him. When he lowered his hands and opened his eyes the body of Gaise Macon had disappeared.

The grass beneath the Moidart's feet shimmered and writhed. Small blue flowers swelled from the earth. All across the battlefield they grew. It was as if the sky had painted the earth.

From the ridge to the south came two riders, followed by thousands of soldiers. The riders approached the Moidart. The first man stepped down. He was middle-aged and sandy-haired. He bowed to the Moidart. 'I am Eris Velroy. I command the army of Lord Winterbourne.'

'Winterbourne is dead,' said the Moidart, still staring at the spot where his son had fallen.

'I guessed that. I do not begin to understand what happened here today, my lord,' said Velroy. 'But it is inconceivable that we should continue the fight. Do I have your permission to withdraw my men and travel south?'

'I lost my son today,' said the Moidart. '*My* son. Do you have sons?'

'One, my lord.'

'Then go home and joy in that.'

The Moidart walked to the spot where Gaise had fallen. Something glinted upon the lush grass. He reached out and picked it up. It was a partially flattened musket ball of solid gold.

The Wyrd moved to him, and laid a hand upon his shoulder. Then she knelt beside him. 'He is still here, Hawk in the Willow.'

'I cannot see him.'

'You will. Did your grandmother teach you the words?'

'Aye, a long time ago.'

'Then speak them with me.'

The Moidart took a deep, shuddering breath, and together he and the Wyrd spoke the ancient farewell.

> *Seek the circle, find the light,*
> *Say farewell to flesh and bone.*
> *Walk the grey path,*

*Watch the swan's flight,*
*Let your heart light*
*Bring you home.'*

As the words tailed away the Moidart saw two ghostly figures in the sunlight. One was Gaise, the other a dark-haired woman in a travelling dress of shimmering green. They reached out and their hands touched. Then they disappeared.

The Moidart remained where he was for a while. Then he stood and walked away, through the silent ranks of Eldacre men and Rigante. There were a great many horses now, standing idle. Gathering the reins of one he stepped into the saddle and rode away across the field of blue flowers.

# CHAPTER TWENTY ONE

IN THE MONTHS THAT FOLLOWED ELDACRE BECAME A CENTRE FOR pilgrims. People travelled from all over the land to see the place where the blessed Gaise Maçon had lived and died. Monks and priests walked the battlefield, gathering blue flowers and pressing them between small sheets of glass.

The Eldacre Company was kept together for three months, while events in the south settled. Then many of them were paid off. Lanfer Gosten returned to his clerical work with a merchant company, and took on Taybard Jaekel as an assistant. Jakon Gallowglass remained with the reduced army, with the rank of sergeant.

Two of the Moidart's new generals, Konin and Mantilan, rode south to take part in the new assembly which Eris Velroy convened. The six hundred men of the assembly, appointed from the surviving nobility and the ranks of the army, were seeking a new king.

The wonders following the death of Gaise Macon did not cease for a long while. It was almost four months before a single person in Eldacre died. For weeks after the battle reports came in of dying people who had been suddenly cured on the day the Stormrider passed from the earth. A tanner in Old Hills, ravaged by cancer, had risen from his bed; an elderly woman, paralysed by a stroke, had the power restored to her limbs; a crippled child had walked again. So many wondrous tales.

Little had been seen of the Moidart since the battle. He had effectively left the running of the castle to Colonel Galliott, and had retired to the Winter House. People spoke of the grief he was enduring at the loss of his son.

Others took the limelight. A little man with golden teeth, named Aran Powdermill, became a celebrity. He had, it became known, aided the Moidart against the evil of the Redeemer devils. He was a man of magic, it was said. A holy man, blessed by the Source.

Garan Beck was also awarded hero status. The burghers of Eldacre presented him with a fine house, overlooking the town.

Huntsekker was also spoken of with awe when word spread of his magnificent fight with thirty Redeemers in defence of the legendary Maev Ring. He, however, did not enjoy the acclaim, and headed north. Some said he was going there to wed Maev.

The clansman Rayster was drawn into the burgeoning legend: the one-armed man who killed the Demon Lord, Winter Kay, and stopped him from acquiring the dread skull. Somehow it became common knowledge that Rayster had no known parents, and had been raised among the Rigante. Already a figure of mystery and heroic nature, it was decided that he had also been blessed by the Source as a man of rare destiny.

But no-one knew of the part Mulgrave the Swordsman had played in the outcome.

People spoke of the last vile act of the Redeemers, the slaying of the god-prince. In church services they prayed that the Source would curse the godless and evil man who had fired that fatal shot, and robbed the world of greatness.

Their curses meant nothing to Mulgrave. The world could offer no greater hurt than the one he carried. He stayed on in Eldacre for some months, assisting in the rebuilding of the war-damaged community. Then he saddled a horse and quietly rode away.

A week later he arrived at the outskirts of Shelding, and drew rein on the high ground from where the enemy musketeers had attacked the Eldacre Company. It seemed so long ago now. Another lifetime.

Mulgrave dismounted and tethered his horse. Taking a canteen from his saddle he drank a little water. He felt light-headed and weak, and realized he had not eaten in two days. He had lost a great deal of weight in the last few months, and was now skeletally thin.

He gazed down at the distant town. It was here that he had experienced the last happiness of his life. It was here that he had served the *real* Gaise Macon, the young man of honour and courage. Not the killer he had become. Nor the god-prince that legend was now creating.

The days in Shelding had become golden in his memory. Perhaps that was why he felt drawn here. He shivered as a cool breeze blew across his rain drenched clothes. I should have died here, he thought, suddenly. Despair engulfed him and he struggled to his feet. Moving to his horse he drew a pistol from the saddle scabbard. Cocking it he pressed the barrel against his throat and pulled the trigger.

There was a loud click.

Rain had seeped into the flash pan, drenching the powder. Sitting down he cleaned out the pan and recharged it.

'This is not your destiny,' came the voice of the Wyrd in his mind.

'Leave me be!'

'Close your eyes, Mulgrave. Join me at the mill.'

'I just want peace!'

'Join me, Mulgrave. If only to say goodbye.'

He sat back against a tree trunk and closed his eyes. The world shimmered and a warm breeze touched his skin. Opening the eyes of his spirit he gazed down on the old mill and the water glittering in the sunlight. 'I am so lost, Wyrd,' he said.

'You are not lost, my friend. You are alone. Sometimes it feels the same.' The Wyrd took his hand. 'You did not kill him, Mulgrave. He was dead from the moment he accepted the skull.'

'I know that, Wyrd. The knowledge does not help me. What hurts me most is that he had no life. A tortured childhood with an uncaring father, and then a war. No wife, no family, no love.'

'*You* loved him.'

'It is not the same.'

'I think you are wrong,' she said, softly. 'Your friendship meant the world to him. You were like the father he never knew, and the brother he never had. You were the rock he could cling to and idolize. You helped a frightened boy become a man of courage. You were his hero always.' She patted his hand. 'Sit here a while, and, when you are ready, return to the flesh.'

Then she was gone. Alone now, Mulgrave stood and wandered down to the mill. The last time the Wyrd had brought him here was to talk in secret with Gaise. He had listened in horror as his friend asked for his help. 'I cannot do it,' Mulgrave had said.

'You must, Mulgrave. There is no-one else. Taybard Jaekel is dead.'

'Then let us fight on, sir. We can win without the skull.'

'Aye, we might – though I doubt it. But what then? The skull cannot be destroyed. One day someone else will be drawn to it. I need your friendship now more than ever before. If you still have love for me after all I have done, then do this one last thing for me, Mulgrave, I beg of you.'

And, in the name of love, he had agreed.

Mulgrave walked away from the mill, and wished himself back to the world of the flesh. When he opened his eyes he smelt woodsmoke. Turning his head he saw the Wyrd sitting by a small fire. 'How did you get here?' he asked.

'By the old ways,' she answered, with a smile. Then she peered at him. 'You look dreadful, Mulgrave,' she said. 'You have no flesh on you at all.'

'I have not been hungry.'

Reaching out she placed her hand upon his head. 'Here is a small gift for you.'

He felt her hand warm upon his skin, and then a wondrous cool breeze seemed to flow through his brain. His muscles relaxed, and all tension fled from him. Opening his eyes he saw the sunlight on the hillside, and joy touched him. Flowers were growing there, and the colours seemed indescribably beautiful. 'What did you do to me?' he asked her.

'I gave you a little earth magic. Are you hungry now?'

'Ravenous,' he admitted.

'Good. Now let us go down to Shelding and eat. We should be in time for the celebrations and the feast.'

'What are they celebrating?' asked Mulgrave.

'It was announced yesterday. Heralds have been riding to every village and town. Have you not heard? We have a new king.'

'I hope he's better than the last one.'

'They elected the Moidart,' she said.

Together they left the river bank and took the road to Shelding. Flags and bunting decorated the buildings, and long trestle tables had been set up in the market square. Mulgrave and the Wyrd moved among the happy crowd.

A young woman recognized Mulgrave, and called out to her friends. 'Here's one of the soldiers of Gaise Macon,' she cried. People gathered around him. Questions were shouted, too many to answer. A tankard of ale was thrust into Mulgrave's hand.

'Tell us about the Moidart,' said a man. 'They say he's a saint.'

For the first time in many months, Mulgrave laughed, the sound rich, joyous and full of life.

# EPILOGUE

IT HAD BEEN FIVE YEARS NOW SINCE RIAMFADA HAD DEPARTED THE world. Feargol missed him still. He would often stare up and out at the stars, wondering if the spirit of Riamfada had ever found the Seidh.

He was thinking of him now, as he strode down the wooded hillside, the morning sunshine glinting on his braided hair. He was a long way now from the great trees. The journey had taken several months. His moccasins were thin and all but worn out.

A huge herd of bison was grazing on the grasslands as Feargol emerged from the woods. He stopped and watched them for a while. Then he began to run, falling into an easy, rhythmic lope. He loved to run, filling his lungs with the sweet cool air, feeling his body stretch and sweat and relax.

He continued on for more than two hours, then climbed to the crest of a low hill and stopped to rest.

Ahead he could just make out the line of the coast, and the blue sea beyond. Across the vastness of that ocean lay the land of his birth. He thought of it little now. *This* was his land. This wondrous continent of magnificent forests and mountains, rivers and valleys. Magic was everywhere, floating in the air, seeping from the earth, bubbling in the rivers. Feargol drew it in with every breath.

Having rested he ran on, moving into sun-dappled woodland.

When he arrived at last at his destination he sat and waited, gazing down at the distant compound. Few people were stirring there. This was hardly surprising. They were dying.

Here, in a land rich with edible roots and game, they were starving to death.

Feargol had waited for this moment for most of the fifteen years he had spent in this great land. Riamfada had warned him of it. The Varlish had finally crossed the ocean. They had come in a great ship, and had begun a settlement on the coast. They had brought books, and chairs, and clothing and guns. They had carried beds and pictures and chests laden with goods from home. Not one of them had brought a fishing line. Nor a horse or mule. Not a single cow, and certainly no seed corn. They had expected to be re-supplied by sea, but those supplies had never arrived. Now they were dying.

And this was the pivotal moment that Riamfada had spoken of. What happened today would ultimately set the destiny of the world.

Feargol calmed himself, allowing his spirit to commune with the land. He felt uneasy, and had done for months now, ever since these few Varlish had landed here.

Towards dusk he rose from the ground and walked out to meet the seven hunters, laden with meat, who were heading for the compound.

The leader, a tall broad-shouldered warrior with a broken nose and a scar across his lips, gave a crooked smile as he saw Feargol. He was carrying a small dead deer upon his shoulders.

'Ha! Ghost Walker. Have you also come to marvel at our foolish visitors?'

'Not to marvel, Saoquanta. You are carrying much meat.'

'They are dying down there. They had one hunter, but he broke his leg. Now they have nothing.'

'And you will feed them?'

'It is a small thing, Ghost Walker.'

'No, it is not, Saoquanta. It is a great thing. I have seen it.'

Saoquanta tipped the deer from his shoulder to the ground. The other six warriors laid down the meat they were carrying. 'What is it that you have seen?'

'I have seen the rivers boil and stink, and the air darken. I have seen the buffalo vanish and the land laid to waste. I have seen the tears of the mountains, and heard the cries of the valleys. The people in that compound will be the fathers and the mothers of the darkness. Their children will outnumber the stars. They will rape and mutilate the land until there is nothing clean left to destroy.'

'These . . . fools will do this?' said Saoquanta.

'And others like them.'

'These words are heavy. They sit like stones upon the heart, Ghost Walker.'

'And upon mine.'

'What is it that you advise?'

'I do not advise, Saoquanta. I merely prophesy.'

The broken-nosed warrior nodded. 'Your dreams are always true. It is well known you walk the spirit paths. The Great Spirit has blessed you.'

'He has.'

'He has blessed me also, Ghost Walker. He has told me to protect my people, and to nurture the land. He has made me a hunter of great skill, and a provider to my people. I need to think on what you have said.'

With that he moved away from Feargol and entered the trees.

For more than an hour the hunters waited. At last Saoquanta returned. He sat once more with Feargol.

'If I walk into my camp and I kill a child with my knife that would be evil and the Great Spirit would be saddened by my actions. Not so, Ghost Walker?'

'It is so.'

'If I walk into my camp and a child is starving and I offer it no food and it dies have I not killed it?'

'Yes,' agreed Feargol, his heart heavy.

'The fools have children with them. They are dying. I have food. If I walk away now will not the Great Spirit be saddened, Ghost Walker?'

'The descendants of these people will have no understanding of the Great Spirit,' said Feargol. 'They will be thoughtless and greedy, merciless and vile.'

445

'It seems to me you are saying that if I do this small evil then great good will grow from it. This may be a great truth. It is not a truth I choose to understand. I am Saoquanta. I am a hunter. I do not let children starve. This is not why the Great Spirit blessed me.' Saoquanta rose and lifted the deer to his shoulders.

Feargol stood. Curiously the sense of unease left him. He felt free of the burden. 'You are a great man, Saoquanta. I shall walk with you, for I know the language of these men.'

Together they walked down the hillside to the compound. There were no guards at the stockade and the gates were open. The hunters moved inside.

Several gaunt men saw them. One of them, seeing the meat they carried, fell to his knees and offered up a prayer of thanksgiving.